CLOAKED

BOOK FOUR

of the

BLIND SERIES

Linda Riesenberg Fisler

All the best!
Thank you for your
Support. Enjoy,
Linda Riesenberg Fisler

Published by Linda Riesenberg Fisler
DBA Kit-Cat Press
Middletown, OH

ISBN: 978-1-7325197-0-1

Author's Note:
This novel and series is a work of fiction inspired by true events. Names, characters, places, and incidents either are the product of the author's imagination or are used fictitiously, and any resemblance to actual persons, living or dead, events, or locales is coincidental.

Cover design by Linda Riesenberg Fisler

DEDICATION

To my husband, Tom, who continues to be the wind beneath my wings.
To all my patrons, thank you for your trust, encouragement, and believing in me,
To my readers, loyal or new, you are the reason I do what I do.
Thank you for keeping the series alive!

Want *Behind the Scenes* information, access to author readings, and special secret meetings?

You can become a field agent on Linda's Patreon page and receive all that and more!

www.patreon.com/LindaRiesenbergFisler

Also by the Author—

Blind Influence-Three-Time Award-Winning novel!

"Interwoven plots of international intrigue propel the storyline through all the twists and turns the author uses solid dialogue and three-dimensional characters to keep the pages turning! This is a visual experience in the words that demonstrated her other talents. Linda is equal parts writer and artist—a rare combination that brings her story to life!" –A.M.

"I just read this book while on vacation. My only complaint is I couldn't put it down to do anything else! The author has written a gem. The characters are compelling and the plot engrossing and fully fleshed out. "It and They" pull the reader in and don't let you out! Looking forward to reading the prequel now…and every book in this series as they appear. Please don't make us wait too long! -M.D.

Blind Persuasion-Award-Winning novel

"Suspenseful, moving and kept my attention. I did not want to put the book down. Intertwined characters & anxious to know how their relationships change in book 3. The author did great research to provide authenticity" -M.F

"I have already finished Blind Influence and now this book. Had to read it straight away. Could not wait. Lots of action and twists. Will read the next book." -R.A.L.

Blind Alliance

"Our book club ordered everyone an autographed copy directly from the author. We had read the first two books in the series and loved meeting Linda at a book signing event. So once they arrived, we moved the selection to the current month's gathering. We couldn't wait to talk about the third book in the *"Blind"* series! The first question asked was "When is the next one coming out?!" *"Blind Alliance"* continues the intrigue, character development, and plot twists so artfully crafted by this author. This series does an excellent job of capturing the undercurrents, intrigue, and power broker maneuverings of political life." -A.M.

"Study the past if you would define the future."

--Confucius

"Abuse of words has been the great instrument of sophistry and chicanery, of party, faction, and division of society."

--John Adams

"Let us not seek the Republican answer or the Democratic answer, but the right answer. Let us not seek to fix the blame for the past. Let us accept our own responsibility for the future."

--John F. Kennedy

CHAPTER ONE
LATE DECEMBER 1980

Moscow, USSR—Kremlin

Colonel Dmitry Leznikov, a former field agent of the KGB, was looking out his interior office window. He studied the bullpen of workers under his command. While some were scurrying to spruce up their desks and office space, Leznikov, a jovial fifty-three-year-old former engineer turned spy, yearned for his days back in Montreal. His daydream was interrupted when one of his men deposited a new bundle of papers on Leznikov's already cluttered desk. As the clean-up continued, Leznikov's paper heap continued to grow. Beyond the bullpen were windowless white metal doors that led to various laboratories. He made a mental note to visit each lab for inspection before President Baranov arrived later in the day. Leznikov leaned out the door and shouted a few more instructions, keeping his smile to himself. He watched as the pace of the men became even more frantic. He could not afford to be too cordial with the men under his command.

Leznikov walked back to his desk and sat down in his comfortable, leather chair. His mind wandered back in time to a few years earlier when he was recalled from his fieldwork and ushered into the Politburo. Leonid Baranov and Leznikov were friends long before Baranov's rise to power. A key player in Baranov's ascent in the 1970s, Leznikov vowed his loyalty to his friend-turned-leader. With each passing year and despite his ill-health, Baranov managed to accrue more power thanks to Leznikov's intelligence information. In 1977, Baranov removed Alexey Palokov as chairman, hence becoming the top man in the Communist party as well as the Soviet Union's ceremonial leader. Baranov was ruthless when he needed to be, and his success emerged from lobbying and the political prowess of a thinking man. Baranov knew how to make the Politburo his ally even during the most arduous times.

In 1972, the USSR accepted the détente offered by President Andrews. The USSR's economy had stalled from the isolation that the leaders before Baranov hailed as the means for their country's success. The lackluster, failing economy was becoming the West's best weapon to undermine communism. However, in the seventies, fear of the USSR's nuclear capabilities was over-reaching at best, greatly exaggerated at worst, by the US government. The two countries signed the détente as a way for Soviet American relations to control the rhetoric of nuclear war and present calm, cool-headed leadership to the rest of the world. The United States did not realize that this détente only confirmed the perception to the rest of the world that these two nations equally possessed the means to obliterate each other—a fact most hoped would deter the other from pushing the button.

Leznikov remembered sitting in the room with his fellow Politburo members and listening to Baranov convince them that détente was necessary. "We communists," Baranov began his speech, "have to become friendly with the capitalists for a while. We need their credits, their agriculture, and their technology. But we are going to continue massive military buildup and increase the number of military programs. We lack in the technology sector. We will use our intelligence community to obtain secrets from the Western companies, improve upon them, and distribute this new technology within our country. Our goal is by the middle of the 1980s; we will return to a much more aggressive foreign policy designed to become more powerful than the West." Cheers and applause rose as Baranov emphasized the latter part of the last sentence.

The détente proved to be the shot in the arm the Soviets needed. The GRU and KGB were set to pounce on every opportunity to steal from the free enterprise systems of the West, particularly the United States. Leznikov smiled as he recalled the many different ways during the 1970s the Soviets had capitalized—pun intended—on the openness of United States businesses to share their science and technology advancements. It was no secret to the Soviet leaders that they trailed the West in computer and microelectronic technology by more than a decade. The discussion of the détente agreement started when the Council of Ministers and the Central Committee established a new unit. This unit was known as the Directorate T and part of the KGB's First Chief Directorate. Its mission was to penetrate the research and development programs of the Western economies. There were many participants in the Directorate T program involving many factions of the Kremlin. The State Committee of Science and Technology, the Military-Industrial Commission, Military-Intelligence (GRU), the Soviet Academy of Sciences, and the State Committee for External Relations supplied Directorate T with its collection requirements. It was no surprise that Baranov would recall Leznikov from Montreal and appoint him to head up Line X, which was the operating arm of Directorate T.

Leznikov prided himself on his genius for collecting the information the Soviets needed to draw even and then surpass the West. The détente provided new, creative ways of Soviet exploitation. Delegations of Soviet specialists traveled to the United States to visit firms and laboratories associated with their commissions. Leznikov inserted Line X personnel masquerading as delegates on these trips. The typical ratio of KGB Line X agents to non-espionage related delegates was three to one. Leznikov himself decided to attend a visit to Boeing. Just before entering the factory floor, Leznikov and a few additional "Line X" delegates excused themselves to the restroom where they applied adhesive to the bottom of their shoes. This method obtained metal samples for the laboratories of Line X to analyze, and thus provided the Directorate with information on the metals used by Boeing to build both commercial and military aircraft. Another example of their collection methods involved ranking scientists and managers of the Soviet computer and electronics industry. The managers requested and obtained a visa to visit the Uranus Liquid Crystal Watch Company of Mineola on Long Island, New York. Three days before the delegation's arrival, Leznikov requested an expansion of the itinerary. The request included nearly all of the US computer and semiconductor firms. By studying the US regulations, Leznikov knew that the Department of Defense would not have time to object to the expansive addition. As a result, Line X agents visited nearly all of the computer and semiconductor firms, acquiring precious secrets through obscure collecting methods as crafty as the adhesive on the soles of their shoe method. These endeavors continued; including proposing to Lockheed and Boeing that the Soviets would purchase fifty transport aircraft if the firms would build and equip a modern "aircraft city" in the USSR. This proposal made to each company resulted in Boeing and Lockheed playing off each other allowing the Soviets to obtain technical data. These were only a few operations, but Line X's reach touched all aspects of military and commercial systems.

Leznikov smirked at how stupid he thought Americans were. His Line X operation continued undetected. Ten years later, information was still pouring into his directorate. To his knowledge, the United States had no idea they were helping to build a more powerful Soviet Union. In fact, each year in the last ten, the United States continued to laud the success of the détente. His smile grew larger when he recalled the Apollo-Soyuz spacecraft joint mission in 1975, and how the Soviets successfully planted a KGB Line X agent among their crew to gain intelligence access to the US space program. Only a few weeks before launch did US counterintelligence discover the Soviet agent. By then, the agent had gathered all the useful information. Leznikov counted that success as one of Line X's most brilliantly executed operations.

Today was the tenth anniversary of Line X. In celebration, Leznikov invited Baranov down to his unit to address his men. He wanted Baranov to boast to his workers how the information they were collecting, reviewing, and passing on to others was strengthening the USSR to surpass its enemies militarily, as well as in technology and science. The USSR was stronger than ever and now possessed the nuclear capability to strike the United States five times over. Leznikov personally informed Baranov that a new cable channel in the United States aired government activities. On this channel, a report given by a five-star general to the US Senate Armed Services Committee proclaimed that the United States military only possessed the ability to strike the USSR four times over. It was a great day in the USSR, and Line X was a huge contributor to the success. Leznikov couldn't wait to see the expressions on his men's faces when Baranov painted the USSR's prosperous future and the demise of their most inept adversary who unwittingly continued to help them. Leznikov felt his heart skip a beat with excitement. *Yes,* Leznikov thought, *the seventies were very good for the Soviet Union thanks to the détente with the United States.*

Moscow, USSR—United Kingdom Embassy

Neither Sean nor Nicole slept well their first night in their new home. It was after eight in the morning when the phone rang. When Sean answered, his chief of staff, Colin Stewart, was on the other end. He informed Sean that there was a matter of importance to discuss and apologized for waking him. Sean dressed quickly telling Nicole to come down to the office when she was ready to practice at the shooting range with her new present—the Beretta that he had given her the night before.

Sean walked into the foyer of the residence. He stopped when he noticed the smashed vase and roses that Nicole had thrown against the wall upon their arrival had disappeared. Puzzled, he looked around the foyer and the adjoining rooms before he exited. He wondered if Nicole had cleaned it up during the night while he dozed. Since he had not been in a deep sleep, any movement would have woken him. He walked down two flights of stairs and continued past offices and the bullpen of lower ranking embassy staff. He greeted all he met along the way. He noted the surprise and sometimes embarrassment of the embassy workers when he engaged them. The whole situation seemed quite strange—as if he expected his staff to be seen and not heard.

"Good morning, Mr. Stewart," Sean said as he opened the door to a suite of offices. Stewart sat in the outer office to greet visitors and other embassy workers. Sean's office door was to Stewart's left. Nicole's office door was to Stewart's right, and Nicole could enter Sean's office by a door that connected them directly.

Colin Stewart, who was about the same age as Sean, measured about five feet nine inches tall with jet black hair, fair complexion, and the bluest sapphire-colored eyes. His looks were striking, and some women found him irresistible. Feeling that proper attire was a requirement of his position in the embassy, his dress was impeccable and something on which he prided himself. Stewart rose to his feet when Sean entered the outer office area. "Good morning, sir."

"Come on in," Sean called as he walked into his office. Stewart picked up his day planner and walked into the inner office, closing the door behind him. "Mr. Stewart, there were flowers in the foyer of our residence last night. Do you know anything about them?"

"If I may, sir, please call me Colin or Stew," he requested as he stood in front of the desk waiting for Sean to sit down.

Sean looked at Stewart a bit puzzled. "I think I rather like Stew if you don't mind."

"Not at all, sir."

"About the flowers—" Sean started to repeat his question, but it wasn't necessary.

"Yes, I don't know the details but would assume that they were placed there by your chambermaid," Stewart interjected. "Would you like me to question her about them?"

"We have chambermaid?" Sean asked, surprise evident in his voice.

"Yes, sir," Stewart replied. "She is Russian and does not live on the embassy grounds. I presumed she introduced herself this morning."

"We haven't seen her," Sean countered.

"Oh dear, that won't do. I will instruct Natasha to introduce herself today before she leaves. Were there something wrong with the flowers?"

"Just who they were from…," Sean's voice trailed off. He was already wondering if this Russian chambermaid was the Serpent's informant. "I'd like to see her file as soon as possible—now actually. And you may want to call up to the residence and warn Nicole that we have a chambermaid." Stewart stood steadfast, making a note in his planner. Annoyed with Stewart's inaction, Sean asked, "How do I call the residence?"

Stewart reached over, picked up the receiver, and dialed the three digits. The phone rang, and when Nicole picked it up, Stewart said, "Ambassador Adkins for you, ma'am." He handed the phone to Sean.

Even more perplexed, Sean accepted the phone from Stewart. He could hear Nicole snickering. "Thank you, Stew," he said. He put the phone to his ear. "Nicole, I wanted to let you know we have a chambermaid. Don't be alarmed if you happen to run into her." He smiled when he heard Nicole give another laugh.

"Seriously, you had to have Mr. Stewart call me?" Nicole responded. "And a chambermaid? We need a chambermaid?"

Sean decided to answer with a flippant response. "Welcome to embassy life. I'll see you in a few minutes." He hung up the phone. He returned his look to Stewart, who was still standing. He motioned for him to sit, but Stewart didn't move. "You have no idea how the flowers got to the foyer?"

"They were presumably delivered to the front gate. One of the guards must have called for the chambermaid to retrieve them. That is the customary procedure for deliveries like that." Stewart was suspicious. He decided to ask again, "Was there a problem with the flowers, sir?"

"It's a long story, Stew," Sean began. "I'm afraid that the sender is someone that neither Nicole nor I would like to hear from again. In her anger, Nicole broke the antique vase. I suppose I'll have to pay for that."

"While that is unfortunate, I suggest that we don't bring it up." Stewart grinned. "I will do some quiet checking to see if it was on loan, but my gut feeling is that it was not. If that is the concern, sir, I wouldn't let it bother you. The former ambassador's wife had a habit of *breaking* quite a lot of things." Stewart's emphasis on the word breaking led Sean to believe the former ambassador's wife had quite a temper.

Sean took a breath and decided to change the subject. "Have a seat, please."

Stewart cleared his throat, which caught Sean's attention. Sean diverted his attention from a piece of paper that was on his desk to Stewart. "I only sit when you sit, sir. It is customary—"

"Oh, right. I'm sorry. I'm not accustomed to this quite yet." Sean smirked but did not sit down. "I don't think we'll be much longer." Sean heard the door open in the outer office and assumed it was Nicole. "But first, Nicole and I are going to the practice range to shoot off a few rounds."

After a few quick raps on the door, Nicole opened it and walked inside just as Stewart said, "I'm afraid that won't be possible." He turned to Nicole to greet her. "Good morning, ma'am."

"Good morning, Mr. Stewart," Nicole, dressed in blue jeans and a loose-fitting blouse, said as she closed the door. She had her gun concealed beneath her blouse and tucked into her jeans at the small of her back. "What is with everyone? I said good morning to some of the staff, and you would have thought I had horns growing out of my head."

"I had the same experience. We'll get to that later," Sean said.

Nicole walked up to the two men who were still standing. Her eyes darted back and forth between them when they did not resume their conversation. "I'm sorry, am I interrupting something?"

"Stew was saying that we may not be able to go to the practice range."

"Sir, you have to present your credentials to President Baranov this morning at ten. After Mr. Baranov received your brother's—" Stewart corrected himself, "the prime minister's letter about the situation in Poland, his secretary called demanding to meet with you immediately. I was fortunate to schedule the meeting at ten o'clock."

"What situation in Poland are you referring to?" Sean's mind was on the Serpent, not politics.

"That is what I need to brief you on before you present your credentials. There is a strike in Poland, and it seems that the Soviet Union is mobilizing troops to intercede."

"Yes, of course," Sean replied, a bit embarrassed that he forgot. "I remember reading about it in the papers you gave me last evening. Have there been further developments?"

"It seems that the prime minister, the president of the United States and the German chancellor have written letters urging Baranov to not interfere with Poland," Stewart informed him. "Copies of the letters are on your desk. They came across the teletype early this morning."

"We still use teletypes?" Sean was surprised.

"Yes," Stewart confirmed. "That's another discussion we need to have. This embassy is deficient in a number of ways, and I believe there is a security risk because of our inadequate systems."

"I see," Sean replied. He looked at Nicole, his apology written on his face. "It seems we have some work to do. What's the proper attire for this sort of thing? I suppose business suits for both of us?"

Nicole looked at Sean. "I'm not needed at your meeting. I am very sure the invitation was extended only to you." She walked up to Sean and gave him a quick kiss on the cheek. "What *is* the ambassador's appropriate attire for this meeting?"

"A suit," Stewart instructed.

"I'll get that out of the suitcase and make sure it is free of wrinkles. What's the chambermaid's name?" Nicole said as she walked toward the office door.

"Natasha," Stewart replied. "And she can press the ambassador's suit."

"I assume she speaks and understands English?" Nicole opened the office door, ignoring Stewart's comment.

"Yes, ma'am," Stewart confirmed.

"Thank you," Nicole responded as she left the room to return to the residence.

Stewart watched her leave and then turned to Sean. "I get the distinct feeling she doesn't like me."

Sean raised his eyebrows with curiosity. The tone of Stewart's voice intrigued him. Was Stewart trying to divide and conquer?

Did Stewart feel threatened by Nicole's role at the embassy—a role yet to be determined? He decided to sidestep any reassurances to Stewart's ego until he knew Stewart better. "Tell me about Baranov and what I'm supposed to do when I meet him."

"Yes, of course," Stewart started. Sean sat down behind his desk. Stewart walked around the desk to stand by Sean's chair. Stewart placed a manila folder in front of Sean. Stewart went over the contents, including how Sean should behave, where to stand, and how to address Baranov. Sean listened intently. Stewart then showed Sean his credentials. He read them over. "What if he doesn't accept them?"

"That rarely happens," Stewart assured him. "Have you ever met Baranov before this?"

"No."

"Then I don't think it will be a problem."

Sean knew the KGB was capable of unearthing well-hidden information on any individual that interested them even if MI6 cloaked the identities of their agents. A new ambassador replacing an overtly Soviet-friendly ambassador would draw the attention of the KGB. He bit his lower lip as he thought about an exit plan. Stewart was rambling on about how to leave Baranov's presence. Sean's attention was brought back to the conversation when he heard Stewart mention walking out of the office. "I'm sorry, Stew, my mind was elsewhere. What did you say about leaving?"

"You are not to show your backside to Baranov. It's considered an insult."

"Yes, well," Sean began, "how do I get out of the room without tripping over something or toppling a table or two?"

"With as much grace as you can muster," Stewart joked. "Believe me; it wouldn't be the first time." Stewart looked at his watch. "You need to dress now, sir. Hopefully, Natasha has some breakfast waiting for you. We should be ready to leave at 9:15."

Sean looked at his watch. He had about thirty minutes to prepare. He took his credentials with him. He returned to the residence to find that Nicole had laid out his freshly pressed navy blue pinstripe suit, white long-sleeve shirt, and a maroon-colored tie. On a table in the bedroom was a tray of food consisting of an apple, orange, some bread, butter and under a dish warmer, some scrambled eggs. Sean noticed a note and walked over to the table. He picked it up and discovered that Nicole had decided to proceed to the firing range without him. Sean wasn't at all happy that Nicole had decided to do this, but he didn't have time to go after her. He sat down to eat the eggs, not interested in the other items. While he was eating and studying the materials in the folder, Natasha entered the room.

"Good morning, Mr. Ambassador," Natasha said after she knocked once on the open door and entered the room. One got the impression that she felt she owned the flat. "My name is Natasha. I help you here."

Sean stood, offering his hand to her. "Hello, Natasha. I assume you met Nicole?"

"Da," Natasha said, ignoring the offered handshake. "She said she was going to shoot a gun, nyet?"

"Evidently," Sean quipped, his displeasure apparent in his tone. "Did you get this suit ready for me?"

"Da," Natasha responded. "I ironed suit when your lady told me you were to wear it."

"Thank you," Sean said. "Her name is Nicole and mine is Sean. You may call us by name." Natasha did not respond. Sean got the feeling Natasha was going to call them whatever she wanted regardless of any instruction to the contrary. "Is there a way for me to call the firing range?"

"Da," Natasha replied as she walked over to the phone. She opened a drawer and removed a small binder. "Here are numbers." She opened it to the page and pointed to the number. "This number, you do this." Natasha pointed to the phone number pad.

"I understand," Sean replied. "Thank you."

Natasha walked over to the tray of food. "As I told the nice Lady Charbonneau, I talk to you about the food you like and other habits. Are you done with this?"

"Yes, thank you," Sean responded, standing by the phone. "I'm afraid I'm not very hungry."

Natasha nodded once and picked up the tray. "I leave now."

"Thank you," Sean called after her. Natasha did not acknowledge Sean's comment. Shaking his head at Natasha's abruptness, he picked up the phone and dialed the firing range. "Yes, I'm looking for Nicole Charbonneau. She has…"

"Yes sir," the guard interrupted. "We know who she is. She is finishing up right now. Can you wait?"

"Yes." As Sean waited, he could hear the rattle of automatic gunfire, some cheering, and then chatter among what he assumed were the other guards watching someone shoot. He smiled when he recalled some of the bets that were placed at Fort Monckton when the recruits were partaking in target practice. He heard the door open and then Nicole's voice.

"There's no welshing on bets here—get your money out," Nicole said as she walked to the phone, now being held by the guard who had answered it. "Thank you. Hello?"

"Nicole," Sean began. "I see you made it to the firing range."

"Yes," Nicole confirmed. "Is everything all right?"

"I don't want you walking around the grounds alone until I have had the opportunity to vet everyone."

"I'm sorry," Nicole responded. She wasn't sorry, and her tone reflected that. "I do have a gun. Remember?"

Sean smiled. "And I can see the headlines if you decide to use it." Sean heard Nicole's sarcastic, lilting laughter and decided to change the subject. "I'll be leaving soon. What's your assessment of our security guards?"

"Well, let's say that I'm getting to know these gentlemen very well," Nicole said. She winked at the guards who were in the room looking at her. "I understand that Alistair will be commanding the squad accompanying you to see Baranov today." Nicole was watching Alistair gear up for the mission. "He and the rest of the men are getting ready now—complete with bulletproof vests and SA80s."

Sean was quite astonished that Nicole even knew what an SA80 was: a new rifle, equipped with a three-position gas regulator. This regulator would allow the shooter to choose between normal firing, adverse condition firing, or launching rifle grenades. It was obvious to Sean that his posting to Moscow came with an upgrade in munitions as the SA80s were not deployed to Her Majesty's embassies yet. Sean cleared his throat. "SA80s? How do you know about SA80s?"

"Alistair was kind enough to show me one," Nicole proudly replied.

Sean heard a Scottish burr voice say in the background, "Show, my arse!" A laugh went up in the office. "Here's your winnings, love."

"Thank you, Duncan," Nicole said as she took the money from him.

"Nicole, am I to understand that you shot an SA80?"

"Yes," Nicole confirmed. "I was dared by Alistair. He didn't think I would be able to hit the target, but I did. It wasn't dead center, not anywhere near it. But the bet was that I couldn't hit the target at all."

Sean could hear the men laughing in the background. He wanted to join them but tried very hard not to do so. He remembered his astonishment in Inverness when Nicole surprised him with her shooting prowess. Holding in his amusement, he changed the subject. "I'm about to leave to meet Baranov in a few minutes. Can we at least plan to have lunch together?"

Nicole smiled. "Don't get jealous," she whispered into the phone as she turned her back to the other guards, who were utterly taken by Nicole.

Sean shook his head. "Obviously you don't know me as well as you think you do. I don't get jealous. It's a wasted emotion."

Nicole smiled at Sean's attempted denial. "Uh-huh."

"I'll see you when I get back," Sean said with a little irritation in his voice. "And please, don't roam around the grounds by yourself. Come straight back here."

"OK," Nicole replied. "Have a good meeting. Love you."

As she hung up the phone, Sean could hear Nicole's question to the guards in the office. She asked them to tell her about the previous ambassador. Sean knew he would be getting a briefing at lunch. He couldn't be mad at Nicole. In her way, she would obtain more information than he could through their personnel files. She had the freedom to ask them any question and the charm to get the truth from them. Sean felt like they were a team and he needed to dial back his overprotectiveness. It was obvious that Nicole wanted more control over her life now that she was feeling stronger. Working as a team only enhanced their chances in any situation.

Sean quickly donned his suit and headed down to the front door of the embassy. He was carrying his shoulder harness and gun with him. He knew he would never be allowed in to see the leader of the Soviet Union wearing his gun, but he felt naked without it. His motorcade, complete with little Union Jack flags on the hood and bonnet of the cars, was waiting for him. The members of his guard detail, which was a subset of the embassy's security force, was standing in a line by the vehicles. Alistair, clearly the highest ranking member of the squad, was standing in front of his men and snapped to attention when Stewart, who was waiting for Sean outside, opened the door.

"Good morning," Sean said as he walked up to Alistair, extending his hand.

Alistair first looked at Sean's hand in surprise, but then shifted his SA80 to his other hand and accepted it. "Good morning, sir." His uneasiness was evident in his voice. "I'm Captain Alistair Delaney. We'll be escorting you to the Kremlin for your visit."

Sean smiled when he heard the name. "Are you the chap that showed Nicole the SA80?"

A few chuckles escaped some of the men's lips. Alistair's quick glance shut them up. He turned his attention back to Sean. "Yes, sir."

Sean nodded his head. "Well, later today I'd like to give it a try if I may?"

"Yes, sir," Alistair replied.

Sean leaned into Alistair and whispered, "Don't feel bad. She has a way of knocking me down a few pegs time and again. It's irritating that she is so damn good at it."

Sean watched a restrained smile dance quickly across Alistair's lips before Alistair regained his stoic composure. "Yes, sir." He noticed Sean's gun and holster. "Sir, if I may, they won't allow you to wear that inside the Kremlin."

"Yes, I determined that," Sean confirmed. "It's going to ride along with me in the car. Shall we go?"

Stewart and Sean walked to the car as Alistair gave the order to his men. Alistair followed Sean and Stewart, crawling into the seat across from them. Sean placed his gun and holster next to him on the seat. Alistair tapped the window that separated the driver from its occupants. When the window retracted, Alistair said, "The quickest route to the Kremlin and inform the others of that." The window rose as Alistair turned his attention back to Sean. "In the future, sir, so that you know, I will always be in the car with you. Think of me as your bodyguard." He looked at Sean's Beretta.

Sean could tell that Alistair was not at all happy with Sean carrying a gun. "Yes, well, tell me if I'm wrong, but didn't you recently lose a bet to Nicole?"

Alistair frowned. "Yes. She said she was a bit rusty, but I assure you that she is quite a shooter. She has game, as they say."

Sean smiled. "Yes, I recently found that out myself. Captain, understand that Nicole and I will be armed whenever you encounter us. I'll explain the reason in the next few days. My advice to you and your men is to get used to that fact. If for some reason we are not armed, let's say for a diplomatic party at the Kremlin or another embassy, we may not be carrying the gun on our body, but we will have it with us en route."

"Yes, sir," Alistair replied. "In that case, Mr. Ambassador, before we reach the Kremlin gates, would you be so kind as to allow me to carry your gun? We are expected to be armed." Sean eyed Alistair for a moment. "You, on the other hand, are not. We should be reaching the Kremlin's front gate in about five minutes." Sean took the gun out of its holster, checked that the safety was on, and handed it to Alistair, who tucked it into his pants at the small of his back. "Thank you, sir."

Sean nodded his acknowledgment and turned his head to look out the window. They were in one of the business centers that led to Red Square. He observed the people in their winter coats and boots, hopping from shop to shop, some in conversation, and some hurriedly completing their errands. He watched the lead vehicle of his motorcade turn as they arrived at the front gate of the Kremlin. The gate opened as their car approached.

The door to his limousine opened, and Alistair exited the vehicle first, indicating he wanted Sean to stay put. Sean glanced around observing the placement of the Soviet guards. Alistair motioned for them to exit the vehicle; Sean emerged first followed by Stewart. Sean had never seen the Kremlin in person, so he took the opportunity to scan the building, taking in its unique architecture and then surmising that it looked very much like the photos he saw while in training at Fort Monckton. Alistair accompanied them as they walked through the hallways that led to Baranov's outer office. Sean walked to the desk of the male secretary and introduced himself. The secretary took the folder from Sean and depressed a button on his desk. He immediately got up to open the door to the president's office. Stewart and Alistair didn't move when the secretary motioned for Sean to enter the room. Sean walked in alone and noticed President Baranov beginning to stand.

The secretary walked toward Baranov, meeting him in front of his desk. As Sean took a few more steps before stopping in the center of the room, the secretary handed Baranov Sean's credentials. Baranov silently read them. While Sean waited for Baranov to address him, he studied the leader of the Soviet Union. Sean noticed the stature of the leader: broad-shouldered, stout, and the face of someone who had become too familiar with war. His dark hair had streaks of gray throughout, and his eyebrows were thick and currently furrowed as he read. His mouth was in the familiar scowl Sean had seen in photographs. It was clear that Baranov was no stranger to the stress of ruling or fighting, as the lines on the leader's face attested. Sean didn't turn his head, but his eyes darted around the room taking in many details. Cigarette smoke rose from Baranov's desk, the cigarette placed in the ashtray when they entered the room. The office décor was sterile and military. The drapes and rug in the room matched the red of the proudly displayed Soviet Union flag.

Baranov motioned for the secretary to leave the room. As the secretary brushed past Sean, intentionally making contact with Sean's shoulder, Baranov reprimanded the secretary in Russian. The secretary stopped, turned, and then apologized as directed by his leader. Sean acknowledged the apology with a quick nod of the head. The secretary walked out of the room, closing the door behind him. Baranov motioned for Sean to approach him and said,

"Hello, Ambassador Adkins. Come here and sit with me a moment or two."

Sean walked up to Baranov, taking the leader's extended hand into his. "I am honored to meet you, sir." Honored was not the word he wanted to use, but Sean knew you gathered more information acting as a friend rather than an enemy.

"Thank you," Baranov said, gently nudging Sean to the chair across from his desk. He signed the credentials and handed them to Sean. "Sit, please." Sean sat down after Baranov had taken his seat. "I could not help but notice your last name is the same as your prime minister's."

"Yes," Sean replied. "He is my brother."

"And your father is Lord Peter Adkins," Baranov stated. Sean nodded his head. "You are aware of the letter your brother has sent me regarding Poland?"

"I'm aware you received three letters, Mr. President," Sean stated. "I believe their counsel is wise."

"You do?" Baranov questioned. "Tell me, Mr. Ambassador, if Scotland decided to go on strike and not send a product that your country was dependent upon, would you not interfere with that strike?"

Sean hesitated. "That isn't my decision to make." Baranov cocked his head, not happy with Sean's diplomatic answer. "Mr. President, I believe the issue is not with having a response to the strike, but it has more to do with how you plan to respond." Baranov's thick eyebrows furrowed over his squinted eyes as he surveyed Sean. "Going back to your question about Scotland, Her Majesty would not send a regiment of armed soldiers. Instead, she would send the appropriate diplomat or even a highly skilled negotiator to bring the strike to an end. Armed soldiers typically are not regarded as good negotiators."

Baranov sat back. "So, you don't approve of sending troops to defend my border with Poland."

"I didn't say that," Sean replied calmly. "I would say that the action is causing concern in the West. It is an escalation that may only lead to war. Can you tell me that you have no interest in invading Poland at a time of civil unrest?"

Baranov gave a stifled chuckle, followed by a few coughs. He looked at Sean, who didn't blink. "You, Ambassador Sean Adkins—you I like. You are the only one with the nerve to ask me directly what the others will not." Baranov stood up, and Sean rose to his feet in response. Baranov extended his hand. "Welcome to my country. We are having a little party here on New Year's Eve. I would like you to attend—no, I command you to attend."

"It would be an honor, Mr. President." Again, the word honor escaped his lips. He made a mental note to find a more appropriate word. Sean shook Baranov's hand. "May I bring a companion?"

Baranov turned his hand to look at Sean's ring finger, noting the absence of a wedding ring. "Are you married?"

"Not quite yet," Sean responded.

"Yes, of course, bring your companion."

"Thank you."

Baranov walked around his desk and motioned for Sean to join him. Putting an arm around Sean's shoulder, he walked him to the door of his office. "I think you and I will get along very well. Welcome again to my country, Mr. Ambassador."

"Thank you for your time, Mr. President," Sean said as Baranov opened the door. Stewart and Alistair saw Baranov remove his arm, and Sean extended his hand once more to the leader. After the handshake, Baranov turned to walk back to his desk. Sean walked out of the office and started for his car with Stewart and Alistair following him. When they were safely on their way back to the embassy, Sean said, "That was the oddest experience. His reaction to me was unexpected."

"It seems you have somehow won his trust in that short time," Stewart observed.

"I'm not so sure," Sean countered. "You know the old saying about keeping your enemies close. In any event, it looks like Nicole and I will be spending a part of New Year's Eve with him. He invited us to his party."

Stewart looked at Alistair, astonished. "You can't be serious."

"I am," Sean confirmed. "Why?"

"The previous ambassador received his first invitation-only last year," Stewart offered and then added, "It raised the suspicions of the home office."

Sean did not respond; he merely raised an eyebrow as he turned his head to look out the window. He realized he needed to learn more about the previous ambassador before attending the party.

Moscow, USSR—Airport

Former Senator Larry Barker and his wife, Louise, arrived at the airport in Moscow and were greeted by his chief of staff. A longtime aide to the senator, Cliff Brown was in his forties and had begun working for Barker close to twenty years ago. Cliff remained loyal during times when others had abandoned the senator. Barker admitted to himself that he trusted Cliff more than he trusted Louise. Cliff knew about the senator's shenanigans—the senator's illegal and legal actions. Cliff graduated at the top of his class at Yale Law School. He latched onto Barker's coattails believing that they would take him to the White House one day as Barker's chief of staff. He was as bitter as Barker was concerning President-Elect Robert Jenkins. Over a whiskey, before Cliff left for Moscow, the two men had made a pact to make life hell for Jenkins at every opportunity.

Louise wasn't happy with her husband's new assignment. She referred to it as banishment to the Soviet Union. She batted back tears all through the flight, and whenever she tried to talk to her husband, he snapped angrily at her. She was on the outside and had no idea why the former-prodigy-now-president-elect would ostracize her husband to such an isolated, unglamorous post. She walked slowly and dejectedly behind her husband and Cliff, accompanied by the only person her husband would allow her to bring: her young, perky, newly appointed social secretary. Louise knew why Barker selected this woman for her. She knew of their affair but turned a blind eye as she had always done. But this time, her resentment of the two of them was almost too much for her to bear silently. Louise's best friend and former chief of staff was her confidante, and Barker fired her. Louise's best friend approached Jenkins at a social event and pleaded with the president-elect to reconsider Barker's posting to the USSR. Barker found out and was enraged, firing her moments after he was informed. Now Louise was in Moscow with no one to trust. She felt utterly abandoned and helplessly stranded.

Barker's group piled into the limousine waiting for them on the tarmac. Hardly a word was spoken as they drove through the streets to the embassy. Upon arrival, the embassy's military force greeted them. Cliff had ordered their presence upon arrival, encouraging Barker to give them a quick inspection. Cliff hoped it might give Barker a much-needed lift of spirit. While it did just that, Barker fell back into his gloomy, angry demeanor as he approached the building. Cliff escorted everyone to their rooms in the residence wing, the Barkers' suite being the last stop. Louise was well aware why Cliff deliberately showed them her new secretary's room first so Barker would know where to find his mistress. Louise would know where to look if she ever decided to go looking for him. Once inside their own suite, Louise walked to the bedroom, dropping her coat on an armchair as she walked by it.

"A staffer will deliver your luggage shortly," Cliff called to Louise as she left the living room.

What Louise did next should have been the first sign that the trouble between Louise and Barker was approaching disrepair. Louise, a sophisticated, almost aristocratic, old-school, prim and proper lady raised her middle finger without caring enough to turn around to see her intended victims' faces. Louise never used the word associated with the middle finger salute, and this was the first time that both men could remember that she had ever flipped them off. While the two men stood astonished, Louise walked into the bedroom, slammed the door and locked it. Louise was sixty-five years old, and she felt horrible. The treatment she was receiving took her back to the day when Barker brought his mistress's child into their home and forced her to raise it as their own. No one knew this happened and no one heard from the mistress again. There had been other times that Barker demeaned her, but nothing came close to that day until now. She threw herself on the bed and let the cry she was holding back for days escape her trembling body. She hated the Soviet Union, and she hated her husband. How was she going to survive this?

Cliff looked at Barker when the door slammed. "You know you need to bring her around. She's your best asset in social settings."

"She'll come around," Barker spat out. "Where's the whiskey?"

Cliff pointed to the bar on the other side of the room. "You know about this place, right?"

"The Soviet Union—of course, I do."

"No," Cliff said. "I mean the embassy. It's history." He explained to Barker in detail the construction of the embassy. William Bullitt, Jr. was appointed the first ambassador to the Soviet Union in 1934. Finding the embassy old and inappropriate for their needs, Bullitt asked Stalin for permission to build another embassy closer to the Soviet Union's government buildings. The request went unfulfilled, garnering little attention until negotiations began in earnest in the 1960s. At this time, the Soviets countered the thirty-odd year request with their request for a new embassy in Washington, DC. Lenin offered a site high atop Lenin Hills, formerly known as Sparrow Hills. Lenin Hills rose above the Moskva River and was the highest point in Moscow. The State Department was not impressed by the offer and opted instead for an eighty-five-year lease on a ten-acre site that was more accessible and centrally located. An agreement was reached in 1969, but more delays kept the new embassy from being constructed. In 1972, President Andrews ordered the State Department to get it done, handing off the control of the design and construction to the Soviets. "Everyone thought we would be able to outsmart the Soviets," Cliff continued the story. "But we failed. This place is so bugged. They hear every word, and so far, there is nothing we can do about it. The Soviets were crafty enough to secure the wires inside the concrete walls. We can't get to them."

"I remember that now," Barker said with a devilish grin that crept across his lips. He made a mental note that the bugging of the American embassy could be used to make Jenkins's presidency a living hell. "There was a lot of discussion in committee about installing countermeasures or even having this building razed."

"That's correct," Cliff started. "While in some places we've been partially successful with those countermeasures, for the most part, this building is considered compromised."

"Indeed it is," Barker agreed. "And you just cheered me up." Barker downed his whiskey and put his glass down. "Where's my office and what's on our agenda?"

"This way," Cliff replied, gesturing to the front door of the residence. "First we need to present your credentials to Baranov, and then there is this New Year's Eve party that you need to attend."

"Who's throwing the party?"

"Baranov," Cliff responded. "You'll have the opportunity to meet fellow ambassadors and the men closest to Baranov."

"Perfect," Barker said as they left the residence headed for his office.

Washington, DC—Blair House

Chris knocked on the door to President-Elect Jenkins's office before he opened it. "Sir, we need to discuss your special guests at the inauguration. Invitations are due out as soon as possible."

Jenkins looked up at Chris and said, "I assume you have a list of guests from both sides of the aisle."

Chris walked into the office, closing the door behind him. "Of course," he replied. "But I am sure you have people you want there. You can invite anyone you want." He opened his folder and produced multiple sets of paper-clipped documents. "The top is the

DNC's list. The second one is a list that President Blackwood sent over. I assume that includes the RNC's request. The third list contains the names of big donors to your campaign. There is also a list from the D-triple-C." Jenkins took the lists out of the folder while he looked at Chris. "The last paper contains foreign dignitaries to whom you may want to extend an invitation."

Jenkins flipped through the lists. He picked up his pen and started to scratch out names. "I know some people may not like the names I'm scratching off of here, but it is my party." Jenkins smiled as he spoke. "Those I scratched off can obtain tickets from the politicians whose pockets they have their hands in. I don't want their names associated in any way with me regardless of whatever side of the aisle they sit." Chris acknowledged Jenkins's comments as Jenkins flipped to the last page. Jenkins handed the paper back to Chris. "Add my parents to the list."

Chris was about to turn, but stopped and looked at Jenkins. He flipped to the last page and glanced down at it. Chris concluded his quick scan and said, "My apologies, sir. Of course, I will add their names. You'll want them sitting on the platform with you, correct?"

"Yes," Jenkins replied. "Unless I can find a date between now and then," Jenkins quipped. Chris hesitated. "What is it?"

"You are within your rights to extend an invitation to Nicole and Sean," Chris stated.

"Invite Her Majesty's ambassador to the USSR?" Jenkins wanted to laugh. "I don't think that would be a good idea. I would like to keep my friendship with Sean and Nicole quiet, in case I may need them in the years ahead." Jenkins stood and stretched. "I'm sure there will be other times when I'll see them. My parents will be proud to be by my side."

Chris had something else he needed to bring up to Jenkins. "Sir, I was asked a question this morning, and I'm not quite sure how to answer it," he started. Jenkins walked out from behind his desk and urged Chris to continue. "The duties of the First Lady providing tours, selecting the china for state dinners and the like, decorating the White House, and so many other duties—who will be doing that?"

Jenkins looked at Chris. He could tell by Chris's awkward phrasing he was uncomfortable bringing up the question. "I haven't thought about it," Jenkins responded truthfully.

"Well, sir, if your vice president were a man, his wife could be asked to step in on occasion."

"But since my vice president is Patricia Samuelson, it is automatically assumed that her husband wouldn't be interested in performing those duties," Jenkins said with a crooked smile on his face. Chris smiled back. "I suppose it would seem chauvinistic for me to ask my vice president to do these things?"

"It might diminish the office of the vice president," Chris responded truthfully.

"I see," Jenkins said. "I do have a social secretary. Perhaps I can work closely with her. We'll give that a try."

"Yes sir," Chris said as he left the office.

Jenkins walked to the window and gazed outside at the barren trees and gray sky. When he had started his run for the presidency, Nicole was by his side, and he had every intention of proposing to her quietly, off-camera, and before he took office. Now his accomplishment seemed empty. He was looking forward to the challenges that awaited him, and he knew he would be kept busy, but he also knew he missed Nicole's wise counsel.

Jenkins sat back down at his desk and picked up the phone. He paused as he thought about what he was about to do. He put the phone back down. After a few seconds, he picked it back up again. He turned to retrieve his little black book from the pocket of his suit jacket which was hanging on the back of his chair. Placing the receiver between his ear and shoulder, he thumbed through the book until he came upon Nicole's phone number at the Moscow embassy. He started to dial the number. When he heard the first ring, he closed his book and grabbed the receiver from his shoulder. He smiled when he heard Nicole's voice. "Hello, Nikki," Jenkins began. "Do you have a few minutes?"

Nicole paused as she recognized the voice on the other end of the receiver. "Is this wise, Bobby, to call the UK's Russian embassy directly?"

"My reason for calling is legitimate," Jenkins replied. "I'll get right to the point. I'm calling to offer you a position in my administration. How does Attorney General Charbonneau sound?"

Nicole didn't respond right away. Finally, she said, "I think that would present some problems for both of us. I'm assuming this is not a secure line so I won't spell them out for you." Nicole was referring to the personal files she had given Jenkins that included information on her clients. "Bobby—"

Jenkins could sense Nicole was going to end their conversation. "Nikki," Jenkins interjected. "I can agree that the attorney general position is probably not a good idea. I have always appreciated your counsel. I'd like to ask you to consider my next offer before you respond. I encourage you to discuss it with Sean. I can even assign Secret Service protection to you. I'm sure there are other things we can negotiate. I would like you to be my communications director." Jenkins paused. "Nikki?"

"I heard you," Nicole responded. "I don't know what to say. I'm honored that you think I could do that job."

"Are you kidding?" There was a bit of a chuckle in his voice. "I believe you could excel in that position. It's why I'm offering it to you."

"That's the only reason? You aren't trying to come between Sean and me?"

"No," Jenkins denied. "I have concerns about you being in the Soviet Union, but I know Sean can protect you and you are very resourceful." Jenkins paused as he gathered his thoughts. "I am offering you the job for a selfish reason. I haven't forgotten how you provided wise counsel to me during my campaign. I'd like to have that available to me now." He waited for a response. "Nikki, I know you love Sean. I'm not trying to come between you. I could use your talents here. I'm asking you to serve your country."

"Bobby, I can't make this decision without talking to Sean," Nicole said. She admitted to herself that she would like this opportunity.

"You would help me shape the policies of this administration," Jenkins enticed her. "At the risk of making you angry, I can protect you here, just as well as Sean can."

"You had to go there, didn't you?" Nicole shot back.

Jenkins laughed. "I don't think the little jabs will ever stop. Seriously, talk to Sean and consider my offer. I think you would do an excellent job."

"I'll talk with Sean, but I do not promise anything. Bobby, I will tell you that I don't want to leave him. The distance and the fact he would be in Moscow would place a hardship on this relationship that I don't think it could withstand. For that reason alone, I suggest you think about other people who could fill this role."

"Talk to Sean," Jenkins repeated. "If you truly love one another, you can make it work. You can call me with your answer when you've decided, but I will add there will always be a spot for you in my administration."

Nicole smiled. "Thank you. I'll talk with Sean. Goodbye, Bobby."

Jenkins bade her farewell and hung up the phone. He hoped that Nicole would take him up on his offer. He looked down at his schedule and realized he had a meeting starting in a few minutes. He needed a quick break and some coffee. He placed his black book back in his suit jacket pocket, put the jacket on, and left the study for the kitchen. He let his mind wander on the thought of Nicole joining his administration. He couldn't keep himself from smiling. He honestly believed that she would accept his temptation.

Moscow, USSR—Outside United Kingdom Embassy

With some disinclination, a woman wrapped in a heavy coat and fake-fur pillbox hat walked ever so slowly up to the gate. One of the guards exited the little shack to the woman's left and approached her.

The Welsh guard spoke quickly. "What business do you have here?"

In a proper English accent, the woman said, "I'm here to work. Colin Stewart said to be here at eight o'clock. I'm here, and you need to let me in."

"Darlin', Mr. Stewart could order up a whole whore-house, but without credentials, you don't get past this gate," the guard retorted. "Now, do you have those or not?"

"It's my first day, you crude-mouthed imbecile—" The woman started to unbutton the top two buttons of her coat.

"Callin' me names will get me to walk away from you," the guard interrupted.

She pulled out her badge, which hung around her neck, from under her coat. "Would this be what you're looking for?"

The guard eyed the credentials without reaching through the gate for them. He jerked his head in the direction of the guardhouse door on her side of the gate. "I'll meet ya inside." The guard walked into the guardhouse and to the door where the woman stood waiting. He unlocked it and opened it for her to walk inside. Once inside, he closed and locked the door again. As he walked behind the counter that separated the small shack in half, he said, "You need to sign this book." He pointed to the ledger in the center of the counter. "And I need a closer look at those credentials." The woman removed her badge and handed it to the guard. He looked at it and then removed a clipboard from under the counter. He looked down the list and found the name that matched the credentials in his hand. He checked the photograph and looked up at the woman in front of him. "Please remove your hat. The photo has you with long hair."

The woman did as instructed and long brunette hair fell from underneath the hat, framing her lily-white face and baby-blue eyes. She looked at the guard with a smirk on her face. "I don't have a coat on in that picture, and don't think for a moment that I'm taking it off."

"Well, Stacy Cambridge, if you want to report to your job here, you will take it off and put it through that scanner over there, along with your briefcase. You'll also walk through that metal detector," the guard announced as he handed her credentials back to her.

Stacy huffed at the inconvenience of taking off her coat and going through the security measures before she was allowed to enter the compound. "I bet you wouldn't ask Baranov to do this."

"You can bet Baranov wouldn't get through the front gate," the guard shot back. "Now, get on with you." After Stacy cleared the metal detector, the guard opened the door, which led to the courtyard inside the walled embassy compound. He gave a loud, ear-piercing whistle to another guard standing at the entrance to the embassy. "She's cleared. First day here," he called. The other guard acknowledged the statements and started to walk over to meet Stacy. He pointed to the other guard. "There's where you'll be going, Stacy. Enjoy your first day of work."

Stacy walked toward the building meeting the guard about halfway. They walked together to the embassy door in silence. He opened the door and walked inside with her. "Wait here," the guard said as he picked up the phone in the foyer. "Mr. Stewart, we have a new hire here." The guard hung up the phone and waited with Stacy. "Mr. Stewart will be right down."

"Thank you," Stacy replied, taking her gloves off and placing them in her coat pockets.

Five minutes later, they could hear the echo of rushed footsteps through the halls. Stewart turned into the corridor leading to the foyer a few seconds later. "Stacy, it is good to see you again. Welcome to the embassy. I'll show you where your office will be."

The guard watched them turn the corner before he walked back outside the building. He looked to his left to see the guard in the guardhouse on the phone. When their eyes met, the man on the phone acknowledged the other with a nod. That was all he needed to know that the guard on the phone was talking with Alistair. He began his scan of the courtyard—the first of many he would do that day.

Alistair was surprised to hear about the new employee. Even though the majority of the new hire's paperwork was secured, Alistair was still bothered. Stacy Cambridge was missing one important piece of paper. Alistair hung up the phone and began searching through his desk and file cabinets for the one page summary of her background check. Before Stacy obtained her badge, he would have conducted that check. When he couldn't find it, he called his second in command, Duncan, into his office and asked if he recalled conducting the search.

"I don't think I did," Duncan remarked. "I'll check my files, but the name doesn't sound familiar." Duncan returned a half hour later to report that he couldn't find a thing on Stacy Cambridge.

"I'll bring it up to Mr. Stewart," Alistair said. "Maybe we gave it to him, and he just hasn't returned it. Thanks for checking, Duncan. Let's get back to work."

CHAPTER TWO
NEW YEAR'S EVE 1980

Moscow, USSR—Kremlin

The ride over to the Kremlin was a stark contrast to the lavishly decorated hall. Nicole took notice of the old, dilapidated buildings with boarded up windows in which she imagined the occupants huddled around a stove for warmth. The guests for Baranov's New Year's Eve party mingled in intimate circles of trusted friends amid marble floors and gold-laden decor. Sean and Nicole entered the hall from above and proceeded to a white marble staircase. A uniformed man stood waiting to receive the invitation before announcing them. Sean was in a tux, complete with tails, a sight Nicole had never seen until now. While she couldn't help teasing him, mainly because Sean kept tugging at the garment which confirmed his discomfort, she had to admit that he looked stunningly handsome.

"Quit fidgeting," Nicole said as they approached the guard who announced each name in a flamboyant, yet eloquent style. Nicole had discovered her bronze evening gown tucked away in a box of clothing that had arrived at the embassy days before. She remembered that this was the dress she had worn the night she met

Jenkins at a White House dinner. She always loved the gown for the way it danced in the light, and Sean had never seen it.

Sean gave Nicole a quick disapproving look for admonishing him before handing the guard his invitation. The man leaned over to Sean asking for the pronunciation of Nicole's last name. Sean provided that and the announcement was made. At the bottom of the staircase were President Baranov and his wife. When they reached the bottom, Sean presented Nicole to the Baranovs.

"Thank you for the invitation, Mr. President," Nicole said, allowing Baranov to kiss her hand. Nicole turned her attention to his wife, Viktoria. A very plain and conservative looking woman, Viktoria was soft-spoken, having no love of political affairs or showy parties. "Mrs. Baranov, I'm happy to meet you. I wish you and your husband a joyful new year." Viktoria kindly smiled but made it clear she did not feel a need to speak to Nicole. Viktoria's eyes moved to Sean.

"Happy New Year, Mr. President," Sean said as he shook Baranov's hand. "Thank you for your hospitality this evening," Sean added, now looking at Viktoria.

"It is good to see you again," Baranov responded. "I hope this New Year brings a better understanding between our countries."

Sean did not smile or make any facial expression as he responded. "A better dialogue, more open and informative, is always preferred to silence." Sean was referring to the Cold War state that existed between the Soviet Union and NATO.

"I wish that your predecessor felt that way," Baranov shot back. "He was most difficult to deal with."

Sean's brow wrinkled. Of all the complaints that he had heard about the former ambassador, difficult to deal with was not one of them. “I’m sorry to hear that. Perhaps someday you can tell me what you found difficult?”

Nicole gave a gentle tug on Sean’s arm, indicating he should not encourage that type of communication.

“Maybe tonight will be a good time. You and Nicole are sitting with us,” Baranov announced.

“Well,” Sean started unsure of what exactly he wanted to say. “This is quite a surprise. We look forward to talking with you.” Sean heard the announcement of the next guest. “Good evening.”

Sean and Nicole moved away from the president and his wife. He scanned the room for familiar faces. Waiters in white tux jackets circulated throughout offering champagne to the guests. At the end of the hall was a set of closed doors that led to what Sean assumed was the dining hall. A waiter approached Sean and Nicole, and Sean picked up two glasses of champagne. Before handing one to Nicole, he took a deep sniff in each glass. Sean looked at her as their glasses met. They clinked the glasses together each taking a drink.

“I can imagine that you did the same thing at those stuffy White House dinners,” he said.

“I did what?” Nicole asked, confused by Sean’s comment. She leaned in close and asked, “And can you tell if the champagne is drugged just by smelling it?”

Sean laughed. “In answer to your first question, turn every man’s head upon entering.” He saw Nicole’s uneasiness at the mention of the attention she garnered as she quickly glanced around the room. “You have no idea, do you?”

"I don't pay any attention to it," Nicole replied as she moved closer to Sean, wrapping her hand around his arm. "It makes me very uncomfortable. It goes back to something that happened to me a long time ago. I put up barriers so that I don't feel the stares or acknowledge them. I'm not seeking the attention, Sean."

Sean reminded himself of how little he knew about her life before their fateful meeting a little over a year ago. He looked down when he thought about it. He took a drink of his champagne and sheepishly looked around the room. "And I wasn't sniffing the champagne for drugs," he whispered. "I was checking its bouquet."

Nicole frowned, only half believing Sean's comment. They both took another drink. "Did you notice that Mrs. Baranov didn't speak?"

"Yes," Sean confirmed. "In case you didn't notice, you are in a country where they barely recognize the working class, let alone bold, brash feminists."

"Thin ice," Nicole said as she raised her glass to her lips. "You are treading on thin ice."

Sean chuckled, knowing the last bit of his comment would bring some ire from Nicole. He started to scan the room again, catching a glimpse of someone who set off an alarm within him. He darted his head back and forth trying to see around groups of people to get another look. He had no such luck. The man seemed to vanish into thin air. *Did I see him?* Sean took another drink of his champagne trying to calm himself.

"What is it?"

"Hmm? Oh, sorry, I thought I recognized someone."

"Would that be a good thing?"

"No, it wouldn't," Sean replied, his attention now being caught by the announcement of the next guests.

"Mr. President, Ambassador of the United States, Larry Barker and his wife, Louise."

Her back to the stairs, Nicole was sipping her champagne when she heard the announcement. At the mention of Barker's name, Nicole coughed down the champagne. Sean placed his hand on Nicole's shoulder to check on her. "I'm all right. Just hearing that name…"

"Yes, I know," Sean agreed. "I can't wait for him to see your face." Nicole sulked, hoping that she could avoid seeing them at all.

Louise and Larry Barker descended the steps with an air of aristocracy that only the old guard of American political nobility could muster. Nicole glanced over her shoulder to see the couple and quickly turned back around. To Sean's surprise, she finished her champagne in one gulp. Seeing their arrogance made Nicole realize that she would have to put on her game face. She knew Barker would flaunt his power and facing him was not going to be easy.

Barker greeted Baranov and his wife. Barker did all the talking, a stark contrast to Sean and Nicole's greeting. Louise and Viktoria knew their place was beside their husbands and they were not to speak or show any independence. It was a quick exchange and very cold.

"Interesting," Sean started. "What garnered their invitation I wonder?"

Nicole looked around the room. "I don't think the party is as small as Mr. Stewart led you to believe. Look around, Sean, most of our NATO allies are here."

Sean did take a quick look around and noted that Nicole was right. "Get ready," he said when he noticed Louise had recognized Nicole and was quickly walking toward her, leaving her husband's side.

"Nikki?" Louise inquired, touching Nicole's forearm to attain her attention.

Nicole exhaled the breath she had taken in when Sean told her to be ready. She turned with a smile on her face and said, "Hello, Louise."

"I thought it was you! I saw you when I was descending the stairs." Louise was ecstatic. She paid no attention to Nicole's body language. "It is so good to see you." She hugged Nicole who tried to break the hug off as quickly as it started. Barker watched his wife as she greeted Nicole. Sean watched Barker. The American ambassador's facial expressions went from arrogance to sinister and back to arrogance as he approached them.

"Why, Nikki, what a surprise," Barker said, attempting to grab Nicole into one of his bear hugs. Nicole stepped back just as Sean interceded by offering his hand to Barker.

"Mr. Ambassador, indeed, what a surprise to find you in Moscow," Nicole said with a coldness in her voice. "May I introduce Lord Sean Adkins, Duke of Guilford and ambassador for Her Royal Majesty here in the USSR. Sean, this is Ambassador Larry Barker and his wife, Louise from the United States."

"Pleasure," Sean spat out, his tone matching Nicole's in coldness.

"No hug, my dear?" Barker questioned, ignoring Sean's offered handshake. "It seems your ex-lover has relegated his enemies to the cold, distant den of the Great Bear. At least we could be cordial to one another." Sean tried his best not to smile at the reference to

Jenkins, no doubt spoken to extract an annoyed response from them. The attempt failed. Nicole, however, did smile. Barker did not break off his intimidating stare. "Moved on to royalty I see," Barker added when no response came.

"Mrs. Barker," Sean said as he offered his hand to Louise. Louise took Sean's hand with an apologetic look on her face.

"It's a pleasure to meet you, Mr. Ambassador," Louise interjected courteously. Her discomfort apparent in her voice. "My husband and I knew Nikki when she lived in Washington, DC."

"Oh, yes. When Nicole was a lawyer with, oh dear, what was that name of that law firm again, darling?" Sean was laying on the charm, his British accent becoming thicker to the delight of Louise.

"Rosen, Shafer, and—"

"Pruett, yes," Sean interrupted. "I remember now. But didn't you leave that firm in December of 1979?"

"Shortly after that, yes," Nicole replied.

"And right before you left that Jenkins fellow for London," Sean added. Nicole was trying hard not to laugh at Sean's high-browed, thick accent. "I still don't understand what you saw in that rather controlling, cocky man." Nicole bit her lip in an attempt to keep from laughing.

Barker wasn't sure what to make of Sean's comments. "That's our president-elect you are referring to, Mr. Ambassador."

"Yes, I know, Mr. Ambassador," Sean shot back. "For a minute, I thought you hadn't noticed me. Besides, it appeared to me that you don't have very high regard for your soon-to-be president considering your initial greeting." Sean extended his hand. "Shall we try this again?"

Barker shook Sean's hand quickly and released it. "How did you meet our *beloved* Nikki?" Barker hissed the word "beloved."

"I thought it was rather obvious that we met in London," Sean quipped. "But then, you were probably too busy trying to intimidate her with that rather rude and awkward stare." Nicole gave a short, gentle but firm tug at Sean's elbow. Sean cleared his throat. "And other than her previous connection to your president, how did you come to know Nicole?"

"Just through her brief affair with Jenkins," Barker retorted.

"That's President-Elect Jenkins to you. Let's not forget how generous the president-elect has been to you considering all you have done," Nicole reminded Barker, who noted Nicole's galling smirk."I think its time to find our seats, Sean."

"Yes, it does appear that way," Sean agreed, noticing people moving to the dining hall.

"Nikki," Louise called. "May I have a word?" She turned to Larry. "I won't be but a moment. You go ahead, and I'll meet you inside."

Barker turned to Sean, "Shall we?"

"I'll be right here," Sean said to Nicole, moving a step away from them. "Have a good evening, Mr. Ambassador," Sean said, making it very clear he wanted nothing to do with Barker through his rejection to walk with him into the dining room.

Barker gave Sean a stern look. "I'm afraid we got off on the wrong foot, Lord Adkins. Considering our countries' history, you may find that I can be quite the asset to you here."

"I'm confident you truly think so," Sean retorted, not willing to add anything else to his remark. Sean took a drink of his champagne while waiting for Nicole to have her conversation with Louise. It was obvious to Sean that Louise wasn't going to have that conversation until her husband was away from her. "I believe your wife would like to speak to Nicole in private." Sean took two steps away from Nicole.

Barker was seething at Sean's dismissal of him. Louise could feel the threatening stare of her husband baring down on her. Nicole could tell that Louise was about to give into that unspoken threat. All her life Louise had obeyed her husband. Nicole wondered if there was ever a time Louise raised her voice to him or denied him anything. Louise started to take a step toward Barker. Nicole took her elbow, exerting a little pressure and pulling Louise back to her. Nicole knew if Barker was capable of ordering her death, he was capable of just about anything with Louise. Nicole turned her back on Barker, bringing Louise around so that Louise's back was also to the ambassador.

Nicole could sense Louise's panic, and she whispered, "What did you want to ask me?"

Louise swallowed, knowing that there was nothing wrong with her husband's hearing. Barker leaned in to listen to his wife's conversation. She said, "It was nothing. I just wanted to know if we could have lunch sometime."

Nicole knew that wasn't Louise's intention. Although Nicole had no real desire to ever speak to either of the Barkers again, she was curious what Louise wanted with her. "Have you ever been to the British embassy?" she asked. "We have gorgeous artwork on just about every wall. You were on the board of the National Gallery of Art, weren't you?"

"Yes, I was," Louise said as she took a quick glance at her husband.

"Well, then, you simply must come over and tell me about the art in the embassy." Nicole leaned into Louise and whispered, "I can't visit the American embassy. That's considered American soil and you know, the Sipes confession tape and all that." Nicole knew she was safe on American soil, just not on the American embassy's soil. She didn't trust Barker. She was not about to give him an opportunity to hurt her again.

Louise looked at Nicole with shock. "I had forgotten," she whispered back. She noticed she had been hunched over, feeling the weight of her husband's glare. Now confident, Louise threw her shoulders back and said loudly. "I'd love to see the artwork. What day would be good for you?"

"How about next Friday?"

"I'll check my schedule and get back with you," Louise responded with a wink. She surmised, although it was falsely done so, that as bad as she thought she had it, Nicole had it much worse. As usual, Louise was naive and never made an effort to educate herself appropriately.

"Wonderful," Nicole confirmed, giving Louise's elbow a little squeeze before she released it. She started a confident strut, crossing right in front of Barker as she took Sean's offered arm. "Shall we?" Nicole placed her hand on the crux of his arm.

Sean smiled at Nicole's moxie, thinking she would have made a wonderful agent. He also knew that her heart had to be beating through her chest. Without biding either of the Barkers a good evening, they turned away from them and walked into the dining hall. Most of the guests were in the process of sitting down when Sean and Nicole entered, followed closely by the Barkers. Quickly and quietly they moved to Baranov's table.

As they reached the table, Sean apologized for their delay in arriving. Sean looked around the table at its occupants. Baranov and his wife had not yet arrived, which explained the two remaining empty chairs. Those already seated were prominent businessmen in the USSR accompanied by their wives, or they were Baranov's trusted allies in the USSR's government. Sean recognized a few men. As they introduced themselves, the Russian businessmen stood to offer their hand to Sean. Sean remained standing as the introduction started around the table. As his eyes moved to the next occupant, Sean almost expelled a gasp of air. Here, in Moscow, it was the last place he thought he would run into someone who knew he was an MI6 agent. Sean gave a little cough to cover the near faux pas. He picked up his napkin with his left hand and coughed into it once. He then offered his right hand to the man who knew him. Nicole caught Sean's unusual behavior and looked at him with concern evident on her face. Leznikov waited, then accepted the hand of the man he had met for the first time in France many years ago. Petrified that Leznikov would tell Baranov that he was with MI6, Sean glanced around the room trying to determine their escape route.

Across the room, Sean noticed another Russian had made his late arrival at Barker's table. Vladimir Valesky could be charming when he wanted to be, but just as evil as he needed to be. The people of Moscow knew him as Baranov's enforcer. If Baranov needed someone to be discreetly taken care of, Baranov directly gave Valesky the order. Valesky had read *The Godfather.* Valesky believed Baranov was the most powerful mafia boss, and Valesky was his most trusted ally—the Luca Brodsky to Godfather Baranov with one major difference: Baranov did not fear Valesky the way Vito Corleone feared Brodsky. Although Baranov retained power over Valesky, Baranov needed Valesky more than Valesky needed Baranov, especially in the last year. Baranov wasn't the strapping, strong, forceful man he used to be. He was getting older, and illness was seeping into his body. Valesky saw it and positioned himself to gain Baranov's most sacred trust and confidence. This maneuvering also gave Valesky the freedom to enforce his terror on the Soviet people. Corruption is never far from those seeking power, regardless of which form of government is in place. As the saying goes, "Absolute power corrupts absolutely."

"You are the American ambassador?" Valesky asked as he walked up to the table to join Barker, his wife Louise, and other officers of the Soviet Union. Valesky was only interested in Barker and, to a small degree, Barker's wife. He had seen the intelligence gathered on Barker over the years. Valesky wondered just how loyal and patriotic Barker would be to his former prodigy and now president-elect. It was Valesky's mission to find out. "I am General Vladimir Valesky, at your service." He snapped to attention, giving a quick but courteous bow to Louise.

Barker stood up and offered his hand. "I am Ambassador Barker, and this is my wife, Louise. It's very good to meet you, General."

Valesky accepted Barker's hand, giving it a firm, but short, shake. "Please sit down," he instructed. The others at the table had also stood as Valesky outranked them. Valesky gestured for them to sit as well. "Imagine our surprise when we heard that a man of your accomplishments was going be here in our country as an ambassador. We can only assume that your president is interested in better relations with the Soviet Union by sending us such a prestigious man."

Barker marked his words. "President-Elect Jenkins is open to conversation with our Cold War adversary, and he recognizes the Soviet Union's strong leadership position. A better relationship would benefit both our countries."

Louise slowly turned her head and looked at her husband as if he had lost his mind. While she didn't utter a word, it was exactly the contradictory action Valesky wanted to witness. Louise's expression told Valesky that the United States had no interest in ending the Cold War or bettering the relations between the two countries. More importantly, the intelligence that suggested Jenkins had banished Barker to Moscow was confirmed—all with the turn of Barker's annoyed, angry wife's head. Valesky raised his glass to toast Barker's statement. He smiled and said, "If that is the case, then I would think we will be seeing more of each other in the coming months."

Barker secured his glass in his hand and clinked it against Valesky's. "I welcome our future discussions."

Louise knew the code spoken between these two men, and it sickened her. "Excuse me," she said, standing up as the two men sipped the wine from their glasses, sealing their clandestine pact. "Which way to the ladies room?"

A colonel sitting next to her piped up, "It is that way." He pointed across the room. Louise briskly turned without uttering a word and walked away from the table.

Outwardly perturbed by Louise's actions, internally Barker knew that it served an important purpose in the conversation between Valesky and himself. Barker had his intelligence on General Valesky, thanks to his old friend, CIA director Douglas Stanton. As compromised as the American embassy was, Barker knew that the CIA was also listening to determine how much of the US's correspondence ended up in Soviet hands. No code between Jenkins and Barker had been established before Barker left the country. Barker knew that Jenkins was exiling him to the Soviet Union with no umbilical cord—no hope of being called back. Barker fully intended to make the best of his situation, even if it was only for his own gain. "Are you married?" an annoyed Barker asked Valesky.

"Yes, and four children," Valesky replied. "My wife is ill this evening. She could not attend due to a virus of some kind."

"I'm sorry she isn't feeling well. Please give her our best," Barker offered.

"How long have you and your wife been married?"

"We're coming up on forty years," Barker replied.

"We must celebrate such a milestone!" Valesky insisted. "That is a long time. You must know each other very well."

"Too well sometimes," Barker responded with a frown. Valesky knew all too well what he meant. Valesky was hardly home, and he preferred it that way.

A lone figure racing from the dining hall caught Nicole's attention. She watched Louise dash from the room and wondered what happened to precipitate her abrupt departure. She looked over at Barker's table, studying the two men in conversation. Barker was laughing and enjoying himself far too much. She didn't expect Barker to be rude to their hosts, but she didn't expect them to carry on like two long-lost friends either. Her mind began to run through scenarios in which Barker could hurt Jenkins. She hadn't gotten through all of them when their salad arrived.

Leznikov grinned while he waited for Sean to recover from the shock of seeing him. Leznikov had crossed paths with Sean only a couple times, but they were memorable times. Occasionally, Leznikov's field work for the KGB in Montreal brought him to France and the United Kingdom. One close encounter with the Serpent outside an airport in France was particularly notable. Sean would have caught the Serpent that day if Leznikov had not absent-mindedly bumped into the Serpent, which in turn ruined Sean's shot. It didn't happen once, but three times, which infuriated Sean and removed all doubt that Leznikov was just a clumsy tourist. Thanks to Leznikov's tactics, the Serpent gave Sean the slip. When Leznikov retreated to a bathroom, a furious Sean approached him. Certain Leznikov was the Serpent's accomplice; Sean conked Leznikov over the head with his Beretta. Sean quickly locked the bathroom door, maneuvered Leznikov into one of the stalls, and dunked Leznikov's head in the toilet waking him. After a few more long soakings in the dirty toilet, Leznikov had the opportunity to talk. Leznikov explained he didn't know the man Sean was targeting, but he saw the laser light on Serpent's body. Another dunk, in outrage, occurred before Sean let Leznikov go. With Sean's Beretta pressed against Leznikov's temple, Sean asked if he was KGB. Finally able to pull a few thoughts together, Leznikov asked if Sean was MI6. Sean explained that his target was the man Leznikov helped to escape. Leznikov didn't ask any further questions but apologized for his interference. Leznikov explained that he was on another mission, which had nothing to do with Sean or the Serpent. Leznikov suggested that Sean leave the restroom first and he would avoid him in the future. "We will act like this never happened, no?" Sean could hear Leznikov asking. Sean agreed. Although they vowed to not interfere with each other's missions, Sean was confident that Leznikov reported the incident to the Kremlin just as Sean had done to MI6.

Sean watched as Baranov approached the table and everyone stood up. Baranov waved acknowledging the applause. When Baranov sat down, the others at the table took their seats. Leznikov leaned over to Baranov and whispered something to him. Baranov looked at Leznikov with a confused, but serious expression. Could it be Leznikov just informed Baranov about Sean—a foreigner Baranov embraced?

"Please to remain seated," Baranov muttered. "The colonel and I have something to discuss. We will return shortly." Baranov stood up and motioned for Leznikov to follow him. They walked to the kitchen, disappearing on the other side of its swinging doors.

Nicole looked over at Sean just as he closed his eyes. She leaned over and whispered, "What's wrong?"

"Not here," Sean whispered back.

Nicole sat for a moment, waiting for Sean to make his move. When he didn't, Nicole removed the napkin on her lap and began to fold it. She placed it next to the side of her plate. She reached for her forehead, gently rubbing it. Baranov and Leznikov rejoined them, their meeting not taking more than a few minutes. Nicole was starting to stand when Sean's hand clasped her thigh; an indication that Sean wanted her to stay seated. She realized just walking away from the table now would be an insult or could be misconstrued as confirmation of whatever was happening. She waited patiently for what was going to happen next. She rubbed her forehead every so often to keep her ruse she concocted as an option for their escape.

The others at the table were holding conversations in Russian, which didn't help Sean or Nicole. After a tense few moments of the staring, Baranov waved his hand alerting the waiters to serve the main course. Viktoria Baranov turned to her husband and asked him a question, drawing him into her conversation with one of the businessmen at the table. Leznikov turned his head and joined the conversation on this left. Sean and Nicole sat quietly as the waiters swarmed around the table. As Nicole placed the napkin on her lap and picked up her fork to eat, Sean again touched her thigh. Sean sighed, unsure of what to do. Nicole knew Sean did not want her to eat. She placed the fork down, reached for her small purse and started to rummage through it. The action caught the attention of Sean and the others at the table, including Leznikov and Baranov.

Even though Nicole had no idea what was occurring, she knew that they couldn't sit at the table and not eat. Sean obviously had concerns about the food. Otherwise, he would have started eating. He would not have stopped her from taking her first bite. Nicole noticeably raised her hand to her head, covering her eyes. "Oh, dear," she mumbled, just loud enough for those at the table to hear. She slouched into her chair in defeat. "I'm so very sorry," Nicole said louder when the conversations had stopped, and she could feel everyone's eyes on her. She sat up, removing her hand from her eyes. She blinked her eyes as if the light was bothering her. She acted like she was trying to focus on Baranov.

"Nicole," Sean said, putting his arm around her. "Is something wrong?" Sean could have kissed her right then and there.

Nicole gave a quick nod. "Mr. President, I apologize. I'm having a migraine, and I didn't bring my medicine. If I don't leave immediately—" Nicole paused, reacting as if a horrible pain inflicted the right side of her forehead. She rubbed the temple. "Sean...please. Take me back to the embassy quickly."

"Yes, sweetheart, of course," Sean said, standing and helping Nicole from her chair. Sean was quite impressed with Nicole's performance.

"I'm sorry, Mr. President," Nicole uttered again, leaning on Sean. "I hope you will forgive me for taking Lord Adkins from your company."

Baranov stood when Nicole and Sean had risen. "We have doctors here who can—"

"Oh, thank you, but I don't want to be a bother," Nicole interrupted. "It's imperative that I take this particular medicine. I foolishly left it behind. It knocks me out, and I don't feel a thing until the migraine is gone. Good night, everyone." Nicole took

Sean's arm. Sean quickly bade everyone at the table farewell and escorted Nicole from the hall. They quickly moved outside after retrieving their coats waiting for Alistair and the motorcade to arrive. Within a couple of minutes, Sean and Nicole were seated safely in their limousine and on their way back to the embassy.

"Are you all right, ma'am?" Alistair asked. "Should we have the doctor standing by?"

Nicole looked at Alistair. "I'm fine." She wasn't sure if she should ask Sean what just happened. "It was a ruse."

"Her quick thinking got us out of a difficult situation," Sean added. "When we get back to the embassy, I'd like you and Duncan to join us at the residence." Sean looked at Nicole. "I think Elliot should join us as well." Elliot, who was Sean's contact while Sean was tracking the Serpent, had arrived days before and was in the process of upgrading the embassy's computer system and tightening the security, which included sweeping the building for listening devices and removing them.

"Yes, sir," Alistair acknowledged without hesitation.

"Tell me again why I thought coming here would be a new beginning?" Nicole asked, her sarcasm dripping from every word.

"I thought you liked adventure," Sean quipped.

They soon arrived back at the embassy. All disembarked from their cars and headed into the building. Sean unlocked the door to the residence for Alistair, Duncan, and Nicole to enter. Elliot was standing in the foyer, a piece of electronic equipment that identified listening devices in his hand. He tilted his head to the living room. "It's still clear," he said as he started to walk into the room with the rest following him.

"How did you know to be here?" Nicole asked Elliot, bewildered.

Elliot pointed to Sean's cuff-links. "Those," was all he said. Sean walked over to him and held up his arms for Elliot to remove the devices.

"What happened at the Krelim?" Nicole asked Sean.

"Let's all sit down," Sean said. Everyone moved to the closest seat. Sean removed his tux jacket and sat down next to Nicole. "Alistair and Duncan, this needs to stay between us. I'm an MI6 agent. My expertise in the field brings along benefits as well as disadvantages." Duncan and Alistair looked at each other and then back at Sean. They did not show surprise at Sean's admission. "Any questions?"

"After watching the two of you at the training facility and the firing range, we had a bet between us that you both had some association with the intelligence community," Duncan said. "Are you CIA, ma'am?" Duncan asked Nicole.

"No," Nicole replied. "I'm along for the ride." Sean smiled at Nicole's response.

Alistair smiled at Duncan's disappointment at losing the bet. "Thank you for confiding in us. It will help with our protection duties," Alistair said. "What happened at the party?"

Sean looked at Nicole. "The man who was sitting on Baranov's left is Dmitry Leznikov. He is a KGB spy." Nicole nodded her understanding. Sean explained how he knew Leznikov to the others in the room. "Now, we all know that Leznikov reported me back to the Kremlin, just as I reported him to MI6. What I don't understand is how we came this far, and no one alerted me that he was part of Baranov's cabinet."

“How do you know he is?” Elliot asked.

“I’m assuming those at Baranov’s tables are his closest allies. Leznikov whispered something to him prompting them both to leave the table. You don’t have that level of trust with an enemy,” Sean replied. “I’ll need background information on Leznikov.”

“Got it,” Elliot confirmed. He stood to leave.

Alistair and Duncan also stood. Sean shook everyone’s hand and, as the three men left the residence, reminded them how important it was to keep his identity quiet. Sean exhaled a sigh of relief. He ran his fingers through his hair, trying to calm his racing mind. What bothered him most was how he had frozen. How he couldn’t find an exit. He looked toward the bedroom where Nicole had retired for the evening. He was thankful Nicole had provided a reason for their departure and her convincing execution. He smiled as he walked back to the bedroom with the full intention of thanking Nicole properly.

Washington, DC—Blair House

President-Elect Jenkins was standing in the foyer with Vice President Patricia Samuelson welcoming their guests for the New Year’s Eve party. Jenkins couldn’t help but remember that the woman in his home a year ago was Nicole. As a senator chatted with Samuelson, Jenkins’s mind recalled embracing Nicole as she looked out the picture window of his condo. Little did he know at the time that Nicole looking out of windows should have been a clue for him. He had no idea she was constantly looking for Sean.

“Isn’t that right, Bobby?” the senator asked.

“I’m sorry,” Jenkins said, turning to the senator. “My mind was elsewhere. What am I supposed to agree with?”

"That Patricia here is as pretty as she is intelligent," the senator said, reaching for Samuelson's upper arm and squeezing it. Samuelson wrenched her arm from his grasp, a defensive move she had executed many times.

Jenkins stared at the male senator. He knew the senator's clumsily disguised compliments and actions were meant to intimidate his vice president. "Well," Jenkins began, his Southern twang becoming more apparent as he chose his words carefully, "I'd have to disagree. I chose my vice president solely on merit. Patricia's intelligence is not dependant on her physical appearance. I admire Patricia for her strength, her mind, and her legislative abilities among many other qualifications. I would highly suggest in the future, Senator, when I dispatch her to call on you for your assistance in promoting our agenda, you focus on her words and show respect for the office that she holds. Any intimidation attempt based on gender will be interpreted as an insult to the office and dealt with accordingly." Jenkins watched as the senator became visibly annoyed. He decided to cut to the chase. "Come now, Senator, you'd never make that comparison with a man, and you certainly wouldn't grab the president's arm the way you just grabbed Patricia's. I expect an apology to Patricia before you adjourn to the living room for a drink."

Samuelson was shocked. In her time in the Senate, no man had ever stepped in to air his contempt for another senator's mistreatment, abuse, or harassment. She had a thick skin, and it served her well. Her female Republican colleagues received the same treatment. There were less than a handful of female senators and only a few more female representatives in Congress. She also knew that no one was above intimidation if one allowed it to occur. Samuelson fought hard for her reputation as a fair, honest, and tough legislator. She didn't complain about the treatment she received from her fellow male colleagues. She knew she was hitting close to the mark or even succeeding in what she wanted to accomplish when the harassment ensued. She looked into the offending senator's eyes waiting for the apology the president-elect demanded from him.

The senator swallowed. "I meant no harm," he said to Samuelson. "I'm sorry if I hurt you." The words were meant to imply a weakness in Samuelson, and she knew it.

"You didn't hurt me, Senator," Samuelson began. "I've become accustomed to your ways and dismiss them much like I dismiss half-hearted apologies."

Jenkins bit his lip to keep from laughing. He watched the senator begin to bristle at Samuelson's comment. Jenkins turned the senator away from Samuelson and began to usher him into another room. "You'll find the bar over there," he said as he gave him a gentle push. "I believe the bourbon will take the sting out of the insult." Jenkins turned back around to resume his spot in the receiving line. He wagged a finger at Samuelson as he walked past her.

She laughed at Jenkins's actions, knowing what he must have been thinking. "You caught me off guard," Samuelson said. "For the first time, I felt I could say what I wanted in response."

Jenkins chuckled. "Ahhh—Patricia! I don't think you have ever held back what you honestly think." Before Samuelson could rebut his statement, Jenkins added, "And that is precisely why I asked you to be my vice president." Samuelson nodded her understanding.

The doorbell rang, and Chris opened the door. Majority Leader Daniel Mercer and his wife, Anne, entered. Anne approached Jenkins, kissing him on the cheek. Senator Mercer shook Jenkins's hand. Jenkins leaned forward and joked, "No kiss?"

“I leave that duty to my wife,” Mercer returned. He extended his hand to Samuelson. “Patricia, it’s good to see you.”

“Thank you, Senator,” Samuelson said.

“Bobby,” Mercer began, “I was wondering if you and I could have a few moments.”

“Of course,” Jenkins replied. He turned to Samuelson. “I think everyone is here now, Patricia. Chris will man the door. Why don’t you and your husband begin to mingle while the majority leader and I have a short visit.”

“Yes, sir,” Samuelson said as Anne took her arm, beginning to whisper some gossip in Patricia’s ear as the two of them walked into the living room.

“There’s a study over here,” Jenkins said as he led Mercer to the room. He closed the door behind him once Mercer had entered. “What can I do for you, Daniel?”

“I’ve just gotten word that Blackwood has sent his secretary of state to negotiate the release of the fifty-two hostages in Iran,” Mercer said as he sat down in a chair.

Jenkins walked to a chair across from Mercer. “That’s good to hear.”

“No, it’s not,” Mercer corrected him. “You could have your first big win if we negotiate the release of the hostages.”

Jenkins looked at Mercer. He was internally fighting his disbelief at Mercer’s comments as well as the little voice that was agreeing with Mercer. He cleared his throat and shifted his position, crossing his legs before he spoke. “I ran on a pledge of bringing bi-partisanship back to this country. If Blackwood’s secretary of state can secure the release of all the hostages, who, in case you have forgotten, are human beings, then I will applaud his actions. I will not try to derail their attempt in any way. We have to mend this country. We can't afford to make this divide any wider. What difference does it make which administration secures the hostages return?"

"It makes a big difference, and you know it. It makes us look weak," Mercer declared. "You have to call Blackwood and tell him that your secretary of state—"

"In case you haven't noticed, I haven't announced my pick yet," Jenkins interrupted.

"Then send a representative of your administration. For Christ's sake, send Patricia!"

Jenkins cocked his head, still staring at Mercer. "I do believe that Patricia could handle it, but don't you think that Iran would look at that as a slap in the face?"

"She's the vice president, and the Middle East is going to have to learn to deal with a Western woman," Mercer quipped.

Jenkins shook his head. "No, I'm not sending anyone."

"I am strongly advising you to change your mind," Mercer said through clenched teeth.

"Daniel, I know you're mad. You don't have to grit your teeth at me. There will be times when I will not listen to your advice. There will be times when I do." Jenkins could see Mercer was about to interrupt him. He held his hand up and finished, "But any mistake I make has to be my mistake. I'm not the president yet. I will not insert myself or any member of my staff, elected or appointed, into the Blackwood administration. If Blackwood calls me and asks for assistance, I will be more than happy to oblige him. And as I said earlier, if the secretary of state secures the release of the hostages before I take office, well then, good for them and good for this country." Jenkins studied Mercer. "Country before party, Daniel. It has to be that way." Mercer didn't say anything. "What is honestly bothering you about this?"

Mercer looked at Jenkins, knowing he was defeated. "Let me paint you a picture."

"Oh, we're artists now, are we?" Jenkins quipped, slightly irritated.

"Don't try my patience any more than you already are, Bobby," Mercer condescended.

"And remember who you are talking to, Senator," Jenkins shot back. "I'm not your prodigy any longer. I'm the leader of your party and the free world."

"Not for twenty more days," Mercer declared.

"I am currently the leader of *our* party," Jenkins replied with a cocky grin on his face. "I believe I mentioned that I am not the president yet."

"With all due respect," Mercer choked out, "if Blackwood and the secretary play their cards correctly, the news story on your inauguration day will be the release of the hostages and not you taking the oath of office."

Jenkins let that image sink in for a moment. His ego didn't like the image of the hostages release overshadowing his inauguration. He got up out of the chair and walked to the bar. He took a glass and poured his favorite scotch into it. He took a drink, then slowly turned to look at Mercer. "Then we'll have to figure out a way to turn the story back to the inauguration *if* that happens."

"Damn it!" Mercer screamed. "Call Blackwood and tell him not to do this."

"I won't," Jenkins sternly replied. "And not you nor anyone else in this party will call him with that demand." Jenkins swallowed the rest of his scotch. "I won't play with the lives of Americans for the appearance of a political win. We have to heal this nation if we are to remain a world power. We can't continue to fight one another. We need to cheer our victories and console each other in our defeats." Jenkins looked at Mercer once again. Eyeing Mercer, he said, "And if you can't accept that, then maybe I need a different majority leader in the Senate."

"Is that a veiled threat?"

"There's nothing veiled about it," Jenkins retorted. "We have to mend this country, or we walk down a path more dangerous than any of us can conceive. With each new generation of politicians, our respect and fortitude diminish. I can tolerate 'losing' if it means we saved American lives. I won't draw a line in the sand in this case." Jenkins put the empty glass down on the bar. "And if you can, then you aren't the man I thought you were." Jenkins walked past Mercer and opened the door. "I ask you, Senator, to think about what I've said. If you can't support me in this, I'll understand, and I think you know what you have to do. Now, let's celebrate the New Year." With that, Jenkins left Mercer standing in the study.

Moscow, USSR—United Kingdom Embassy

The next morning, New Year's Day, Nicole woke before Sean. She slipped out of bed, secured her thick, warm robe around her, and walked to the kitchen to prepare a quick breakfast. Nicole had succeeded in convincing Sean to throw an informal New Year's Day party for the embassy staff. Nicole had some food trays to prepare and champagne to chill. She placed the teapot on the stove and turned on the burner. Checking the coffee maker and finding it ready to go, she poured water into the receptacle and turned on the machine. She walked to the refrigerator and found the food trays already prepared. Nicole smiled as she determined Natasha had put in a little extra time on New's Year's Eve to arranged the platters as a thank you for giving her the day off.

Sean shuffled into the kitchen yawning and running his fingers through his hair. His emerald-green eyes were bloodshot. He walked to Nicole, embracing her and then kissing her. "Sorry if I kept you awake last night."

"You were tossing and turning a lot," Nicole replied. "What's wrong?"

"I can't believe I froze like that," Sean said, referring to his actions when he realized Leznikov could identify him.

"I don't think you did," Nicole offered. "I think you were going through all the scenarios."

"I think you are too kind," Sean said as he walked to the coffee maker to pour himself a freshly brewed cup. "I can't help but think I've lost my edge." He walked to the kitchen table and sat down.

"Oh, please," Nicole pleaded. "You are not losing your edge. You're just in a new role and a new environment. You've been to the range, and I know that you went through the obstacle course that Alistair put together to provide extra training for the security force. Duncan told me everyone was quite impressed with you."

Sean looked at Nicole. "I was thinking last night that it might be better if you took that job in Washington. It might be safer."

Nicole sat down at the table with her tea. So many thoughts were running through her mind. She knew Sean wasn't saying this to hurt her or because he had fallen out of love with her—not after their lovemaking last night. She dunked the teabag a few times while she gathered her thoughts. She took her spoon, scooped the teabag in it, and squeezed out the remaining water. She set the teabag-ladened spoon next to her cup. "I'm not going anywhere without you."

"I'm not sure what's going to happen here."

"If you are that worried about it, then you need to call Jack and have him extract us," Nicole responded. "I'm not leaving you here, and I'm not going to take that job in Bobby's administration."

"You don't understand, Leznikov could come to the embassy at any time and have me arrested," Sean pleaded.

"What have you done wrong?"

Her question took him by surprise. "What do you mean?"

"Since being in Moscow, what have you done that would cause Baranov or the KGB to come here and take you away? Have you done any spying? Have you killed anyone? Have you acted in any way that indicates you are anything else but an ambassador?"

"No."

"Then I think it would be outrageous for them to storm this embassy, basically committing an act of war. You've given them no reason to suspect that you are anything except an ambassador. Will they up their game in monitoring your movements and bugging this place? Absolutely. But they aren't going to just burst into this embassy and snatch you out of here." Nicole placed her hand in Sean's. "We'll be fine, and if it comes to it, we leave together." Sean smiled at Nicole's reassurance. "You'll know when that time comes. In the meantime, I think it would be wise to tell Jack about Leznikov."

"Yes," Sean started. "I suppose your right."

"But first, breakfast, and then we have a party to get ready for," Nicole said as she stood to make their breakfast. "Eggs?"

"And toast," Sean said. He went to refill his coffee cup. "It's bloody freezing in here." He turned in the direction of the draft he felt. "There's a draft—" he stopped mid-sentence when he noticed the door out the back to the fire escape was slightly ajar. "Bloody hell," he said as he walked over to it. Nicole followed him. "I know I locked this door last night." He pushed it open by the frame, not touching the doorknob. "Call Elliot," he whispered in Nicole's ear. She ran to the living room while he looked out the door. Sean found nothing out of the ordinary on the fire escape or in the courtyard. He managed, with some difficulty, to close the door without touching the doorknob, hoping the doorknob would provide some fingerprints for Elliot to lift.

Nicole returned from the living room. "He's on his way."

Sean sat back down at the table. His insecurities that Nicole had just put to rest were now resurfacing. He could only hope that somewhere in some database was a set of Leznikov's fingerprints. Sean wondered if Leznikov would be foolish enough to plant the devices himself, or if he would have sent someone. Sean sighed as he realized he didn't have the answers.

The knock on the residence door pulled Sean out of his thoughts. He stood to walk to the foyer but realized he was too late. Nicole walked into the kitchen with Elliot by her side. In Elliot's hand was his black canvas bag of gadgets. Nicole walked him to the back door, and Elliot began to dust for fingerprints. No one spoke a word. Sean walked over to Elliot and bent over to look into the bag. Elliot knew what he was looking for and handed the bug detector to Sean. Sean began sweeping the kitchen. He found one device. He opened a drawer and rummaged through it for some tape. After locating it, he marked the spot and continued his sweep through the rest of the residence. When Elliot finished lifting the prints off of the door, he started to remove the three listening devices that Sean had marked. They all met again in the living room.

Elliot tossed the now destroyed devices onto the table. "They were KGB models."

Sean slowly closed his eyes. "How long will it take to find a match for those prints?"

"It depends," Elliot replied. "If we have the prints in the database, not long. If the prints aren't in the database, we may never know." Elliot looked at Sean. "I doubt it is Leznikov."

"What makes you say that?" Sean inquired, somewhat defensive.

"Why would he risk coming here to plant bugs if he is that close to Baranov? I'm not saying he didn't send someone, but I don't know. It doesn't feel right to me."

"I think we need to sweep the offices again," Nicole added. "I think it is safe to say that if they were here, they are there, too."

"I'll get busy doing that now," Elliot said as he gathered his bag of gadgets together. "Sean, keep in mind, this is an embassy of an adversary to the Soviet Union. We'll constantly be finding bugs."

"Is someone who works here doing it?" Nicole asked.

Elliot shrugged. "Your guess is as good as mine."

"Until we catch them in the process, we don't know," Sean said. Sean stood up and walked with Elliot to the foyer. Nicole followed behind the two men. "We'll see you at the party. Get started on those prints as soon as you can."

"Will do." Elliot stopped. "I feel a need to say this: There may not be prints from whoever planted the devices. They could have—"

"Worn gloves. Yes, I know," Sean interrupted. "But let's have a look all the same." Elliot smiled as he walked through the door opened by Sean. "Thanks, Elliot."

Nicole and Sean started down the hallway to their bedroom to dress for the party. After dressing, they grabbed the trays that Natasha prepared and headed for the Great Hall. After several trips to the cafeteria for a few remaining trays of food and drinks, the staff started to arrive.

The dress was casual for the informal party. Nicole had heard from a few of the staffers that some of the office members had formed a band. Nicole asked them to bring their instruments. After an hour or two of mingling, the band members began to play. Sean, Nicole, and the others sat encircling the musicians and sang along. For a few hours, the burdens of serving their country in a foreign land lifted. The security force meandered in and out of the party, Alistair making sure that each of his men enjoyed the food, friendship, and singing. Duncan, Alistair's trusted second in command and Nicole's bodyguard, was stationed in the party room. Alistair roamed the grounds and relieved the guards so that they could join the party for a short time.

After cleaning up the hall used for the staff party, Sean and Nicole walked back to the residence. They settled in the living room, Sean offering to fix them each a gin and tonic. Nicole accepted the drink as Sean sat down next to her. Just as Sean settled in, there was a knock on the door. Sean set his drink down on the table as he walked into the foyer.

It was Elliot, who ran the prints through the intelligence database during the party. "I've got some results," he said, holding up a folder. "You aren't going to be happy."

Sean opened the door further, inviting Elliot inside. He closed the door and continued to the living room. "What did you find?" Sean inquired.

Elliot nodded to Nicole as he sat down. "I don't understand why Stewart's fingerprints would be on the outside and inside of that particular door."

Nicole and Sean looked at Elliot. Nicole spoke first. "Are they fresh prints?" She cleared her throat. "I mean if he had an affair with the former ambassador's wife, as our security team has indicated, it would make sense."

"True," Elliot replied. "I don't know how fresh they are. There weren't many prints on the doorknob. Who uses that door?"

"No one that I know of," Nicole said. "Natasha enters through the front. I've never opened that door."

"What other prints did you find?" Sean asked.

"The previous ambassador's and his wife's were there. A few of the guards' prints were on the outside. Even Stewart's prints aren't a 100 percent match. The prints on the outside of the door were partial prints, but the inside match was better. I have more confidence in that print. He could have taken it as a shortcut or something."

"So, we're nowhere," Nicole said, a frown closely following her statement.

Elliot nodded his agreement. He stood to leave. "And Sean, your office was bugged again. Same model as the ones planted here. I removed and destroyed them. My advice is to check these places often. I've ordered another detector from headquarters for you. It's a matter of time before we catch whoever is planting the bugs."

"Thanks for your help," Sean said as he walked Elliot to the door. He closed the door and walked back into the living room, snatching his gin and tonic up along the way. He held his glass up and said to Nicole, "It's going to be an interesting few months."

Washington, DC—Blair House

Jenkins was alone on New Year's Day. He had given Chris and his staff the day off. Samuelson was flying back to Colorado to spend some time with her family before the inauguration. He even ordered his chief of staff, Fred Whittaker, not report to Blair House or to call him. Jenkins looked forward to some solitude and watching football on the television. In fact, he was even toying with staying in his pajamas, robe, and slippers for the entire day. This was a welcomed break in the hustle and bustle of the last year. He needed to recharge.

He made himself a pot of coffee, scrambled some eggs, and was sitting down with the newspaper when the phone rang. He looked at it as his mind ran through the possibilities. He determined it was either Chris or Whittaker. The next question was whether he was going to answer it. He knew if he didn't, the Secret Service would bust through the doors to make sure he was in fine health. He swore as he stood and walked to the wall-hanging phone. He snatched up the receiver.

"I'm perfectly fine," Jenkins snapped. "Now leave me alone."

"I can only hope that you become sicker than a rabid dog, you little prick."

Jenkins recoiled from the vile, all too familiar Texan drawl on the other end of the phone. "What the fuck do you want?" Jenkins was in no mood to deal with his nemesis today.

Barker sat quietly for a moment as he pondered his next sentence. "I see the love of your life has found herself a new beau," he taunted. "And right here, in Moscow, where I can have my way with her too."

"We both know what you're capable of, having failed once already. Did you tell Louise why I exiled you to Moscow?"

"I'll be back in Washington soon. Putting your lover here wasn't a smart thing to do," Barker replied.

"She is not my lover any longer, thanks to you," Jenkins said, calmly. "And if I find out that you made one move toward harming her or if you plan any attempt on her life, I'll have your ass. I don't think you'll find a remote Moroccan jail cell to your liking." Only those with the highest of security clearances knew about the place Jenkins was referencing.

"You wouldn't dare," Barker declared. "I have too many contacts, and that would come back to haunt you. If you want her safe, your best move is to recall me to Washington."

"No," Jenkins said. "That won't be happening. And if you don't stop trying to weasel your way back here, I will have no problem arresting you for the attempted murder of Nikki." There was silence on the other end. "Yes, I just said that out loud. Are my phones tapped? Are you on tape?" Jenkins smiled. "Face it, Barker. You are irrelevant. Now be a good ambassador. Stay out of trouble and don't make me come after you."

"Wait," Barker urged. "You don't have any evidence."

"I don't?" Jenkins questioned. "Are you sure about that?" Jenkins could almost hear Barker squirming in his chair. Jenkins cleared his throat. "Don't ever call me directly again. Your chain of command is through the State Department. If you threaten me again, I'll report you to the Secret Service. We both know what will happen then. Do you understand, Mr. Ambassador?" He paused, waiting for Barker to comment. When none came, Jenkins hung up the phone. He returned to the table and sat down. He opened the paper and took a drink of his coffee to help calm him. He took a bite of his eggs and found himself wishing that Nicole would seriously consider the communications director role he had offered. He smiled when he realized that he felt he could protect her better than an MI6 agent in Moscow.

CHAPTER THREE
END OF JANUARY 1981

Washington, DC—Oval Office

Jenkins had been in office for six days. The first few days were busy with introductions and meetings. His next appointment was to be a briefing with the Joint Chiefs of Staff. Whittaker informed Jenkins that the commanders wanted to bring him up to date on a situation in the USSR. At first, Jenkins wondered what Barker could be up to then realized that he was overreacting. Whittaker informed Jenkins that the meeting's subject was in regards to a reconnaissance mission over Murmansk—the Russian nuclear submarine base that bordered on the North Sea. The rumor was that the Soviets were introducing new electronic countermeasures and the need for the submarine's identification signature was paramount to national security. The Joint Chiefs were sitting on the couches with Jenkins and Whittaker sitting in armchairs on opposite ends in the conversation area.

The Joint Chiefs and a few others discussed details of the operations involving an SR-71, a submarine, and a Blue Ridge class command ship to aid in the gathering of intelligence. It was a risky mission because the aircraft would fly very close to Soviet airspace.

"The mission will take approximately ten and half hours to execute," the Air Force general said.

"And it is imperative that we obtain this information?" Jenkins asked.

The chairman of the Joint Chiefs, Admiral Clifton, cleared his throat. "Yes, sir. The Soviets are about to launch its newest submarine, and we have no intelligence on how to track it. This mission will provide information needed to build the appropriate electronic signature for that sub."

"Without it—" General Richard Babcock, the commandant of the Marine Corps, started but the chairman raised his hand, stopping him from completing his sentence. There was a tense moment in the room. Jenkins and the commandant were in a stare down.

"The Soviet sub is scheduled for launch in a few weeks according to our latest intelligence. Perhaps you'd like to think about it?" Clifton inquired.

Jenkins sat forward in his chair and continued to look at the marine commandant. He recalled the commandant's attendance at Barker's social affairs and other gatherings. Jenkins wondered for a brief moment if Babcock was the person Barker had blackmailed to put the hit out on Nicole. "Gentleman, remember my prior experience–both as a Navy SEAL and as chairman of the Senate Intelligence Committee. We have seen each other in briefings, meetings, and social events." Jenkins continued to stare at Babcock. He stood and buttoned his jacket. The Joint Chiefs also stood. "Some of us have mutual friends and, well, let's say, former friends. What I am about to say may shock some of you, but it needs to be said. Gentlemen, you can't serve two masters."

"Excuse me, sir?" Clifton was confused.

Jenkins gave Clifton a quick look, returning his glare to Babcock. "If you can't see that Barker is destroying our democracy—just as Stevens and his gang of five tried to do—then it is with regret that I say you will not be serving as a Joint Chief in this administration. I'll accept your resignations within the hour." Jenkins was wondering how far Barker's reach was, especially since he had not ended the Mockingbird Operation. Barker simply took it out of the hands of the CIA and constructed a web of deceit from which Barker prospered. Jenkins turned and walked to his desk. When behind it, he added, "My motives are simple. We—together—fix our country and our political system by ridding it of personal agendas and greed, or we will surely murder this democracy. Each of you, like myself, have taken an oath. I know that some of your loyalties unwillingly rest with someone else. So, I ask you again, if you can't serve your country without the fear of exposing something dreadful in your past, then I ask you to do the country a favor and submit your resignation." Jenkins broke off his stare and quickly glanced at the other Joint Chiefs. "That's all for now."

"Thank you, sir," Clifton said, still bewildered at what he just heard. The Joint Chiefs followed Clifton out of the Oval Office.

"Admiral Clifton," Jenkins called to him before he left the room. "One moment, please." When Clifton was by his side, Jenkins asked, "How long will it take to execute this mission?"

"Twenty-four hours," Clifton replied. "It will take time to get the naval vessels in position."

"Thank you," Jenkins said. "I will let you know in the morning, Admiral." Clifton nodded and left the room.

"Sir," Whittaker began when they were alone, "may I ask what that was about?"

"Babcock is in Barker's back pocket. Barker has something on him. It was a Marine sniper that fired the shot that almost killed Nikki. Anyone Barker can blackmail, especially on the Joint Chiefs, I want them out of my administration. Is that clear?"

"I think you made that pretty clear, yes," Whittaker replied, not at all happy with Jenkins's actions. "I think we could have dealt with it a bit differently."

Jenkins first smiled, but it quickly disappeared as he reached his boiling point. "I have only been here for SIX DAYS. It seems that you and the rest of my advisors think I can't do the job!" Jenkins threw the pen in his hand and rested the knuckles of both hands on the desk trying to steady his nerves. "Is this the way it is going to be? Are you going to doubt every decision I make?" He stared at Whittaker, who stood silent, not flinching from the glare. Jenkins took a deep breath. Mind reading was not a skill Jenkins possessed, but in this case, he knew what his chief of staff was thinking. He took another breath before he said, "Don't worry, Fred, I'm going to authorize the operation. I plan on calling Clifton this afternoon to ask for a full briefing on the operation in the Situation Room. I do not doubt that these men are good. I do, however, believe some of them are harboring ill feelings toward me because of what happened during the campaign, and I can guarantee you, General Babcock will resign within the hour."

"I hope you're correct in your assumption," Whittaker said. "Or we just pissed off the Joint Chiefs—a group of leaders you don't want to have on your bad side, in case you haven't figured that out yet."

"We'll be fine," Jenkins countered.

"Is that all, Mr. President?"

Jenkins looked up from a paper he had started to read. "Let me know when his resignation comes through. Tell Clifton to get ready to brief me in the Situation Room an hour after that. Thanks, Fred." With that, Whittaker left the Oval Office.

Puy-l'Évêque, France—Le Château du Vipère

Maggie had just returned from the market. She walked into the kitchen to find Kent sitting at the little table in the nook. He was looking out the window deep in thought. Maggie greeted him, but he didn't respond. She started to put the items she bought in their proper place: the cheese into the refrigerator, the fresh fruit into a basket, she went to the sink rinse the fresh vegetables. When she turned the faucet on, the running water caught Kent's attention. "Are you OK?" she asked him.

Kent looked at Maggie. "Yes," he said and then paused. His face revealed his predicament. "Maggie, can I trust you?"

Maggie gave Kent a strange look. Her heart skipped a beat. She had waited for this question for a long time. Her whole objective was to win his trust. She turned the water off and gently asked, "What's wrong, Kent?"

"I've received a job offer. It's a bit complicated, but I never thought I would do anything against my country," Kent said, quite aware he was making no sense.

Maggie instinctively knew she had to play this correctly—too eager and it could tip him off to her double life; too little interest and all that she was trying to establish with Kent would vanish. "If I can help you, you know I'm willing." She wondered if that sounded too ambitious. She kept the space between them, intentionally not moving toward him.

Kent found her words supportive and wondered if she had developed feelings for him. He eyed Maggie with suspicion, not for her words, but because of his insecurities. He had been enjoying her company for almost six months, and she had proven her loyalty. She had also displayed good business sense, improving the wine business Saverio, the former Serpent, had started as a cover. She waited at the château patiently when he went on a job, but most importantly, any little secret he had shared, as far as he knew, remained a secret. If he could trust anyone, it had to be her. Was he willing? Did he want to let her into his world? Was he falling in love with her? He always thought that Sean's weakness was his ability to love. How could he have that same weakness? How could he let himself fall in love?

Kent shook his head, wanting to dismiss his thoughts. He was beginning to understand the loneliness that Sean endured while tracking down Kent's predecessor.

Maggie stood her ground. Kent kept his gaze locked on her. "What do you mean 'against your country'?" She hoped the question would ease some of the tension she was feeling.

Kent still sitting kicked a chair away from the table. The action made Maggie jump. He looked at her, remembering the one night he was agitated and took it out on her. "I'm not going to hurt you. I want you to sit down here." He pointed to the chair.

Maggie remembered that night as well. He had hit her, and it was all Maggie could do not to retrieve her gun and kill him. He had hit her, not once, but several times. Her bruised right eye swelled with the discoloration extending to her cheekbone. Her upper arms were ringed with bruises where he had grabbed her. Her only defense was to kick him in the balls so that he would release her. She thought that he had found out that she was with MI6, but that turned out not to be true. It remained a mystery to her. "If you don't mind, I'd rather stand."

"Maggie, come sit down. I promise I won't harm you," Kent urged her. "As I said that night, I won't touch you again in that way. Please believe me."

Maggie tucked her long blonde hair behind her ears and cautiously moved to the chair that Kent had kicked away from the table. She moved the chair so that it faced Kent, giving her more room to escape from him if he tried to hit her. "I'm sitting," she said, still wary.

Kent exhaled a small breath; a brief frown crept across his lips as he looked down. "If you can't sit next to me after I have asked you if I can trust you, maybe I have my answer."

"I don't think the question of trust is whether you can trust me. I think it is whether I can trust you," Maggie corrected. "I've never done anything to make you distrust me. You, on the other hand, beat me for no reason."

Kent shook his head. "So you hate me?"

Maggie smiled. "No, I didn't say that. You get this look on your face. I don't know where you go, but I know better than to push any further."

Kent looked at her. "It has to do with an old colleague. Someone I could live without and someday I will make that happen."

"Make what happen?"

"Live without him being in this world. I will kill him and his lover," Kent declared, the hate evident in his voice.

"Can we not talk about him, whoever he is?" Maggie asked, as she shifted in the chair, showing her discomfort. She knew Kent was speaking of Sean and Nicole. "You asked if you can trust me. Tell me what's bothering you."

Kent ran his fingers through his hair. He massaged the back of his neck with one hand and repeated. "I have a job offer. It involves travel to the Middle East."

"The last time you were there, you returned so ill," Maggie stated.

"Yes, it is not my favorite part of the world. But this job offer, it is big and could be the offer that sets me up for the rest of my life."

"I don't understand." Maggie was curious if Kent would tell her he was an assassin. She wanted to know how much he trusted her. She also wanted to know who offered him the job hoping that he would inadvertently tell her.

"Do you know what I do for a living?"

She knew she had to be coy. "You're involved in the wine trade." She hated playing the ditzy blonde.

"No, that is a cover." Kent looked her in the eyes. "Maggie, what I tell you has to stay between us. If you ever tell anyone, I can't let you live."

Maggie played along. She sat back in her chair, acting scared. She widened her eyes as she said, "I don't think I want to know."

"I'm the Serpent. I'm a professional assassin," Kent stated. He studied her reaction.

Maggie turned her head as if she didn't believe him. She gave a little chuckle as if the words were starting to register. She shook her head in disbelief. She studied him while he studied her. Her brow furrowed. "An assassin?"

"Yes," Kent said. "People hire me to take care of their problems." Maggie didn't respond. She just looked at him judgmentally—as anyone would do. "Say something."

Maggie licked her lower lip and then bit it. She cocked her head and coquettishly asked, “Are you good at it?”

Kent laughed. “The best,” he replied.

“There are more than one of you?” Maggie asked, still playing her role. “I mean, saying you’re the best indicates that there are more than one of you.”

“There are many of us.”

“How does this offer set you up for life?” Maggie asked. “Does it mean you can stop doing it?” She thought someone with no experience would want to know if the person could stop killing.

“No, it actually will do the opposite. It would drum up business and prove—” Kent stopped. “It’s complicated. There were two other Serpents before me. Before the death of the second assassin, he was training me because he wanted to leave and enjoy his riches. This job would stop the speculation.”

“I don’t follow, but I’m not sure I need to,” Maggie responded. She knew precisely what Kent was telling her. She knew Sean killed Saverio. She knew Kent assumed the Serpent’s identity and that most of the world believed the Serpent was dead. “I don’t understand what you need from me.”

“If I accept this job, I’d like you to come with me,” Kent said. “It will take some time to scout it out. I’d like you to take care of me.”

In a way, Maggie felt touched by his sentiments. Those feelings made her doubt herself. Could she love someone like Kent? She swallowed as if she was squelching the thought. “Am I allowed to know where in the Middle East and who is hiring you?” As soon as she asked, she wanted to pull the words back. She quickly sought out a lock of her hair and started twirling it around her fingers. She needed to convince Kent the information was of no real importance and that she was asking out of curiosity. Toying with her hair provided that impression, she hoped.

Kent thought for a moment as the doubts surfaced. Why would she care to know? She would need to pack appropriately. She already knew the information that would serve her well if she ever decided to leave. Of course, leaving alive would never happen. She had to stay expendable. Kent decided he could trust her. The rest of the information was just details. "We will be traveling to Syria. That's all I can tell you."

Maggie gave a quick, almost indiscernible, nod of her head. "When do we leave?"

"In a few days," Kent said. He leaned forward and kissed her. She welcomed the kiss as she traced his chest with her fingers. She slipped her right hand down his pants and firmly grasped his testicles and then started rubbing his penis. Kent snatched her to him, standing as she embraced him, wrapping her legs around his waist. They continued to kiss as Kent carried her to the bedroom. Maggie could think of no other way to solidify the trust she had earned from him. She knew she had him right where she wanted him.

Moscow, USSR—United States Embassy

Barker was sitting at his desk looking over some papers, all of which were of little importance. He finished the last paragraph and dropped the paper from his grip. His mind turned yet again to his relegation to what he described as a hellhole. *How did this happen?* His prodigy was in the White House. The Democrats had control of both houses of Congress, while he sat in Moscow. He could only hope his well-placed spies could influence the agenda of his prodigy-now-nemesis. He stood and walked to the makeshift bar located in the hutch across from his desk. He snatched up the crystal-bottled bourbon and removed the top. He poured himself a generous amount before he returned the top and bottle to the spit-polished silver tray. He took a drink when the door to his office opened. "Damn it, Cliff! I said no—"

"I don't give a rat's ass what you told him," Louise spat out as she entered the office.

"I'm sorry, sir," Cliff said, walking in behind her.

"It's OK," Barker consoled him. "Close—"

"That won't be necessary," Louise interrupted. "I just came to tell you that I'm going out for a while. I don't expect you to wait for me for lunch or dinner."

"Where are you going?" her husband barked. Louise pursed her lips and looked him right in the eyes resolute in not answering his question. "Didn't I tell you that you will not meet with her?"

"Yes," Louise started, nonchalantly looking at her nails. Louise had stopped caring about her husband's demands after Baranov's New Year's Eve party. "But I have an appointment with her anyway. If you won't tell me what happened, then I will find out from her." Louise was referring to the reason for their exile to Moscow.

"And you'll believe her story? Have I ever—"

Louise let a taunting laugh leave her lips. "Don't even think about finishing that sentence. You'd be surprised by my answer." Louise began to put her gloves on and turned toward the door that Cliff was holding open. "I doubt you'll even miss me. Tell your whore—I mean my so-called social secretary—that she can remove her shit from the desk outside my office. I won't be needing her. I'm sure you'll find a place for her. You always do." Louise left the office, forcibly bumping Cliff into the door he was manning.

Cliff regained his balance with very little effort, but Louise's intent was noted. Cliff looked back at Barker as Louise slammed the outer office door. Barker was downing the drink he had in his hand. "You need to fix this."

"She's here with me. Just what damage do you think she can do?"

"You under-estimate her," Cliff said. Barker's phone began to ring. Cliff walked to his desk without closing the door. "United States of America Embassy, Ambassador Barker's office, how can I help you?"

"This is General Babcock. I need to talk to the ambassador."

Cliff was aware that Babcock was on the Joint Chiefs and an ally. "One moment, please." He put the general on hold and walked back into Barker's office. "Commandant of the Marine Corps, General Babcock for you."

Barker walked back to his desk as Cliff started for the door. "And I'm going to remind you again that we are not alone."

Barker huffed at Cliff's reminder. He snatched up the phone saying, "Hello Rob, how's everything in Washington?"

"Changing," Babcock replied. "I'm handing in my resignation."

"You can't do that," Barker almost shouted. "You're my eyes and ears there. What happened?"

"We were briefing the president on a mission. To make a long story short, he knows."

"Knows what, dammit?" Barker demanded.

"Jenkins knows that someone on the Joint Chiefs ordered the assassination of Charbonneau. He put it together. I can't stay. I'm leaving before this comes out and ruins everything. He gave me an out, and I'm taking it. I repaid you with that favor. We're even," Babcock told him. The tone of his voice sounded more like begging than delivering an ultimatum.

"We are even when I say we are even," Barker retorted, his anger audible in his harsh tone.

"Then this is our final conversation. What I'm about to tell you is the last favor I do for you," Babcock started, not giving Barker a chance to counter. "There is a military operation the president will be briefed on later today. It involves the country you are in, and you will have the opportunity to make it a success or failure. Sonic Stroll is all I am going to say. You should be able to get what you need through your other stoolies. What you do with the information is your decision." Babcock swallowed. "I'm handing in my resignation within the half-hour. If you decide to intervene, then God help us." The line went dead.

Barker held the phone for a moment. "Cliff!" When the door opened, and Cliff was close to his desk, Barker added, "We need to find out all we can and quickly." Barker wrote the codename on a piece of paper and handed it to Cliff. "I suggest you get your coat and make the necessary calls elsewhere." Cliff acknowledged the order and left his office for the secure surroundings of the apartment he was renting across town just for this kind of situation.

Moscow, USSR—United Kingdom Embassy

Sean was working at his desk when Nicole quickly stopped in to let Sean know she was meeting Louise at the Intourist Hotel restaurant. Sean voiced his concern. Nicole quickly interrupted him noting that Duncan and a few other guards were going with her.

She had no intention of staying long, and if she saw any glimpse of Barker, she would not step one foot in the restaurant. She was out the door before Sean could say another word. He returned to his work but for only a few minutes. Stewart knocked on his open door, a sharply dressed woman by his side. Not looking up from the paper he was reading, Sean said, "Yes, Stew, what is it?"

"I have someone here, sir, I'd like you to meet," Stewart said, motioning for the woman to move into the room. "Her name is Stacy…" Stewart's voice trailed off as he caught the quick glimpse of Sean's reaction as he looked up from his paper. Sean's jaw almost dropped open, only to catch himself and internalize his surprise within seconds. "I'm sorry, have you met before?" Stewart asked.

"No," Stacy said, moving forward with a walk all too recognizable to Sean. "I don't believe so. My name is Stacy Cambridge." She smiled at Sean, now in front of his desk. She extended her hand, palm-down as if inviting him to kiss it rather than shake it.

Sean stood up, took Stacy's hand in his, turning it sideways once their flesh met. His intention was clear. He would not kiss her hand. He cleared his throat. "Welcome to our embassy, Ms. Cambridge." He looked at Stewart.

"She is working in the bullpen. She came very highly recommended, and I couldn't let her credentials slip by us. She knows Russian, so I thought starting her with translations would be appropriate," Stewart replied to Sean's unasked question.

Sean smiled as he looked back at Stacy. Their eyes met, and Sean could almost feel his knees buckle. "Translations, yes," he mumbled.

"Unless, of course, you would like her to work more closely with you," Stewart added, noticing that Sean had not released Stacy's hand and was still gazing into her eyes. He cleared his throat.

"No," Sean said, snapping back into the conversation. "Translations would appear to be the appropriate place. Tell me, Stacy, what part of England do you hail from?"

"Just outside London," Stacy replied.

Sean acknowledged her answer with a quick nod. "Aren't we all," he quipped. He released her hand and broke his gaze. "Well," he started. "I'm sure that Stew's thoroughness will get you up to speed quickly and you'll feel right at home in no time."

"She has already been here for a while, starting last month," Stewart said. "It was just a convenient time to introduce you. She dropped off a report that she translated." He motioned for Stacy to hand it directly to Sean.

"Yes," Stacy said, presenting the report to Sean. "I hope you find it written well, but if you should have any questions, I've written my extension on the front page."

"Very well," Sean said. Her forwardness caused him to blush. He was still stricken with her. He set the report down on his desk and cleared his throat. He was starting to feel foolish. "Thank you for introducing us, Stew. Will there be anything else?"

Stacy moved closer to the desk. "Hopefully we could have a chat someday soon. I miss London, and from what I've read, your family has quite a history." Stacy was almost whispering her invitation.

Sean looked at Stacy, taken aback. "I'm afraid I'm quite busy. Give it a bit more time. I'm sure you'll find friends among your co-workers." Sean smiled. "I need to get back to this…" His voice trailed off as he sat back down. When she didn't move, Sean looked up at her. "Thank you."

Stewart cleared his throat. "Stacy, this way please." He motioned through the open door. Stacy backed away from the desk, still holding Sean's stare. She then began to flip her long brunette hair between two fingers. She turned and walked out of Sean's office.

"Stew," Sean called. Stewart poked his head back in the door. "Close the door, please. I wish not to be disturbed until Nicole returns."

"Yes, sir," Stewart confirmed. He shut the door behind him and gave a smile to Stacy, who was also grinning from ear to ear. He leaned into Stacy and said, "Well played. You got to him." Stacy simply gave Stewart a seductive smile and walked out of his office.

Moscow, USSR—Intourist Hotel Restaurant

"I'm not sure I like this," Duncan said, as he opened the door of the hotel. He quickly glanced around the vicinity as he waited for Nicole to enter. "Tell me again why she couldn't come to the embassy?" The original date set on New Year's Eve had been canceled and rescheduled for a drink at the Intourist Hotel.

Nicole smiled at Duncan's concern. "It will be OK. Sit next to me," Nicole said removing her gloves as they entered the restaurant. She arrived at the table where Louise was waiting and took her coat off. She was about to throw it over her chair.

"I'd prefer if you would sit in this chair, ma'am," Duncan said, pointing to a chair whose back was against the wall. This allowed Duncan to sit with an unobstructed view of the entry and rest of the restaurant. He caught a quick glimpse of her Beretta in her shoulder holster. Nicole obliged his request. Louise ignored

Nicole's bodyguard, stood, and gave Nicole a quick hug and kiss on the cheek. Her hand brushed the holster of her gun. It surprised Louise who was about to question Nicole.

"How have you been, Louise?" Nicole asked, stopping Louise before she could ask her question.

"I'm fine, dear," Louise responded, sitting back down. "Thank you for meeting me."

"Of course. Is there something wrong?" Nicole inquired.

"You mean other than being exiled to this dreary place?" Louise asked rhetorically. She fidgeted in her chair when Nicole offered no response. "I don't understand what happened. Larry and Bobby were such good friends. They worked so well together. I expected Larry to be in his cabinet, not sent here to Russia." Louise paused. She noticed that Nicole wasn't responding to her statements at all. In fact, for the first time, she noticed how cold and distant Nicole was. She cleared her throat. "Well, I won't waste your time. I just wanted to know if you could talk to Bobby about getting us home. I also wanted to know if you knew what happened between them."

Nicole looked down before her eyes settled back on the wife of the man who had ordered her assassination. "Louise, it is obvious that Ambassador Barker doesn't tell you everything. I think the person you should be asking is your husband. He knows what he did to earn Bobby's mistrust."

"So you do know," Louise muttered. "I have tried to get him to tell me. He won't."

"I don't think I should be—"

"You have to be! Please, tell me," Louise begged her. "I have been with Larry for a long time. It won't be the first time he has done something I can't forgive. I doubt it will be the last." She looked at Nicole, who was still stoic. "Nikki, I don't know what happened between you and Bobby, but obviously it was something you couldn't forgive, or you wouldn't be here with that adorable Ambassador Adkins."

Nicole briefly smiled at Louise's short, but she felt accurate description. "Bobby hasn't done anything to me," Nicole stated. "It's a long story, but the truth is that I love Sean. I always have even when I was with Bobby. If anyone is to blame for my breakup with Bobby, it's me."

"Could you talk to Bobby—ask him to let us return?"

"I won't do that," Nicole said. She pulled her elbows off the table. "I won't ask Bobby for favors that I don't want him to extend. Quite frankly, Louise, I wouldn't lift a finger to help your husband."

Louise sat back. In the short time that she knew Nicole, she had never seen Nicole be so heartlessly cruel. "What *has* he done? Please tell me."

"I don't think that would be a good idea," Nicole replied, shaking her head. "If he won't discuss it with you, I should not be the one who does."

"I can't stay here, Nikki," Louise pleaded. "I hate this place, and Larry leaves me alone all day long." Louise decided that it was time to bare her soul. "It's like a prison. He dismissed my staff and brought his whore here as my social secretary. We are barely speaking, and I can't live like this. Give me the reason to leave him, please."

Nicole looked at Louise. “If you aren’t happy, you don’t need any other reason. If he is mistreating you, you don’t need another reason to leave.”

“Oh, yes I do,” Louise said with a hint of anger in her voice. “I need something to hold over him so that he doesn’t come after me. I stopped loving him when he forced me to raise his first whore’s son as our own. We made a pact then, and he cut me off from knowing the details of his schemes. If I leave now, he will make sure my life is a living hell. I want to be free of him for good. I want to go home to the United States and be free of him. Can you understand that?”

Nicole nodded her head.

“Then tell me what he did,” Louise implored.

“He leaked the story concerning Bobby’s Vietnam record,” Nicole said.

“That’s what he did to Bobby,” Louise said. “What did he do to you?”

“He tried to kill me,” Nicole whispered.

Louise leaned in closer to Nicole; sure she hadn’t heard correctly. “I’m sorry—”

Nicole glanced at Duncan who sat stoically, acting like he wasn’t listening to the conversation. She leaned a little closer to Louise and whispered again, “He tried to kill me.”

“What?” Louise was horrified and shocked. She sat back. “Nikki, he adored you. Why would he want you dead?”

Nicole was still whispering, uncertain she wanted any of this said out loud. “I influenced Bobby during the campaign, and it was a thorn in your husband's side. Bobby sided with me on most issues, and Barker couldn't tolerate that. We fought all the time, and he threatened to kill me once in South Carolina when I rewrote one of Bobby's speeches. I didn't think he would go through with it, but when I was in London…" Nicole paused. "The sniper was ordered to kill me by your husband. He bribed a Joint Chief. Bobby knew he couldn't keep Barker in the Senate, plotting to ruin his presidency, so he sent him here, where he would be forgotten. Bobby has all the information he needs to keep Barker in line."

"He tried to kill you," Louise repeated, trying to make herself believe it.

Nicole could see Louise was having a hard time accepting her answer. "He despised my relationship with Bobby, my ability to work with Bobby for the betterment of his campaign and the nation," Nicole added. "I was in the way. I was a threat to everything Barker ever wanted to achieve. With me there, he couldn't control Bobby."

"I can't believe you," Louise began. "Larry has never killed anyone."

Nicole became angry. "I wouldn't be too sure of that. You think a man who could force you to raise his whore's son isn't capable of killing someone?" As a waitress made her way to the table, Nicole sat forward, taking Louise's wrist in her hand, and whispered. "He may not have pulled the trigger, but he has killed many people with his bribes and threats. His power is knowledge. What does he have on you that you would come begging to me to free you? What does he have on you that is preventing you from walking out on him without some knowledge to keep you free of him?" She stood up, waving to the waitress to leave them alone. "You have the nerve to doubt me after I tell you what he did to me." She looked at Duncan as she grabbed her coat. "We're leaving," she said.

"Louise, you played your hand well for years and lived the fantasy of the powerful man's wife to perfection. Your husband is the monster you think he can be. I doubt he even knows how to love anybody. You have no one to blame but yourself for the situation you are in now. I can only hope you have the courage to do what you know you have to do. But, I fear you are just a pawn in his game. So, tell him for me, that I know he tried to kill me once. But now, I'm prepared to protect myself." Nicole threw her coat around her, letting Louise catch a glimpse of her gun. "Duncan," Nicole said as she started for the door.

Louise's eyes began to tear up as she watched Nicole leave the restaurant. She knew in her heart what Nicole had told her was true. Her husband tried to ruin his prodigy. When Nicole and the others outwitted her husband, they punished him for what he did. A single tear escaped her eye, and she quickly wiped it away. She stood, put on her coat, and told her security detail that she was ready to leave. The only thing on her mind was whether she was going directly to the airport, leaving Larry Barker once and for all, or if she wanted to confront him. The only thing she knew for certain was that she needed to be brave.

Washington, DC—Situation Room

Jenkins was seated at the head of the long table listening to his advisors argue the merits of launching Operation Sonic Stroll. Babcock's resignation had been received, and Jenkins moved the briefing up on his schedule. The Soviets were about to launch its latest and greatest submarine—a new class of warring machine. The intelligence provided few facts and much suspicion on what that technology was. Jenkins had all the typical questions. Did it put the US in immediate danger? Did the new technology damage any advantage the US had? More information was needed, and this trolling mission off the coast of Murmansk was designed to provide that.

"Trolling?" Jenkins asked.

"Trolling is an action by which we manage to light up the Soviet defenses, forcing them to use their radios and radar. We overload them with electronic information, which causes them to reveal telltale electromagnetic signatures. These signatures would reveal types of equipment, modes of operation, and their limits," Clifton informed him.

"Besides the SR-71, we will have Navy vessels offshore increasing the amount of data we can secure in one pass," the Navy admiral added.

"And we have done this successfully in the recent past?" Jenkins asked. "How safe is it?"

"We've done it successfully many times, sir. It is the recommended method now," Clifton responded.

"How quickly can this be done?" Jenkins looked at each of his remaining Joint Chiefs.

"We are waiting for your command, sir," Clifton stated. "We need your order after which naval vessels will be directed to move into position. The SR-71 would lift off within forty-eight hours of the vessels arrival."

Jenkins thought for a moment. His gut was churning, and he wondered if he should wait a few more days. He stood up, and everyone in the room quickly got to their feet. "Make it happen," Jenkins ordered. As he started to leave, he added, "Keep me informed of the progress."

"Yes, sir," came a collective response from the Joint Chiefs. They immediately grabbed the phones in front of them. Almost in unison, "Sonic Stroll is now operational. It's a go!" came out of the Joint Chiefs' mouths.

Jenkins gave a quick glance over his shoulder as he turned the corner heading for the Oval Office. All he could do now was wait.

Moscow, USSR—United Kingdom Embassy

Nicole was sound asleep until Sean's tossing and turning woke her. She lay still for a moment, not sure what was happening. Sean flailed to the left, then to the right before he sat straight up in the bed. Nicole reached over to turn on the light. She turned and looked at Sean before she spoke. The edges of his black hair were wet with sweat as was his face and naked chest. The palms of his hands were at the temples of his eyes as if he was trying to squash his torment. "Sean?" She placed her hand on his back, feeling the perspiration.

Sean jumped at her touch, gasping for air. It was then he realized the light was on in the room. He blinked his eyes repeatedly. Nicole determined that Sean was not fully awake. His confusion was obvious. She started to move from the bed slowly. Although she truly believed Sean would not intentionally hurt her, it was clear wherever his mind was it was not in their bedroom. As she placed her feet on the floor and exited the bed, she called his name again. Sean was now rocking and mumbling as he looked at his hands, then brought them back up to his temples. Nicole called his name a third time, a little louder.

Sean's reaction was to cover his ears and shout, "Sarah! No, Sarah!"

Nicole moved to a chair and sat down. She watched Sean for a few minutes, as she realized that Sean was reliving Sarah's death. "Sean," she started, waiting to see if her voice penetrated Sean's darkness. It did not, so she yelled, "Sean!" He stopped rocking. "Sean!"

Nicole's voice finally broke through Sean's nightmare. He removed his hands from his ears, noticing how wet they were and that they were not covered in the blood as they were in his nightmare. His eyes darted from side to side, as he gathered his bearings. He started to slow his breathing as he silently told himself he was in the embassy. His eyes finally rested on Nicole, still sitting in the chair.

"Are you awake now?" Nicole asked.

"Yes," Sean replied. "I'm sorry. I hope I didn't frighten you."

"You scared the shit out of me," Nicole exclaimed, as she stood up. "What were you dreaming about?" She sat on the edge of the bed.

Sean watched her move toward him. When her question registered, he just looked at her. He finally said, "I think you know."

"Sarah?" Nicole questioned.

"Yes," Sean replied.

"But why now?" Nicole asked. Her confusion was evident. "I don't understand." Sean looked away from her. Sean wasn't ready to tell Nicole. He knew they had said no secrets. Nicole asked again. "Sean?" Sean didn't look at her. "Sean, you're scaring me. What's going on?"

He couldn't lie to her. "I don't know." It was the best he could do. He saw her concern and placed his arm around her, taking her with him as he reclined back on the bed.

"Was this an anniversary or some special date for you and Sarah?" Nicole pressed.

"No. Maybe. I don't know. Nicole, let's not analyze this," Sean pleaded. "I'm sorry I scared you. It will be all right. I want to go back to sleep." Sean kissed her forehead. "Can you turn the light out, please."

Nicole turned away from him, reaching to turn the light out. When she turned back around, wanting to cuddle with him and hold him tightly, Sean had turned his back to her. Nicole gave him the space he sought, lying on her back. She bit her lip as her mind raced with possibilities that she had no way to dispell. It was early morning before she finally fell back asleep.

CHAPTER FOUR
FEBRUARY 1981

Moscow, USSR—United Kingdom Embassy

It was morning, and Nicole walked into the breakfast room where Natasha was adorning the table with freshly baked scones, coffee, and tea. "Good morning, Natasha," Nicole said as she sat down at the table.

"Good morning, ma'am," Natasha greeted her. "I will retrieve the newspapers now."

"Take your time," Nicole offered. "Sean is still sleeping. These scones smell wonderful!" Nicole poured her hot water in her cup and laughed when she thought of Sean admonishing her for not putting the teabag in the pot and allowing it to steep there versus repeatedly dunking it in the cup. Nicole adopted a new technique, first dunking it in her cup then transferring it to the teapot after it reached the desired strength in her cup. This technique infuriated Sean even more—the effect she was looking for in the end.

Natasha returned to the table with the newspapers. "If it is OK with you, I would like to go to the market and get some items. We are low on things."

"Yes, of course," Nicole replied. "Do you need money or transportation?"

"No, ma'am," Natasha responded. "There is a code—"

"Oh, yes, I keep forgetting about that," Nicole interrupted. "I'm sorry." Nicole knew the code was a way for the KGB to keep tabs on what was coming into the embassy. It was a thought that Nicole detested. She was eternally thankful that Sean had agreed to allow shipments of some of Sean's favorite foods from England, which in turn lessened their reliance on the Moscow food chain. She called it one of their comforts for being abroad. Nicole's thoughts turned to her homeland. She missed having an American hamburger. Her mouth watered as she pictured herself sitting in Old Ebbitt Grill, one of her favorite restaurants in Washington, DC, and biting into the thick, juicy sandwich.

Natasha snatched up her list and left the residence. She hummed as she walked on her way to the market, never stopping, but thinking how her life had changed since Sean and Nicole arrived. She was home in time to see her children. She had to admit to herself, as hard as it was, that she possibly liked these two foreigners. They were fair and just in her eyes, something a true Soviet may not like to admit. As she moved through the market, Natasha became aware of a gentleman who was following her. At first, she thought it was merely a coincidence.

Natasha moved to another section of the market. She turned to find the man directly behind her. She gave him a look, which conveyed her irritation with him. As she started to speak, she was interrupted.

"My dear lady," the man began, speaking in Russian. "My name is Vladimir Valesky, and I would like to buy you a cup of coffee. Will you allow me that honor?"

"I don't drink coffee," Natasha shot back annoyingly. "And I have no time for men." Natasha wasn't lying. Ever since the untimely death of her husband, her life was work and her children. She still longed for the man she loved with all her heart. The thought of someone else never entered her mind. She took a step back from the man she felt was invading her personal space and caught a whiff of his cologne. It triggered her memory. Her mind returned to the morning of her late husband's last birthday. She surprised him with the cologne worn by the previous ambassador. It was not available in the Soviet Union, and she inquired about the possibility of getting it for her husband. The ambassador's wife graciously had a bottle shipped from England. She would never forget that scent: Musk by English Leather. She did not doubt that Valesky was wearing that scent. But where did he get it? She scanned the man from head to toe. His clothes, his grooming, his build, and even his shoes provided clues that this man was well traveled and had money. Natasha then recognized the man's name. Valesky's reputation preceded him. The man waited while Natasha scanned his body, her eyes first stopping at his belly which was slightly bigger than a fit young man (indicating he enjoyed good food) but firm as the rest of his muscles. Natasha's eyes reached his face, and he smiled. She knew then that the rumors she had heard about Valesky's infidelities were true.

"A nice hot chocolate, perhaps?" Valesky enticed her.

Hot chocolate was an extravagance in the Soviet Union for people like Natasha. She only indulged herself at the embassy when Nicole had received a new shipment from England. She thought that Nicole didn't notice, but Nicole did. Nicole knew too well the pleasure of its silkiness as the warm, velvety liquid enveloped the throat and chest on its way to the belly. Nicole couldn't deny Natasha that simple pleasure. Natasha licked her lips in anticipation. Then she remembered she was on an errand. She needed to get back to the embassy. She needed her job. Her face reflected her return to the present, much to Valesky's displeasure. "No, I must get back to work," she said.

"Perhaps we can meet when you are off work? What time would that be?"

Natasha paused for a moment. "You know where you can buy me hot chocolate?"

"Yes, I do." Valesky pointed down the road toward a very expensive hotel that Natasha only dreamed of seeing the inside of. The Intourist Hotel always held a fascination for Natasha. She had seen rich people and foreign dignitaries walk into the hotel, their furs wrapped around their designer dresses. She imagined herself stepping from a limousine, wrapped in a luxurious fur, barking orders at the bellhop, who removed suitcase after suitcase from the car. She nonchalantly sashayed her way to the imagined front desk with everyone's eyes on her. "Would you care to join me? I will wait for you there," Valesky urged.

"I don't know you," Natasha said, not at all convincing. While she recognized the man's name and reputation, she was not sure she wanted to get to know him better. She certainly didn't want to owe Valesky any favors.

"As I said, I am Vladimir Valesky," the man said as he offered his hand. Natasha put her hand in his, and he brought it to his lips, gently kissing it. "And might you tell me your name?"

"Natasha," she said, captured by his gentle kiss. "Natasha Kirakov."

"It is a pleasure, Natasha," Valesky said. "What time shall I see you?"

"I get off work in an hour," she said. Valesky's gentleness was the opposite of the cruelty she had heard about him. Besides hearing of Valesky's infidelities, she heard countless tales of the cruel murders committed by Valesky at Baranov's instructions. Valesky seemed kind and caring. The difference between the man and the myth surrounding him intrigued her.

"I will see you then." Valesky kissed her hand again before releasing it. He smiled and gave a half bow before leaving her.

Natasha smiled. Her cheeks flushed. When he was out of sight, Natasha's senses returned. She cursed the cologne for throwing her off-balance. She finished her shopping and quickly headed back to the embassy. She completed her work, and then looked around the residence for Nicole. When she determined that Nicole was not there, she cursed. She didn't know why at first. She decided that she was seeking advice—no, that wasn't the right word. She thought for a moment, searching for what it was she wanted from Nicole. Was it Nicole's permission she was seeking? Frustrated, she decided that whatever it was, she ultimately was responsible for her actions. Nicole was her employer, not her friend. Natasha had lived her life for everyone except herself. One or two hours enjoying a conversation and hot chocolate with a handsome man was a luxury she wanted to give herself. She would meet Valesky once.

She walked to the Intourist Hotel and entered the lobby. She wrapped her worn coat around her plain clothes as the stylishly dressed concierge turned her nose up at her. Natasha felt out of place. She began to question why she came as she scanned the lobby looking for the man who promised her hot chocolate.

Valesky was reading a newspaper while smoking a cigarette. He felt the wisp of fresh, brisk air when the doors opened. He was now peering over the paper while Natasha was looking for him.

Pleased that he had succeeded in luring Natasha to the hotel, he smiled and stood when their eyes met. He greeted her with a kiss to her offered hand. As they walked through the lobby to the restaurant, Valesky hoped he could persuade her to visit with him longer and in the privacy of one of the hotel's rooms.

As Natasha walked to the restaurant her eyes examined the pristine marble floors, the artwork hanging on the walls, and the plushness of the furnishings. They were shown a table and seated. Valesky ordered the hot chocolate for Natasha as promised. He wanted to order vodka but settled on coffee instead. He had to play this correctly, or he would lose the opportunity. Valesky had to maintain just the right amount of flattery to keep Natasha off-balance, more importantly, interested. He had to woo her if this affair was to reap the reward he was seeking. He thought it shouldn't be too hard, but then worried he might be under-estimating his prey.

The hot chocolate and coffee arrived. Natasha smelled her treasure, closed her eyes, and imagined she was somewhere else. She searched the corners of her mind seeking that perfect place to which the aroma transported her. The memory of a garden near the Mediterranean Sea was the image on which her mind settled. The chocolate drink reminded her of the pleasure of being with her deceased husband in this garden. The thought of the warmth of his body next to her, his sweetness toward her, and of a happier time caressed her as she took her first sip. She stayed lost in the memory for a moment before Valesky's voice invaded, urging her not to burn her tongue. She suspiciously eyed Valesky. What could this well-to-do man want with her? She sipped the chocolate again, almost as a protest against his invasion of her daydream. She enjoyed the silky texture of the chocolate in her mouth and the comfort it gave her, all the while eyeing this handsome yet mysterious man. She quickly glanced at the ring finger of his left hand. No ring was present. Natasha had her doubts about him, but she believed she deserved an extravagance now and then.

From the look he received from Natasha when he spoke to her, Valesky knew that he would have to move slowly. He cursed that she would not be an easy conquest. He was well experienced at what he was doing. He remembered to remove his wedding ring when he was in the market earlier in the day. Valesky caught her quick glimpse of his ring finger. He knew she didn't believe he was single by the furrowed brow and smirk on her lips. Natasha was going to take more effort and more research, much to his dismay. This rendezvous would consist of chit-chat between them, ending with Valesky asking to see her again. He hoped he could convince her to accept another date.

Valesky made Natasha the center of attention. There were compliments given at appropriate times, talk about her children and family, and he gave very little information about himself. When pressed for information, Valesky convincingly provided lies. Natasha drank the last of her hot chocolate and looked at the clock on the wall. She announced that she had to leave to meet her children. She thanked Valesky for the treat and the conversation; both were equally delightful. Natasha stood up.

"I hope we can do this again soon," Valesky said, standing to join her.

She suspiciously eyed him. "Something tells me you are trouble," she remarked. Valesky played the fake, hurt man perfectly. Natasha, still wary, gave a quick laugh and said, "I would entertain your offer if you should make it again. But now, I honestly must go and quickly. Thank you for a pleasurable time. Goodbye." Natasha turned and walked out of the hotel.

Valesky watched her leave. He slipped his hand into his pocket retrieving his wedding band. He motioned for the waiter before placing the ring on his finger. Reaching into his pocket again, he removed his money clip and paid the bill. As he walked from the restaurant, a bellhop approached him.

"There is a phone call for you, General Valesky," the bellhop said. "You may take it over there." The bellhop pointed to the front desk.

"Thank you," Valesky responded, the tone of his voice showing his annoyance at being tracked down. He walked to the front desk and was handed the phone by the desk clerk. "What is it?" Valesky snapped into the receiver.

"I have some information for you," Barker stated. "But if you don't want to be bothered…" His voice trailed off as if he was about to hang up the phone.

Valesky recognized the Texan accent of his new friend. Since the New Year's Eve party, Valesky and Barker had met regularly for lunch. "What possible information would I want to get from the American ambassador? Whatever you have to offer, I probably already know."

"I doubt that," Barker replied. "It involves your new submarine in Murmansk."

Valesky paused. For once, Barker did have some information that interested him. He sighed when he realized that he would not be going home for a quickie with his wife. He glanced around the lobby for someone he could quickly enjoy himself with before meeting Barker. His eyes met the gaze of a maid standing at an elevator. He smiled when their eyes met. "Meet me at the Intourist Hotel, room 213." Valesky had secured the room in hopes that Natasha would fall for his charms swiftly. "Don't hurry." Valesky handed the phone back to the desk clerk and walked confidently up to the maid. The elevator arrived just as Valesky started oozing his slick charm on the inexperienced maid. By the time the elevator doors closed, Valesky knew he had his prey. The young maid cooed at every comment and giggled at his advances. As the elevator began to ascend, Valesky selected the second-floor button and slipped his arms around his mark. By the time the maid realized what was going to happen, it was too late. Her struggles to evade him only heightened his desires. Never releasing his grip, he opened the door to his room and forced her inside while smothering her with his sloppy, sodden kisses. He ripped the underwear from her as he thrust her onto the bed.

Valesky dismounted the disheveled, half-dressed, and shocked maid. He rolled onto his back on the bed, his pants and underwear around his ankles. The maid brushed the tears from her eyes as she sat up. She held her cheek where Valesky had slapped her after she bit his lip. She found her underwear ripped in two on the floor a few feet from the bed. She didn't bother to pick them up as she ran from the room. Valesky knew it would not be the last time he forced himself on this girl, especially if the conquest of Natasha took too long to materialize. The violence of rape satisfied him on many levels. It was victory and dominance. It fed his ego and reinforced his hoodlum persona. He was untouchable. He reached for his pack of cigarettes, removing one, lighting it, and taking a long, satisfying drag.

Ten minutes later, Valesky was dressed and seated at the little round table in the room waiting for Barker to arrive. He barely recalled the conversation they had exchanged earlier on the phone. He only knew that his main concern now was why Barker felt a need to tell him something about the Soviet submarine and what Barker wanted in return. Valesky waited five more minutes and was about ready to leave when Barker knocked on the door.

Valesky strolled to the door, opened it, and said, "What took you so long?"

"There are police in the lobby talking to one very hysterical young girl," Barker told him and gave him a knowing smile. "I couldn't risk being seen coming to this room. I had a drink in the bar and waited for the police to leave."

"You know we have agents here all the time," Valesky said. "For example, I know your wife met with the UK ambassador's whore in the restaurant a few weeks ago. Where is your wife now, Ambassador Barker?"

Barker slowly took in a breath. In actuality, he had no idea where Louise was. She left for that meeting with Nicole and never returned. He phoned family and friends, but no one had seen her. "She's back home in Texas." That was the cover story for now.

"Is she?" Valesky asked. He could see through Barker's weak attempt to convince him. He had no interest in Louise. She had served her purpose in letting him know her husband was approachable at the New Year's Eve party with her disapproving stare at Barker's ingratiating comments. He waved his hand as if to dismiss the conversation. "I'm a busy man. What is it you want to tell me?"

Barker looked at Valesky. "I have some information that you may find useful. But first, I need to know what you are willing to do to ensure that we continue to work together."

Valesky studied Barker. After the New Year's Eve party, Valesky had gathered intelligence on Barker. "You know, Ambassador, we are not that different. I will give you an example. We both know that information is more powerful and can take you further than any material thing. I know that you have a lot of information on people in your government. I know you hate Jenkins and why he exiled you here. So, for me, the information you have will do me no good with Jenkins. Why do I know that? Because he somehow has information to neutralize you or he would not have sent you so far away from him." Valesky shook his head. "So what good would you be to me? No good. We have your embassy bugged. We know what goes in and out every day." Valesky picked up his coat from the bed.

"I suppose that ripped pair of underwear means nothing to you," Barker countered, pointing to the underwear in the trash can.

Valesky gave a few quick laughs, insulted that Barker thought of blackmailing him. "She is of no consequence." Valesky looked Barker in the eye. His light mood vanished in the cold stare. "The last person who tried to blackmail me is floating face down in the Moskva. I advise you to be very careful."

"You have a new submarine in Murmansk, do you not? I would hate to see something happen to it before it is launched," Barker mocked. There was no reaction from Valesky. "I can see you are not interested in what I have to say."

Valesky shrugged his shoulders, unwilling to take the bait. He brushed past Barker as he walked to the door. "You must be leery of a man so desperate to commit treason." Valesky opened the door, turned, and looked at Barker. "I am not desperate, but I am very suspicious. Thank you for the tip. We will see what happens next." Valesky left the room, closing the door behind him. Valesky had enough information to follow up with his informants. He laughed as he heard Barker swear on the other side of the door. He left Barker to fume in private.

Washington, DC—Oval Office

It was time again for the weekly intelligence briefing. All the players were present, including Kevin Thompson, who was now serving as director of the FBI.

As the men entered the room, Jenkins walked out from behind his desk to greet each with a handshake. Thompson was the last to shake his hand. Jenkins was surprised, although he didn't show it when he felt a folded piece of paper Thompson covertly left behind in Jenkins's hand. Jenkins stuck his hand containing the paper immediately into his pants' pocket and moved to the chair to direct the meeting.

"Gentlemen, what do you have for me today?"

"We're keeping an eye on Afghanistan," Douglas Stanton, director of the CIA, began. "There seems to be an elevated level of interest on the USSR's part. We've also intercepted some chatter about the transport of weapons to the region in the coming weeks."

"Soviet weapons, I assume," Jenkins stated for clarity.

"Yes," Stanton confirmed. "We are trying to determine if it is in response to some new equipment we sent to the region." Stanton went on to inform Jenkins with snippets of other intelligence collected. He finished with, "It's been a rather slow week."

"We're continuing surveillance on a few white supremacy groups who had threatened to bomb a sporting event. There are some drug trafficking cases we are monitoring as well. In short, it's business as usual, which after the past year is a good thing to report," Thompson said.

"Would it be a fair statement to say the international scene is a bit more active?" Jenkins questioned, looking for confirmation.

"Yes, sir," Stanton replied as Thompson nodded in agreement.

"I don't expect anything to change after green-lighting Sonic Stroll," Jenkins added.

"Yes, sir," Stanton confirmed.

"Well, keep up the good work," Jenkins said as he stood up. All the men exited the room. Jenkins asked Chris to give him a minute before the next briefing. He walked into the bathroom and pulled the folded-up paper that Thompson had given him out of his pocket. He unfolded it and began reading.

"Mr. President, I wanted to alert you to a situation that has come across my desk involving the CIA and Ambassador Barker. It appears that Barker has requested all information they have on Ambassador Adkins. The same request crossed the desk of one of my agents. He found the request suspicious given these requests are typically vetted through the State Department. The FBI has not responded, and the agent was ordered not to reply. I have stepped up surveillance on outgoing information. The agent is aware that I doubt his loyalty to the FBI since Barker contacted him directly. I do not want to embarrass the CIA director by bringing it up in the meeting. I also want to see if he will inform you." The note was not signed.

Jenkins tore up the paper and then threw it in the toilet. He flushed it, waiting to ensure that all the paper disintegrated and nothing remained. He wondered what Barker was up to, but Jenkins knew exposing Sean's past was not an option. He walked into the hallway, hoping to catch the director of the CIA. He was too late.

"There you are," Whittaker said as he entered the hallway. "Are you looking for someone?"

Jenkins turned to look at his chief of staff. “No,” he started. He pointed at the door he had just exited. “I was curious where that door leads. I can’t recall walking out of it before.”

Whittaker looked at Jenkins. “Mr. President, we walked out that door two days ago to meet with staff in the Roosevelt Room.”

“So we did,” Jenkins said, turning to walk back through the door to the Oval Office. “Is there something I can help you with, Fred?”

“Amon Seddik is on the phone,” Whittaker said. “He says it is important. When you didn’t answer your phone, Chris phoned me.”

“Seddik?” Jenkins asked, surprised the Egyptian president was calling him. They entered the room, and Jenkins walked to his desk and sat down.

The phone on the desk buzzed. Jenkins looked at his watch; it was already close to four in the afternoon. He picked up the receiver and said, “President Seddik, it’s getting late in Egypt. Is there a problem?”

“Hello, Mr. President. Thank you for taking my call,” Seddik replied. “I would like to talk to you about the peace accord I signed with Israel under the previous administration.”

“Yes, an accomplishment my predecessor achieved before his assassination.” Jenkins knew about the accord.

“As you may also know, I am facing strong resistance here because of the agreement.”

Jenkins spoke up. “I hope that you will continue to honor it.”

“I have every intention of keeping my word. However, I need to have some visible support from your administration. It would help my people to understand that the United States has not abandoned us," Seddik explained.

"I see," Jenkins replied with skepticism. "And what would this show of support look like to you, Mr. President?"

"That depends on how much you support our position and understand how exposed my country is to those opposed."

"Are you suggesting that there is activity from another country to shatter the work done to date?"

"Honestly, yes," Seddik confirmed. "I have unverified reports that the Soviet Union is active in Syria and Libya recruiting their allies to rise against Egypt. There have been some indications that pro-Soviet rebels have backed some of the rioting and uprisings."

"I understand," Jenkins replied. He pondered his response. "Mr. President, allow me to check with my secretary of state—"

"No, Mr. President, I don't want the secretary to come here. I want the president to come here. President Andrews demanded we journey to Camp David, so I demand you show how strongly the United States backs us by coming here," Seddik said adamantly.

"Amon, we both know my first foreign trip cannot be to the Middle East," Jenkins stated. "My visit would have to occur with visits to other countries first—meaning our European allies, which have always been the traditional first trip." Jenkins paused for a moment. "I will talk with my secretary of state and make it clear that Egypt should be a part of our first trip."

"We would welcome you here regardless of where it falls on your itinerary, Mr. President," Seddik said. Jenkins could swear he heard a sarcastic tone in the Egyptian president's voice.

"I appreciate your understanding on this matter," Jenkins returned. "I look forward to discussing the agenda of our meeting. The sharing of the intelligence that is fueling the speculation that the Soviet Union is behind the rioting would be extremely helpful. I will have my secretary of state coordinate with your office and arrange the meeting."

"Thank you, Mr. President. Egypt will await the call," Seddik responded before he hung up the phone.

Jenkins looked at Whittaker. "I just had a security briefing, and they didn't mention the uprisings in Egypt. Fred, I was the chairman of the Senate Intelligence Committee. Surely they know I have contacts. Surely they know better than to hide information from me."

"Would you like to see the director of the CIA and NSA again?"

"First thing tomorrow morning," Jenkins demanded. "And get in touch with Secretary Alboreto and tell him we need to get Egypt and Israel on the itinerary for the first trip overseas."

"A full day for both places?" Whittaker asked.

"Yes, I think it will have to be an overnight stay," Jenkins said. "I am sure both will want my undivided attention."

Moscow, USSR—United Kingdom Embassy

A few days had passed since Sean had received a phone call with an accompanying demand. It had happened so quickly; Sean wasn't sure if he even recognized the voice. Hurriedly, the man on the other end of the phone said, "February 12 at noon, Sokolniki Park, chess club."

Now Sean found himself walking toward Elliot's secured office, swiping his badge, and entering after keying in his security code. It was a little after ten in the morning on the twelfth, and Sean still had not made up his mind. Was he going to meet this Soviet?

"Good morning, Sean," Elliot said a few seconds after Sean walked into his room. Elliot was standing by the new mainframe computer, looking over some electrical cords. "Sean?"

Sean was deep in his thoughts. Did he recognize the Soviet's voice? Was it who he thought it was? Was it a trap? When Elliot called his name a third time, Sean looked at him. "Hello, Elliot."

"Is there something I can help you with?"

"Yes," Sean began as he walked over to Elliot. "I'm in a bit of a quandary."

"Really?" Elliot joked. "I couldn't tell."

"Funny," Sean chided. "I got a phone call a few days ago. The person on the other end was Russian, asking me—well, demanding me—to meet him in Sokolniki Park today at noon."

"Did you recognize the voice?"

"I'm not sure, but I think it was Leznikov."

Elliot stopped messing around with the cords, stood, and looked at Sean. "Did he say what it was about?"

"No," Sean replied. "Eight words were spoken—the date of the meeting, the time, and the place before he hung up."

"I'm not sure I like that," Elliot countered. "It sounds like a trap."

"Or a call for help," Sean retorted. "If it is Leznikov, he can't be seen coming or going to this embassy. He isn't in a position to summon me to the Kremlin. What if he wants to warn me or, better yet, tell me something that would prevent an incident between our two countries? I keep thinking, Elliot, I can't ignore this call."

"What if it *is* a trap?"

"He has to know I won't go anywhere in the Soviet Union without a contingent of security guards."

"He could have an army behind him," Elliot replied.

"So you think I shouldn't go."

"That depends on how much you believe it was Leznikov and how safe you think it is," Elliot countered. "Do you think Leznikov would set you up?"

"Anything is possible," Sean said, frustrated.

"But your gut says you should go anyway."

"Yes," Sean admitted.

"Don't go alone and don't go unarmed," Elliot offered. "Where's the meeting again?"

"Sokolniki Park," Sean replied. "There's a chess club that meets there in the rotunda at the far end of the circle."

"How do you know that?"

"He said to meet him at the chess club," Sean began. "I did some checking. Evidently, it is a very public place, and anyone can go to watch them play. It's, perhaps, a great place to have a sniper take out an MI6 agent."

"Here's my suggestion: go to the meeting. Have Alistair search the premises as quickly as he can, stationing guards in the places where snipers could be." Elliot retrieved an earpiece and handed it Sean. "You don't enter until Alistair gives you the all clear. If Leznikov wants you dead, he will realize you have taken precautions. I doubt Leznikov shows up for your meeting after he sees Alistair has done his job. If he wants to see you for any other reason, he shouldn't be surprised by your precautionary measures. It should be enough for you to exchange in private what it is he wants with you. You are both agents. You'll both be armed. I doubt this is an attempt on your life. I think he wants to talk to you in a place that has less of a chance of being overheard."

"I think you're right about that," Sean said, referring to where Leznikov wanted to meet. "If indeed it was Leznikov that phoned."

Elliot tilted his head. "That's why you have Alistair with you."

"It should look more casual—as if we just happened to bump into one another." Sean looked away in thought.

"Take Nicole," Elliot suggested.

Sean's head snapped around to look at Elliot. "Are you insane?"

"No, think about it." Elliot walked to his desk. "It gives you a second gun close by, and it makes it look like you are out exploring Moscow."

"In the middle of winter?"

"Why not?" Elliot countered. "You are out for a hike and see the rotunda. You walk in to check it out, and you bump into Leznikov—if indeed he is there. If he isn't, you leave shortly after you arrive." Elliot had a point. It would be a rare occasion when Sean wouldn't have Nicole by his side. "And I would still have Alistair there to secure the place beforehand."

"Right," Sean said as he turned toward the door. "Thanks, Elliot."

"Sean," Elliot called before Sean opened the door. "Are you all right?" He noted Sean's confused look. "Normally this would be nothing for you to figure out. What has you rattled?"

Sean looked down at his feet for a brief second. He walked back over to Elliot. "I need a favor. Walk by the bullpen and look up a woman named Stacy Cambridge. If you are as surprised as I am, you'll know what you need to do next."

"Are you fucking kidding me?" Elliot asked. The last thing Elliot needed was to check out a woman.

"No. You'll see why I am asking," Sean replied. "And don't mention it to Nicole."

Elliot shook his head. "It's not like I'm busy upgrading your embassy—"

"It's important to me," Sean interrupted.

"OK," Elliot replied, raising his hand to make Sean stop talking.

"It's not what you think," Sean assured him. He saw Elliot shake his head again. Elliot turned back to the mainframe. "Thank you. I'm off to see Alistair and then try to convince Nicole to take a walk on this cold, snowy day." He walked out the door and headed to meet with Alistair before returning to his office.

Nicole was on the phone when Sean peeked his head around the door-frame. Nicole waved him into her office as she finished her conversation. "That's wonderful! Set the closing for the beginning of March, and I'll begin to make arrangements. Thank you for all your hard work. Goodbye." Nicole hung up the phone and smiled at Sean. "My condo sold and at a very nice price, too. The closing will be the beginning of March. I'll know more about that in a day or two."

"You have to be there?" Sean asked.

"Yes," Nicole said. "Well, I could get a proxy or an attorney, but I'd rather be there. I have to make arrangements to get the furniture I left behind put in storage." Nicole looked at Sean. She could tell he was not enthusiastic about her return to Washington. "Sean, we knew this day would come. You knew the condo would sell and that I would need to return to Washington to tie up loose ends. You are more than welcome to come with me. You know that."

"We'll see when the time gets closer. I do want you to take Duncan and a small number of guards with you if I can't break away," Sean added.

"Of course," Nicole replied. "Did you need something?"

"Yes," Sean replied. "We need to take a stroll through Sokolniki Park and check out the chess club. I've been requested to meet someone there at noon."

"Who?"

"We'll find out at noon," Sean said. "Let's change into some warm clothes. It's a bit cold outside." He offered his hand to Nicole and they quickly walked to the residence before leaving the embassy.

Leznikov arrived at the Sokolniki Park rotunda fifteen minutes before noon. He did not enter the building, instead choosing to sit on a bench and feed the pigeons. He watched out of the corner of his eye the people entering and leaving the rotunda as well as walking on the trails leading to and from the building. He knew it was impossible for him to know every KGB agent. He knew the risk he was taking.

Sean and Nicole arrived at the rotunda a few minutes before noon, with no apparent security force. Leznikov breathed a small sigh of relief when he noticed Sean had only his woman with him. Sean opened the door for Nicole, and they entered the rotunda. It was not unusual to have strangers enter the rotunda to watch the chess matches. No one turned to look at them. The players concentrated on their dream: to become the next Boris Spassky. Among the players were a few grandmasters, who were always looking to identify their up-and-coming challengers.

Sean took Nicole by the arm and started further into the rotunda. Nicole kept her hands in her coat pockets, the palm of her right hand lying against her Beretta. Sean had urged her to keep it in her holster. Nicole refused his request, saying it would take her too long to retrieve it if she needed it. Sean turned his head and noticed Alistair in a strategic position and nonchalantly watching a chess match. He was in plain clothes as were all his scattered men stationed around the rotunda. Sean didn't acknowledge Alistair when their eyes met. He did, however, admit to himself that their clothing blended in well with those attending the chess club.

After a few minutes, Sean was rather rudely bumped into by a man who seemed to be in a hurry. The man realized his abruptness and turned as if he was going to apologize. It was Lezinkov, and he played his surprise perfectly. "Ambassador Adkins, I am amazed to see you here."

"Colonel Leznikov," Sean acknowledged, offering his hand to shake. "Do you play chess?"

"Yes, but never against these professionals," Leznikov replied, releasing Sean's hand. "Do you?"

"No, I've never found the time for board games."

Leznikov looked at his watch. "Allow me to introduce you to the game." Leznikov walked over to an empty table where a chessboard was waiting for players. Sean and Nicole followed.

"I'll even let you go first." Sean sat down, and Nicole looked around, trying to find a position that would allow her to protect them both. She let out a small sigh when she determined there was no such place. Leznikov looked at her, kicked a chair out from the side of the table and said, "Join us, my dear."

"Thank you," Nicole said with a condescending smile. Sean recognized the tone and tried not to acknowledge it.

"Chess is all about strategy. It is like planning a war. You deploy your men, and you have to have the ability to understand your enemy. You need to look many steps ahead. Of course, the opening says so much about the person," Leznikov started. Sean sat looking at Leznikov, blinking his eyes in disbelief. "For example, you don't want to move too many pawns. While their movement is restricted when compared to other pieces, they are the strength in defending your king."

Sean leaned forward and quietly said, "I don't have time to play a game of chess with you."

Leznikov barely moved his lips. "Indulge me." Louder he said, "Control of the middle ground is good." Leznikov pointed to four squares at the center of the board. "I won't go into all the different openings. For now, move a pawn."

Sean looked at Nicole. Nicole's eyes darted quickly between the two men. She leaned into Sean. "Move the pawn in front of your king," she instructed. Sean put his finger on the pawn and looked at Nicole. "Yes, that one. Move it up to the next white square." Sean executed his move.

Leznikov looked at Nicole. "Perhaps I should have asked you to play."

"It's a package deal," Nicole responded.

"Tell him why he made that move so he can learn."

Nicole kept her gaze on Leznikov. "The queen is the most powerful piece on the board. She is free to move in any direction to protect her king." Nicole's choice of words was deliberate. With this description, Nicole had made it known to Leznikov that she could act the same as the queen. Sean brought his hand up to his chin and stroked it while he tried not to react to the warning that Nicole just uttered to Leznikov.

Leznikov executed the same move, which resulted in the two pawns meeting in the center of the board. Leznikov leaned forward and quietly said, "I have become aware of the true mission of my directorate and its intended use." Leznikov sat back and said in a normal voice, "Now it is your turn again."

Sean placed his elbows on the table and looked down at his pieces. He spoke quietly. "You are putting me in a no-win situation."

"It is only the second move in the game. You have many options," Leznikov said.

"Move the horse, your knight, up two spaces and over one." Sean did as Nicole instructed. He watched Leznikov move his knight; a reflection of the move that Sean made. "Move your bishop here." Nicole pointed to the bishop first and then to the white square to the left and a row before Leznikov's black knight.

Leznikov's next move was to extract his second knight, landing it two squares to the left of his first knight. "Look at the whole board."

Sean knew this was not only a clue to the game they were playing but also a prompt to think beyond just his situation in Moscow. He pointed to the queen. "She can move freely?"

"She can move any number of squares vertically, horizontally, and diagonally," Leznikov replied. He leaned in as if he was looking at the board more closely. "The risk of this is far greater to me, yet I am willing to accept this."

"Move your king here and your rook here," Nicole said. Sean executed the move.

"I need more," Sean replied.

Leznikov moved his queen's bishop next to Sean's queen's bishop on the board. Both were leaning into the board where they could speak quietly and seem to onlookers to be studying the board. "My position in Line X allows me to see the whole board. I have seen what Baranov wants to do and I do not agree with it. I want to stop this."

"Line X?" Sean asked as he waited for Leznikov's move.

"I cannot go into details," Leznikov replied as he castled his king.

Sean looked at the board. He whispered his two-word question. "Double agent?"

"It is up to you now. It is your move," Leznikov replied. His answer was an affirmative to Sean's question. "Make a safe move. The game is in your hands to win or lose."

Nicole wanted to scream. This veiled conversation was infuriating. She looked at Sean who was now looking at Leznikov. He looked back down at the board and sat back. It was obvious to Nicole that Sean knew what Leznikov wanted. She could see his mind churning out the possibilities.

"Dmitry, did you receive your invitation to our embassy's open house?" Sean asked.

"No," Leznikov replied. "I don't recall seeing it."

"Well, consider this your invitation. The doors open at five o'clock ten days from now, but maybe you could drop by a little early, and we can have a go at another game."

"I accept your invitation, but I'm afraid I can't come any earlier," Leznikov responded. He felt uneasy about being at the embassy, especially if Baranov would be attending the open house. "It's your move."

Sean stood up and looked down at his pieces. He reached for his king. He laid it down on the board, surrendering it. "I will see you in ten days." Sean looked at Nicole and back to Leznikov. "I have a meeting I need to get to, Dmitry." Nicole stood up. "Thank you for an introduction to this fascinating game."

Leznikov watched Sean surrender his king, a hint that perhaps Sean was well versed in the game of chess. "I will see you soon. Thank you for allowing me the opportunity to enlighten you."

Nicole's brow furrowed at Leznikov's extensive vocabulary and choice of words. Sean motioned for her to start walking to the door, Sean reaching for her elbow as she passed. They left the rotunda without saying a word.

Leznikov repositioned the game pieces to their starting positions. He looked at his watch and then stood up. He scanned the area around Sean's chair and the board as if he was looking for something. Leznikov then scanned the rotunda for familiar faces. Not seeing any, he left the building and headed back to his office.

Alistair and his men waited fifteen minutes before they started to leave the rotunda individually. There was no set pattern or length of time between their exits. Alistair was the last to leave, knowing he would be a few minutes late to the meeting Sean called for that afternoon.

Alistair met Sean and Nicole in Elliot's office. "He didn't want to get together for a friendly game of chess," Alistair said upon gaining entry into Elliot's office. After a few steps, Alistair stopped and looked at the mainframe computer that took up half the room as well as the three other computer terminals to his left. "Whoa."

"Impressive, isn't it?" Sean said. "Even if we don't know what it does."

Alistair gave a quick chuckle. "I don't want to know either."

Elliot wheeled a couple of chairs out from the desk and encouraged everyone to sit down. "What did Leznikov want?"

"He is offering us information on his department, which is Line X," Sean replied. "I don't know what that is."

Elliot stared, in shock, at what Sean had just said. Elliot blinked his eyes a couple of times. "Did he say that—directly?"

"Nothing was said directly," Nicole chimed in showing her frustration.

"He wasn't that direct, but his intention was as clear as it gets in our game," Sean replied. "He wants to become a double agent, providing information from his department to us."

"That's incredible," Elliot said. "We were beginning to wonder if Line X even existed."

"What does it do?" Nicole asked.

"It gathers technology information for the Directorate T of the KGB," Elliot responded. "In other words, we would know precisely what technology the Soviet Union was interested in acquiring, why they want it, what information they have obtained, and what they are possibly developing. We can't pass this up."

Nicole looked at the three men almost salivating and certainly chomping at the bit to make this happen. "Wait a minute," she cautioned. "Sean, this could be a setup, and you know it. You said yourself that Leznikov knows you are MI6. You take one shred of information from him in this country, and you might as well slap the handcuffs on now!"

"She's right," Sean admitted. "This could be a trap."

"We can't collect it here no matter what," Elliot told them. "It's got to go to someone outside the Soviet Union and, since he made contact with you, someone not in the United Kingdom. It's all too traceable now."

The four sat despondently for a few minutes until Sean said, "We have ten days to figure out how this happens. I invited him to the open house."

"I doubt you would get more than a few minutes at the party, and I doubt you'll be able to talk details," Elliot flatly stated.

"Yes, that's true, but I could tell him where we can meet. Possibly France…" Sean's voice trailed off as he slid into his thoughts. "If he can travel freely, then this might work."

"What might work?" Nicole asked.

"I think it is best that our next meeting occurs in Paris," Sean replied. "I have a contact there. Elliot, I'll need a secure way to talk to my contact. Can you make that happen in the next couple of days?"

"Give me his name and number. I'll get started."

"His name is Pierre Beaumont," Sean began. He picked up a scrap piece of paper and wrote the phone number to a flat that Beaumont rented for his mistress. He often called that number to arrange meetings. "This is the number I have for him."

"I'll let you know when I have the line established," Elliot said. Nicole, Sean, and Alistair left Elliot to do his work.

CHAPTER FIVE
MID-FEBRUARY 1981

Damascus, Syria

Kent enjoyed the restaurant that Maggie had selected for them. He ate a good meal and drank bottled water at Maggie's urging. Upon arriving in Damascus, Kent was feeling ill from dehydration. After drinking some soda that Maggie retrieved from the gift shop in the lobby of the hotel and a short nap before dinner, Kent felt well enough to walk around the city with her. The call for evening prayer sounded, and Kent was just as bewildered as Maggie. He watched some people disappear into mosques while others continued with their business. Foreigners stood silently, as did Kent and Maggie, listening to the soothing sound of the male's voice. When it ended, he looked at Maggie and gave a quick shake of his head. They began walking again, heading back to the hotel to turn in for the evening.

The next morning they ate breakfast in the room. Maggie studied a map of the city while Kent reviewed the small amount of information he had received back in France.

Securing a taxi, Kent and Maggie arrived at a nondescript building where he was to meet Hayyan al-Ashear. Upon exiting the taxi, a man greeted and escorted them to the outer office of the leader of Syria. The escort gestured for them to sit down. He walked over to the secretary explaining who the two were. The secretary acknowledged them with a quick, almost indiscernible bow of the head and smiled. Maggie deduced that the drab surroundings reflected the chaos of the government of Syria. While Ashear had secured his position of leader and deradicalized the Arab Socialist Ba'ath Party, the country was still fighting a civil war. The Seige of Aleppo was persisting, having started in February of 1980. The clash between the Muslim Brotherhood and Ashear's government had reached a fever pitch in April of 1980. The government forces regained control in May, only to have more clashes that summer. Intelligence reports disclosed two massacres during the summer. In both cases, people were forced from their homes, rounded up by Ashear's forces. In one case, after an attack on the government forces the day before, orders were given to randomly extricate people from their homes in the neighborhood of al-Masharqah. A forced march to a neighboring cemetery ensued. Close to one hundred citizens were executed, including children. The following day, Ashear's Third Division occupied Aleppo, killing an additional thirty-five citizens. No one could deny the brutal inhumanity of President al-Ashear.

Maggie looked at the photo of Ashear hanging behind the secretary's desk, and she felt a cold chill shiver down her spine. She thought for a second that she wasn't thrilled with Kent becoming involved with such a ruthless man. There was never a moment in her life that Maggie felt the urge to flee as much as she did now. She was glad the private meeting with Ashear did not include her.

After a few moments, the door to Ashear's office opened. Three men started to exit the room. Ashear shook the hand of only one of those men. A tall, thin man with a seemingly peaceful demeanor, smiled and nodded as Ashear finished his conversation with him. The well-groomed, black-bearded Saudi Arabian-looking man wore the traditional dress of a pristine white thobe. Maggie intensely watched this man, as he moved from Ashear and through the exit door. He looked directly at her and gave a small bow of his head. It was not a reverent bow; it was a simple acknowledgment of them. Maggie noted that he had a mystic or charismatic aura about him, and then she realized she had previously seen a picture of him. After a few seconds, she gave into the fact that she couldn't remember the man's name, but she did recall that he was indeed from Saudi Arabia. The two men who accompanied the Saudi flanked him, and one moved quickly to open the door for him. As quickly as they entered the room, they were gone. Maggie knew it was a face that she would see again. She wasn't sure why she felt that way, but she knew he would command more attention in the years to come.

The secretary waited a few moments before he addressed Kent. Kent stood and followed the secretary into Ashear's office. Ashear greeted Kent with a handshake. He walked with Kent to his desk, indicating to Kent to take a seat across from him.

"Welcome to my country," Ashear said.

Kent skipped over the formalities and said to the president directly, "It is my understanding you have a proposal for the Serpent, and you are willing to pay two million dollars for its execution?"

Ashear was amused at his choice of words. "Yes, only if it is successful."

"Who is the target?" Kent asked.

"That will be transmitted only to the Serpent," Ashear declared.

"If you do not tell me who it is, I don't see how I can agree on behalf of the Serpent," Kent replied calmly.

"I was lead to believe that this was not an issue."

"This?" Kent asked.

"The target's name transmitted after we reach the agreement," Ashear responded.

"It is merely a confirmation step that the Serpent demands. Think of it as a code word confirmation to make sure there are no mistakes. If you are uncomfortable with telling the Serpent's most trusted confidante the deal is off." Kent stood to leave.

"Seddik," Ashear said. "Amon Seddik is the target."

Kent sat back down. He tried not to show any emotion. In his mind, he was questioning why Syria would want the president of Egypt killed. The scenarios began to run through his head. In the end, the reason why Ashear wanted Seddik dead was of no concern to him. It was a job. It also occurred to him that he couldn't possibly say no and expect to leave Syria alive. "Four million dollars and the Serpent will require months of surveillance before the hit will occur."

Ashear looked at Kent. "We can send the Serpent intelligence reports on Seddik's movements over the next few months."

"That would be helpful, but the Serpent prefers to do his own surveillance and will cultivate the necessary informants if he doesn't have any in place," Kent said as nonchalantly as he could manage. "Is that all?"

Ashear shook his head. "When will the assassination take place? Will we know in advance?"

"You will know when you hear about it on the news, not before," Kent said. "I am done here. The Serpent will want to hear the deal is secured. You will transfer half the money as instructed." Kent stood up. He didn't offer his hand to Ashear. "Good day." He turned and walked out of the room.

After the door closed, a man's voice broke the silence. "He will do nicely," the thick Russian accent cracked over the speakerphone. "I will forward our part of the payment to you shortly."

Marysville, CA—Beale Air Force Base

Two pilots geared up and walked to the SR-71 Blackbird, their office for the next eleven hours if everything went to plan. Lieutenant Colonel David Smith and his Reconnaissance Systems Officer (RSO), Lieutenant Jay Anders, had just finished their steak dinner. They needed to complete their pre-flight inspections before starting their mission.

Smith had previously completed a trolling mission two months prior. Sonic Stroll was his fifth such mission. Anders, on the other hand, had just transferred to the unit and was about to experience his first mission aboard the SR-71. Smith and Anders had completed training exercises over the last two months, and Smith expressed complete confidence in his RSO's capability to complete this mission successfully.

The SR-71 Blackbird was a long-range reconnaissance aircraft built by Lockheed and its "Skunk Works Division." The aircraft was designed to fly at speeds of over Mach 3 for the sheer purpose of evading enemy artillery or aircraft. Its design was an early attempt at stealth technology, dismissing its detection by minimizing its radar cross-section. With a crew of two pilots, sitting in tandem, one pilot would face forward, flying the aircraft, while the RSO would face backward focusing on navigation. In the rear of the aircraft was the recon and surveillance equipment. The SR-71 was painted dark blue, almost black, to aid in the emission of internal heat due to the elevation of its flight. The color also provided camouflage against the night sky, hence its nickname of Blackbird.

The SR-71 possessed the capability of flying at eighty thousand feet, which presented engineering challenges with the expansion of key equipment required to keep the aircraft in the air. Little things, like O-rings and gaskets, became important to the success of the aircraft. The engineers would design the critical fuel equipment for optimal conditions in flight, meaning the SR-71 leaked like a sieve while parked on the ground. Upon take-off, the Blackbird would ascend to eighty thousand feet to achieve optimal operating conditions and then descend to twenty-six thousand feet to rendezvous with two tankers to fill its fuel tanks. The Blackbird was a thirsty aircraft, especially when flying at Mach speeds.

Smith and Anders climbed aboard their aircraft and reviewed their flight plan. The Blackbird would fly over the Soviet Union, snap the photos, and then hit the afterburners accelerating to Mach 3 to evade the aircraft that would surely be launched to intercept. Trolling into the USSR's claimed territory would ignite all the electromagnetic systems, including those on the submarine in the dock.

As the Blackbird lumbered out to the runway, Smith asked for confirmation that the tanker aircraft was in position and ready. The airman in the tower confirmed the position of the tanker. Sonic Stroll began as the Blackbird took off and climbed into the night sky.

When the tanks were full, Smith and Anders made one last check of their instruments and headed to Goose Bay, Labrador, where they refueled again before skipping across the Atlantic Ocean at Mach 3. The third refueling happened over the North Sea, northeast of Scotland. Up to this point, the mission was routine. Feeling confident, Smith alerted his mission cohorts that all systems were a "go." They accelerated to Mach 3.5 to penetrate the Soviet air defense region of Murmansk.

They flew west of Norway and north of Finland, heading to the Soviet coast. Their path over the Barents Sea allowed them to take a ninety-degree, head-on approach inbound. Smith and Anders announced their arrival, as the Blackbird usually did, with a double sonic boom traveling twenty-two hundred miles per hour. Because of a dispute about how far the Soviet Union's sea territory extended, these types of missions got a bit tricky. The Soviets declared one hundred miles as their territory. However, the international norm is twelve miles. Smith and Anders flew to within twelve and a half miles of the Soviet coast.

Smith executed a thirty-degree right bank turn while Anders obtained radar imagery and recorded Soviet countermeasures. A naval vessel sitting just outside the one-hundred-mile range in the Barents Sea was also picking up electronic signals in unison with the aircraft. Just as Smith was about to turn back out to sea, a master warning light sounded, and a red light on Anders's dash began to blink.

"What's that?" Smith called to Anders.

"Master warning light," Anders calmly reported.

Smith looked down at his panel, to check the flashing warning light. "Confirmed—master warning light. I am notifying Navy vessel of the warning light." Smith switched his communications link to send a quick message to the Navy vessel.

"Intercepts launched," Anders called. "We need to get out of here."

"SAM or MIG—hold it together Anders. Give me information so that I know how to react," Smith called back, the warning light's audible alarm still ringing out.

"SAM," Anders started, "coming in at three o'clock."

"Turn that damn alarm off," Smith yelled. "Taking evasive—" Just as Smith tried to take an evasive maneuver, another failure occurred. "Shit!"

"We're dead," Anders yelled. "The emergency checklist said we should land as soon as possible. This second failure—Smitty—we can't go to Mach speed!"

"Damn it; I've lost all instruments!"

While the two men frantically tried all they could think of to evade the incoming SAM, their plane traveled deeper into the Soviet Union. Two MIGs were scrambled from a base just outside Murmansk and headed their way.

"Get ready to eject. I'm going to try to head to those mountains. With luck she'll crash there," Smith ordered.

"Eject?! Are you fucking crazy?! We're over the Soviet Union!"

"You have your orders!" Smith yelled back. "Ready…NOW!" Smith ejected himself and his RSO just after they completed a turn that set the plane on a course that Smith hoped would keep its technology from falling into the Soviets' hands. The two men stayed in freefall, too high in altitude to deploy their parachutes. Smith tried to watch the plane crash, but his fall prevented him from following the plane. They stayed in free fall for what seemed like an eternity. Smith was the first to deploy his parachute. The two men floated down to the Soviet ground beneath them. Even though they didn't think so, luck was on their side. Below them was a dense wetland with forest located in the Smolensk region, approximately 230 miles from Moscow.

Smith hit the ground after cutting himself out of the parachute that caught on the limbs of a tree. He stood up, aching from the fall, but no broken bones. After catching his breath, he started to search for Anders, who was a few hundred feet away. Anders was hiding behind a tree and peered out to see who he heard approaching. When he recognized Smith, he stepped out and quietly called to him.

Smith turned around and walked up to him. "Let's get away from those chutes," Smith said.

"What are we going to do?"

"Walk," Smith mumbled. "I hope this little thing works." Smith pointed to his watch, which included a small tracking device, activated by pushing a button on its side. It ran off the watch battery. The technology was new and untested in the field. Smith wasn't holding his breath that it could save their lives.

"You know we don't have any weapons," Anders whispered as they began walking.

"Then we better hope that we are walking out of the Soviet Union and not deeper into it."

"Do you speak any Russian?"

"Not one word," Smith whispered back. He was looking at the stars, wishing he had paid more attention to astronomy. "Let's try this way." Anders didn't argue. The two men walked quietly away from their parachutes in the dark and only able to see a few feet in front of them. Smith wanted to be far away from their current position before he activated the tracking device.

Washington, DC—White House

"What the hell happened?" Jenkins yelled as he entered the Situation Room.

"The last communication with the Navy vessel was that the SR-71 experienced a master warning light," the Air Force general reported. "That wouldn't have been enough for the plane to crash, but they would have had to land as soon as possible."

"Surely these men realize landing an SR-71 in the Soviet Union isn't something you do as soon as possible," Jenkins replied, sardonically.

"They didn't land," Clifton said. "The SR-71 crashed into the mountain. They ejected." The chairman walked to a map of the Soviet Union in the front of the room. Jenkins joined him. "The SR-71 went into the side of a mountain here. The Navy vessel in the Barents Sea tracked it. We believe the two pilots ejected over Smolensk. That's here."

"So, you are telling me I have two pilots somewhere in the Smolensk region after ejecting from our spy plane that crashed into the side of a mountain in the USSR. Basically, we've just committed an act of war. You are aware of that?"

"Yes, sir," Clifton confirmed.

Jenkins shook his head. "I am surprised that Baranov isn't calling me right now," Jenkins mumbled to himself. Then, losing patience, he yelled, "Could we have fucked this up any worse?" Everyone, except Whittaker and Jenkins, looked down. Jenkins rolled his eyes—something not lost on Whittaker. "What do we do now?" Jenkins moved back to his seat. "And don't tell me to call Baranov. I'm not doing that."

"We wait," Clifton said.

"I had a feeling you were going to say that," Jenkins responded, not at all impressed. "How will we know these two pilots are alive? Can they signal us in some way?"

"I was told that Lieutenant Colonel Smith has a tracking device. We are waiting to see if we can pick up a signal."

Jenkins shook his head and stood up. "Let's pray he does and the device works." He left the Situation Room and headed to the Oval Office. Whittaker was following him. "Fuck," he yelled as he stormed into the office. "Damn it!" As he paced back and forth, he looked at Whittaker. "You realize this means I have to work with Barker." He kept pacing. "I will end up owing that jackass a favor."

"Let's see how this plays out," Whittaker said.

"What do you mean?" Jenkins asked, stopping to focus on Whittaker.

"They may not have survived." Whittaker's voice trailed up at the end as if he were asking a question. Jenkins tilted his head, his mind racing and not wanting to believe the inference that his chief of staff had just made. Cool and calculating, Jenkins responded, "Tell me that you aren't suggesting we leave them there."

"It gives us options," Whittaker stated coldly.

"No, it doesn't," Jenkins countered. "They are coming home, dead or alive. I prefer they be alive."

"I'm just saying—"

"I know what you're saying," Jenkins yelled. "And I'm going to pretend you weren't stupid enough to make that suggestion. Have you forgotten if it weren't for John Spencer, I would have been left behind in Vietnam?"

"No, sir," Whittaker replied, although admitting to himself he hadn't thought about that before he spoke.

"We leave no man behind," Jenkins ordered. "I thought the objective of the mission was to light up—I believe that was the term the Joint Chiefs used—the Soviet radar and electronic systems." Jenkins's voice got a little louder. "Well, the Soviets are on full alert now! You can bet your last dollar the Soviets are hunting those two pilots." Whittaker was about to speak when Jenkins cut him off again. "Get out of my office," he commanded with a wave of his hand. Whittaker started to leave. "Fred," Jenkins called to him in a calmer tone. "Let me know when they know something."

"Yes, sir," Whittaker said.

"Close the door," Jenkins called to him. Jenkins was now alone. He sat down behind his desk. Deep in thought, he found himself staring at the phone. He didn't have time to spare. He retrieved his little black book of phone numbers. He picked up the phone with one hand while he began to dial with his other. "Sean," he said when a sleepy Sean answered. "I apologize for the late hour, but I need your help. I'm running out of time."

Sean sat up in bed, turned on the light by the nightstand. "Bobby? I mean, Mr. President?"

When Nicole heard Sean speak Jenkins's first name, she rolled over in bed. "Bobby? At this hour?" Sean acknowledged her questions with a quick nod.

"Mr. President, is this a secure line?" Sean asked, fully awake now.

"I'm not sure," Jenkins replied. "I just dialed—"

"I'll call you back," Sean said as he hung up the phone and threw the covers off him as he got out of bed. He grabbed his robe and his gun.

"I'm coming with you," Nicole added, getting out of bed and following the motions of Sean.

"Stay here," Sean advised but knew he wouldn't be able to convince her to stay. "I'm just going to my office."

"And I'm coming with you," Nicole stated again, with a little more conviction. "I'm already awake, and I won't go back to sleep until I know what is wrong."

Sean smiled. "I don't even know what he wants."

Nicole walked to the door of the bedroom and opened it. "Let's go."

Sean grabbed his key ring and slipped it into the pocket of his robe. He took Nicole's hand as he walked past her and into the wide, dark hallway of the residence. He switched on the foyer light when they arrived there. Out the door, locking it behind them, Sean and Nicole headed for Sean's office. When they arrived, Sean instructed Nicole to lock the outer door. While Nicole did as instructed, Sean obtained a secured phone line and dialed the White House—directly into the Oval Office via the phone number that Jenkins had provided some time ago. "Mr. President, how can I help you?" Sean asked when Jenkins picked up the phone.

"You will probably hear shortly that one of our planes crashed in the Soviet Union this evening," Jenkins began. Sean pointed at the television and the computer on his desk. Nicole turned them both on. "We believe our two pilots ejected before the crash."

"Where and what were they doing flying over Soviet airspace?" Sean asked. Nicole looked at Sean after she turned on his computer.

"It was a recon mission. The Blackbird was never supposed to fly over land. There was a malfunction—"

"There always is," Sean interjected with a hint of sarcasm.

"Anyway, the pilots ejected in the Smolensk region," Jenkins continued. "We don't know the exact location yet."

"Bobby, you realize the Smolensk region is a good four-hour drive from here," Sean said. "It will be light here in a couple of hours."

"I know," Jenkins confirmed. "That's why I'm running out of time."

"What exactly do you want me to do?" Sean asked.

"Find them," Jenkins pleaded. "I can't ask Barker to do anything. He'll end up expecting a favor or intentionally blotch this up. I want those pilots home alive."

Sean's eyes were darting about as he tried to come up with a plan. "Do you know how big the Smolensk region is?" He put his hand over the receiver and said to Nicole, "Wake Alistair and have him come here." He brought the receiver back to his mouth. "I don't have a lot of freedom to move about here."

"Sean, since when did you need the freedom to move about a country?"

"This is a bit different, Bobby," Sean began. "For starters, the Soviet military is going to be combing the area. Additionally, you don't even know where they are."

"My Joint Chiefs believe they will activate their trackers when they feel they are in a secure location."

"And you don't think the Soviets won't be looking for that?"

"Sean, I can argue this all night, but we are running out of time," Jenkins said, irritation apparent in his voice. "You could be on your way. When you get close to them—"

"How would I know I'm close?"

"They went down in the Lakeland region. You could start for that area and call Nikki for the location. I will phone her when I know."

"Bobby, I just had Nicole wake my security commander here," Sean said. "Let me talk with him about options. He knows this country better than I do. I have never operated in the Soviet Union until now. I can't make a promise at this time. But know this, if I can help you, I will."

"I understand," Jenkins said.

"Call Nicole when you have more information. Bye for now," Sean said and hung up the phone.

"Alistair is on his way," Nicole said, as she reentered the office. "What's going on?"

"Mind if we wait for Alistair?" Sean asked. "I need a map." Sean logged onto his computer and starting reading through his electronic mail. "Can you check the teletype in the other room?"

"Yes, but for what?"

"You'll know when you see it," Sean replied. His adrenaline had kicked in, but so had frustration. He felt as if he couldn't do anything, but also knew that rushing into the area without some plan was suicide.

Nicole returned a few minutes later, Alistair right behind her, and announced that she found nothing of interest on the teletype. She also had a map in her hand. "I found this in Stewart's desk."

"Perfect," Sean said taking the map from her and walking to the table across from his desk by the window. "Thank you, Alistair, for joining us. Sorry about the hour."

"No worries," Alistair said as he stood in front of the table watching Sean smooth out the map. "What's happening?"

Sean informed Alistair and Nicole of the failed mission. Alistair looked at his watch. "It's going to be light soon."

"Yes," Sean agreed. "We need to get on the road. Jenkins will call Nicole with their location once they activate their trackers."

Alistair shook his head. "That sounds a bit like shooting for the moon."

"Do you know this area?" Sean asked Alistair.

"Amazingly, we do," Alistair responded, scratching the back of his head. "The former ambassador used to travel to the Lakelands on holiday. He stayed with a Russian oligarch who has a place up there." Alistair looked at the map. He found the approximate location and pointed. "It was in this area. The bad news is there are not a lot of paved roads there. A limo won't be able to traverse—"

"We aren't taking the limo," Sean interrupted. "One vehicle and just three of us, no more."

"Would you mind if our third is Duncan?"

Sean looked at Nicole, who patted her robe pocket which contained her Beretta. "I think that Duncan would be an excellent choice."

"Then let's get on the road," Alistair declared as he started for the door. "We have better maps of that region in our office. I'll grab them. Meet us out front in five minutes."

"Confirmed," Sean replied. "Fold that up and stash it somewhere," he told Nicole, who did as he asked. "Stay here in case Bobby calls. We'll call you when we get closer to the region."

"Sean," Nicole said right before he walked out of the room. "I wouldn't count on that call. You don't have a plan."

"I know," Sean responded. "I have a feeling we'll be in the thick of the Soviet's search. We'll be making this up as we go."

"Make sure Alistair packs…" Nicole's voice trailed off as Sean shot her a look. She resigned herself to sitting by the phone waiting for a call from Jenkins. She walked to the window that overlooked the courtyard where Alistair and Duncan were waiting for Sean. She took some solace when she saw the vehicle they were taking on this mission. There were no markings on it, and it looked rugged enough to tackle the unpaved forest roads Alistair spoke of earlier. She saw Alistair step out of the vehicle. Alistair's fatigues were complete with bulletproof vests and helmet. Sean exited the embassy and walked up to Alistair who handed him a bulletproof vest and a helmet as well. They climbed into the car and left the compound. Nicole silently wished them everything she could think of: speed to the Lakelands, a quick rescue, and the pilots would activate their trackers indicating their precise location soon. Above all, she hoped all would be coming back to the embassy unharmed. She walked back to Sean's desk, sat down, and laid her head down on her crossed arms. She turned her head so that she could watch the images on the television to her left. She switched the channels, finally locating a local Soviet news station, but found she couldn't concentrate on the images as her thoughts always returned to Sean, Alistair, and Duncan.

A couple of hours later, the Soviet news station began coverage on the Blackbird's crash. While she didn't speak Russian, the photos were all she needed to know that the search for the pilots was in full swing. The phone on the desk rang. She grabbed it on the second ring. "Hello, this is Nicole."

"Nicole, it's Sean." The three men had stopped at a gas station for Sean to use a public phone to call Nicole. "Have you heard anything?"

"No, and Sean, it's all over the news now. They have their military everywhere, and from the photos, there are roadblocks on the major roads. It doesn't look promising. Have you formulated—"

"I'll call you back in a little while," Sean interrupted. He was not going to share their plan, even if they had one, via a public phone.

"Sean, it's daylight now," Nicole said, the worry evident in her voice.

"We'll see you soon. I'll check back in when we stop again," Sean said. There was a pause, and then he added, "I love you."

"Oh, God!" Nicole exclaimed. "Don't do that. That makes it sound like you aren't coming back."

Sean smiled and looked down, knowing she read him correctly. "You aren't getting rid of me that easily. I'll see you soon."

"You better," Nicole shot back. "Or I just won't be able to forgive you." She heard Sean exhale some breath, keeping a laugh from escaping his lips. "I'll talk to you in a little while."

"Yes," Sean said. "Till then." Sean hung up the phone.

Nicole placed the receiver back in its cradle. She was still in her pajamas. She walked over to the adjoining door to her office. Ellen, her aid, was sitting at her desk. She looked up when Nicole opened the door. Nicole arranged to change her clothes and ask Natasha to bring some food to her office. Time seemed to stop. It was sheer agony how slowly it ticked by, and Nicole was getting anxious. Three hours after Sean and the others had left, Jenkins finally called.

"Nikki," Jenkins said. "They haven't activated their trackers. Our intelligence can't pinpoint them. Have you heard from Sean?"

"He called a while ago. They are still on the road."

"When you talk to him again, tell him to return. It's like looking for a needle in a haystack, and I don't want to drag him into this incident. Barker has called a couple of times and seemed to think he can work a deal with the Soviets."

"You know Sean isn't going to come back here without trying to find them first," Nicole said.

"Nikki, you need to tell him that the Soviets are all over the forest. If something happens to him, I couldn't bear it. I over-reacted. I should never have called."

"I don't blame you not wanting to owe Barker any favors," Nicole began. "But I know Sean, and if he can keep two of his allies from falling into our enemy's hand, he'll do whatever he can. Thanks for calling, Bobby. We'll call you back when we know something." She hung up the phone more worried as her eyes drifted back to the images on the television.

Washington, DC—Oval Office

Jenkins knew Sean was flying blind in Smolensk and if anything happened to him, he knew Nicole would never forgive him. He cursed when he realized any unfortunate outcome would move Nicole further away from him. He began to question why he had called for Sean's help. Was it to put him in danger, presenting an opportunity for Sean to be removed from Nicole's life forever?

Jenkins spun his chair around to look out the window as he examined his conscience. He convinced himself that his call to Sean was desperate, but the thought that this was a way to win Nicole back had never entered his mind. He shook his head and spun his chair back just as a buzz on his speakerphone sounded.

"President Baranov is calling for you, sir," Chris said. "Would you like me to inform him that we need an interpreter present and that you will call him back?"

"He knows I don't speak Russian," Jenkins replied. "Get one here quickly, but I'm sure his English will be good enough to say the words 'act of war.' Tell Whittaker to get in here and then patch him through."

Whittaker burst through the door just as the phone began to ring. "Don't answer that. Let's call him back."

"No," Jenkins said. "Get on the extension there." Jenkins pointed to a phone set by the chair in the conversation area. "We know what he wants and delaying this conversation will only make him angrier." Whittaker put his hand on the phone and waited for

Jenkins. "On three…one…two…three." Jenkins and Whittaker picked up the phone at the same time. "Mr. President—"

"What a stupid thing you have done," Baranov yelled. "Are you deliberately trying to test me? Because I have no problem going to war with the United States!"

"President Baranov, you have every right to scream and yell at me. But let's keep our heads," Jenkins started. "I will not deny that we were on a mission tonight outside your borders. Our aircraft suffered a mechanical failure."

"You were not outside our borders. Before the aircraft had its failure, it was within twelve miles of my coast, in our territorial waters," Baranov declared. "You committed an act of war."

"It was never our intention to fly over your territorial waters or your land," Jenkins patiently responded. "And before you decide to yell at me again, Mr. President, I suggest we take a breath and remember that we both routinely run covert operations to gather intelligence on our latest and greatest equipment. This time our aircraft had a mechanical failure that puts us both in a precarious situation. You have two of my pilots in your country and a media calling for war. I suggest we work together to show the world that we can and to ease the tension that is escalating with every minute my men are missing."

"Mr. President, if you are suggesting that I simply hand your men back to you free of consequence, then you are dumber than my intelligence on you indicates." Baranov had a certain smugness in his voice that irritated Jenkins.

"I don't believe that comment was warranted, Mr. President," Jenkins began, but was interrupted before he could continue.

"Acting like this was an accident is an insult," Baranov shouted. "I know what your Sonic Stroll operation was intended to do."

Jenkins looked at Whittaker. His face turned red from anger, not from embarrassment. Jenkins did not respond as he tried to gather his composure. Could he bluff? "Mr. President, just what do you think this Sonic Stroll—is that what you called it—was supposed to do?"

Baranov wasted no time. "I have a new submarine, and you needed its electronic signatures. That is why you committed an act of war."

Jenkins could only think of one thing to say. "Tell me how that is different than your country positioning your new class of submarine in our territorial waters to gather information?" Baranov didn't answer. "Come now, Mr. President, we both know this game goes on constantly. If one of your submarines malfunctioned and your men needed assistance, I would do everything in my power to make sure they were safe until their return to your country."

"Before or after you tortured them for information?"

Jenkins paused. "They would not be harmed." There was a brief silence again before Jenkins spoke. "Mr. President, if you capture my men, can I expect them to be returned to the United States unharmed?"

"If you publicly admit that you invaded my country, then I might be persuaded to do so," Baranov pushed back.

Jenkins let a small laugh leave his lips as he exhaled. "And if you were in my situation, would you do such a thing?" he asked. There was no response. "The United States did not intentionally invade your country. If I were going to invade your country, Mr. President, I wouldn't send one aircraft. You know the strength of our armed forces. If you intend to announce that we invaded your country this evening, I will have no problem telling my news media that one aircraft doesn't constitute an invasion and that I'm concerned about your mental state of mind if you sincerely think that it does."

"You better hope, Mr. President, that we don't find your men," Baranov retorted. "And you should not forget that I have the details of Sonic Stroll. There was more than one aircraft involved, and you know it."

"And if the Soviet Union is terrified of one aircraft and two naval vessels, then the United States has already won the war," Jenkins shot back. "If you injure or killed those pilots, you will have more than just an aircraft and two naval vessels to worry about, Mr. President." Jenkins hung up the phone. He shot out of his chair and yelled, "That fucking bastard!"

Whittaker was well aware that Jenkins was referring to Barker, not President Baranov. "What do you want to do? Recall him?"

"Try him for treason sounds good to me," Jenkins rebutted.

"You'll need some evidence for that," Whittaker said. "I don't think having a Russian testify is a good idea."

Jenkins eyed Whittaker. "Get me Secretary Alboreto first. Then I'll call Barker." Whittaker started to walk to his office. "And Fred, find out if any of the US embassy security force has been deployed to find the pilots."

"Yes, sir," Whittaker said as he left the office.

Smolensk, USSR—Lakeland Forest

Sean, Alistair, and Duncan were stopped just outside the Lakeland forest region after being on the road for approximately four hours. Sean had just hung up the phone and exited the restaurant where they had eaten. He approached Duncan and Alistair, who were looking at a map on the hood of their vehicle. "Nicole said that Jenkins called. They don't know where they are. He wants us to abort and return to Moscow."

"Not surprising considering all the military vehicles we passed on the expressway here. We need to get out of here," Alistair declared, ignoring Sean's comment about scraping the mission. "I suggest we head toward Belarus."

"Why?" Sean asked.

"If I were one of the pilots, I wouldn't want to get farther into the Soviet Union. Finland is a long way from here and, frankly, where the Soviets would expect me to go. Belarus is closer than Finland, and while still in the Soviet Union, I might find someone sympathetic. If I keep walking, I get to Poland. We all know what's going on there."

"You think they would make it all the way to Poland in their uniforms, with no money and no weapons?" Sean asked.

"I think that is the way they would go," Alistair replied. "It gives them a fighting chance. Finland is out of the question."

Sean looked at the map. "I doubt they got very far. Let's start looking on that edge of the forest."

They got into their vehicle and started out of the parking lot headed toward the western edge of the Lakeland National Park. When they entered the park and came upon a dirt road, Alistair decided to take it. Hours passed, driving down dirt road after dirt road, avoiding the Soviets, and making no real progress. They located a restaurant in a small town, not even on the map, and they decided to stop. There was a petrol station across the street. Alistair and Duncan fueled up the vehicle and then joined Sean at the restaurant. He checked in with Nicole again, who was frantically worried.

Alistair and Duncan sat down at the table Sean had commandeered after talking to Nicole. "Still no word," Sean told them. Out of the corner of his eye, he noticed two men looking at him oddly. "I don't think they get many English-speaking visitors here."

Alistair casually looked over his shoulder at the two men. "I think you're right. Best to get something to go."

Sean and Duncan nodded their agreement. They tried their best to communicate what they wanted, but it was becoming hopeless. The older of the two Russian men stood up and walked over to their table. "I speak little English. You want American hamburger, no?"

"No, I don't," Sean replied. "We're not Americans. We're British."

"Get them some stroganoff," the old man said to the waitress in his native tongue, pulling a chair out from the table. "They will like that."

Sean looked at Alistair, whose hand was starting to move to his holstered gun. Sean shook his head once. "Thank you for your help." He smiled at the waitress and handed the menus to her. "That will be fine." Sean looked at the man. "We would like to take it with us."

The man explained in Russian Sean's request to the waitress. When the waitress walked away, the Russian man folded his arms on the table, lowering his chin to his forearms. He started to whisper. "I know where they are."

"Where who are?" Sean asked.

"Don't be stupid. You are here for the Americans," the man said. Sean noticed his English got remarkedly better.

"Who are you?" Sean asked.

"Who are you?" The man shot back. Sean didn't answer. "I didn't think we wanted to get into that game." The man's eyes gestured toward his friend. "We had gone out to fish, and we caught them." Sean was beginning to think this sounded like an old wives tale until the man added, "One has been shot by the Soviets. It was in the leg, here." The man gestured to his thigh. "He can't walk very good."

Sean didn't respond. He looked at both men. "How do you know English so well?"

The man smiled. "I was captured during the war."

"What do you want?" Sean asked.

"For you to get these two men out of here before all the Soviets arrive here and disrupt our way of life." The old man looked at Sean. "I don't want any trouble, and, of course, if you have some money, that would be helpful."

"Of course," Sean said, a sardonic grin on his face. "It always comes down to money."

"We are poor and forgotten," the old man started. "Forgotten we can live with, poor—not so much."

"I don't have much on me, but I'll give you what I have," Sean said. "If what you say is true, I can make other arrangements."

The man turned to the cook and spoke in Russian, then turned back to Sean. "You're food—it will be in box—how do you say?"

"We understand," Sean replied. After getting the food and paying for it, Alistair, Duncan, and Sean met the men outside. The two Russians walked to their car and started driving down a dirt road behind the restaurant. Sean, Alistair, and Duncan got in their vehicle and followed them to a hut back in the woods. It was desolate and off the beaten path. Alistair voiced his concern that these men were setting them up, and Sean said he hadn't ruled that out. He asked them for all their cash, save a few rubles. When they reached the hut, Sean told Alistair to stay with the vehicle. Duncan and Sean went into the hut with the two Russian men.

After a few minutes, Duncan was helping Anders into the car. Sean was paying the older gentlemen, and Smith, the other pilot, was standing next to him. They were walking back to the vehicle when a shot from the forest rang out. The men ran for cover—the closest being the vehicle they came in—and were surprised when they heard return fire coming from the hut. A quick hail of bullets pinned Sean, Smith, and Duncan next to their vehicle. Alistair threw Duncan an SA80. Duncan switched the mode and launched a few rifle grenades as Sean ordered Smith to retreat inside the vehicle, his Beretta at the ready. Duncan then indicated he wanted Sean to get inside the car. Duncan fired a few more rifle grenades and dove into the front seat.

"Go! Go!" Duncan screamed as he shut the door.

Alistair floored it, spinning around to head down the dirt road that had led them to the hut. Gunshots pinged the armored vehicle, but that didn't stop Alistair. Anders winced as the car bucked up and down on the bumpy road. Sean started throwing bulletproof vests to the airmen. After a few hundred feet on the bumpy road, the gunfire stopped. There was an explosion, and Sean turned to look out the back window. The fishing hut was in flames, no doubt suffering a mortar attack.

"Keep the pedal down Alistair! That wasn't a flamethrower!" Sean yelled, his knowledge of Soviet military grade weapons lacking.

"No shit!" Alistair yelled back in the heat of the moment. After a couple hundred feet, they reached the main road that dissected the little town. "Hang on!" Alistair declared as he made the sharp turn, tires squealing, without slowing down. He sped through town, noticing a few Soviet military trucks parked at the restaurant they had just visited. "This is going to get worse!"

"Keep going!" Sean yelled. Sean looked at Duncan, who was now in the passenger's seat and noticed blood on his clothes. "Duncan, are you hit?" Sean indicated where the blood was.

"No, I don't think so," Duncan said. He started to investigate the area in question. It then dawned on him the blood was from Anders. "Sir…" His voice trailed off as he looked at Anders.

Sean leaned over Smith and started to feel around Anders's side. He found a wound above his hip. "Shit," Sean said. "How long have you had this one?" He asked Anders.

"Not very long…" Anders responded, weakly.

Sean looked at Smith, who shook his head and said. "I only knew about the one on his leg. We haven't had much time to look for—"

"Are you injured?" Sean asked Smith as he grabbed a first aid kit out of the back of the vehicle.

"No," Smith replied.

"It's time for you to play doctor," Sean instructed Smith. He gave the kit to Smith and started to reach in the back for something else.

His eye was caught by the Soviets standing outside the restaurant. "They are putting it together, Alistair!"

The Soviets standing by their vehicles were looking at the smoke from the burning fishing hut rising above the trees. They looked at the vehicle that was screaming past them with perplexed looks. When they finally put the clues together, they started screaming at each other and scrambled for their combat vehicles.

Alistair kept his foot on the accelerator, thankful he had a full tank of gas. He made his way to the express route while Sean grabbed two duffle bags out of the back of the vehicle. "Gentlemen, if you please. We need to get you out of those clothes."

"Who are you?" Smith asked, having just finished playing doctor. He began to change into the black trousers and shirt Sean handed him. "Not that we aren't thankful."

"I'm Ambassador Sean Adkins," he said. "These are two of my embassy security forces—Alistair Delaney and Duncan Davies."

"We sure are happy to see you," Smith replied.

"We aren't out of the woods yet," Sean responded. "Pun intended."

Alistair found a roundabout route back to the expressway. After being on the road for thirty minutes, Alistair pulled off, entering what Americans refer to as a rest stop. Sean glanced around before he spoke. "Is something wrong? I don't think it is a good idea to stop."

"Trust me, sir," Alistair replied.

As they reached an area protected by a building between them and the expressway, Alistair came to a stop. By now it was obvious to Sean what Alistair had done. The rest stop was empty except for Sean's diplomatic limo and two escort vehicles, complete with their flags. Sean looked at Alistair, who acknowledged the unspoken compliment and said, "Two words: diplomatic immunity."

"Brilliant," Sean responded. A member of Alistair's security force walked up to the vehicle. Alistair rolled the window down, and the man reported the area secured. Sean, Smith, Anders, Duncan, and Alistair vacated their current vehicle for the limo. Sean turned, looking at the vehicle he had just exited. Riddled with bullets and knicks, it would never make it past a military checkpoint. "We can't take this with us. Blow it up," Sean said as he walked to the limo.

When all the security forces were in their vehicles, just before pulling out, Alistair instructed one of his men to fire rifle grenades into the vehicle that saved their lives. A well-placed grenade found the gas tank and the car exploded into flames. Satisfied that the car would provide little evidence to the Soviets, the diplomatic entourage left the rest stop for the three-hour drive back to Moscow. Smith was given a gun and told to blend in with the security force, sitting next to Alistair and across from Sean. Duncan was in the front with the driver. Anders was sitting next to Sean, his condition worsening. Every stop at the checkpoints went smoothly as no lower rank Soviet officer wanted any trouble as a result of questioning a diplomat. The window that separated the driver from the ambassador was up; the darkened windows kept prying eyes from seeing anything. Alistair's plan for getting back to Moscow was perfect.

It was dark now, and there was still no sign of Sean and his crew. The phone on Sean's desk rang, and Nicole quickly snatched it up with both hands. All Nicole heard was that Sean was in the infirmary before she dashed out the door. She ran to the infirmary's waiting room, opening the door where four of the five men were sitting. When she spotted Sean, she rushed to him. Sean stood up as Nicole reached him. She threw her arms around his shoulders and neck. The fear that she was suppressing for more than twelve hours exploded into a few sobs. Sean held her tight thankful for the show of raw emotion by Nicole.

“I’m all right,” Sean whispered. Nicole quickly regained control of her emotions but was not quite ready to let go of him. It was starting to embarrass Sean, who again reinforced that he was unhurt. Nicole finally loosened her grip on him, which allowed Sean to pry her away to look at her face. He didn’t speak but smiled and winked at her.

Nicole wiped the tears from her cheeks and turned to see Alistair standing with his arms open, expecting a hug from her.

“Don’t we get a hug, too?” Alistair asked, a dash of a joke in his voice. “We were in danger as well you know.” The others started to chuckle, which turned into a roar of laughter when Nicole surprised him by rushing toward him. She threw her arms around his neck, hugging Alistair in much the same way as she had hugged Sean. Alistair blushed at the action, not at all ready for Nicole to call his bluff.

“That will teach you,” Duncan said, giving another laugh.

Nicole joined in the laughter as she moved back to Sean’s side, taking his hand in hers. It was then Nicole noticed there were only four of them. “Where’s the fifth? There was suppose to be five of you.”

“Anders is in surgery,” Sean informed Nicole. “It doesn’t look good. He’s lost a lot of blood.”

Nicole looked at Smith, who was now looking at the floor. “We have excellent doctors here,” she consoled him. “They will do all they can.”

"Thank you, ma'am," Smith responded.

Nicole and the four men sat back down to wait for news from the doctor. Thirty minutes later, just as one of the doctors walked into the room, Stewart rushed in and announced, "Ambassador Barker just exited his car and entered the embassy. He is outraged for some reason I can't explain."

Nicole looked at the doctor, who was waiting patiently to give his news. She opened her jacket to show Sean and Duncan that she was armed. "I'll head him off and bring him to your office."

"Go with her, Stewart," Sean demanded.

Nicole didn't argue. She and Stewart briskly walked out of the room and in a direction that would intercede Barker's journey to Sean's office. Nicole was walking in front of Stewart, ignoring the many questions he was asking.

"If someone would be kind enough to tell me what is going on, I'm sure I would be a great help," he said as they rounded a corner.

Nicole couldn't help but run directly into Barker. She tried to step away from him but was unsuccessful in getting out of his reach.

"Where are they?" Barker screamed as he tried to regain his balance from running into Nicole, grabbing her upper arms.

"Where are who?" Nicole shouted back, trying to rid herself of his grip on her.

"The pilots," Barker yelled. "The god-damned pilots!"

Nicole successfully wriggled out of Barker's grip and regained her composure. "Ambassador, if you will follow me to Ambassador Adkins office, we can calmly discuss this."

That was more than Barker could handle. He grabbed Nicole by the neck with both hands, swinging her around and into the wall. The thud of Nicole's body hitting the wall made Stewart wince. Nicole tried to stop the exhale of breath that Barker's action knocked out of her. He applied a small amount of pressure around her throat at first. *Just enough to scare her*, he thought.

Stewart's eyes bulged at the site. He was frightened for Nicole's life. Out of the corner of her eye, she could see Stewart disappear down the hallway from which they came. Nicole managed a quick eye roll and thought about how useless Stewart was. Her attention returned to Barker. His eyes trained on her, and all the hate he held for her was beginning to show. The man's face wrinkled up in disgust. His skin turned red from the winching of muscle. He looked every bit the hideous man that Nicole knew he could be.

"Tell me where the pilots are," Barker demanded, applying more pressure around her neck.

Nicole now started to gasp for air. She knew he would have no problem killing her. He had ordered it before. Her mind flashed back to the campaign trail. All their arguments and his threats returned to haunt her. The hallway was empty—there was no one to intervene. She felt the pressure increase as Barker looked to his left and right. He returned his vicious glare to her.

"I should have done this in South Carolina," Barker hissed. Barker had committed one mistake, though.

Nicole's arms were free. She slowly, while taking another gasp, moved her arm to her gun holster. She gasped again, taking in as much breath as she could and held it. In one swift movement, she retrieved her gun, unlocked the safety, and brought it up to Barker's temple. She cocked it and then rested her finger on the trigger.

Sean, Duncan, and Alistair rounded the corner just as Nicole's gun reached Barker's temple. They slid to a stop. The noise drew the attention of Barker. Nicole held the gun forcefully against Barker's head. Barker held Nicole in his grip, his mind racing for an explanation that the three men would accept. He didn't release her.

There was a part of Sean that wanted Nicole to pull the trigger. He almost told her to do it. But he didn't want her to live with the torment that came with taking a life. Sean took a breath to calm his racing heart. "Ambassador," Sean started. "I suggest you remove your hands from Nicole's throat, slowly." No one moved. "She will kill you. I do not doubt that, and personally, I wouldn't blame her." There was still no movement. Nicole took another gasp as Barker's grip loosened slightly. "Considering what you ordered up in London and what I see now, I'd tell your State Department and my country that this was self-defense."

"It most assuredly is self-defense," Duncan chimed in to support Sean, who waved off Duncan's support.

"Nicole, don't do it," Sean said. "Ambassador, she rarely listens to me, so I suggest you release her."

Barker did not attempt to do as Sean suggested. His hands were still firmly around Nicole's throat.

Sean grabbed his Beretta from his holster, cocked it, and trained it on Barker. "I'm getting very tired of saying this." Barker's eyes shifted to see Sean's gun on him. "Release her. Now!"

With two guns now directed on him, Barker released his grip and lowered his hands. Nicole moved the gun from Barker's temple to the front of his forehead, just above and between his eyes. She tried to control her breathing, still taking in short gasps. She tried to steady her gun.

"Nicole, move toward me, slowly," Sean said calmly. "He's not worth it." Duncan started to move toward her. "Duncan, Nicole is going to move toward us. She doesn't need our help."

After a few seconds, Nicole started to move toward Sean, staying against the wall. Her gun stayed trained on Barker as she moved. When she reached the three men, Duncan, who was standing closest to the wall, lowered Nicole's gun.

With his gun still pointed at Barker, Sean seethed, "Now, Mr. Ambassador, get the fuck out of my embassy." Barker didn't move. "Alistair, Duncan, please remove Ambassador Barker from our premises." Duncan and Alistair started toward Barker. "With force if necessary." Sean lowered his gun. "Don't ever put your foot on this property again. If you do show up here, my security forces will be instructed to fire first and ask questions later. Is that understood?" Barker turned away from Sean without saying a word. "And don't think your president won't hear about this incident."

Alistair and Duncan walked toward Barker, their guns at the ready. When they turned the corner, Sean put his arm around Nicole and asked, "Are you all right?"

Nicole was rubbing her throat. She stopped, turned toward Sean and asked. "How red is it?"

Sean looked at Nicole's neck. "It's pretty red. It may bruise."

"We should get a picture of this," Nicole said as she put her arm around Sean. "How is Anders?"

Washington, DC—Oval Office

Jenkins was watching WNN's coverage of the situation and waiting for another report from the Joint Chiefs. It had been over fourteen hours since his first call to Sean. WNN's correspondent in the USSR was reporting from the Smolensk region. Jenkins's ears perked up when the reporter described gunfire and a fire in a remote area of the forest. Jenkins closed his eyes and hoped that Sean, the pilots, and any security forces were not mortally wounded.

He jumped out of his meditative thought when the phone on his desk rang. He gathered himself before he picked it up. "Yes?"

"It's Ambassador Adkins on a secure line, sir," the operator declared.

"Put him through," Jenkins ordered. "Sean, are you all right?"

"I'm fine," Sean replied. "I'm afraid I have some bad news." Sean paused a moment. "Lieutenant Anders didn't make it. He was shot in the leg by Soviet forces. What we didn't know until we were in the clear was that he secured a second gunshot wound in his back—the lower back more toward his right side. We tried to save him when we arrived back at the embassy, but he had lost too much blood." Silence met Sean's report. "Mr. President?"

"I'm here," Jenkins replied. "I don't know what to say. I thank you for your efforts, of course."

"I appreciate that sir," Sean responded. "Lieutenant Colonel Smith is in fine health and is waiting to talk to you."

"I'd like to hear his voice," Jenkins said.

"When your conversation is complete, I have more news," Sean added. He stretched the phone out to Smith. "Your commander-in-chief would like a word."

Smith moved to the phone, taking it from Sean. He stood at attention when he spoke. "Mr. President?"

"Lieutenant Colonel Smith," Jenkins started. "Thank you for your service. You're safe with our friends there at the British Embassy. Ambassador Adkins and Nicole Charbonneau will take good care of you until we can get you both home safely." Jenkins paused. "I will call your families in a little while. Is there anything I can say that would ease the burden on Mrs. Anders?"

"He performed his duties with excellence, sir. You would have been proud of him."

One side of Jenkins's mouth curled up quickly and just as quickly returned to a frown. "That is good to know. Anything I can say to your family?"

"I'm looking forward to seeing them soon," Smith replied.

"You represented your country well."

"Thank you, Mr. President," Smith replied. He handed the phone back to Sean.

Nicole, who was also present, indicated she wanted Smith to follow her out of the room. Nicole walked into her office through the inner office door that directly connected to Sean's office. She closed the door behind her. "Have a seat." She walked to her desk, picked up the phone and called Alistair. After requesting his presence in Sean's office, she hung up the phone. "Why don't you stretch out on the couch and get some rest? We'll be with you shortly." She walked to the door that connected directly to Sean's office. "Oh, and whatever you do, don't answer that door." She pointed to the door that led to the outer office where Stewart sat. "That man drives me crazy," she mumbled as she left her office, closing the inner office door behind her. Sean was finishing up with the story of the incident between Nicole and Barker.

"I managed to talk Nicole down, although I have to say every bone in my body was shouting for her to pull the trigger," Sean concluded.

"If I were her, I'm not sure I would have had the same restraint," Jenkins agreed. "I received a call from Baranov earlier. He referred to our mission by its code name. I know Barker gave someone over there the information and it made it all the way to Baranov."

"It was probably through General Valesky. He was far too cordial with Barker at a couple of gatherings we've been at lately. I'm not sure what you know about him."

"Valesky? Nothing," Jenkins admitted.

"He is Baranov's enforcer. That's the best way of putting it. Whatever Baranov orders, Valesky does it," Sean informed Jenkins.

"Well, it makes sense that Barker would align himself with someone like that."

"What are you going to do?"

"I'm calling Barker to tell him he has one more chance to help. He's going to take the heat of the Soviet government, pretending to have the pilots."

"And if he doesn't?"

"Alboreto will recall him," Jenkins said.

"That's it?"

"I can't prove he told the Soviets about the operation. I can't put him on trial for treason," Jenkins conceded. "I don't like it either."

Nicole had picked up an extension and was listening to the conversation. “Bobby, I’m sure you could leak something to the press,” she interjected. “There’s always someone in the White House more than happy to talk to the press.”

“Ruin his reputation via the media?” Jenkins questioned.

“Why not?”

Jenkins considered it but quickly made a decision. “It will draw him into this more if we don’t ignore him. How are your going to hide my pilots?”.

“I haven’t given it much thought,” Sean admitted.

“I have,” Nicole replied. “I asked our chief of security to come to your office, Sean. I thought that we would disguise Smith as one of our security forces.”

“I think that’s an excellent idea,” Sean said. “We’ll prepare Anders’s body, of course. We’ll need to get a plan together for the journey home and release to your government. I have to say; I think you should consider Nicole’s thought of releasing Barker’s betrayal to the press.”

“I don’t want to give Barker any opportunity to spout off in front of the press,” Jenkins retorted.

“Too late,” Sean said, looking at his television. Barker was holding a press conference from his embassy’s press room.

Jenkins looked up at WNN to see what Sean was seeing. “That son of a bitch! I’ll call you back, Sean.” He slammed the phone down and turned up the volume on the television to hear Barker’s final statement.

"As I said, the pilots are safe and at an undisclosed location to ensure their safety. I'm offering my services to President Jenkins. I'm willing to work with the Soviet government to ensure their safe return to the United States."

Upon seeing Barker on WNN as well, Whittaker scrambled through the door that led from his office to the Oval Office. He looked at the desk first and then to the conversation area just as Jenkins was sitting down in front of the TV. Whittaker closed the door and moved toward Jenkins. He could see Jenkins wasn't happy. "What is it?"

Jenkins turned his head and looked at Whittaker. "Safe return, he says. That jackass is doing nothing to ensure their safety. Anders died of a gunshot wound he received while evading capture. They aren't at our embassy. They are at the UK embassy."

"How did they get there?"

"I called in a favor," Jenkins responded. He stood up as a reporter shouted a question at Barker.

"Where are the pilots? Are they here at the embassy?" the reporter yelled

"No, they are not here," Barker replied. "At this time, I don't want to disclose their location. As I said, they are safe."

"Now I understand why Stevens hired a hitman," Jenkins quipped as he turned the volume down. "What am I going to say to the Anders family? 'I'm sorry, the ambassador was wrong'?"

Whittaker looked at Jenkins. "He didn't make it?" Jenkins nodded once. "That's exactly what you say."

"Chris!" Jenkins yelled. Chris opened the door a few seconds later. "Tell the commander of the Joint Chiefs that I want the phone number of Smith's and Anders's families."

"Yes, sir," Chris said as he returned to his desk to make a phone call. A few minutes later, Jenkins was on the phone talking to the commander, answering his questions.

After calling the two families of the pilots, Jenkins was about to call Alboreto when Chris buzzed his phone. "President Baranov for you, sir."

"Thank you," Jenkins said. He knew exactly how he was going to play this conversation. He picked up the receiver. "President Baranov," he began.

"Mr. President, I demand that you turn the two pilots over to my government immediately."

"No," Jenkins firmly said.

"You are forcing me to make a public statement. One you will not appreciate. You are purposely escalating this situation. I may be forced to call your illegal activity an invasion. It will incite the Politburo who are calling it an act of war."

Jenkins sat quietly for a moment. "Mr. President, what information do you have on the two pilots?"

"I know you found the two pilots. One of my generals told me," Baranov reported. "You have no choice but to accept my terms."

"That is where you are wrong," Jenkins calmly replied. "Ambassador Barker doesn't have the correct information. It is my duty, Mr. President, to inform you that your government—your military—has committed a grievous act that will probably have the citizens of my country calling for war." Jenkins paused, waiting for a reaction from Baranov. Jenkins could hear Baranov speaking in his native language with someone else in the room.

Baranov cleared his throat and returned to speaking English to Jenkins. "You are bluffing. You invaded our country—"

"Mr. President, your military killed one of my pilots," Jenkins interrupted. "He was not armed. Your actions were uncalled for and will ignite the American people against a country they do not like and do not trust. I don't know which general gave you the information, but I would have to doubt his intention. We know our embassy there is compromised beyond repair." Jenkins paused. "Since you killed one of my men, here is what is going to happen: You will permit the return of the surviving pilot and the body of the dead pilot without any interference from your military or government. I will allow you to do it quietly. Your only comment will be that we've worked out our differences in regards to this incident and no further action will be needed. Is that understood?"

"In return for doing what you ask, you will lift the sanc—"

"You don't understand. In return for your non-interference in bringing my two Air Force officers home, we will not pursue any further action against the Soviet Union—no condemnation at the United Nations and no calls for an investigation under the Geneva Convention."

"You ask too much," Baranov said pridefully.

"My men were not armed," Jenkins stressed. "Your military shot and killed an unarmed man. If anyone has the right to escalate this situation, it is me, sir. I suggest you take the deal I'm offering, or I will whip this nation into supporting whatever action I deem necessary. The last thing you need on the world's television screen is a grieving widow holding her baby to her breast while standing over her husband's casket." Allowing the image he painted to sink in, Jenkins finally asked, "Do you agree to let my men come home without interference?"

Baranov was angry—an emotion not lost in the tone of his voice. "The pilots will be returned without interference." He paused as he tried to determine a way to save face. "The least you can do—"

"I am doing the least I can do," Jenkins spat out. "Don't try my patience, Mr. President. We will handle the details of their extraction. I will call you when I know they are home safely." Jenkins hung up the phone. He looked at Whittaker who reinforced Jenkins's actions with one simple nod of his head. Whittaker returned to his office.

Moscow, USSR—United Kingdom Embassy

It was the next morning. Sean was sitting at his desk when a call came from the guard at the gate of the embassy. "Sir, I'm a bit concerned," the guard said over the phone, "General Vladimir Valesky is here. He has seven armed soldiers with him and is demanding to enter the compound."

"For what purpose?" Sean asked.

"He said that he would like to meet with you, but from the looks of it—"

"I'm sure it is his way of trying to search the embassy. Don't let them in. Inform the general that I will be right down," Sean replied. He hung up the phone. Nicole overheard Sean's comments and walked into his office as he was slinging his winter coat over his shoulders. He started out the door, and Nicole followed him. "Get down to the firing range and take Smith with you," he told her. "Make sure he is in one of our guard uniforms. I have no intention of letting them in, but if Smith is in uniform and firing a gun, at least, he will look the part. If asked, he is part of your security team." Nicole nodded her head. They parted ways as Sean turned for the front gate.

Sean stopped to talk with Alistair before he approached the car containing Valesky. When Valesky recognized Sean, he got out of the car. Valesky's men exited their vehicle, all bearing arms. Alistair and the majority of his men stood at the ready several yards away from Valesky's car. It was a considerable show of force, exactly what Alistair wanted.

Sean waited for the two snipers on the roof of the embassy to get into position, before he approached Valesky. Sean quickly looked up at them before engaging in conversation. "General," Sean said, extending his hand. "What brings you to my embassy unannounced?"

Valesky shook Sean's hand, looked at the men standing in front of his car, and then glanced up at the roof. "We have received information that you are hiding the two American pilots. We want them, and we are not leaving without them, even if I have to enter this embassy without your consent. Your embassy is in my country."

"You are aware, General, that your action would be considered an act of war," Sean stated.

"I was hoping that you would agree to a tour, in the hopes that our countries could become friends."

"Friends?" Sean questioned. "Do friends show up at the door armed?" Sean gestured to the armed men now standing behind Valesky's car. "I don't think the queen would be happy to know that you showed up here clearly threatening her sovereignty of this embassy. You have no right to search these ground, either by invitation or by force. Since I did not invite you here, I suggest you get back in your cars and leave." Alistair started to move forward to stand next to Sean. Sean raised his hand, causing Alistair to stop.

Valesky gave a cold eye to Sean. "You are hiding something."

"I'm not hiding anything. You are not welcome to search the queen's embassy. If you would like to visit and meet sometime, we can arrange that. I highly suggest that we make an appointment and you can return on that day to speak with me."

Valesky shook his head. "No. By then you will have moved the pilots."

"As I have already said, if you enter without an invitation, you will be committing an act of war. I wouldn't give the queen a reason to invade your country. In case you have any questions, your invasion of our embassy by force would trigger article 5 of the NATO agreement, which means you would also have to face our allies. Are you sure President Baranov ordered you here?"

Valesky shifted his weight to his other foot. It was the sign that Sean was looking for all along. He stared Valesky in the eye and saw his hesitation. Valesky, ever a pompous ass, decided to up the ante. He ordered his armed men forward. Alistair ordered his men to be ready to fire. Sean's eyes moved toward the gates of the embassy, noticing that Valesky's car and his small contingent of men were inside the gates.

Sean turned to the guard in the guard shack. "Close the gates," he commanded. As the heavy, iron-reinforced gates began to close, shutting off the Soviet's only escape route, Sean cocked his head and said, "I suggest you surrender." Valesky looked at the gates as they clanged shut. "You're a bit out-numbered and clearly on British soil. No court in the world would find me wrong in ordering my men to open fire since you are armed and threatening to invade this embassy. Surrender your arms, and I'll open the gates so that you can leave without incident."

"They won't fire while you are standing here." Valesky was calling Sean's bluff.

"Oh, I don't intend on standing here much longer," Sean responded. He turned to Alistair and ordered, "Captain Delaney, prepare your men." Sean motioned for the guard in the shack to move out to join Alistair's men. "So sorry it ended this way, but you gave me no choice." Sean started to walk away from Valesky, facing him for the three or four steps that he took. Alistair ordered his men to aim. It was a tense few seconds that seemed to last an eternity. Sean started for the cover of the guard shack when Valesky threw up his arms.

Frustrated, Valesky shouted, "Wait! Open the gates. We will leave." Sean walked up to Valesky after instructing the guard to open the gates. "General Valesky, if ever you want to meet with me, I suggest you call ahead, arrive at my office unarmed, and I would be more than happy to show you our magnificent embassy." The gates were now open. "Order your men to their vehicle." Sean waited for Valesky to do so, staring into Valesky's dark brown eyes. Valesky finally backed down and gave the order. When the men were in their transport, Sean said, "Have a good day, General." He turned and walked away from Valesky, Alistair keeping his gun trained on Valesky until Sean was safely among Alistair's men. As the Soviet's cars were backing away, Alistair ordered his men to stand down. Sean kept walking to the embassy. As he reached the steps, he heard the clank of the iron gates shutting. It was only then that Sean took a deep breath and exhaled in relief.

He continued to his office. He stopped first at Elliot's office and knocked on the door once before swiping his key card. He typed in his code, opened the door, and said, "Elliot, would you be so kind as to accompany me to my office?" Elliot gave Sean a confused look—mainly because of his overtly polite request—stood up and walked with Sean to his office without saying a word. A minute later, Alistair arrived after retrieving Nicole from the firing range. They acknowledged Elliot when they entered Sean's office. After Sean informed them of the incident and Valesky's intention to find the pilots, he said, "It is obvious that Smith isn't safe here. We need to get him home as quickly as we can."

"I'm not sure exactly how we would get Smith and a coffin to the airport, but my condo closing is in a few days, that could be the excuse for me to fly to Washington. Smith could be part of my security detail," Nicole offered.

"We wouldn't transport Anders in a coffin," Alistair began. "We could, just for the trip to the airport, put him in a shipping crate, in a body bag. They load the crate on the plane, and we could—"

"Why make a switch?" Nicole asked. "Why not put the coffin in the shipping crate? I'm sure we could ask Bobby for permission to land at Dover Air Force Base. He could meet us there for the exchange. I go on to my condo closing and fly back in a week."

Sean was thinking it through. "The only part of the plan I don't like is the drive to the airport here in Moscow."

"You could accompany us to the airport," Nicole suggested. "Doesn't your motorcade have diplomatic immunity?"

"It does," Sean began. "But sometimes things happen, and it usually doesn't end well." Sean looked at Nicole to assess her comprehension. "We are in an adversary's country. They know we have the pilots. I'm sure Barker told Valesky."

"We could request a helicopter land on the roof," Alistair suggested.

Sean shook his head. "That requires too much planning and would draw too much attention. I like the idea of Nicole going to Washington to close on the sale of her condominium as a cover story." A brief thought of Nicole spending time alone with Jenkins entered Sean's mind. He gave Nicole a quick glance. "I have some reservations about it, but nothing I can't resolve." Nicole crinkled her brow at Sean's statement but didn't interrupt him. "Let's take some time and think about the travel to the airport. What options do we have, and is there something else we could do to ensure a safe journey? Those are the questions we need to concentrate on right now."

Elliot cleared his throat. "Leznikov."

Sean looked at Elliot. "What about him?"

"I think if we are going to trust him, he has to show his intention to work for us before we do anything else. He is friends with Baranov. He tells Baranov that allowing us to get the pilots out of the country without anyone knowing about it allows Baranov to save face. Baranov's problem dies down in a week or two. We'd need Jenkins to not make a big deal out of the return."

"A private reunion at Dover," Nicole said, thoughtfully. "I think he would go for that. It's a bittersweet reunion, and this wasn't exactly a victory. I do think Jenkins would be open to that." Nicole tried to reassure herself.

"It's not Jenkins I'm worried about," Elliot said. "The press is my concern."

"He can't control the press," Nicole replied. "But if it is a private affair, he can keep them at bay. They can unload the aircraft in a hangar with the doors closed. But something will have to be released—a formal statement, maybe a photo or two. He also can't keep the families, or Smith for that matter, from talking to the press. We can only ask for their cooperation."

"Quite frankly, I don't care what happens once they are out of this embassy and safely home in the United States." Sean looked at Elliot. "The idea that Leznikov has to prove his sincerity in becoming a double agent is brilliant. He is coming to the party tomorrow. I can present him with the dilemma and see how he reacts. I think that's it for now." Sean watched as Alistair and Elliot left his office. Sean looked at Nicole. "We better call Bobby."

"I can do that," Nicole said, standing up. "You look exhausted, and I know you had another nightmare last night. Why don't you try to get some sleep?"

"I would like to lie down for a bit," Sean said.

Nicole hesitated and then gently asked, "Why do you think that Sarah is haunting you again?"

"She isn't haunting me," Sean snapped, the irritation evident in his voice. He took a breath and stood up to hug Nicole, realizing his tone was harsher than he wanted it to be. "I'm sorry. I have a lot on my mind, and I'm not sure why they have returned." Sean kissed her cheek to hide his lie. He knew exactly why they had started again. "Let me know if Bobby has a problem with our plan."

Nicole watched Sean move away from her. She wasn't sure, but she had a feeling that Sean did know why the nightmares started again. When Sean turned at the door to look at her, she snapped out of her thoughts. "I will," she said with a reassuring smile on her face. "Get some rest." With that, Sean left his office. Nicole retreated to her own office to call Jenkins.

CHAPTER SIX
END OF FEBRUARY 1981

Moscow, USSR—United Kingdom Embassy

When Sean and Nicole had first arrived in Moscow, Stewart suggested opening the embassy up for a social gathering. Since that time, the event had morphed into a grand ball, then a dinner party, and finally an early evening black tie optional open house and cocktail party. Sean decided that Stewart would be in charge of tours since he was more familiar with the embassy's artwork and collectibles. The guests would enter the Great Hall, extravagant with its gold and crystal chandeliers, large paintings of the current and past British monarchs, and oval tables with floral centerpieces atop their white linen tablecloths. Nicole had hired an eight-piece band to play a mixture of jazz, swing, and standards while the guests mingled and munched on a lavish buffet that sat between the two entry doors. The guests would enter and exit the party through one set of doors and would leave for tours through another set of doors to the right of the buffet.

Sean was tugging at the cuffs of his tux as they walked into the Great Hall ten minutes before the start of the party. "All I am saying is that the arrangements for leaving could have waited until after I have spoken with Leznikov."

Nicole, dressed in a glamorous emerald-green velvet evening gown with a sweeping floor hem, rolled her eyes. The jeweled front and back V-neck had both on-and-off shoulder straps, which were also jewel laced. Nicole lifted her dress up enough to keep up with the quick walking Sean. "Sean," she finally said in exasperation, "will you please slow down?" He walked to the center of the hall where he stopped to take in the decorations and staging. "I have the closing in four days. I have told my agent that I will be there. So, I'm going regardless. I'm sorry that you don't like that fact, but it is what it is." Sean turned his head to look at her. She knew what was troubling him; it was that she would be in Washington with Jenkins without him. "I would like to think that you trust me, because if you don't, then I'm not sure why I am here."

"This has nothing to do with trusting you," Sean finally said. He knew when the words left his lips they were not convincing.

Nicole smiled, rolled her eyes, and shook her head. "I leave tomorrow morning, regardless of whatever you can arrange," Nicole said as she brushed past Sean to speak to the band leader. "Honestly, if the two of you can't accept how I feel about each of you, I may have to decide to live my life without either of you." As she walked to the stage, she was still mumbling. "Such childish bullshit—why I put up with either of them is beyond me."

Sean watched Nicole walk away, hearing every word she not-so-quietly mumbled. He turned and walked to the door where the guests would enter. Stewart was waiting for him.

"Is everything all right, sir?" Stewart asked.

"Not exactly," Sean replied.

"What do I need to change?" Stewart questioned, believing there was something wrong with the hall's setup or other arrangements.

"I wasn't referring to this," Sean responded, waving at the lavishly decorated hall.

"Oh," Stewart nodded. "Well, I can't help you there."

Sean suppressed a smile when he heard Stewart's answer and the sardonic tone that accompanied it. "The hall looks perfect. Are you ready to be the tour guide for the evening?"

"Absolutely," Stewart replied. "It's not too bad. We are running them every half hour, and as you suggested, it is very limited. I want to confirm; there will be no access to the office areas."

"Thank you," Sean said. The staff of the embassy was requested to attend, and many were starting to arrive. Sean greeted them as they entered. He looked over at Nicole, who was talking with Ellen, her chief of staff. When he caught her attention, Sean made it obvious he wanted her to be by his side. Nicole ignored the unspoken request by turning her back on him. Sean bit his lip as he turned to find Stacy walking into the room. "Good evening, Stacy. Thank you for coming."

"My pleasure," she replied as she presented her hand for Sean to kiss.

Sean accepted her hand, giving a slight bow of his head, but not kissing her hand. His lips came nowhere close, and his head bow never intruded on Stacy's personal space.

Nicole turned to see the interaction, noticing the flirtatious mannerisms of the woman who now moved closer to Sean and whispered in his ear. Ellen touched Nicole's arm to get her attention. Ellen informed Nicole that she was taking her leave to check on the few items they had just discussed. Nicole turned to thank Ellen, and when her attention returned to Sean, Stacy was gone.

"Mr. Stewart," Sean began, now realizing that all of the embassy staff had arrived and were assigned various duties or stations, "On your way to your station, if you would be so kind as to inform Nicole that our guests are starting to arrive, I would be most grateful."

Stewart couldn't resist. "Chicken," he said with a laugh. "What did you do this time?"

Sean, however, was not amused. "Do it, please."

Stewart acknowledged Sean's request and walked over to Nicole, who just looked at Stewart, not giving him a verbal answer. Her look told Stewart he'd better move along. Nicole's gaze fell upon Sean. Nicole was not about to join him, still feeling the sting of their angry exchange while they were dressing. The flirtatious mannerisms of Stacy and the fact that Sean didn't reject them added to Nicole's anger. Maybe her departure to Washington the next day was what they needed. Was selling her condo the right move? Nicole tried to shake the thought from her head.

Sean started to walk toward Nicole, who didn't move. When he was standing before her, he extended his hand to her. "Would you please join me in welcoming our guests?"

"I'm not a citizen of the United Kingdom," Nicole began. "Technically, they are not my guests."

"Nicole, please," Sean implored her. He wasn't begging. His frustration with her actions was very clear in the tone of his voice. "Can we put the argument on hold until after this party?"

Nicole took Sean's hand in silence. They walked to the door just as Duncan arrived.

"Hello, Duncan," Nicole said. "Are you ready for tomorrow?"

"Oh, yes, ma'am," Duncan said. "I've never been to the United States. I'm rather looking forward to it."

"It's not a vacation, Davies," Sean snapped at him.

"No, sir," Duncan responded, snapping into attention. "I didn't mean to make it sound like it was, sir."

"I want to talk with you this evening, directly after this shindig is over," Sean instructed him.

"Yes, sir," Duncan replied. "I'll be announcing the guests. Alistair is heading up security today, sir."

"Very well," Sean said.

Nicole had crossed her arms when Sean snapped at Duncan. "What has gotten into you?" she questioned when he turned his attention to her.

"I don't have the foggiest idea what you are referring to," Sean replied. "Even if I did, this is not the time to go into it." He smiled as he greeted the first guests.

The next few hours entailed welcoming the dignitaries from the other embassies in Moscow. To cover for Barker's absence, Jenkins informed Alboreto that he would schedule a training session for Barker that addressed the roles of being an ambassador and see to it that he attended the teleconference personally along with Barker's chief of staff. While the United States had a presence at the party, it was a lower ranking official that attended.

Duncan checked a clipboard and announced, “Everyone has arrived, sir. I’ll man the door. You can mingle now if you like.”

Sean looked at Duncan. Nicole took Sean’s arm and said, “Thank you, Duncan. I appreciated your stylish announcements of our guests.” She was referring to his Scottish burr.

“Thank you, ma’am,” Duncan said with pride. It was a duty he enjoyed doing, having done so for the previous ambassador.

She looked at Sean, knowing she cut him off from making yet another rude comment to Duncan. Nicole knew Sean was taking his anger out on others. “I think we both need a drink.” She led Sean to the bar where she ordered two double gin and tonics. She thanked the staffer manning the bar as she and Sean walked away. “I think now would be a good time for you to talk to Leznikov. I saw Valesky leave with Stewart on a tour.”

“Right,” Sean simply said as he walked away from Nicole and she began to mingle.

Leznikov was sitting at a table with other dignitaries of the Soviet bloc countries. Sean set his drink down as he approached the table. Ever so slightly he brushed up against Leznikov’s chair, just enough to get his attention. To anyone sitting at the table, it looked as if Sean was merely stepping out of the way of two women who were walking toward him. After a few seconds, Leznikov excused himself and walked to the bar where Sean was now ordering another gin and tonic. Leznikov requested a double vodka, neat, and then said to Sean, “The artwork is splendid. You must educate me on the monarchs. It seems I can never keep them straight.”

“It would be my pleasure,” Sean said. “Shall we start with Queen Victoria?” He gestured to the painting on his right. The two men moved toward it.

After they arrived at the painting, Leznikov quietly asked, "Are you prepared to accept some documents from me?"

"Not today," Sean replied. He waited a second before he added, "Dmitry, I have a favor to ask, and I've arranged a meeting in Paris."

"I suppose this favor is for your Nicole to be free from interference on her trip tomorrow," Leznikov said. He took a sip of his vodka to suppress his smile.

"How did you know—"

"It is my job to know," Leznikov replied. "It is already arranged. I know that the pilots will be with her. Baranov is anxious to put the unfortunate death of one of the airmen behind him. Valesky—not so much, but he made an error, and Baranov is not happy with him. So, I have the president's ear for a little bit."

Sean wasn't sure how to respond. "Dmitry, does Baranov know I am with MI6?"

"No," Leznikov replied as he admired Victoria's portrait. "Do you think I am stupid? It is better for everyone that no one knows."

"I agree. I can't run the risk of having your intelligence come through my embassy. I've set up a contact for you in Paris. Can you take a trip there in July?"

"It would be better if we could do something sooner," Leznikov replied.

"I need time to meet with your contact and make other arrangements," Sean informed him.

"If that is the best you can do, then I will plan a few trips to Paris before July. I think I need a vacation," Leznikov said. "There is a hotel in Paris I like very much. It is not in the tourist area. I have a good friend I have not seen in a long time. I need to visit her before she forgets me." Leznikov smiled, winked at Sean, and gave a hearty laugh.

"That sounds lovely," Sean said, somewhat at a loss for words. He moved to another painting as if he were giving Leznikov the information he requested. Sean put his free hand into his trouser pocket and whispered, "At the Gare du Nord train station there are lockers. I will leave instructions for you in a locker there. When I return from Paris in April, I will find a way to get you the key to the locker." In a louder voice, Sean said, "Perhaps, we could play a game of chess in the near future?"

"I am always interested in a good game of chess," Leznikov stated.

"It was good to talk to you. Unfortunately, I must end my history lesson here." Sean extended his hand, and Leznikov shook Sean's hand. Sean leaned into the handshake, again whispering, "If we don't have unimpeded access tomorrow, the deal is off." Sean walked past Leznikov to meet up with another ambassador, who was on his way to talk to Sean.

Leznikov turned his attention to the painting in front of him. He took another sip of his vodka before he moved onto another painting. Leznikov then looked at his watch and moved to the area where Stewart was starting another tour. Valesky was returning from the previous tour. Leznikov could tell by the frown on Valesky's face that he was not successful in locating anything of value. However, the quick glance between Stewart and Valesky gave Leznikov a moment to pause. Was there something between these two men? The interaction between them indicated that there was. Leznikov made a note to himself to have Valesky followed.

"Are you ready for the tour?" Stewart asked the group that included Leznikov. Some nodded their heads; others gave verbal agreement. "Fantastic! Let's get started." Stewart led the small group out of the Great Hall. Just before Leznikov left the room, he scanned it. He watched as Sean joined Nicole who was now talking with the Polish ambassador and his wife. He caught a glimpse of Valesky as he left the party through the other door. "You'll have to keep up if you please," Stewart called to Leznikov.

"Yes, of course," Leznikov replied, knowing that remark was for him. "I apologize. I thought I recognized someone in the hall. I will have to check when I get back. An old friend from Canada—"

"Yes, well, if we make this quick, you'll hopefully be back before the party ends," Stewart said, ushering his group forward.

Washington, DC—Oval Office

Jenkins was sitting at the Resolute desk. It was a gray, rainy day which made his amputated lower leg ache more than usual with phantom pain. He was waiting for the CIA director. While he waited, he read over the morning briefing notes. He studied the information that the CIA had collected on planned demonstrations in Egypt. He picked up a pen and added his thoughts in the margin.

Chris knocked once on the door and opened it. "The CIA director is here."

"Send him in," Jenkins said as he stood up and buttoned his suit jacket. As the director entered, Jenkins walked around the desk and extended his hand. "Director, thank you for coming over."

"Mr. President," Stanton said, accepting the handshake.

"Have a seat," Jenkins said as he motioned to the chair across from his desk. Jenkins leaned back on the front of the desk, crossing his feet at the ankles with the palms of his hands resting on the desktop. "Doug, we've known each other for many years now and worked well together when I was in the Senate, so I want to be upfront with you. I understand that the CIA received a request from Ambassador Barker."

Stanton's brow furrowed. "Yes, there was a request."

"Barker requested information on Ambassador Adkins, is that correct?"

"Yes," Stanton replied. "How did you know?"

Jenkins smiled. "Let's just say that Barker is under scrutiny. I sent him to the Soviet Union for a reason." Stanton looked at Jenkins, confusion apparent on his face. "I think we both know why." Jenkins waited for Stanton to realize the reason. When he continued to act confused, Jenkins simply said, "Mockingbird." Stanton looked down, knowing Jenkins now knew about Stanton's connection to Barker. "You haven't sent any information, have you?"

"Not yet, sir. We were preparing the report."

"There won't be a report. I have received requests from members of Parliament and the prime minister asking that the ambassador's identity remain undisclosed," Jenkins told a little white lie, but he knew Geoffrey Adkins would back him up if asked. "You need to tell Barker that you have nothing in your files concerning Ambassador Adkins. Any further requests from Barker for any information goes through the proper channels. In the future, if he makes any requests to our intelligence community, I am to be made aware of them. Barker works as an ambassador now, and he needs to channel his requests through the State Department. Is that clear?" Jenkins had made Alboreto, who was part of the Phenom Five (which was Jenkins's inner circle, led by Barker, before their falling out), Secretary of State for this very reason. Alboreto was ecstatic with the appointment in spite of having to deal with Barker.

"It's clear, but I don't understand why Barker has to go through the State Department," Stanton pressed. "He's a former senator and has connections that others don't. He has the proper security clearance—"

Jenkins cocked his head. "He *had* the proper security clearance. We downgraded his clearance because of our compromised embassy in the Soviet Union, as I am sure you know." Jenkins smiled coyly. "Doug, I know you and Barker are very good friends. I know you were key in continuing Operation Mockingbird after I ordered its shutdown when I was chairman of the Intelligence Committee. I know you helped him get dirt on just about every person in Congress." Jenkins folded his arms. "What I am asking you to do is follow the proper procedure. Any ambassador asking for information—intelligence information—goes through the State Department to the CIA. Barker will have no more access directly to you." Jenkins paused while he watched Stanton fidget in his chair. "I sense you are uncomfortable with my request."

"Request? It sounded like an order," Stanton stated. "I wasn't aware of Barker's downgraded clearance, but if he requests something from me, I can answer that request. There is nothing wrong with that."

Jenkins's brow furrowed. "What does Barker have on you?" Stanton smiled but did not respond. "How far does this go?" Jenkins paused. When Stanton did not speak, Jenkins said, "Do I need to ask for your resignation?"

"If you are in a firing mood, then my deputy should be asked to leave as well," Stanton shot back, resentful of being put in this position. Stanton's thoughts turned to his wife and family. Barker's information on Stanton's many indiscretions would hurt them deeply. In the last year, he realized how deeply he cared for his wife after he almost lost her due to breast cancer. He didn't want to risk the rekindled relationship with her. "I would look outside the agency for our replacements. Until then, move the chief operating officer into the deputy position. That should buy you some time to get someone who is Senate-confirmable."

"Doug, I need to make sure that the UK's ambassador is safe," Jenkins said. "I can't afford to anger our oldest ally. I need Barker neutralized. I can't have him meddling in my administration or with my intelligence agencies. He has already shown we can't trust him in the Soviet Union. For Christ's sake, Doug, he gave the Soviets the code name of the mission."

Stanton stood up. "The CIA, FBI, and NSA didn't give Barker that information," he said as he buttoned his suit jacket. "You know who did and he is no longer a threat." Stanton was referring to Babcock. He turned to walk toward the door from which he had entered the Oval Office. "You'll have our resignations by the end of the day." He extended his hand. "In a way, this is a relief. I won't cause you any problems. Thompson's appointment secured the FBI. Thompson has done a remarkable job weeding out the moles. That was a good move, and you have no worries there. My replacement should be untouchable. I know you worked with Thompson, but his loyalty is to the country first. That's what you need at the CIA."

"Thank you, Doug," Jenkins said shaking his hand. "Can I trust that the report—"

"—Will be sent over to you, along with my resignation letter," Stanton interjected.

Jenkins shook his head. "The letter has to be handed to me, in person."

"Then I'll bring the report over with my letter," Stanton corrected himself. "I'll bring the deputy director with me, and he will have his letter of resignation as well."

They walked to the door together. "Thank you, Doug. I have every intention of putting a person who is country first into your position."

"Thank you, Mr. President," Stanton said as he exited the Oval Office.

"Chris, I need to see the communications director, Whittaker, and the press secretary immediately."

"Yes sir," Chris said, picking up his phone and dialing the number of the communications director.

Moscow, USSR—United Kingdom Embassy

It was raining with intermittent lightning and thunder. Suddenly a red strobe light blinded Sean's eyes. His breathing quickened. "No," he whispered. "No, NO!" He started running toward the familiar house. It was his home—a quiet sanctuary—that the police now invaded. An ambulance, sirens blasting and lights flashing, drove past him. "NO!" he screamed again. He ran to the house and out of breath; he reached the door. He felt as if his heart was being ripped from of his chest when he saw them. "Sarah! Kate!" There was blood on the walls and carpet. Sean's wife and child were lying in their own blood.

Nicole watched as Sean's head thrashed on the pillow as if he was looking for someone. His body jerked a few times, and his eyes were in rapid movement beneath his eyelids. With a violent jerk, Sean forced himself awake. He placed his hand on his forehead and reached for Nicole. When his searching hand couldn't find her next to him in bed, he lifted his head. She was sitting in the chair across the room. "I never know if I should wake you when you are experiencing their deaths," she said with a calm, but cold, voice.

Sean brought his hand down from his forehead, wiping the sweat from his face. He threw the covers back, turned on the light by his bedside, and sat on the edge of the bed. Still feeling vulnerable and, if it was even possible, more naked than he was from their lovemaking after the party, Sean grabbed his robe off the floor and wrapped it around him.

"They are getting more frequent," Nicole added. "I think it might be a good idea for you to talk to someone."

"It won't do any good," Sean spat out. "The doctors tried, but the nightmares didn't go away until after I killed him." Sean was referring to Saverio the Serpent.

"He's still dead, and yet here we are," Nicole countered. The resentment in her voice was noticeable. "Has Kent been in touch with you?"

"No," Sean replied, the angry tone still in his voice. "I can deal with this."

Nicole sighed. For the last few weeks, Sean's temperament had changed. He was angry and short-tempered with her. She disliked this new wrinkle in their relationship. She looked at the clock on her bedside table. It was five thirty in the morning. "I'm going to take a shower." She stood up and walked toward the bedroom door.

"The shower is that way," Sean said as he pointed in the direction of the master bath.

"I'm going to get a cup of tea. Then I'm going to call the barracks and have them wake Duncan and the other guards that are leaving with me. I'm up. I won't get back to sleep, so we might as well get going." Nicole disappeared into the hallway.

When she returned, Sean said, "Nicole, don't be mad."

"I'm not mad," Nicole returned. "You refuse to tell me what you think is triggering the nightmares. I know there has to be something causing them. You know what it is, and I know you are keeping it from me." She continued to the bathroom. "You are acting as if I'm not here, so I might as well leave now." Nicole closed the bathroom door before Sean could reply.

It was like a dance. Sean and Nicole prepared for the day, each trying hard not to get in each other's way. Nicole finished in the bathroom, opened the door, and walked to her closet. Sean had placed her packed suitcase at the bedroom door. When she vacated the bathroom, Sean entered. She could hear the water for the shower running. She dressed, picked up her suitcase, and moved it to the front door of the residence. She walked on to the kitchen, grabbed a couple of pieces of bread, and smothered them with butter. It was her comfort food. She could remember eating it in times of stress. A few minutes later Sean entered the kitchen.

"Do I have time for coffee?" Sean asked as he grabbed a scone.

"It's my understanding that the plane isn't exactly on a schedule," Nicole retorted. She hated the cold distance between them.

"I'll get some when I get back," Sean replied. Nicole finished the last bite of her bread and butter just as there was a knock on the door. Nicole walked to the door and opened it to find Duncan.

"Good morning, ma'am," Duncan said as the door opened. "I can take your luggage to the car. Anders's coffin is on the truck in the shipping container. Smith is waiting with the other guards. We're ready to go when you are."

"Thank you, Duncan. I'm sorry about the change of plans."

"Don't be," Duncan replied. "I prefer leaving in the dark if possible. Our airport contingent is servicing the plane now."

Nicole smiled her acknowledgment. She retrieved her suitcase, handing it to Duncan. "I have a briefcase, but I'd like that to stay with me."

"That will be no problem, ma'am," Duncan said, as he turned to leave.

Nicole closed the door and walked back to the master bedroom. She grabbed her shoulder holster, checked her gun, and placed the gun back into the holster. She slung it into place. She grabbed her suit jacket and put it on, noticing that Sean was standing at the door. She picked up her purse and briefcase. "I'll get my coat and meet you in the foyer." She didn't move, knowing that Sean wanted to embrace her.

Sean swallowed when he realized that Nicole didn't want his touch. He stared at her, trying to think of the right thing to say. He moved to his closet to grab a pullover sweater. "I'll miss you," he said as he walked toward the closet.

"I doubt it," Nicole replied as she left the bedroom. She walked to the foyer and retrieved her coat from the closet. Sean was now walking to do the same. After she put on her coat, she walked to the front door.

Sean managed to grasp her arm gently. "Nicole, don't do this. Don't leave like this," Sean pleaded. "I love you. I will work it out, I promise."

"I do not doubt that you will," she agreed. She removed her arm from Sean's grasp. "But we said no secrets, and this feels like a secret. It's a wall you built, and I can't accept that." She moved toward the door. "I have a lot to think about while I am gone. So do you."

Sean exhaled as he watched Nicole leave the residence. He didn't have the heart to tell Nicole what he suspected was the cause of the nightmares. Sean cursed as he put his coat on and walked out of the residence. He shut the door behind him and quickened his pace to catch up to Nicole.

As they rode to the airport, Nicole looked out the window into the obscure, dim streets and buildings. She couldn't help but feel lost in the darkness. She thought about how she gave up her life for the man sitting next to her. She wondered if love blinded her, seeing only the dashing Brit and what she envisioned would be a calm life in the service of the Foreign Office. A single thought kept returning to her mind. *I gave up everything to be with him. Everything.* She sighed. *Am I that stupid?*

Sean stealthily maneuvered his hand to take Nicole's into it. She didn't resist. Sean watched as she batted back a few tears. He realized this would be the first time since their reunion in London that they would not be together. He wondered if the lure of a position in Jenkins's administration would be too much for her to resist especially with the current friction between them. Sean knew Jenkins would make the offer again. The entourage arrived at the airport just as Sean began to wonder if he would ever see her again.

They exited the cars, which were permitted to pull directly up to the plane that was bound for Dover Air Force Base. They stood and watched the loading of the shipping container that contained the coffin into the cargo area of the plane. Nicole had instructed the men to remove the coffin once inside the plane, out of the sight of any prying eyes. She had informed Jenkins upon their arrival to have a flag available to drape over the coffin. She noted American flags in the Soviet Union were a hard find. All instructions were carried out. After the removal of the cargo container from the plane's cargo hold, Duncan climbed out along with the other guards. Sean walked up to Duncan, had a brief chat with him and then walked back to Nicole.

"Everything is ready," Sean began. "You'll need that American flag."

"Bobby's staff is taking care of that," Nicole responded. "Take care of you." Nicole swallowed, not at all sure she wanted to kiss him goodbye.

"You take care of you," Sean echoed back. He took her hand and gently tugged her toward him. "I am still deeply in love with you," he whispered. "The thought of not having you by my side is paralyzing." He kissed her on the cheek.

"Damn you," Nicole said as she brought her hands up to Sean's chest. She buried her face in the crux of his neck and shoulder. Sean wrapped his arms around her, smiling at her curse, knowing she didn't mean it. "I love you, but I can't live like this." She pulled back and looked him in the eyes. "I'm worried about you. Why you insist on living like this and not talk to me, I can't understand." There was an additional thought that Nicole wanted to add. It was that she didn't have to live with someone who couldn't trust her enough to tell her what was happening, even if it was just a theory. "Fix it," she said.

"I will, but give me time," Sean pleaded. He could see that Nicole was skeptical. "Come back to me. I will fix it." He kissed her quivering lips, knowing she did not fully believe him.

Nicole pulled away from him when the kiss ended. She quickly picked up her briefcase she had set by her feet when they were watching the guards load the crate. She walked up the steps to the plane's cabin, not looking back.

Sean called to her, "Tell the president hello for me." There was no answer. Sean turned to Duncan. "I don't know if she'll be able to call once in Washington. I would appreciate someone letting me know you arrived safely and how it is going there."

"I have to check in with Alistair throughout the day while we are gone. I'll have him pass the word on to you," Duncan said. "I'll take good care of her, sir."

"Thank you," Sean said. "Have a safe trip." Sean turned and walked to the car as the engines of the plane started. When Duncan and his accompanying guards were safely aboard, the door to the cabin was closed, and the stairs retracted. Sean tried to peer through the plane's windows to locate Nicole, but the attempt was futile. What he didn't know was that Nicole purposely chose not to sit by the window or on the side of the plane that faced him.

The plane rolled away from Sean and onto the taxiway, heading for the runway. He sighed, hoping he would see her again. So far, Leznikov had kept his word. Now he would see if he could return to the embassy without being stopped.

Dover, Delaware—Dover Air Force Base

Jenkins arrived with a few minutes to spare. Chris took care of all the details, including notifying both families of the change in time for the arrival of their loved ones. Both families were flown to

Washington, DC, the day before and their expenses paid by Jenkins personally. Jenkins's communications director had requested television time later in the day. Jenkins would announce the return of Smith and Anders's body, sharing a few photos of the arrival at Dover, particularly the photo of Mrs. Anders and her baby grieving next to the flag-draped coffin.

The plane touched down and taxied into the hangar. When the engines were shut off, Jenkins moved from a soundproofed room to the hangar itself. After the stairs were moved to the main door of the aircraft and in place, Jenkins walked to them with the American flag in his hands. He was met by Duncan who had just traversed the stairs reaching the bottom.

Duncan snapped to attention and saluted Jenkins. "Good morning, sir," Duncan began. "If you'll allow me, sir, I'll take that flag and prepare the coffin for presentation."

"Yes, thank you," Jenkins said. "May I?" Jenkins gestured toward the cabin door.

"Yes, sir," Duncan said. "She's expecting you." Duncan left to join the other guards who were now opening the cargo door.

Jenkins climbed the stairs and entered the cabin. He walked around the bulkhead and paused when he saw Nicole. He smiled when she stood and walked up to greet him.

"Mr. President," Nicole said, extending her hand. "I apologize for throwing everything off schedule by arriving early."

Jenkins looked at her hand. He shook his head and extended his arms, asking for a hug. "It's good to see you, old friend." Nicole smiled as she moved into Jenkins's arms. "Is everything all right?" Jenkins whispered in her ear.

"Not now," Nicole replied. She broke off the hug. "Are the families here?"

"Yes."

"Lieutenant Colonel Smith," Nicole began as she turned to see Smith standing at attention, holding the salute his hand snapped to when Jenkins entered the cabin. "Mr. President, this is Lieutenant Colonel Smith."

Jenkins saluted Smith, then walked toward him. "Welcome home, Lieutenant Colonel." He extended his hand.

Smith accepted the handshake and said, "Thank you, Mr. President."

"Your family is anxious to see you," Jenkins added. "Shall we go?"

"If you don't mind, sir, I'd like to be present when you present Anders's coffin to his wife and child."

"I think that would be appropriate," Jenkins replied. "I suggest we deplane and be present for that."

"Duncan has instructions to wait until we are ready," Nicole said as she snatched up her purse and briefcase. She walked to the door, allowing Jenkins and Smith to exit before her. Jenkins motioned for Chris to escort Anders's wife and 6-month old baby to stand beside him. Duncan looked at Nicole, who gave a slight but discernible nod of her head when all were in place. The coffin was lowered down a ramp and met by eight airmen and one officer. When commanded, the eight airmen lifted the flag-draped coffin from the ramp. With each command, the airmen responded with precision and respect. Smith and Jenkins snapped to attention, complete with a salute, as the coffin and honor guard walked to the hearse, which was within the hangar. The honor guard solemnly marched past Nicole, Smith, Jenkins, and Anders's wife and child. Mrs. Anders bit her lip in an effort not to outwardly sob. The honor guard placed the coffin by the tailgate of the hearse on a bier. Nicole heard Mrs. Anders's stifled cry, and Nicole tried to stop her own eyes from filling with tears.

The airmen backed away from the coffin, leaving a space for the family to approach. Jenkins and Smith completed their salute. Nicole turned to Smith, cleared her throat, and said, "Lieutenant Colonel, would you please escort Mrs. Anders and her baby to pay their respects?"

Jenkins took a step back, allowing Smith to offer his arm to Mrs. Anders. Jenkins looked at the teary-eyed wife. "Take as much time as you need," he gently said to her.

"Thank you, Mr. President," Mrs. Anders managed to say.

Nicole and Jenkins watched as Smith escorted Mrs. Anders to the coffin, physically supporting her the closer she got to it. When she reached the coffin, she laid her head on the top of it, clutching her baby in her arms. Smith just held them both as they said their goodbyes. A White House photographer took one photograph. Smith leaned over and was speaking quietly to the widow. Nicole and Jenkins watched the exchange for a few minutes.

Finally, Jenkins said, "Let's go inside." Jenkins escorted Nicole, who was now dabbing away the few tears that she shed, to the soundproof room at the back of the hangar.

"Where's Smith's family?" Nicole asked when they were inside.

"In there," Jenkins said, pointing to the door to his left. Chris had waited in the windowed room that allowed him to watch the proceedings. As Jenkins and Nicole entered the room, he said,

"Chris, have the car ready for Mrs. Anders." Chris acknowledged Jenkins's comment and left to execute the given command. Jenkins turned to Nicole. "I think we should tell Smith's family what is going on."

Jenkins and Nicole walked to the door of a second soundproof conference room. Jenkins opened it and allowed Nicole to enter. He closed the door behind him. The Smith family consisted of Smith's wife and their three children. The oldest son was twelve, the middle daughter was nine, and the youngest son was six. Mrs. Smith stood up and then motioned for her children to do the same.

"Mrs. Smith, this is Nicole Charbonneau," Jenkins began. "Your husband was staying at the United Kingdom's embassy in Moscow. Her Majesty's ambassador and security forces did an excellent job of protecting both men."

"I know Ms. Charbonneau," Mrs. Smith said.

"I'm sorry, have we met?" Nicole asked, studying the face of the woman before her.

"Oh, no. I'm sorry, I know you from exposing the Sipes confession tape. That was incredibly brave," Mrs. Smith clarified.

"Not as brave as what you face on a daily basis. Who have we here?" Nicole asked, referring to the children. Mrs. Smith proudly introduced them. Nicole shook each of their hands. "Your father is a very brave man. You should be proud of him." She was met with three embarrassed and mumbled thank-yous. She looked at Mrs. Smith and smiled. "Your husband is paying his respects with Mrs. Anders. I would venture to say that he is telling her how brave her husband was."

"Yes, ma'am," Mrs. Smith agreed.

"It shouldn't be too much longer," Jenkins added. "We'll wait out here." Jenkins started to move to the door. "We don't want to intrude…"

"Mr. President," Mrs. Smith started, "thank you for keeping the press away."

Jenkins smiled. "That feeling—I know it all too well." They all laughed. "There are times when I don't want to talk to them either. But it goes with the job." Jenkins opened the door and allowed Nicole to leave.

As Jenkins closed the door behind him, Mrs. Anders, with her baby in her arms, and Smith entered the windowed room. Jenkins walked up to Mrs. Anders. "Mrs. Anders, I wanted to convey my deepest condolences. As much as I appreciate and honor the service of your husband, I want you to know that I am aware of your sacrifice. If there is anything I can do in the future, don't hesitate to call the White House and ask for my assistant, Chris. He'll make sure to get the message to me directly." Jenkins paused before adding, "I'm so sorry I failed in bringing him home to you..." His voice trailed off as he didn't want to add the word "alive" to the end of his sentence.

Mrs. Anders looked at Jenkins. "Thank you, Mr. President." Looking past Jenkins to Nicole, she asked, "Do you know what happened?"

Nicole looked at Smith. "Didn't the lieutenant colonel tell…"

"I wasn't sure…" Smith began before his voice trailed off; inferring that he didn't know how much information was considered classified.

"Oh, yes, of course," Nicole responded. "One moment, Mrs. Anders." She leaned over to Jenkins and whispered, "Is any of this classified?"

Jenkins whispered into Nicole's ear, "Just the mission. I don't care what comes out about what happened in Moscow."

"Mr. President, why don't you and Lieutenant Colonel Smith…" Nicole pointed to the door leading to Smith's family. "I'd like to talk with Mrs. Anders."

"She is the only person who can tell me what to do," Jenkins joked as he motioned for Smith to join him.

"Mrs. Anders," Nicole said as she motioned to a couple of chairs along the wall. "There isn't much I can tell you. He arrived at our embassy and went directly into surgery. He had lost a lot of blood from a gunshot wound that he sustained while evading the Soviets. From what Smith has told me, he performed his duties honorably, and I'm sure the president and this nation are indeed proud of him."

"Was a deal made?"

"A deal?"

"For my husband's return?" Mrs. Anders asked.

"Not to my knowledge," Nicole said.

Mrs. Anders nodded her acknowledgment. "There's just this incredible amount of anger at the Soviets for his…not returning to us." She chose her words carefully.

"I can't imagine what you are feeling. I wish I could help you in some way," Nicole replied, searching for the appropriate words.

"You brought him home," Mrs. Anders said. "That's better than wondering where he was or what they did with him." Nicole looked down. "I think I'd like to go now."

"Of course. Chris?" Nicole called. Chris walked up to Mrs. Anders and escorted her out of the hangar and to the car. After five minutes, the Smith family with Jenkins left their room. Smith thanked Nicole again for their help and wished them well. With that, the Smiths left for home.

"Are you ready?" Jenkins asked Nicole. "I told Chris that we'd drop you at your hotel."

"That's not necessary. Just call me a cab, Bobby."

"No, I'd feel better taking you there," Jenkins countered. "Besides, this gives me an opportunity to visit with you a while." He pointed to the door. They both started walking toward it. "How long will you be staying?"

"At least a week," Nicole said as they walked to the limo. "The closing is in three days, and I have some furniture to move to storage. There are a few other things I need to take care of as well." When outside, she saw Duncan waiting with their luggage. Nicole climbed into the limo, setting her purse and briefcase between her and Jenkins. Duncan loaded their cases into one of the cars. When everyone was in place, the motorcade left for the hotel.

"Anything I can help with?" Jenkins asked when they were seated.

"No," Nicole replied. "But if I remember correctly, there might be some additional information I can pass off to you before I leave."

"Now you have me intrigued," Jenkins responded. "More of what I previously received?"

"Possibly," Nicole said. "I have to look them over."

"I understand," Jenkins responded. "Nikki, I know this is awkward, but my first state dinner is in a couple of days. I'd love for you to attend. At the very least, look over the arrangements for me."

Nicole looked at Jenkins. "I don't know, Bobby."

"Please. It would mean a lot to me," Jenkins said. "Look, I know you are with Sean. I'm not asking for you to be my date. I'm just asking that you attend. I could sit you at the United Kingdom's embassy table if you wanted."

Nicole smiled. "I'll agree to look over the arrangements."

"And keep thinking about attending?"

"I'll think about it."

Before they realized it, the limo had arrived at the Carlton Hotel. Jenkins insisted on escorting Nicole to her room, saying Sean would never forgive him if he didn't. Duncan, his men, and the Secret Service accompanied them to the third floor and down the hallway to Nicole's room.

"I'm looking forward to a nap before I have to meet with my real estate agent—" Nicole looked at her watch—"in just a couple of hours," she said to Jenkins. She looked at the door to her room and inserted the key. When she opened the door, she noticed a bouquet of deep red roses sitting on the table. She looked slyly at Jenkins first.

"I swear I didn't send them," Jenkins responded in his defense. "I know better!"

Nicole laughed. "Well, that leaves only one other person." Nicole walked up to the roses, sniffing a few of them before she took the card out of the holder. She opened it, trying to guess the clever message that Sean had written. She extracted the card from the envelope.

Jenkins watched her smile turn to anger. "Nikki?"

"That bastard," Nicole said. "That fucking bastard!" The last time she received roses from this person they were yellow. To her knowledge, Jenkins and Sean were the only two men who knew her favorite rose color was deep red. She swore again at her naivety. Given the state of her relationship with Sean, she should have known these were not from him.

Jenkins looked at Duncan. "I don't understand."

Nicole swept the vase and roses off the table and marched past Jenkins to the hallway. She paused for a second not finding the desired trash can. With not one in sight, she marched back into the room. She found the room's trash can and dropped them from shoulder height into it.

"Nikki, what's going on?" Jenkins implored. "Are you and Sean doing OK?"

"They aren't from Sean," Nicole shot back. She pointed at the trash can as she looked at Duncan. "Somebody get rid of these damn things!"

"Who are they from?" Jenkins asked.

Nicole looked at Jenkins. "The Serpent—Kent," Nicole spat out.

"What?!" Duncan exclaimed, his Scottish brogue tongue very pronounced as he drew out the word longer than usual to convey his surprise.

"Somebody in the embassy knew I was going to be here," Nicole snapped.

Jenkins drew in a slow breath. He looked at Duncan and then Nicole. “You can’t stay here.”

“I agree,” Duncan confirmed.

“There is no safer place than the White House. You aren’t going to argue with me about this,” Jenkins firmly stated, stopping Nicole’s protest. “Your men are welcome to stay there as well. But you are not staying anywhere else—that’s final.” Jenkins started to leave when he noticed that Nicole was not going to follow. Jenkins looked at Duncan. “I’ll order my agents to carry her out of here if you can’t talk some sense into her.”

“He is right, ma’am. The White House would be the most secure location for you. I have no intelligence on the location of Kent and the White House takes you out of public access the majority of the time.”

Nicole rolled her eyes and sighed. “I have to come and go—”

“That’s not a problem,” Jenkins interrupted. “Your security detail will escort you. I won’t intrude. Don’t argue with me, Nikki. Don’t make me carry you.” Nicole tried to suppress her laughter. “What’s so funny? You don’t think I could do it?”

“No,” Nicole began. “I’m trying to figure out how the communications director would explain a photo of the president carrying his former girlfriend out of a downtown hotel.”

Jenkins tried to keep his determined, straight face, but couldn’t. A small burst of laughter escaped his taut lips. It was a snort more than a laugh. That noise prompted a laugh from Nicole. After a few seconds, Jenkins said, “Let’s spare my communications director the heart attack. C’mon, let’s go.” Jenkins extended his hand. Nicole took it. “Gentlemen,” Jenkins addressed the Secret Service and Nicole's security guards, "the next stop will be the White House."

Nicole left with Jenkins, surrounded by her guards and his Secret Service agents. It reminded her of the time she spent with Jenkins on the campaign trail.

Moscow, USSR—United Kingdom Embassy

Sean awoke drenched in sweat from the all-too-familiar nightmare. He glanced at the clock on the nightstand next to him. It was five in the morning. He wiped the sweat from his face and contemplated the horror he had just experienced. This time the ordeal moved past discovering Sarah's and Kate's bodies. He was standing at their graves. He was alone, staring at the tombstone when Sarah appeared before him. She walked to him, not speaking a word. When standing close enough for Sean to take her in his arms, Sarah raised her hands to Sean's face and dug her nails into his skin pulling down from his temples to his chin. She smiled at the pain she was inflicting on Sean. Blood began to seep from between Sarah's teeth. She opened her mouth exposing her bloodied forked tongue—the Serpent's calling card. He tried to grab her hands to stop her, but his hands could not grasp hers. He screamed his displeasure. That's when he forced himself to wake and heard the last of his anguished scream as he sat up in bed.

Reclining back down, Sean ran his fingers through his damp hair and stared at the ceiling. He thought of Nicole and how he missed her. He looked at the clock again. Only ten minutes had passed. He threw back the covers and sat on the edge of the bed. He knew he wouldn't sleep. He showered, dressed, and walked into the living room. He walked to the bar, not thinking of anything except the nightmare. He grabbed the gin bottle and poured a glass half full. He set the bottle down and picked up the glass. He had it to his lips when the phone rang. The sound jarred him out of his trance. He looked at the glass, surprised it was in his hand. The phone rang again. He looked at it and then back at the glass again. He closed his eyes, realizing the same demon that had haunted him in North Carolina was tempting him again.

On the sixth ring, Sean answered the phone. “Yes, what is it?”

“It’s Alistair, sir. I wanted to report that Nicole arrived safely in Washington. However, there has been a change of plans. It seems they are staying at the White House now.”

Sean pulled the phone from his ear in confusion. “The White House,” he repeated, mumbling. “Why? Did Duncan say why?”

“Apparently upon their arrival at the hotel, two dozen red roses were waiting for Nicole in her room,” Alistair informed him.

Sean’s first thought was that Jenkins put them there. He knew Jenkins would never stop trying to win her back. He bit his lower lip. “Who sent them? I know I didn’t.”

“They were from Kent.”

Sean felt his knees go soft as if they were going to buckle. He put his hand on the table to brace him. “Kent,” he mumbled.

“Yes, sir,” Alistair confirmed. “Duncan said that the president declared the White House the safest place for her since there is no intelligence readily available on the Serpent’s whereabouts.”

Sean hung up the phone. He cursed as he leaned with both hands on the table. He looked over his shoulder at the glass of gin he had left on the cocktail cart. It was calling his name. “Just where the hell are you, Kent?”

CHAPTER SEVEN
MARCH 1981

Cairo, Egypt—Outside Seddik's Palace

Kent and Maggie arrived in Cairo a week after Kent's meeting with Ashear. Kent spent most of the day complaining about the heat since he spent the majority of his time outside trying to connect with someone who worked in the presidential palace and on Seddik's personal staff. Kent needed to find someone he could trust and that involved finding the right amount of naivety and eagerness. He knew this was going to take some time.

He was leaning against his car, the hood up, just a block from the palace. He had watched a few of the servants employed there walk home this way. Three men were approaching him. Kent stood up and played the helpless traveler, not speaking the language and trying his best to look completely helpless. A man named Amsu stopped. Amsu spoke English, and the other two called to him when he stopped. Amsu told them to go on with a wave of his hand and a few words in his native tongue.

"Thank you for stopping," Kent said, acting exasperated. "Do you speak English by chance?"

"Yes," Amsu said. "What is the problem?"

"I can't get it to start," Kent said. "I've tried several times and it just won't. I'm not mechanically inclined."

"Get in and try it once more," Amsu said, walking over to the car and peering under the hood. Kent tried to start the car. Amsu jumped back as he was standing by the battery which gave a little spark. "Do you have any tools?"

"This is all I have," Kent said, showing him a channel lock wrench and a screwdriver.

"This should work," Amsu said, grabbing the wrench and walking back to the battery. After a minute passed, Amsu instructed Kent to try it again. The engine chugged and rattled before it turned over. "The battery wire was loose." He handed the wrench back to Kent, who got out of the car. "The roads tend to cause that."

"Let me pay you something for your trouble," Kent said. At first, Amsu refused. Kent pulled a wad of money from his pant's pocket. Amsu's eyes bulged. "I insist." Kent pulled off a generous amount of bills and tried to hand it to Amsu, who again declined. "Well then at least let me give you a ride. Your friends are gone, and it is the least I could do." As Amsu tried to refuse the offer, Kent kept sweetening the deal. "Do you have a wife and children?"

"No," Amsu replied.

"Then let me take you to dinner. Why do you have to hurry home? No one will miss you. Get in, we're going to dinner, and then I'll take you home. Get in," Kent urged, opening the door to the car.

Amsu finally accepted, realizing Kent would not relent. Kent asked the location of Amsu's favorite restaurant. With Amsu providing the directions, they started out. During the drive, Kent played the role of a friendly tourist. Amsu enjoyed the chance to practice his English.

They arrived at the restaurant and walked to a table. Amsu had a passion for learning. His openness to learning about different cultures was one of the reasons he obtained the job on Seddik's staff. He was a fine young man, took care of himself, read a lot, and attended university in the evening, taking a variety of classes but mostly focusing on languages. Even with all of these cherished activities in his life, he was still lonely. Kent spent most of the night with Amsu, inquiring about him, trying to find weaknesses that he could utilize. As educated as Amsu was, his eagerness to learn about the Western cultures and his loneliness were weaknesses Kent could exploit to recruit Amsu as his informant.

Washington, DC—Oval Office

"I'm heading up to the residence," Jenkins told Whittaker. He had just finished a conversation with Seddik and needed a break. Whittaker had just arrived in the office to share a report with the president. "I'll study these while I'm there." Taking the report from Whittaker, Jenkins added it to the stack of papers he was putting in his briefcase. He started for the door, fully aware of the scowl on Whittaker's face.

"Mr. President," Whittaker started. "How long will Nikki be here?"

Jenkins didn't appreciate the tone in his chief of staff's voice. He slowly turned to look at him. "Is there something you want to say?"

"Some issues need your attention, Mr. President. I feel Nikki may be a distraction you can't afford."

Jenkins felt his blood pressure rising. "Tell me, Fred; is there a nuclear war about to break out anywhere?"

"No, sir."

"Has Wall Street crashed?" Whittaker shook his head. Jenkins continued, "Perhaps there is a famine that I could magically fix, or maybe make it rain to help the farmers around the world save crops? Has something that will bring the Earth to a staggering halt occurred that I don't know about?"

"No, sir, just the typical day-to-day things that need your attention to keep moving forward," Whittaker stated candidly.

"There is no crisis, correct?"

"That's correct, sir."

"Then I think I can walk from this office to the residence, in full confidence that if something of grave consequence occurs—" Jenkins paused and pointed to the phone— "I can be reached by picking up the phone and calling me. In fact, I believe that is why there is a residence here. Yes, I think it is because I am only seconds away from being alerted or giving a command." Jenkins stared at Whittaker. "I assure you, Fred; Nikki is not diverting my attention on any matter. However, it seems my cabinet could be dropping the ball on some issues. I suggest you get the word out that I expect full and accurate reports when they walk through the door to this office—the people's office. Is that understood?"

"Yes, sir," Whittaker said, taking the verbal backlash in stride.

"And don't ever question my loyalty to this country again," Jenkins added as he opened the door to leave. "The last person who tried to come between Nikki and me ended up in the Soviet Union."

"Yes, Mr. President," Whittaker said as he started for his office.

Jenkins walked down the hallway to Nicole's suite. The door was open. Nicole had just finished going over the paperwork for the condo closing in the morning. As she set them aside, Jenkins walked into the room, collapsed into the nearest chair, dropping his briefcase beside it. He placed his thumb and index finger above his eyebrows and rubbed.

Duncan stood to enter the room. Nicole also stood and gave a quick wave to Duncan to stay where he was. She walked over toward Jenkins, standing behind a small couch and within Duncan's sight. Duncan couldn't see Jenkins and felt uneasy about that, remembering Sean's instruction not to let them alone. He stood up and walked to the hallway, positioning himself so that he could see them both.

"Nikki, I swear, if your bodyguard doesn't back off, I'll have my agents arrest him," Jenkins said without removing his fingers from his forehead.

Nicole flicked her head indicating to Duncan that he needed to return to his chair out of Jenkins's sight. Duncan reluctantly obeyed Nicole. "What's wrong?"

"You would think people would refrain from withholding information from this office," Jenkins started.

Nicole didn't move. "What information?"

Jenkins removed his fingers and turned his head to look at Nicole. He smiled. "Nice try."

"I wasn't trying to get classified information from you," Nicole began. "I was wondering if you were able to determine Kent's whereabouts."

"All I know is that he is not, as far as we can tell, in the United States," Jenkins said. Nicole frowned and walked around the end of the couch to sit. "What's wrong?"

"I think I should move to a hotel," Nicole said.

"No," Jenkins said flatly. "You are much safer here."

"You just said—"

"I know," Jenkins interrupted. "But Nikki, that doesn't mean he isn't on his way. We don't know where he is, but we do know he is not in France. The minute he enters this country, we'll know."

"What makes you so sure?"

"Because Kent lacks the one thing the other Serpent had and used to his advantage," Jenkins replied.

"What is that?"

"Anonymity. We know what Kent looks like. The Secret Service and the FBI have put out bulletins with his description. He won't make it through that front gate." Jenkins pointed out the window toward the front gate of the White House. "I doubt that Kent has suddenly become a master of disguise."

"That's not the only reason I shouldn't be here," Nicole added.

"You spoke with Sean," Jenkins stated, although the inflection at the end made it sound like a question.

“Yes,” Nicole responded with some hesitation. “And while he isn’t happy with me being alone under the same the roof with you, he did agree that the White House is the safest place.”

Jenkins leaned forward and turned his head to look at Duncan. “We are hardly alone.” He turned back to look at Nicole; a frown planted firmly on his face.

Nicole wanted to laugh but suppressed it. “I’m afraid that Sean gave him an order not to leave me unattended with you.” She heard Duncan cough the water he was drinking when she spoke. It confirmed her suspicion.

Jenkins sat back. “It’s a shame that he feels he can’t trust you.” It was a truth that Jenkins felt he needed to voice.

Nicole shook her head. “It’s not that.” Nicole brought her hand to her brow and scratched it, trying to etch the thought from her mind. Internally, she was questioning if she wanted to confide to Jenkins that Sean’s nightmare had returned. “There are some issues. I don’t know. Something is going on, and I’m not sure what it is. He won’t tell me.”

“What happened to no secrets?”

“I know,” Nicole said. “It’s been a recent development. It will work itself out.”

Jenkins studied Nicole for a moment before he spoke. “Nikki, a place for you in my administration is there for the asking—anytime. If your safety is the only thing keeping you from leaving the Soviet Union, then let my offer ease that concern.”

Nicole smiled. “I appreciate that, Bobby. If things don’t improve, I might take you up on that.”

“I’m more concerned now than I was previously,” Jenkins said.

"I'm fine," Nicole tried to reassure him. She cleared her throat. "Besides, I'm sure you've noticed that the press is having a field day with me staying here."

Jenkins feigned surprise. "I hadn't noticed." A smile crept across his face. "Honestly, I can't understand the press's interest in my very boring love life. I mean—do you know how many bedrooms there are in this place?"

"I have no idea," Nicole replied.

"Come to think of it, neither to do I," Jenkins said with a laugh. "But that's not my point. Compared with Kennedy, this residence is a monastery. He had more women in this White House in one month than I could ever possibly have here. I should be a priest!"

"Bobby," Nicole laughed. "You aren't even Catholic!"

"Exactly," Jenkins replied with a laugh. "My right hand has seen so much action that I think I may go blind."

"Oh, Bobby," Nicole said, her hand quickly covering her mouth. "That was too much information! Can we change the subject?" Her words were slightly muffled, and her face became flushed as she pondered his words.

Jenkins looked down. "I'm sorry. I didn't mean to embarrass you." When he looked up again, a devious smile was present. "You know, I'm great at keeping secrets." He raised his eyebrows at the unspoken invitation. "No one would ever know."

"Bobby!" Nicole howled. After a few seconds of amusement, Nicole had to admit that she found his desire for her refreshing and touching in light of her current situation. Her hand found its way to her necklace as she began to toy with the temptation. She quickly remembered the more amorous times between them. She looked down and then at Jenkins. "I would know." And then, she couldn't resist adding, "And everybody in the press would know."

Jenkins exhaled. "You're right." The moment of closeness between them did not go unnoticed. "I could see there was a second or two that you considered it. Thank you for that. It is nice to know that you still care for me."

"I always will," Nicole confirmed.

"I brought with me the information on the state dinner," Jenkins said, feeling the need to change the subject. "Will you go over them with me?"

Nicole thought she saw a devious smile cross Jenkins's lips. With reservation, she agreed. She stood up and moved to the desk. She grabbed a chair and placed it next to the one already there.

Jenkins grabbed his briefcase. "And since the press already has us sleeping together, you might as well sit at my table."

Nicole shook her head. "You know Sean will go crazy," she said, then bit her lip. "Bobby, this isn't the time to tease him. I'm worried about him, and I don't want to cause him any more pain." Jenkins sat down next to her and removed the papers from his briefcase. Placing the papers in front of him, he looked at her with the obvious question apparent on his face. "The nightmares have returned."

Jenkins thought of his demons and how certain things set them off. "They never go away," he said, trying to console her. "The strangest thing can trigger them. They are always lying just below the surface."

"When they first started up again, they were sporadic. Now, Sean has them every night. He won't tell me what he thinks is triggering them," Nicole confided.

"He may not know."

"He knows," Nicole countered. "He asked for more time to take care of it. I can only hope he has taken care of it before I get back."

Jenkins watched Nicole trying to keep her bravado intact. He swallowed. "Do you think he'll hurt you? I mean not intentionally, but during…" His voice trailed off.

"The thought has crossed my mind. When it starts, I carefully slip out of bed and sit in a chair. It is such torture to watch him. It scares me. I don't dare wake him. There have been times when he has sat up with his eyes open, and he doesn't see me." Nicole stopped talking. She felt she shouldn't be confiding in Jenkins. "As if you don't already have the weight the world on your shoulders." She looked away. "We'll work it out."

"And if you can't?" Jenkins asked. He wasn't trying to manipulate her. Nicole knew Jenkins was concerned with her safety and her happiness. "I have some experience with this. Nikki, I'm serious. It never goes away. Sean has to come to terms with it, or it will always control him. He let it control him for ten years or more." Nicole looked at Jenkins. "Did I ever tell you how I met him?"

"No."

"It was at Jack Kensington's vacation house just after his wife's and child's murders. I was on a trip with Mercer and others. I had met Jack a few years before that. Anyway, I was just getting started in politics, and it was taking its toll. Jack offered his vacation house to me for a week. I took him up on it. A few days before I arrived, Jack told me another person was staying there. He told me that he wouldn't bother me. Sean did just that—or he tried to. I would hear him scream at night. I knew too well those torturous screams. I began to talk to him. We shared our horror stories, our battle wounds, and became great friends. Sean wouldn't be alive today if it weren't for his one sole purpose in life after that horrific night—that purpose was to kill the Serpent." Jenkins paused for a moment. "That purpose is gone now. He has to find a new direction. You can't save him, Nikki. He has to save himself. He has to let go of the guilt. He has to let go of whatever he thinks he did wrong, or it will kill him." Jenkins watched Nicole as she stared at him. She was breathing deeply; the exhales signaling that she was trying to hold back the tide of emotions. "Take it from someone who had to learn this lesson. No one can do it for him. Not even you."

Nicole was touched that Jenkins confided in her. "I've never heard you talk like this. I've never seen you struggle with your demon."

Jenkins smiled. "There were a couple of times I wrestled with it. What I did and didn't do confronts me every morning when I wake up. I have to believe that I can make a difference being here." Jenkins opened his arms, indicating that he meant serving as president. "Nikki, I'll tell you again. I'm not joking about a job here. If you can't bear it any longer, stay here. Don't go back to the Soviet Union."

"I'm sure your current communications director would not appreciate me taking his job," Nicole joked. She tried to cover her feelings with the comment. She felt as if she was betraying Sean in some way by confiding in Jenkins. She shrugged it off and took the top paper from the stack. "Let's have a look at these arrangements."

“Don’t worry about my communications director. He’d land on his feet. As for the state dinner, I would like to have you attend,” Jenkins said.

“I think that time would be better spent getting the furniture out of my condo,” Nicole replied. “Besides, I don’t have anything to wear.”

“Your favorite shop isn’t calling your name?”

“It is a tiny bit,” Nicole admitted.

“Then go shopping, and you are joining us. It’s settled. You can sit wherever you like as long as it is here.” Jenkins pointed at the head table. “I won’t take no for an answer. If Sean gets pissed off, tell him to call me.” Jenkins took Nicole’s hand in his. “I think you deserve a good time. It sounds like you haven’t had one in a while.”

Nicole could only sigh.

Cairo, Egypt—Kent’s Hotel Room

Kent and Amsu spent a lot of time together in the days that followed their first encounter. Kent pretended to be interested in learning more about Egyptian culture and customs. Amsu, always eager to learn about the West, badgered Kent for information about England and Europe. Kent would meet Amsu at a bar down from the palace. Amsu’s trust in Kent grew quickly. Kent would casually slip in a question or two about Seddik’s schedule. Amsu disclosed that Seddik’s staff was planning the annual victory parade that was to occur seven months from now. He told Kent how Egypt celebrated the crossing of the Suez Canal to seize the Bar-Lev Line, a fortification held by the Israelis. The operation took place on October 6, 1973. Amsu described how Syria launched an attack on the Golan Heights at the same time. The coordination of these two assaults marked the beginning of the Yom Kippur War.

Kent was not interested in the history lesson but acted as if he was. His attentiveness delighted Amsu, and he continued with the tale. After a few minutes more, Kent turned the conversation back to the parade and what usually occurred at the event. Amsu provided details of the previous parades, indicating that very little changed from year to year. Kent made a mental note to look into this event as a possible time to assassinate Seddik. Amsu continued to describe the event and then talked about the celebration that occurred back at the palace later in the evening.

In the days that followed, Kent inquired about Amsu's feelings toward Seddik. Was Amsu loyal to Seddik even though the leader of Egypt paid him barely enough money to keep his little apartment and put food on his table? Amsu was single. Kent pointed out that the married servants with children received more pay than Amsu. Every inequality Kent could discover turned into a discussion about how Seddik discriminated against Amsu. At first, Amsu denied it, but as the discussions continued, he started to become bitter.

The night that Kent announced he was leaving, he brought Amsu to his hotel room. Kent initially asked Maggie to seduce him, but Maggie resisted the idea. Using all her persuasion, Maggie was able to convince Kent that a few Egyptian whores would be a better option. The more Kent thought about it, the more he realized he wasn't willing to share Maggie; a thought that both delighted and terrified him. Was he becoming too emotionally involved? Was it a good thing for an assassin to have a steady girl? Could she hamper his work and make him vulnerable? These thoughts would haunt him over the coming months.

Maggie could almost read his mind and acted in a way that would convince Kent that she was not in love with him. On the night of Amsu's visit, she took the initiative to laud affection on Amsu, even though she found the man revolting. A Western woman touching him excited Amsu, and he encouraged more. Amsu took every opportunity to caress Maggie, touching her breasts, his hands following the curves of her body, and even at one point petting her. Maggie kissed Amsu on that occurrence, then looking at Kent after the kiss, ran her tongue along her bottom lip seductively. She left Amsu's side to retrieve more alcohol for the men. As she approached the counter, there was a knock on the door. You could almost hear the sigh of relief from Maggie. It was the three prostitutes she had recruited earlier in the day. Maggie answered the door and ushered them into the room. She introduced them to Amsu, indicating he was their primary concern. She looked at Kent, who had also been aroused by Maggie's actions with Amsu, and then she turned away from them to retrieve the drinks. She placed them on the table, still standing. Kent had taken the hand of one of the whores and was pulling her toward him. Maggie knew this was an attempt to make her jealous, but she ignored it. She walked back to the counter, picked up her purse, and left the room. Kent watched her leave, noting that she showed no emotion at all. Maggie closed the door behind her, elated that she would not be participating in the orgy. She looked in her oversized purse, checking that her camera was present. The only thing left for her to do was capture the event with pictures, which would be used to bribe Amsu before they left for Syria. She exited the hotel and walked to the room secured earlier in the day across from Kent's hotel room.

The plan, though not very imaginative, worked. Amsu fell for their lies, one of which was that Seddik would fire Amsu if he discovered what Amsu had done. Kent even went so far as to tell Amsu that Seddik would execute him. It fed into all the distrust and bitterness Kent had bestowed in Amsu. When sufficiently fearing for his life, Kent threw Amsu a lifeline. Spy for Kent, become the Serpent's informant in the region, and Kent would pay Amsu handsomely. What Amsu did with the money was of no concern to Kent, except that Amsu would need to keep up the appearance of living on the salary that Seddik paid him. But anytime Amsu wanted, he could come to the hotel with as many women as he desired. Kent continued to plot and scheme until Amsu finally broke down, seeing only the option that Kent provided. They shook hands when Amsu agreed to be the Serpent's informant. It was then that Kent gave him instructions on how to contact the Serpent daily with the information on Seddik. Before leaving, to sweeten the deal, Kent told Amsu if he was successful with his work, the Serpent would see to it that Amsu would leave Egypt. Kent, however, didn't tell him how he would leave.

With that settled, Maggie and Kent returned to Syria to inform Ashear that all was in place. "The Serpent will need some time to obtain intelligence on Seddik and his movements," Kent told Ashear. "The Serpent will be in touch as needed." Ashear was pleased. He informed Kent he would wire half the fee to the Serpent immediately. Maggie and Kent were on a plane back to France that night.

Washington DC—White House Residence

Nicole hung up the phone, just finishing her conversation with Sean. She told him the condo closing occurred with no issues, the furniture movers had begun to move items to storage, and she had culled through the last set of her work files. The small, but informative, legal notes meticulously typed up were returning home to Moscow with her. She needed to box up the rest of her clothes that she had brought from the condo and ship them to the embassy. She told Sean how she found her favorite pair of blue jeans and she had forgotten how comfortable they were. They had become her attire for the last few days as she worked around the condo after the closing. Sean's demeanor was bordering on cruel. It wasn't until Sean told her the press pictures snapped while removing some clothes from a car parked outside a back entrance to the White House did she understand his sentiments. Harsh replies and disbelief was Sean's response to every attempt Nicole made to reassure him she was flying home to him soon.

Nicole chose to sit with the Mercers at the state dinner. Jenkins wasn't happy that she wouldn't sit at the head table, but he respected her decision. She had made several adjustments to the arrangements, all of which Jenkins and his social secretary accepted with no arguments. Nicole spent many hours with the social secretary, providing insight into the image that Jenkins wanted to cultivate for himself as president and how important the little touches delicately placed would reinforce that image. The social secretary was immensely grateful for Nicole's input stating that Nicole had a natural knack for planning occasions.

With all that had occurred over the past four days, Nicole still managed to find time to visit her favorite shops and purchase a few items including a dress she couldn't live without—a black silk evening gown designed by Halston complete with silk evening gloves. She was in that dress as she talked to Sean but decided, because of his disposition, it would be better not to mention her attendance at the state dinner. Sean easily became irritated with her now and snapped at the smallest comment or insinuation. The distance between them, both mentally and physically, was making it hard for Nicole to look forward to returning.

She walked to the mirror and applied her lipstick, primped her hair, and did one final check of her outfit. She walked to the door and started down to the East Room for dinner. Earlier, she had informed Jenkins that she would not walk into the party on his arm. It was the only condition she had in exchange for her attendance. The press was already having a grand time snapping photos of her at every opportunity, and Sean made it clear that those photographs had made it back to him in Moscow. That was another discussion that didn't end nicely the day before. She knew she would regret not telling him about attending the dinner, but for just one night she wanted the enticing luxury of her old life back.

When Nicole arrived at the East Room, there was a noticeable acknowledgment of her entry. It wasn't a gasp, but more of an approving, gleeful confirmation of her presence. It shocked her. She swallowed her reluctance to move forward, taking a few steps toward the receiving line as she had done so many times with her former boss and friend, Tony Shafer, by her side. She glanced around the room, looking at familiar faces smiling at her.

"Mr. President," Nicole said, offering her hand to Jenkins as she was announced to him by the Marine by his side.

"Good evening, Nikki," Jenkins said, taking her hand and giving it a quick, subtle kiss. "Allow me to introduce Prime Minister Geoffrey Adkins."

Nicole was so busy scanning the guests in the room; she hadn't noticed Geoffrey. Nicole's face drained to a whiter shade of pale. Nowhere had Geoffry's name appeared during the planning and discussions of the dinner. At one point, Jenkins insisted the honored guest's identity was something she didn't need to know. Nicole was too busy to watch the news and Sean had no idea his brother was going to be at the White House. Nicole was certain that due to Sean's detachment, relevant things escaped him in the current dark state of his existence. "Prime Minister," Nicole managed to choke out of her now dry mouth. "It is a pleasure to see you again."

Laughing, Geoffrey opened his arms and engulfed Nicole into his arms. He cut the hug short, smiled, and stepped back to see an even more horrified Nicole. Geoffrey said, "Relax, Nicole. The president told me you were going to be here."

Nicole looked at Jenkins and then back at Geoffrey. She leaned into him. "Did you say anything to Sean?"

"No," Geoffrey replied with a hint of concern on his face. "Is there something wrong?"

"No," Nicole said as she took a few short steps sideways to allow Jenkins to greet his next guests. "I just haven't told him…"

"Well, you'll be sitting next to me at dinner. We can talk then. I'm sure he won't mind you being in my presence this evening." Geoffrey gently kissed her forehead. "It will be all right."

Nicole was even more confused now. She wondered what empowered him to kiss her forehead when they were barely comfortable enough to hug each other back in London. Geoffrey couldn't help but laugh at Nicole's obvious bewilderment.

"I owe you a hundred dollars, Mr. Prime Minister," Jenkins said quickly to Geoffrey, as he turned back to engage with the next guests.

"Yes," Geoffrey began. He winked at Nicole. "You certainly do." The two shared a brief snicker at Nicole's expense.

Nicole's confusion dissipated when she realized there was a bet between them. She stood looking at them both with a suspicious eye, plotting how she could return the favor.

Jenkins caught the look as he turned to introduce the next guests. Jenkins leaned in and whispered to Geoffrey, "We're in for it now."

Geoffrey looked at Nicole. "And I believe you owe me more money, sir."

"You know her better than I thought," Jenkins replied. "Nikki, go grab something to drink and say hello to Anne. She can't wait to see you." Jenkins was referring to Anne Mercer, who was standing off to the side impatiently waiting to greet her.

Nicole simply shook her head, turned, and walked into Anne's hug. "Hello, Anne."

"Nikki, I missed you so much," Anne said as she hugged Nicole. "How are you?"

Nicole ended the hug, stepping back. "I'm fine. I'm in Moscow with my new beau, the prime minister's brother, as a matter of fact."

"Yes, I know," Anne said. "I ran into Louise Barker the other day. I was shocked to see her. I was even more shocked to find out that she is divorcing her husband."

Surprise took Nicole. After processing the information, Nicole smiled. "Well, good for her," she mumbled to herself. She cleared her throat and said to Anne, "I see."

"No, you don't," Anne replied. "There is so much to tell you." She took Nicole by the hand and led her into the dining hall. "Louise told me that she couldn't go into the details, but after she talked to you, she couldn't go back to Larry. What did you tell her?"

"Anne," Nicole began. "I really can't say." Anne stopped and looked at Nicole. "You know I was never one to gossip, and I don't intend on starting now. Louise made her decision. I'm happy for her. I hope she finds some peace."

Anne frowned. "You always were a hard one to get to talk."

Nicole apologized. "I'm sorry it's the way I've always been. I don't see me changing." She took Anne by the arm and began walking to the bar. "Let's get something to drink."

After Nicole got her gin and tonic and Anne her chardonnay, the two women walked to a quiet area of the room by a window. Nicole took a sip of her drink thinking about the many times she and Sean enjoyed the beverage together. She had to admit, despite everything, she was beginning to miss him.

"You know," Anne began. "You still hold sway over Bobby. Daniel told me that he was supposed to be with Karen Grayson this evening."

"The movie star?" Nicole asked.

"Yes!" Anne said, the excitement evident in her voice. "He's been with her a couple of times now, and they seem to hit it off quite well."

"Karen Grayson—are you serious?" Nicole felt the pangs of jealousy, and she didn't like it. "What could they possibly have in common?" She looked at Anne. "Have you been with them? I mean, when they have been together?"

Anne smiled at Nicole's jealous reaction. "I told Louise that you still loved Bobby, and this is proof. You can't stand it, can you?"

Nicole took a stiff drink of her gin and tonic. She looked at Anne, then at Jenkins. She finally looked down at her drink, realizing how she was behaving. "I care for Bobby very much. He'll always have a place in my heart, but I'm in love with Ambassador Adkins." She paused a moment, wondering how serious this new relationship was. Could she be so easily replaced by a movie star? "If Bobby cares for Karen and they are happy, then I'll be happy for them both."

Anne gave a quiet, but detectable huff. "You will not. I saw that look. You still love him. Admit it! You are still in love with Bobby!"

Nicole looked at Jenkins again. She did still love him, and she could see herself adapting quickly to life in the White House with him. The evening felt strangely like a homecoming. All the usual suspects were in attendance. Nicole smirked at that thought. "I won't deny that it's complicated, but as I told you, I'm with Sean. I can't expect Bobby to wait for me. I hadn't heard he was seeing someone and that surprised me. I'm happy for him."

"I doubt he'll be seeing Karen after the week the press has had with you being here and then him canceling his date with her," Anne spat out. "If I were Karen Grayson, I wouldn't want to follow you."

Nicole cocked her head at Anne's last statement. "Anne, you don't think we've been…" Nicole's voice trailed off as she searched for the appropriate word. "Intimate this week, do you?"

"Honey, it isn't what I think that counts in this town," Anne replied. "The only thing I can tell you is that some people hope that you return to Moscow. They have enough trouble dealing with Bobby without you being around." Anne took a drink of her wine when she saw her husband motion to her. "Excuse me. Daniel wants me to join him." She took two steps before she turned back to Nicole. "All I can say is good for you. Keep both of them off balance." Anne winked as she quickened her steps to take Mercer's offered hand as Jenkins and Geoffrey entered the room.

Nicole took her seat next to Geoffrey at the head table after the president and the prime minister had arrived at their seats. She wondered how long Geoffrey had known she would be at the dinner. Was Sean testing her? Did Sean know and wanted to hear from her that she would be at the dinner? Her thoughts turned to the conversation with Anne. Did Jenkins break a date with a Hollywood starlet because she was here? She closed her eyes when she realized the media storm that was sure to hit in the morning. She wished now that she had mentioned the event to Sean. She scanned the room and realized she was only a few steps away from walking back into the life she had left behind. Was this a door opening for her? Was fate telling her she could step back into the life she missed? Could she leave Sean behind and embrace the opportunity before her with no regrets? Why was the thought of being back in Washington so enticing? She drew in a deep breath and exhaled.

Geoffrey heard her sigh even though he was listening to Jenkins address the attendees. He leaned over and whispered, "Are you all right, Sis?"

Nicole smiled at Geoffrey's attempt to make her comfortable with the situation. "Just peachy," she replied, sardonically.

"You mentioned you didn't tell Sean about this affair," Geoffrey spat out, then quickly regretted his choice of words. Nicole looked at him, about to give him a piece of her mind. "No—No—I didn't mean it that way. I mean the dinner."

Nicole wanted to laugh as Geoffrey realized his guffaw. "No, I haven't told him. There's a very good reason, and it has nothing to do with my friendship with Bobby. I hope—"

"That it doesn't get back to him?" Before Nicole could answer Geoffrey was called upon to give a few remarks. Nicole joined the applause a few seconds late as Geoffrey made his way to the podium. "Thank you for such a warm reception. I'll keep this short as I know you all must be famished. We have enjoyed a long history with our brothers and sisters here in the United States. We look forward to working with President Jenkins and his Congress to make both our countries attain their individual goals. On a more personal note, I have to say that I was both surprised and grateful that I get to spend some time with my brother's significant other and someone who has demonstrated her love of country with her bravery. My brother, Sean Adkins, who is Her Majesty's ambassador to the Soviet Union, couldn't be here this evening but sent Nicole Charbonneau to make my welcome here more reassuring. So, to everyone I heard whispering where Nicole had disappeared to, you now know that not only did she have the courage to expose a conspiracy, we in the UK grew quite fond of her and decided you can't have her back." The room gave a few laughs and scattered applause. Geoffrey pretended to wipe sweat from his brow. "My father is a much better storyteller and public speaker. So, to lower the risk of putting you all to sleep before your meal arrives, I'll simply add that I appreciate and am grateful to be President Jenkins's first state dinner, an honor not lost on this prime minister. Thank you for making me feel welcome." Geoffrey turned from the podium, shook Jenkins's hand, and returned to his seat.

"That was nice," Nicole began. "But Sean won't buy a word of it."

"You can't fault me for trying to help. I know you are looking out there and wondering if you made the right decision. But I don't know why you are pondering it. Is Sean all right?"

"It's not the right place, Geoff," Nicole said. "And don't worry, I'm going home to Moscow tomorrow evening."

A server arrived at the start of the five-course meal. The salad course was delivered to Nicole and Geoffrey at the same time. Following the salad was lobster bisque and then, the main course consisting of filet mignon, steamed asparagus with cheese sauce and a twice-baked potato. A cheese course fell between the main course and dessert. The waiters poured a tawny port for those who desired it. The port also accompanied the dark chocolate mousse dessert. At the end of the night, Nicole started to her bedroom after bidding Geoffrey and Jenkins good night. They invited her for a nightcap, but Nicole declined, preferring to let the two of them discuss the politics of the world. She also knew that she had some errands to run and boxes to pack the next day before she climbed aboard the plane to leave.

"Bobby," Nicole called to him just before the two men left for the study. She walked back to them so that she didn't have to speak loudly. "I almost forgot. Sean wants to meet with you in Brussels if you can make it happen. All I can say is that it is very important. I'd appreciate you taking some time to do so."

"Of course," Jenkins responded. He indicated with a hand gesture he wanted Geoffrey to continue to the study.

Nicole hugged Geoffrey. "Good night, Geoff," she said as she kissed his cheeks in the traditional European style.

"Good night," Geoffrey said, taking her hand. "Whatever it is, Nicole, he'll be all right. He loves you dearly, and he'll do anything to keep you."

Nicole was grateful for Geoffrey's reassurance even if she didn't believe him. "I expect that I'll see you in the morning before I leave."

Geoffrey nodded and said, "I'll see you then." He left for the study.

"You know I would never say no to meeting with Sean. Tell him I look forward to seeing him. I'll share my European trip with you over breakfast, and you can pick a time. I'll make whatever changes are needed."

Nicole gave him a quick smile, kissing him on the cheek. "Thank you."

"My pleasure," Jenkins replied, returning a kiss on her cheek. He smiled at her scrutinizing gaze. "What?"

"Karen Grayson? Honestly Bobby," Nicole said, shaking her head in disbelief.

"I doubt that will be of anyone's concern any longer," Jenkins quipped.

"So it is true," Nicole countered. "You did break a date with her this evening because I was here." Jenkins only smiled at the accusations. Nicole shook her head. "My ego isn't that fragile. You know you are free to see anyone you want."

Jenkins gave Nicole a sheepish look. "Am I?" She reached again for Jenkins's hand, giving it one last squeeze. She could see the love in Jenkins's eyes and was deeply touched. Jenkins did not release her hand. Looking her in the eye, he whispered, "May I?" He gently brought Nicole to him.

Nicole put her free hand on Jenkin's chest, stopping short of accepting his embrace. "I can't," she whispered, breathlessly. "It's not that I don't care for you, I do, but I love Sean. I can't do this." Nicole pulled away from Jenkins. The temptation to kiss him still taunting her. When Jenkins broke their eye contact, Nicole withdrew her hands and turned for her suite. "Geoffrey's waiting for you. I'll see you in the morning." She smiled when she heard Jenkins's anguished sigh; no doubt expressed loudly for her to hear. Jenkins turned to join Geoffrey in the study.

The next day, Nicole looked over the European tour with Jenkins at the breakfast table. She jotted down a few dates and indicated to Jenkins that it might be better to add a day in Brussels to accommodate the meeting with Sean. Jenkins agreed to Nicole's request. After a few minutes, Nicole and Jenkins parted. The president had a full day of meetings. Jenkins hugged and kissed her on the cheek as he left the breakfast room for his office. Nicole looked at Duncan, sighed, and announced they should leave in the next two hours to run some errands before boarding the plane. With that, both quit the room to finish packing.

Moscow, USSR—United Kingdom Embassy

Sean was sitting at his desk with Stacy leaning over him, her long brunette hair tickling his cheek. Stacy's right hand and arm rested on Sean's chair back. Her left hand was placed on the desk, just a whisper of space between her hand and Sean's. Stacy's body language and sweet laughter tempted Sean. As Stacy's breathy voice tickled Sean's ear, she informed him of the contents of a report she had prepared for him. It was nothing important, and it certainly didn't require his immediate attention. More and more, Sean found himself seeking her company. Nicole's absence and subsequent attendance at Jenkins's state dinner didn't help Sean's misdirected desires.

Sean turned his head, almost nose to nose with Stacy as he felt her warm breath caress his face. He smelled her perfume, and its scent heightened his desire. He paused just long enough.

"I can see I was not missed," Nicole said, shattering the silence in the room. She was leaning against the door frame, arms crossed. She saw Sean's surprise drain from his face as it flushed with embarrassment.

"Nicole," he said, as he pushed his chair back and started to walk toward her, avoiding walking past Stacy, who was now standing up straight with an arrogant, defiant look on her face. She looked happy that she and Sean were caught in their intimate moment.

Nicole shook her head. "Don't you dare," she said as she unbuttoned her coat, turned, and walked back through Stewart's office. Stewart looked up from his work as she passed his desk. She quickened her pace.

"Nicole wait," Sean said as he followed her into Stewart's office. Sean was not pleading; he sounded angry.

Nicole opened her office door, turned, and said to Sean, "If you know what's good for you, you will stay away from me right now." She then slammed the door in Sean's face.

Sean stood there for a minute, his eyes closed as he tried to gather himself. He brought his right hand to his mouth as he contemplated entering Nicole's office. The anger he felt that morning when he saw the pictures and headlines regarding the state dinner rose up inside him. It fortified him enough to ignore Nicole's warning. He opened the door and walked confidently into her office, slamming the door behind him. "You're warning me after you attended a state dinner—"

"With your brother—the prime minister," Nicole shot back. "I was not Bobby's date. I walked into the room alone, and on no man's arm. I was not whispering in Bobby's ear or presenting my breasts to him like that," she said, gesturing to Stacy in Sean's office. "At no time did Bobby turn his head with my head only centimeters from it. NOTHING like I just witnessed in your office occurred the entire time I was at the White House." Nicole's lips curled in revulsion. "How could you even think I would betray you like that?" Sean stood looking at her. "Maybe I should have stayed in Washington. Maybe I don't belong here."

"Nicole," Sean began but stopped when she raised her hand, turning her head and allowing her long, cinnamon-red hair to hide the hurtful tears welling up in her eyes.

"Just go," Nicole whispered breathlessly, her left hand still in the air as her right lay flat against her chest in the region of her wounded heart.

"I will for now," Sean started as he walked to the door that joined their offices. "I'll be in the residence when you are ready to talk."

Nicole didn't answer or look at him. She heard the door close. She sat down at her desk, grabbed a tissue, and dabbed her eyes. She knew there had to be something special about Stacy that drew Sean to her. She knew she had to find out, but she didn't know how to do that. She sat back in her chair and stared out the window. "I should have stayed in Washington," she said wistfully.

CHAPTER EIGHT
APRIL 1981

Moscow, USSR—United Kingdom Embassy

Seven days after she caught Sean in an intimate moment with Stacy, Nicole stood outside and watched as Sean's motorcade departed for the airport. Both Nicole and Sean were supposed to travel to France and then on to Brussels to meet with Jenkins. In the past seven weeks, however, Sean's demeanor had become worse; anger and bitterness seemed to spring from his lips no matter how hard Nicole tried to present her conversations to him calmly. The nightmares returned every night, and now it seemed Sean couldn't close his eyes for longer than an hour before the horror would commence. Sean's face seemed to have aged before Nicole's eyes. His disposition returned to the man she had seen when they first met, with one major difference: Sean's ability to deal with his demon had diminished. Last night, while Sean tossed and turned in their bed, Nicole had slipped out, dressed, and walked to the security complex of the embassy. She met with Alistair and changed the arrangements for the trip. She alerted Alistair to Sean's condition and urged him not to leave him alone no matter how much he complained or demanded. Alistair voiced his concern but ultimately agreed to Nicole's request. She also asked that Duncan remain behind.

In the morning, Nicole pretended that she was still accompanying Sean. She watched how his mood seemed to lift with the thought of being away from the embassy. As they walked to the limo, Nicole announced that she was not joining him. Sean snapped at Nicole for what appeared to be a last-minute decision. Alistair watched with consternation the interaction between them. Nicole explained that they needed a break. She couldn't continue to be his punching bag. She motioned for Alistair to join their conversation. "I've instructed Alistair not to leave your side, just as you instructed Duncan not to leave mine." Sean's face contorted with anger, his lips taut, brows furrowed, and his eyes glared at her. "Have a safe trip," she stated. She motioned to the limo with her arm and hand, her stubborn demeanor indicating that Sean was not going to win this argument. "Duncan will stay here. Now go before I say something else that we'll both regret."

Sean's angry huffs started to decrease when he realized that maybe being away from Nicole again was needed. He didn't recall being annoyed when she was in Washington, except for when he talked to her directly. He turned for the limo without attempting to kiss her goodbye. As much as that hurt Nicole, she didn't show it.

Nicole knew she had very little time to determine the reason for the return of Sean's demon. As the gates to the embassy closed, Nicole walked inside the building closing the door behind her. Stewart had also escorted them to the limo as was the custom. After discarding her coat, she handed it to Stewart and said, "Please take this back to my office. I have some things I need to attend to elsewhere."

"Yes, ma'am," Stewart replied. "Is there anything I can do to help you?"

Nicole looked at Stewart. "No, this is something I need to figure out on my own. I'll be back in my office shortly."

"Can I ask where you'll be?"

"With Elliot," Nicole blurted out as she started to walk away from him. She immediately wished she hadn't told Stewart where she was going. She quickly walked to Elliot's office, swiping her identification card upon reaching the door. She typed in an additional code and opened the door when it buzzed. When safely inside Nicole said, "Elliot, I need your help."

Elliot was sitting at his computer desk. He pushed his thick black-rimmed glasses back up his nose. His thick hair looked like it hadn't been combed in days not an uncommon condition to anyone who knew him. "I thought you were going to Paris and Brussels," he commented.

"Change of plans," Nicole countered. "Sean just left. I need you to get me information on Stacy Cambridge," Nicole said as she grabbed a chair and sat it next to Elliot.

Elliot smiled. "I was wondering when this was going to come up. Sean had asked me some time ago to check her out."

Nicole looked at Elliot with confusion. "Sean asked you to do this," she questioned. "When? Why?"

Elliot looked at Nicole. "He asked when he first met her. I think why is pretty evident."

"Maybe to you," Nicole retorted. "Has Sean seen the information?"

"No," Elliot replied. "I've told him several times I have it, but he hasn't made it down here to look it over. He made it clear he didn't want it anywhere near his office."

Nicole looked at Elliot. It was now clear to Nicole that Sean was making a concerted effort to keep the information from her. "May I see the information please?"

Elliot stood up, walked to a door behind him, and unlocked it without saying a word. The opened door revealed a small room with a safe taking up most of the space. He inserted another key in the safe door and then dialed a combination of numbers on the wheel located next to a lever. He opened the safe and removed a manila folder. He went through the procedure in reverse to close the safe. Nicole watched Elliot walk back to his seat without saying a word. "After I saw her, I confirmed Sean's suspicions. He asked me to find any information on her, and I also spoke with the home office a few weeks ago." Elliot hesitated.

"I need you to trust me, Elliot," Nicole urged him. "I know you probably aren't allowed to show me that, but I have to know." Elliot sat quietly. "Sean used to have these nightmares—"

"I know all about the nightmares," Elliot interrupted.

"Are you aware that they have returned?"

"I thought they might have," Elliot said. He set the manila folder on the desk in front of Nicole and sighed. He did not attempt to hand Nicole the information.

"Please," Nicole beseeched him. "You aren't the one who is sleeping next to him. He isn't pushing you away from him. We said no secrets. He is lying to me. I know he knows what is causing the nightmares. I need to understand why we are living in this hell and how I can help him. I can't do that if I don't know what has happened to create this predicament." Elliot looked down, gritted his teeth, and shook his head. Nicole added, "You can leave the room if need be."

Elliot scratched his head. He thought about Sean's recent changes and how happy he was with Nicole before coming to Moscow. He, like Nicole, preferred the other Sean—the happier Sean. "Oh, fuck regulations!" Elliot scooted his chair in and grabbed the folder. "Stacy Cambridge is Katrina Natalinsky. This—," Elliot opened the folder and picked up a black and white photograph—"is the way she looked in the summer of last year. In the fall, she started having a series of operations. In November, she looked like this." Elliot handed her the photo of Katrina, who had transformed into Stacy. There were some scars still apparent from the nose job, accompanied by some bruising around the eyes and cheekbones.

"So, Katrina is a spy?" Nicole asked, holding the photograph of Stacy after the surgeries.

Elliot swallowed. "She's more than a spy. She's the spitting image of Sean's wife, Sarah."

Nicole turned white as a ghost as the blood drained from her face. It explained the return of the nightmares and the guilt Sean felt in failing Sarah. It explained Sean's attitude, and how he was pushing her away from him. She looked at Elliot, her eyes searching for an answer in his. She looked back at the photograph. "His wife…"

"You've never seen a picture of her?"

"No," Nicole said. "I never asked to see one either. He made it clear it was in the past."

"There's more," Elliot said as he reached for a third photograph and handed it to Nicole. With the shock apparent on her face, she looked at Elliot.

"That was taken in Nice, France, two weeks before you and Sean arrived at the embassy."

Nicole pointed to a man who had his back to the camera. "Who is this?"

"I don't know," Elliot replied. "But look closer. Look at the person who is walking off to their right."

Nicole brought the photograph closer to her eyes. When she recognized the person, her mouth dropped open, and the photograph slipped from her fingers landing askew on the floor. Her breathing started to quicken.

Elliot could sense her fear as it started to engulf her. He reached out and secured one of Nicole's hands in his. "Nicole, look at me." Nicole's eyes were searching the room, not focusing on anything as her mind started racing through a thousand scenarios. "Nicole!" Elliot shouted. Nicole's eyes rested on Elliot. "Listen to me. Are you listening?"

"Yes," Nicole said.

"That was months ago," Elliot said. "Take some deep breaths." Elliot waited. "Here's what we don't know. We don't know if Kent met Stacy and this other person. We don't know if they are working together."

"Bulshit!" Nicole exclaimed. "Do you know the odds of those two people being in the same place at the same time in a photograph? Jesus, Elliot! If your intelligence agents are lucky enough just to happen to catch Stacy and Kent in a photograph together, then they should buy a fucking lottery ticket!" Nicole took her hand from Elliot. She bent down and picked up the photograph she had dropped. "Whoever this third person is, they know each other. Look at Kent's eyes. He is looking at this person!" Nicole pointed to the unidentified man. "No one knows who this is? Are they Soviet too?"

"We don't know," Elliot replied. "The fact that we can only see part of the back of his head isn't helping, not to mention the hat he is wearing."

Nicole sat for a moment looking at the photograph. "Sean is going to Paris. This meeting took place in Nice. Is he walking into a trap? If we assume this other man is a Soviet spy, how can we be sure Leznikov isn't compromised or setting a trap for Sean?"

"Sean is well aware that Saverio lived somewhere in France," Elliot said. "And thanks to Maggie, we know exactly where Kent lives now. When you decided not to go, how much of a fight did Sean put up?"

"He wasn't happy I went behind his back and asked Alistair never to leave his side. But he didn't seem as upset as I thought he'd be," Nicole replied. "You think Sean felt better knowing I was here, far away from the country Kent lives in now?" Nicole was seeking confirmation.

"That's my guess," Elliot replied.

"I don't get you guys," Nicole began. "If you know where Kent lives, why don't you go take him out?"

"We might need him," Elliot stated flatly.

"OK—you think that makes sense, but it doesn't," Nicole countered, her frustration showing. "It makes no sense at all. If MI6 would go in there and arrest him or kill him, my life would be a whole lot easier." Elliot smiled at her rant. "How—just how—could Kent be useful to us?"

"With Maggie providing information, we might be able to stop certain assassinations before they happen, direct his movements if she can gain his trust, or even get something as small as a piece of intelligence we didn't get somewhere else."

Nicole sighed. She could see how that might be useful. She knew when she was defeated. "It would make my life easier. That's all I'm saying."

Elliot laughed. "I know it would."

"I want Katrina, or Stacy—whatever we call her—out of here," Nicole asserted. "Can I do that?"

"Do what?" Elliot asked, wanting to make sure he understood exactly what Nicole wanted to do.

"I want her out of the embassy and out of our lives," Nicole said, clearly irritated.

"Out of the building and revoking her credentials you can do," Elliot said. "Out of your lives might be a little harder. We can't just kill her."

"She's a spy in our embassy. Why can't we?" Nicole knew she wouldn't get an answer. "Is there a way to have her sent to SIS for interrogation? Maybe she would tell us who this third person is."

"She'll kill herself before that happens," Elliot stated.

Nicole looked at Elliot knowing he expected her to change her course of action. Without showing any emotion, she replied, "Problem solved." She started to leave when Elliot called to her.

"You realize that means we don't find out who this third person is."

"Who said questions wouldn't be asked? I'm a former prosecutor. I think it is time Stacy and I became acquainted." Nicole opened the door. "Call Duncan and tell him to bring a security team to my office." With that, Nicole left Elliot's office.

She walked to the bullpen where the lower-ranking members of the embassy staff worked translating Soviet newspapers and other documents. She walked into the open area of cubicles and scanned the large room for Stacy. When she located her, she walked over to her.

"Excuse me, Stacy," Nicole said, interrupting a conversation between Stacy and two other British staffers. "Could you accompany me to Sean's office? He wanted to follow up on the report you gave him some days ago." Nicole managed to have just the right amount of animosity in her voice to make her sound jealous.

"Yes, of course," Stacy replied. The defiant, yet confident tone in her voice was apparent. Stacy was playing her role well. She turned to her colleagues and said with a smile, "Excuse me."

Stacy and Nicole left the bullpen area. The two did not talk on the way to Sean's office. Nicole wondered how long it took Stacy to refine her British accent. She wondered if Kent had anything to do with it. She also wondered if Stacy sounded anything like Sarah. Nicole was surprised when she arrived at the locked outer office door. She briefly wondered where Stewart had wandered off to or if he had even bothered to deliver her coat as instructed. Nicole unlocked the outer office door. She smiled as she motioned for Stacy to enter. She left the door open and walked into her office unlocking the door. "Sean will be down in a moment. Would you mind?" Nicole gestured with an open hand, indicating she would like Stacy to enter her office. Stacy smiled and obliged, albeit hesitant at first. Nicole noticed her coat lying on a chair just inside the door. So, Stewart had returned to the offices but left again. She shrugged off her thoughts of Stewart to focus on Stacy.

Stacy walked in and took notice that Nicole left her office door open as well. "Please sit down," Nicole said as she passed Stacy continuing to the front of her desk. Stacy sat down across from her. "I was telling Sean the other day how remiss we have been in getting to know everyone here at the embassy. How long have you worked here, Stacy?"

"Only a couple of months," Stacy replied.

"And before working here, you worked where?"

"I worked in London."

"In the Foreign Office or another occupation that gave you the experience for a job in an embassy?"

Stacy squirmed, feeling as if she was under interrogation, which, of course, she was. "Is there something wrong?"

"No, not at all," Nicole said with a smile. "It's just that you look so familiar. I'm trying to place you. I was curious if perhaps we met at one of the parties thrown by the members of Parliament. There were always so many people at those parties—the MPs, of course, and their staffs, not to mention the prime minister himself."

Stacy smiled, "That must have been it."

Nicole nodded her head, for effect not agreement. "Whose staff?"

"Well, I didn't exactly work for—"

"Oh, you were dating someone?"

Stacy was almost too relieved that Nicole provided her with an out in the conversation. "Yes, I was."

"I think I remember now. Was it Kent? He was the staffer to Prime Minister Wharton." Nicole waited for Stacy's reaction. "I have to say; I wouldn't blame you if you were a bit embarrassed. Kent never quite fit into Wharton's staff." Stacy smiled and gave a quick nod of the head. Nicole acknowledged Duncan and his men just as she asked, "Wouldn't you agree, Katrina?" Nicole watched as the blood drained from Stacy's face. "Come in, Duncan. We were finishing up."

"I don't know what you're talking about, ma'am. My name is Stacy, not—"

"Drop the act, Katrina," Nicole responded as Duncan and the two other men surrounded her. The third man stood blocking the door. "Sean isn't here. In his absence, I get to deal with you. I've seen intelligence reports, and I know you know Kent Chapman. I know you had your face altered so that you would look like Sarah Adkins. And I know you are a spy. What I don't know is who placed you here. Were you sent here by Kent to inform him of our movements or are you solely working for someone in the KGB?"

Katrina smiled. "I don't have to tell you anything." Her perfect British accent morphed into her native Russian.

"No, you don't," Nicole said. "And you won't see Kent again, so I suppose there is no reason to tell me. Since you will probably take your own life, there's no reason to exclude torture during your interrogation…" Nicole was pretending to think about the many ways she could get her to talk. She let a devious smile slowly appear on her lips as she gazed off into the distance as if she could see the pain and agony Katrina would endure. Nicole allowed a sinister laugh to leave her lips. It was all an act, a performance well done as she saw a quick, surprised look appear briefly on Duncan's face. "Duncan, you need to make sure that she has nothing on her before you put her in her cell. I don't want to find out that she took a cyanide pill or cut her own throat."

"Yes, ma'am," Duncan said.

"Of course, Katrina, if you would tell me who Kent is working with, I'd allow you to take your life in a more dignified and less painful way," Nicole said, looking at Katrina. "Any way you look at it, you're dead."

Katrina threw her head back in defiance before she brought her sinister eyes to rest on Nicole. Katrina suppressed the surprise she felt when Nicole wasn't flinching an inch at her attempt to rile Nicole. "You American women are all alike," she began. "You think your Sean is so exceptional." Her face gnarled as she spat out, "You think you are something special to him. That there was Sarah and then you. Have you asked him how many women he has raped on the trail of the Serpent?" Katrina sneered. "I would rather be dead than seduce such a vile creature again. Having him inside me made me want to die. You think you do me a favor by finding out I am a spy? Ha! You do me a favor that I don't have to suck his cock!"

Throughout Katrina's tirade, Nicole didn't blink, move, or make any sound. Nicole noted the comment about them fucking, but she didn't react to it as Katrina wanted. Nicole was stoic. She waited, glaring at Katrina, anticipating the moment when Katrina would squirm under Nicole's unspoken treachery. Finally, Katrina did fidget. Nicole wanted to smile, but she just continued to cast an evil eye at Katrina. Coldly, Nicole finally said, "Tell me who Kent is working with here."

Katrina's mouth scrunched up as she gathered saliva. She stood up quickly and tried to spit in Nicole's face. Duncan and the other guards grabbed Katrina before she could successfully land her spit on her adversary's face, landing on Nicole's neck instead.

Every muscle in Nicole's body wanted to attack Katrina. Slap her! Hit her! Shoot her! Her mind was screaming. But instead, Nicole watched Katrina try to free herself from the guards. "Take this bitch to the brig." Nicole grabbed the jaw of the still-struggling Katrina. "You have two hours to tell me what I want to know, or I truly will make your life hell." She released Katrina.

"It was hell when I had to fuck your precious Sean," Katrina yelled back as the guards began to drag her out of Nicole's office.

"Then I will certainly help you find a fate worse than hell," Nicole shot back as the guards dragged Katrina down the hallway. She sat down at her desk, grabbed a tissue, and wiped the spit from her neck. She tossed the tissue in the waste can and buried her head in her hands, resting her elbows on her desk.

Unbeknownst to Nicole, Elliot was standing at the door watching all that had occurred. "Nicole, are you all right?"

Nicole looked up at Elliot. She ran her fingers through her hair. "Yeah," she said as she turned her head to gaze out the window.

"Nicolc, interrogating spies is different than prosecuting thcm in a court of law," Elliot offered.

Nicole gritted her teeth and turned her gaze back at Elliot. "Oh really? Have you stood toe to toe with a Ku Klux Klan member who has no problem showing his hatred for women and minorities, spitting on you at every opportunity and is only satisfied when they have either broken you, raped you, or hung you?"

"No," Elliot replied. "I prefer working with computers."

"Then don't lecture me about interrogating spies," Nicole uttered. "I've been here many times. I just forgot how ugly it is."

"We should have waited for Sean. That's all I'm saying. Let Sean deal with her."

Nicole looked at Elliot with disgust. She stood and removed her Beretta from the small of her back. She removed the magazine and checked the number of bullets before she replaced it. She prepared the gun, checking to make sure the safety was on before tucking it back into her pants at the small of her back. She decided that Katrina would not have two hours. She pushed her way past Elliot and headed down the hallway to the brig.

As she entered, she saw that Duncan was searching Katrina's clothes. Without saying a word, Nicole walked directly into the holding cell area. Katrina was in a hospital gown, which tied in the back. Duncan had handcuffed Katrina's wrists to the holding cell's bars. Seated on a hard metal bench, her back against the wall, she scoffed when she saw Nicole walk into the area. Nicole drew her firearm, unlocked the safety, and took aim—an inch to the right of Katrina's head. She didn't hesitate to fire.

"What the fuck!" Katrina screamed as Nicole aimed at the same spot. "Bitch—stop it!"

Duncan ran into the room as Nicole took her second shot, the bullet striking the hole made by the previous bullet. "Tell me what I want to know."

"Nicole—"

"Shut up or get out of here, Duncan," Nicole yelled, not taking her aim or eyes off Katrina. "I know what you're asking yourself, 'Is she that good of a shot? Could she hit that small hole twice?' Do you want to find out?"

Elliot ran into the holding area and stopped dead in his tracks when he saw Nicole pointing her gun at Katrina. "Nicole!"

"Elliot, like Duncan, you can shut up or leave," Nicole said as she changed her aim for the center of Katrina's head. "Have you figured out that I put those bullets right where I intended them to go? Tell me what I want to know."

"You won't kill me. You want to know what I know too badly," Katrina dared her.

"Wanna bet?" Nicole asked rhetorically, her voice even, yet threatening. Katrina scoffed. Nicole squeezed the trigger, quickly changing her aim to graze Katrina's shoulder.

Katrina screamed, yanking her handcuffed hands, a reaction of wanting to cover the wound. "Fuck!" she painfully screamed in Russian. "Fuck you!"

"You said you fucked my man. You don't think I'm pissed? Tell me what I want to know." Nicole moved the aim of her Beretta to just below Katrina's belly. "This one will really hurt."

Blood was soaking Katrina's gown where the bullet had grazed her. She had no doubt now that Nicole was as good as she professed. With her eyes, Katrina lined up where Nicole was aiming: Katrina's sacral area. "Wait—" she yelled when she saw that Nicole was about to pull the trigger. Katrina was not about to finger her comrade, but she knew she had to give Nicole a name. She thought of the one person who would end her life quickly. Katrina also knew that Nicole could not touch this person. "Valesky is my contact."

"Why?"

"Why what, bitch?"

Nicole shot another bullet into the wall an inch to the right of her head. "I don't like your attitude. Why Valesky?" She moved the gun to Katrina's sacral area again.

"You think he tells me why he does things? He's Valesky. He wants information on you and to fuck with you," Katrina spat out. Nicole started to pull back on the trigger. "I'm telling you the truth."

"Nicole, Valesky wouldn't tell her everything," Elliot calmly stated.

"How many times did you meet with Kent?" Nicole questioned. When the answer wasn't forthcoming, Nicole pulled the trigger hitting the hole next to Katrina's head a third time.

"Once—in Nice," Katrina exclaimed.

"Nicole," Duncan calmly said. "Enough."

Nicole slowly released the trigger. "Drop this whore outside the gate."

"They'll kill me!" Katrina yelled.

"You think I honestly give a fuck?" Nicole shot back. "Get rid of her!" Nicole walked out of the brig. Duncan and Elliot moved aside to let her pass.

Elliot looked at Duncan, shocked at what he had witnessed. He motioned to Duncan to carry out her order.

Duncan took Katrina out of the cell. He started down the hallway with the handcuffed and barefoot Katrina.

Elliot ran after Nicole, catching her in a hallway on the way back to her office. "Sean is going to be furious!"

"I guess that's my problem, isn't it?" Nicole said as she continued to walk back to her office. She and Elliot stopped when they reached the bullpen area. They watched the reaction of the aides who were looking out the window. One of the aides noted that the woman looked like Stacy. A collective gasp escaped their lips and told Nicole that she would never have to worry about Katrina Natalinsky again. She didn't engage any of the staffers who turned to look at her.

"Who called Valesky?" Elliot whispered his question to Nicole.

"I don't know," Nicole replied. "But someone in this embassy did. Get me the phone records—outgoing calls made in the last hour." Elliot nodded as he left Nicole's side for his own office.

Nicole slowly walked back to her office in silence. She sat down behind her desk. She took in a deep breath and exhaled. She repeated this a few more times. It was then that she realized that Sean was no longer a conundrum to her.

Brussels, Belgium—The Hotel Brussels

Jenkins was in the middle of his first overseas visit that included the United Kingdom, Germany, Belgium, Egypt, Isreal, and France, staying an extra day in Brussels to meet with Sean and Nicole. Jenkins was returning to his hotel after meeting with the Belgian prime minister a second time. While the trip was going extremely well, the most worrisome part was about to occur. After Brussels, Jenkins was flying to Egypt to calm the nerves of Amon Seddik, who was under growing pressure to throw aside the peace accord he had signed with Isreal. But Jenkins didn't want to think about that yet. He was eager to see Nicole, and he had to admit, he wanted to see Sean too, especially now that he knew Sean's nightmares had returned. Because of his discussion with Nicole in the White House residence, Jenkins needed reassurance that Sean and Nicole's relationship was still intact. He wanted to assess Sean himself and determine if Sean was capable of protecting Nicole and, more importantly, could be in a relationship with her. *If he can't, then I'll voice my concerns and encourage Nicole's return to the United States*, he thought.

He arrived back at his hotel, moved quickly to his penthouse suite, and grabbed a bottle of water off the table. He sat down on the couch, sighed, and assumed his familiar pose with the index finger and thumb of his right hand above his eyebrows. "Dear God, give me strength," he murmured. Jenkins was tiring of the constant need to reassure his allies that he was a competent leader despite his comparably young age and recent events.

Whittaker walked into the room with a manila folder in his hand. "Is your headache still bothering you?"

Jenkins removed his fingers and looked at Whittaker. "It hasn't stopped since the meeting in Germany. If I hear one more time how our allies' governments are concerned about the strength of our government given the previous administration's damaging behavior, I think I'll scream." He saw Whittaker choke back a chuckle. "It's not funny." Jenkins opened the water bottle in his hand and took a drink.

"No, sir," Whittaker agreed. "But this is the first time in a very long time that they get to gloat a bit."

"It's not gloating," Jenkins started. "They think the United States is weak and our attention is on other things. They see us becoming an isolationist nation." Jenkins paused as he thought for a moment. He turned his head, looking out the window but not seeing the view. "Given all the latest rhetoric and shenanigans by our Congress, I can't say that I blame them for that impression."

"That's why you are here," Whittaker said. "To reassure them that the US is fully capable and welcomes any opportunity to aid our NATO allies if the time comes."

Jenkins slowly turned his head to look at Whittaker. "Please tell me you haven't been writing my speeches."

Whittaker laughed. "You know I haven't." He walked over to the president and handed him the manila folder. "This is the latest security report for our trip to Egypt."

"You look concerned," Jenkins said as he accepted the folder.

"I think it would be better to make this stop at a different time," Whittaker said. "There are some riots, and Seddik has reason to be concerned."

"All the more reason to go," Jenkins said. "He signed a peace accord with Isreal, brokered by the United States. There is a lot of resistance. It was a huge risk for him to do so, and I have no doubt that he has received death threats." Jenkins tossed the folder onto the table in front of him. "I think I must visit him in Egypt. We can't abandon him now if the peace accord is to have any chance of success."

Whittaker acknowledged the decision with a quick nod. "The ambassador from the United Kingdom who serves Her Majesty in the Soviet Union is here to see you."

Jenkins laughed at Whittaker's tone of voice. "I take it you don't like that I am meeting with him."

Very tongue in cheek, Whittaker said, "Whatever gave you that idea?"

Jenkins smiled. "Send the ambassador in, please." Jenkins stood up and buttoned his suit jacket. Sean entered the room and waited for acknowledgment by Jenkins. Jenkins started to walk toward Sean and extended his hand. “Mr. Ambassador.”

“Mr. President,” Sean greeted, taking Jenkins’s hand in his.

“Is Nikki not with you?” Jenkins asked, looking past Sean.

“No, she is not. She decided at the last minute to stay in Moscow. She said she had something to attend to that couldn’t wait.” Sean noticed the disbelief on Jenkins’s face. Jenkins noted the small amount of anger in Sean’s voice. “I assure you it was not my idea that she stay behind. I’m only here for today, leaving in a few hours for home. I have full faith in our security force.”

“That’s not what that look was about,” Jenkins countered. “It is unlike her to not be by your side.” Sean agreed by nodding his head. Jenkins didn’t want to tip Sean off that Nicole had confided in him. “What was so important?”

“I have no idea,” Sean admitted. “She wouldn’t tell me. I’m not sure I’ll find out either.”

“Another secret between you two? I find that even harder to believe,” Jenkins responded.

“Another secret?” Sean questioned. Jenkins’s comment was enough for Sean to know that Nicole did indeed disclose to Jenkins the return of his nightmares. “I assume Nicole took the opportunity while in Washington to cry on your shoulder?”

At first, Jenkins didn’t like Sean’s tone. He wanted to lash out but decided to keep his manner civil. “We both know Nikki doesn’t cry on anyone’s shoulder.” Jenkins’s words were bitterly true, and Sean knew that. “She’s concerned about you, Sean. I am too. Tell me you have this under control, and I’ll back off.”

Sean shrugged his shoulders, preferring not to enter into that conversation at all. “My only course of action is to hope I find out upon my return what was so urgent.”

“That isn’t reassuring,” Jenkins countered. He looked Sean in the eyes. “What can I do?”

“Stay out of it,” Sean told him.

Jenkins allowed the conversation to end knowing that he made it clear to Nicole that she had options. He stepped aside and motioned to the couch.

“I was rather hopeful that you fancy some fresh air. It’s a very pleasant day, and I doubt you have had the opportunity to enjoy the view,” Sean stated.

Jenkins nodded his head, and the two men started for the balcony. The Secret Service moved quickly outside, one agent informing Jenkins they wanted to secure the location. The canvas canopy that provided both shade and cover from prying eyes had been extended earlier in the day in case Jenkins wandered outside. An agent moved the table and chairs closer to the wall and then indicated where he wanted the president to sit. Jenkins moved to the indicated seat. Sean glanced around and moved a chair closer to the wall and Jenkins. Both men were looking out at the cityscape.

“We have an opportunity to wreak a little havoc on our Soviet adversary that could take them years to recover from if we do this correctly,” Sean teased.

Jenkins was taken aback and turned his whole body to face Sean. “Are you still in the intelligence game?”

Sean smiled, “It was never a game, and I was never out.”

"What if they find out you're MI6?" Jenkins questioned. "I don't think this is very fair to Nikki. I know that sounds somewhat ridiculous, but honestly, Sean, I thought the whole idea was to keep Nikki safe. Now I find out you are still spying, collecting espionage—"

"Do you want to hear what I have come to tell you?" Sean looked briefly at Jenkins before he returned his gaze to the cityscape.

Jenkins fidgeted in his seat and finally said, "Your disregard for Nikki's feelings and your recent treatment of her is beginning to piss me off." Jenkins caught a glimpse of Sean's anger out of the corner of his eye. He exhaled his frustration the best he could. "Tell me."

"There is a chap named Leznikov who is with the KGB. I ran into him a few times when I was tracking down the Serpent. We always stayed out of each other's work, and, well, now he is in Baranov's cabinet and recognized me at the first party we attended."

"You're compromised?!"

"No, not really. That's the odd part," Sean replied.

Jenkins scoffed. "You either are or aren't compromised. There is no in-between. You know that. Get out of there."

"As I mentioned earlier, I have full confidence in our security detail at the embassy. I do know how to take care of myself. I have killed people, remember? And prepare yourself for this one: Nicole knows how to shoot a gun, so I have full confidence in her abilities as well."

"What?" Jenkins exclaimed, surprise written all over his face.

"You heard me. Nicole impressed our security detail with her display of marksmanship shortly after we arrived."

"She killed someone?" Jenkins was in total shock.

"No! God no!" Sean retorted. "But she did practice with the Beretta I bought her, and she shot an SA80. She won a bet." Sean bragged his pride of her on display. "I've seen her shoot. She has game. So, between the security detail, my skills, and knowledge that Nicole has some skills, I'm not worried."

Jenkins shook his head. "I'm glad you're not. Quit playing games, and get out of there."

"Bobby—I mean—" Sean stopped when he realized he didn't refer to Jenkins as Mr. President.

"Bobby's fine," Jenkins said.

"Bobby, trust me, we have to get this right. Leznikov came to me and told me that he has some information he wants to share with us."

Jenkins was still angry with Sean. "I can't believe you are that naïve. I can't believe you are putting you and Nikki at risk. I can't believe that you are so irresponsible."

"I'm not," Sean replied. "I'm not going to do it."

"You want me to enable you," Jenkins mumbled.

"No," Sean replied. "I want France to do it, and I want the USA's help, preferably the CIA and Thompson's help at the FBI."

"Why France and why our help?"

"A contact of mine, who is in the Direction de la Surveillance du Territoire, will meet with Leznikov and set up an operation to acquire the stolen documents from him. I need to meet with Leznikov again, and it needs to be Leznikov who is our contact inside. Any new personnel in his area will be under intense scrutiny. Either Leznikov is all in, or the operation doesn't go forward. I have the DST's support."

Jenkins looked at Sean. "Are you the contact for this Leznikov?"

"Only in a dire emergency," Sean avowed. "Look, ask Thompson or Stanton if they have heard of Line X. It's part of Directorate T."

Jenkins shook his head in disbelief. "What is it?"

"If the Soviets do this correctly, it's the way they win the Cold War," Sean proclaimed. "I'm not kidding." Jenkins studied Sean's face. "This whole thing is new to me, but I have a coworker who understands this new technology, and when he tells me that this is a game changer, I believe him. At some point in the future, President Millet will contact you saying he has obtained some information. That's when we reap the rewards of what we are putting in place in the coming months."

"Is this just the beginning of this little pet project of yours?"

Sean could see that Jenkins was annoyed, but he wasn't sure if his continued annoyance was with the lack of detail or with the current state of his relationship with Nicole. "I've never led you astray before, why would I do that now?" Sean paused and looked at Jenkins. "Especially since Nicole is still with me." Sean was referring in an indirect way that Nicole had returned to him in Moscow. Although he intended it to be humorous, Jenkins was in no mood to joke.

"Fuck you," Jenkins quickly responded, his irritation very apparent in his voice. "And given my knowledge of your current situation, I wouldn't call your relationship with her all that certain."

Sean gave a hearty laugh, ignoring the second half of the president's remark. "I'm sorry, I couldn't resist that one."

"Well, try next time, jackass," Jenkins shot back. He eyed Sean for a moment. "Your emotions are all over the place, Sean. You better work this out and quickly."

Sean chose to ignore Jenkins's coaching. "Seriously," Sean began. "This little pet project, as you call it, has a name. It is Eagle."

"Why such a strange name?"

"If the Soviets discover this operation, they will uncover the American codename of Eagle making the Soviets believe the United States is directing the operation. Their paranoia will lead them to the CIA and not to the DST. While the Soviets are tracking down false leads, the DST can then extract Leznikov before the Soviets reach a dead end. The United States can deny any affiliation." Sean looked at Jenkins. "Besides, it will be your FBI and CIA that will be doing most of the undercover work."

"With what?"

Sean smiled. "Let's say technology for now." There were a few moments of silence as the two men looked in different directions. "We've worked with each other over a very long period of time. I would hate to think we'd destroy our alliance because of our relationship with a woman." Out of the corner of his eye, Sean saw Jenkins's head whip around to look at him. Jenkins bit his lip. "Do we have a deal?" Sean asked without looking at Jenkins.

"I get no information or updates until Millet approaches me?"

"That depends on your intelligence agencies," Sean replied. "Of course, if you have any questions, you know how to reach me. Are you heading home after this?"

"No," Jenkins began. "I'm heading to Egypt to meet with Seddik."

"Why?"

"He is getting a lot of resistance because of the peace accord. We need to show that we support his government," Jenkins explained.

"Bobby, Kent is in Egypt. Is there any way you can postpone this?"

"Why is Kent there? And if he is there, that only confirms that Seddik life is in danger. I have to go," Jenkins said, basically answering his question.

"Kent may not be there for Seddik. Barker is fuming, and we know he is capable of ordering up a murder," Sean told him.

"I'll tell my agents," Jenkins replied. "I'm not calling off the trip. If Kent is there for me, it is no different than any of the other threats made since my inauguration."

"Be careful," Sean said. "Do we have a deal? Will you wait for Millet to approach you?"

"Yes, I will." Jenkins turned to face Sean. "Just one more thing."

"Yes?"

"Stanton is no longer the CIA director. He and his deputy resigned. They were in Barker's pocket."

"Then I would think it is imperative to let this operation play out according to the plan I put in place with the DST," Sean responded.

Jenkins nodded his head. "Do what you need to do, Sean. Be careful, and if anything points to you or Nikki being in any danger—"

"We appreciate your concern, Bobby," Sean interrupted. "We'll be fine."

"Does Nikki know that you are doing this?"

"Yes," Sean responded. "We said no secrets."

"Yet, you have no idea why she backed out of this trip, and you haven't told her why your nightmares have returned. For a spy, you are a lousy liar," Jenkins pointed out.

"As for my nightmares, I'm working on alleviating that problem, not that I believe that is any of your concern. Nicole said there was something she had to do. I'm sure she will tell me what that was when I return."

"And if she doesn't?"

Sean shook his head, a smile creeping across his lips. "Then I will simply ask." Sean stood up. "I've taken enough of your time, Mr. President. Thank you for your assistance."

Jenkins stood up and followed Sean into the room and to the door. "It was good to see you."

"Thank you again, Mr. President," Sean replied shaking Jenkins's offered hand. "I'll give your best to Nicole." Sean started to leave.

"Just one question," Jenkins called to him. Sean stopped in the hallway and turned to look at Jenkins. "Why don't you call her Nikki? She told me to call her that when we first met."

Sean shrugged his shoulders. "I find Nikki simply too boorish for such a cultivated and complex lady." He winked and finished with, "I rather prefer Nicole."

Jenkins just shook his head as he turned from the doorway and walked back into his suite.

Moscow, USSR—United Kingdom Embassy

Late in the day, Nicole walked into Elliot's office. Elliot looked up when she entered. "I need the information you gathered on Katrina for Sean," she directed.

Elliot stood up and retrieved the information from the safe. "Destroy it after Sean sees it," he said, a cold tone to his voice. He handed the folder to Nicole.

"If you think Sean would have done something dif—"

"He would have," Elliot interrupted.

"Is the world all nice and tidy where you sit, Elliot?" Nicole asked, annoyed. "Because where I sit, it's pretty fucked up. Have you ever seen Sean work? Or did you update information already sterilized by Sean? *Operative is no longer alive, killed by 005*—is that the pristine entry you make into that database of yours? Followed by a *job well done*?" Nicole swallowed. "You've never pulled the trigger. You didn't see the life, albeit an evil one, leave the shell of a body. You didn't experience the psychological warfare that Sean experienced. You didn't suffer the loss of your child at the hands of a satan. You were never in the crosshairs of the Serpent." She turned to leave. As she reached the door, she turned to look at Elliot and said, "You didn't experience lying beside him when he sat up in bed, screaming her name and realizing the demon had returned. Don't you dare judge me." She left Elliot's office for the residence.

Upon entering the residence, Nicole placed the manila folder on the foyer table. She knew Sean would see it. She locked the door to the residence before walking to the master bedroom and onto the bathroom. She started the water in the soaking tub and began to undress. After placing her gun on the table next to the tub, she walked to her closet to retrieve her robe and finish undressing.

She walked back to the bathroom, her robe open and swayed as she walked. She pinned her long hair up on her head, removed her robe and climbed into the tub. She turned off the faucet and lay back, allowing the warm water to envelop her. She rested her head on the tub's edge, and she looked up at the ceiling. She sighed as she acknowledged that a part of her life that she had tried to suppress from a long time ago had resurfaced. Memories of her work in Mississippi during Freedom Summer began to flood her mind. The faces of the hateful vigilantes rose up, taunting her. They spat on her as they screamed their vile sentiments. She whispered to herself, "You didn't kill anyone." It was the truth. But she didn't hesitate to injure them if only in self-defense.

She heard Chief Bailey's voice: "How can you stand to look at these homicide photos?" Chief Bailey, the Washington, DC, police chief, was always amazed at what Nicole could handle. She answered that the homicide photos were nothing compared to unearthing the dead bodies in Mississippi of the three young men in what would later be referred to as the Freedom Summer Murders.

Nicole let all the emotions and memories play out. She understood what drew her to Sean and, in a way, Jenkins, too. All their pasts were similar. She had concealed her past effectively and tried hard not to let those memories rule her life. She had over-compensated to the point of paralyzing herself to inaction. She smiled when she recalled her arguments with Tony, her boss at the law firm. She decided inaction wasn't the correct word. She learned to use her assets, her intelligence, for example, and she discarded the gun she had acquired in Mississippi. She recalled how close she came to shooting someone on one of those hot, confrontational summer nights. It was getting too easy to pull the trigger, and that troubled her.

She sat up in the tub and splashed water on her face. She sat back again. Now, the new Serpent was hunting them. She cursed at how naïve she had been, thinking Kent would leave them alone. That somehow the iron curtain would protect them from him. She sat up when she remembered something from the information on Katrina. She grabbed the washcloth and soap that were sitting on the table next to her gun. She quickly washed her face and body. She unplugged the drain, stood up and grabbed the towel to dry herself quickly. She slipped on her robe and placed her gun in one of its pockets. She hurried to the foyer where the manila folder was waiting for her.

She opened the folder and looked at the first photograph, the untouched Katrina before her transformation into the Sarah look-alike. She flipped over the other two photographs and looked at the type-written report. It confirmed her suspicion. They still were not safe. Everything that had happened to date proved they were not safe. She placed the information back in the folder and returned to the bedroom. She dressed for bed. She looked at the clock and determined that Sean would be home shortly. She climbed under the covers and prepared herself for the confrontation that was inevitable.

Sean entered the residence a few hours later, placing the small overnight bag he had packed for the quick trip on the floor just inside the door. He closed the door behind him, locking it, and turned back around. He walked to the foyer table and noticed the manila folder. He opened it to see the photo of Katrina. Not recognizing the woman, he turned it over, placing it face down on the other side of the opened folder. The next photograph was the bruised and stitched face of Stacy. He turned the first photo back over and compared them. He then turned to the third photo. An unidentified man in a hat and Stacy seated at a table. Sean's eyes moved to the man walking up toward them. He picked up the photo to get a closer look as he felt his eyes were deceiving him. It was Kent. Sean dropped the photo and quickly picked up the report that accompanied them. He read through it briskly. He looked to his right. Nicole had gotten out of bed and stealthily walked to the end of the hallway that led to the foyer. She watched him as he studied the materials. Sean looked back at the photograph of Kent and Stacy. He tried to gather his thoughts, but there was only one question he wanted to ask. "What did you do?"

"I removed her from the embassy," Nicole started. "But not before I interrogated her."

Sean closed his eyes. "Tell me exactly what you did."

Nicole told him everything. With each word, she could see Sean shake with rage. "She said her contact was Valesky. I don't understand how Kent knows Valesky. Katrina Natalinsky is dead. I don't know if it was Valesky who shot—"

"That's just *marvelous*, " Sean snapped at her.

"I know you're mad," Nicole began.

"Mad? I'm fucking furious!" Sean shouted. He had so many questions to ask; he could only begin to form the first words of the sentences with his lips. No sound escaped him. "Damn it, Nicole!" It was the only thing he could finally say. "Do you know what you've done? This is an embassy! What happens here reflects on the nation I am representing. How am I going to explain this?"

"You were out of the country," Nicole deadpanned while she folded her arms in front of her. She was trying to remain calm and collected. She wasn't going to scream back at Sean.

Sean exasperatedly rolled his eyes and scoffed. “Did you not even consider that I knew she was a spy? Did you even stop to think for one second that I would take care of this at the proper time? Jesus, Nicole, do you realize the trouble you have caused?” Sean pounded his fist on the table as a string of curse words left his lips. “What the fuck were you thinking?”

Nicole had never seen him this angry. She gathered her robe around her and tied a knot securing it. She slowly walked up to him. Standing toe to toe, she said, “Maybe, if you weren’t such an asshole, you would have noticed that Katrina’s transformation into Sarah started six weeks before we arrived here. Six weeks before we knew we were going to be assigned here. Maybe then you’ll realize, hot shot, that someone at MI6 or in Parliament informed Kent where we were going. I don’t think it stops with Katrina. Let that fact sink in and then fault me for taking care of an issue that entirely engulfed you every night in the shroud of a nightmare you endured for ten years as you hunted the Serpent.” Nicole turned and started for the door. “She said she fucked you. For your sake and the sake of our relationship, I hope that was a lie.” She walked out of the residence, slamming the door behind her.

Sean picked up the report and studied it again. Nicole was correct. Someone had informed Kent where they were going. Sean tossed the report onto the table and walked into the living room. He continued to the cocktail cart where he poured himself a shot of gin. He downed it and poured more into the glass. He turned, jumping at the sight of Elliot, who was standing in the doorway. “Shit!” Sean said, catching his breath. When he calmed down, he asked, “Do you want a drink?”

“No, thanks,” Elliot replied. “I heard the door slam. I thought it would have been you that left.”

“Why didn’t you stop her?”

Elliot chortled, "She had a gun." He walked to a nearby chair and sat down. "And she is a damn good shot."

"Yes, I know," Sean uttered as he walked to the couch.

"What are we going to do?"

"Nothing," Sean replied.

"We can't do nothing. This affects Eagle."

"No, it doesn't," Sean asserted. "If anything it reinforces it."

"How's that?"

"Leznikov can't afford to be seen with me or at this embassy," Sean began.

"It will make him very suspicious."

Sean frowned and looked at Elliot. "He's a Soviet spy in Baranov's cabinet. You don't think he's already suspicious?" Sean shook his head. He looked at his glass of gin and took a sip. "Besides, other than Valesky's resources to transform Katrina into Sarah, I think this was all Kent's doing."

"How's that?" Elliot asked, not following Sean's logic.

"Just before Nicole blasted out of here she revealed to me something both of us failed to uncover," Sean said, taking another sip. "Katrina's transformation started six weeks before we got here. It began before I even knew where I would be assigned."

Elliot thought for a moment and realized Sean was correct. "Damn."

"We have a lot to go through," Sean muttered. "Starting with who in MI6 or the Parliament has a connection to Kent. Who knew I was coming to the Soviet Union? Was this whole thing with the previous ambassador orchestrated by Valesky and Kent? Is there someone else here involved?" Sean looked down. "That's just the beginning."

"We would have ended up here anyway," Elliot said. "I mean, you would have determined that it wasn't a coincidence that a Sarah look-alike just happened to show up here." Sean turned his head and looked at Elliot with confusion. "You just would have handled it differently."

Sean studied him for a moment before he spoke. "I can't decide if you are defending Nicole's actions or opposing them."

"I'm not sure either." Elliot laughed. "By God, Sean, you should have seen her. I honestly never thought she could be that cold." Sean huffed and then smiled. He took another sip of gin. "I'm serious. She even scared Duncan."

Sean turned his head and looked at Elliot. "How?"

"She didn't threaten him if that is what you are asking. She was…" Elliot's voice trailed off. Sean stared at him, not letting him get off that easy. "She was frigid, uncaring, determined, and it was a side of her that I never in a million years thought existed. I think she would have tortured her to death to get the answer she wanted."

"Which was?"

"Stacy's contact was Valesky," Elliot replied.

"We don't know for sure that Stacy's contact was Valesky. She could have just blurted out his name," Sean said. He slowly shook his head while in thought. Had he cultivated this side of Nicole? Were his instincts affected by Kent's psychological play? Sean shook the questions out of his mind. “It’s getting late. You better get some sleep. We have a lot of work to do tomorrow.”

Elliot stood up and walked to the door. He turned and asked, “How was the meeting with Jenkins?”

“Hmm?” Sean began, snapping out of his thoughts again. “It went fine. He isn’t happy that he has to wait until Millet approaches him before they can get involved.”

“You called that one,” Elliot said, trying to reassure Sean of his abilities.

“Yes, I did,” Sean confirmed as he started to slide back into his thoughts that were ranging from next steps to self-doubt. “Good night, Elliot,” he muttered. Elliot left after he bade good night to Sean.

After a few hours of careful reflection on all that had happened, Sean looked at his watch. He was so deep in thought that he wondered if Nicole had slipped in without disturbing him. He walked to their bedroom. The light was still illuminating the chamber, and thc bed was empty. He walked to the bathroom, and it was also empty. Sean checked the kitchen and the other bedrooms. All were empty. He looked at his watch again and determined it had been three hours since he arrived home. He sighed when he decided he better find her.

It wasn’t until the wee hours of the morning when Sean found Nicole asleep in the hall where they had entertained weeks ago. He opened the door and walked into the hall. He noticed a sea of unadorned tables and chairs in the center and back of the room. More comfortable chairs and couches were along the side. He didn’t see her at first. Back in the corner, sitting curled up in an oversized chair, her head propped up on the winglet, was Nicole. He had to squint to separate her figure from the chair itself. He quietly tip-toed across the dance floor. He observed her sleeping for a moment before he knelt down in front of the chair. He stroked her hair out of her puffy eyes and gently whispered, "Nicole."

Nicole roused on the second murmuring of her name, opening her eyes and focusing on Sean. She didn't speak at first, not sure what to say. She broke the gaze between them, looking around the hall before her eyes settled on Sean again.

Sean took her hand in his. Unsure of what to say, he gently muttered, "Let's go back to the residence." As he started to stand, he kissed her forehead. Nicole recoiled at first, not at all sure she was ready to forgive him let alone forget. Sean stood up, still holding her hand. "It's late. A lot was said, but I'm just completely worn out. Can we talk in the morning?"

She looked at the clock on the wall. "It is morning," Nicole retorted. "Three a.m. to be exact."

"You win," Sean shot back. "I don't have the energy to fight with you right now."

Nicole stood up and started to walk away from him. Her hand slipped from his. "What did I say now?" Sean was exasperated. He hadn't slept well for weeks. Between his nightmares and preparing for the meeting with his contact at the DST, President Millet, and Jenkins, he was exhausted. A thought that he wished Nicole was with Jenkins at this particular moment dashed through his mind. He bit his lip trying not to laugh.

"That I'm not worth fighting for," Nicole replied as she headed for the nearest door.

"Blimey, that is not what I said!" Sean returned. "I said I don't have the energy to fight *with* you. With you, Nicole, I don't have the energy to fight with you right now." He started to walk toward her.

"You did?"

"Yes, I did," Sean replied as he reached her side.

"Oh," Nicole said. "Are you feeling OK?"

"I'm fine," Sean returned. "I'm tired."

"You've always had the energy to fight with me," Nicole said, bringing a hand to his forehead.

Sean intercepted it before it reached its destination. He put his arm around her waist. "I need some sleep." They started to walk out of the ballroom to the residence.

"Did the meetings go well?"

"Yes. Bobby sends his love." Sean was being facetious.

Nicole smiled at Sean's remark. There was a time when Sean would have conveniently forgotten to convey any sentiments Jenkins sent her way, and she knew that Jenkins didn't send his love. She knew Jenkins sent his regards. Sean was trying hard to be magnanimous. They walked into the hallway, Sean opening the door for Nicole.

"I understand that you scared the shit out of Duncan and Elliot," Sean said as they turned down the hallway.

"I thought you didn't want to argue," Nicole responded.

"I'm not trying to argue. I just heard that—"

"Heard? Did you wake everyone up?"

Sean scratched his head. “Never mind.” After a few steps, he said, teasingly, “Yep, a real badass.” The corners of his mouth curled as he tried not to laugh.

Nicole teasingly butted him with her shoulder. “Don’t laugh. I got the information, didn’t I?”

“Yes, you did,” Sean returned. “Almost started an international incident at the same time, but yes, you got the information.”

“I thought we weren’t going to fight about this tonight,” Nicole said defensively.

“Who’s fighting?” Sean asked as a smile quickly crossed his lips.

“You’re trying exceptionally hard to set me off again.”

“Set *you* off again? You said three or four sentences. I was the one who was off the mark.” He looked at Nicole, who now knew it was his way of apologizing. She placed her head on his shoulder. “From what Elliot told me, I need to make sure you don’t have your gun the next time we fight.”

“That would probably be wise,” Nicole said with a sly grin. Sean nodded his head. Nicole kissed his cheek. His apology was accepted.

Alexandria, Egypt—Montaza Palace

Jenkins arrived in Egypt late at night so that his motorcade could move through the city unimpeded. He arrived at the Montaza Palace gate shortly before midnight. The palace guards were expecting Jenkins and opened the gates immediately. The cars proceeded to the Al-Haramlik Palace located on the Montaza gardens where Seddik waited for him outside on the portico. Seddik preferred the Al-Haramlik Palace over the Abdeen Palace in Cairo and spent as much time in Al-Haramlik Palace as he could. Most foreign dignitaries met with the president of Egypt here, where Seddik felt the quiet and beautiful surroundings led to fruitful conferences. The door to Jenkins's limo was opened by a Secret Service agent when given the all clear signal. Jenkins exited the car, climbed the steps and shook Seddik's offered hand.

"Welcome to my home and my country," Seddik greeted Jenkins.

Jenkins's Secret Service agents matched the number of guards placed around the portico and colonnade of the palace. "Thank you," Jenkins responded. "I apologize for my late arrival. My last meeting ran over."

"It is of no concern," Seddik stated as he gestured for Jenkins to enter the palace. "If you are hungry I can arrange for something to be sent to your suite."

"Please, don't go to any trouble," Jenkins said. "I ate something on Air Force One, and I would like to get to sleep so that we can meet at our scheduled time in the morning." Jenkins stopped in the foyer and looked around. Its beauty was beyond words. "Exquisite," was all he could manage.

"It is meant to be intimidating," Seddik joked. "The height and expanse were supposed to intimidate my enemies."

Jenkins cocked his head and looked at Seddik. "The USA is a friend of Egypt. Hopefully, your allies find it impressive." He let a smile cross his lips.

Seddik smiled back. "I am glad to hear my friend finds it impressive." He clapped his hands, and a man walked to his side. "This is Amsu Sambra. He will show you to your room and escort you to our meeting in the morning. If you should need anything during your stay, Amsu will get it for you." Jenkins acknowledged

Amsu with a quick nod of the head. “We shall start our meeting at nine o’clock.”

“I look forward to talking with you, Mr. President,” Jenkins stated, offering his hand again.

Amsu started for Jenkins’s guest room in the palace. Two guards flanked Amsu and Jenkins followed them. The remaining agents followed behind the president.

Jenkins arrived at his room, walked inside, and the Secret Service went about its business. An advance team had already arrived and secured the room: One of the agents greeted the president upon entry. After a brief discussion on protection details and confirming the agenda for the next day, the agents left the president alone in his room.

Jenkins was exhausted. It was a long day in France before the flight, and it was going to be another long day tomorrow. The business meeting would be in the morning, followed by visits from various cabinet members and military officers. All he wanted to do was make sure that Egypt knew the United States still supported the peace accord. Jenkins knew Seddik was to ask for certain assurances that would publicly display the USA’s support. Jenkins took off his suit jacket and tie. After a knock on the door, Chris entered.

“Mr. President,” Chris began. “Is there anything I can get you?”

“No, Chris, I’m going to bed.”

“Yes, sir. I’ll be right next door.”

“Thank you, Chris,” Jenkins said as he headed into the bedroom. “I’ll see you in the morning. Wake me at six please.”

“Yes, sir,” Chris replied as he left the room.

Jenkins slept soundly for six hours, falling asleep as soon as his head hit the pillow. The next morning, Chris had woken Jenkins as instructed and then attended to duties in the living room area of the suite where Jenkins would eat his breakfast. Whittaker would join him later to brief him before his meeting with Seddik.

After showering and dressing, Jenkins walked out of his bedroom to find his favorite breakfast, complete with eggs, biscuits, and bacon waiting for him on the table by the balcony. A servant poured his coffee handing the cup and saucer to him. "Thank you," Jenkins said as he accepted the morning brew with his right hand. He placed it on the table next to his plate. "This is wonderful. Thank you. I won't require anything else." The servant bowed and left the room. Jenkins looked at Chris. "If I continue to eat these breakfasts, I'm going to die of a heart attack. I'm beginning to think there is a secret plot. Where do they get this idea that I eat this kind of breakfast every morning?"

Chris laughed. "Blame the morning news programs. I think they mentioned it a couple of times during the campaign."

"Would you like some of this?"

"I've already eaten, sir. Thank you."

Jenkins shook his head and began eating. "Can we let it slip," he said with some bacon in his mouth. "That I no longer have a favorite breakfast?"

"I'll see what I can do, sir," Chris replied. There was a knock on the door, and Chris left Jenkins's side to answer it. It was Jenkins's chief of staff.

"Morning, sir," Whittaker said as he entered the room, acknowledging Chris with a nod of his head. "Ahhh, I see you also got the chef special this morning."

Jenkins laughed. "Where did they get the bacon?"

"I have no idea," Whittaker admitted. "You don't think it's made from something else besides a pig, do you?"

Jenkins looked at Whittaker, smelling the bacon while continuing to look at him. "Like what?"

"I've seen an awful lot of camels," Whittaker opined. One side of his mouth curled up into a smile, just enough to make Jenkins think he was serious.

"You are not funny," Jenkins quipped. He looked at the bacon and slapped his hands on his thighs, declaring, "Now I'm not hungry. It will be considered an insult if I don't eat this."

Whittaker laughed. "I was kidding. It tasted like regular bacon to me."

Jenkins gave Whittaker a disbelieving look. He put down the bacon, picked up his fork, and opted to eat the eggs instead. After swallowing the first bite, he asked, "Is anything going on at home I need to know about?"

"You mean other than the Joint Chiefs calling to tell me to keep you from giving away the store?"

"Are you serious?"

"Yes," Whittaker confirmed. "They don't want to deploy any more people here."

"We have people here?" Jenkins said as he tried the bacon again. "Now it tastes like a camel."

"Well, we don't have a base here," Whittaker dodged. "And you've had camel before?"

"We have people here?" Jenkins asked again, ignoring the question about eating a camel.

"We have people helping with intelligence and security," Whittaker stated vaguely.

"We don't have a base here." Jenkins looked at Whittaker. Whittaker shook his head. "Do you think I'm that stupid?"

"No, sir," Whittaker promptly said.

"Yes, you do," Jenkins said, wiping his hand with a napkin. "You think I'm that stupid. Need I remind you that I was a Navy SEAL?"

"In Vietnam," Whittaker replied. "Not in Egypt."

Jenkins rolled his eyes. "I know we don't have a base here. What I can't grasp is *why* we don't have a base here." Jenkins always enjoyed bantering fine details with Whittaker mainly because he knew it drove Whittaker a little crazy.

"Because President Seddik thought it would make Egypt appear weak," Whittaker noticed Jenkins's brow furrow. "He feels his forces can protect Egypt."

"Can they?"

"It's done a pretty good job so far," Whittaker confirmed.

"Are you done prepping me for this meeting? I mean, I've only been reading up on this for—oh, I don't know, years," Jenkins said sardonically.

"I think you're ready," Whittaker deadpanned. "Finish your breakfast."

"I beg your pardon," Jenkins started, jokingly. "Are you ordering me around?"

"Somebody has to," Whittaker quipped as he walked to the door. "Thank you, Mr. President."

Jenkins looked at a Secret Service agent, who was the head of his detail and bodyguard. "You see how they treat me, Rick?" Rick smiled but didn't respond. Jenkins sipped his coffee and finished his breakfast.

CHAPTER NINE
JULY 1981

Paris, France—Avenue des Champs-Élysées

Leznikov retrieved the meeting information early in the morning from the locker at the Gare du Nord train station with the key that Sean had passed him at the chess club in Sokolniki Park in June. They had met to play a quick game of chess. When the two men shook hands at the conclusion of the game, Sean palmed the key to Leznikov, who quickly put his hand and key in his trouser pocket. Now, Leznikov was strolling along the Champs-Élysées occasionally stopping to look at the shop windows. He walked into a bakery and purchased a pain-au-chocolat. He continued his walk as he ate the divine pastry. Leznikov stopped and started his walk many times, glancing with his eyes to make sure no one was following him. He finished the pastry and tossed the paper napkin in the trash can freeing his left hand. In his right hand was a small attaché. Its contents were just a small example of the documents he wanted to give his new contact. He knew he had to be careful and he wanted to make sure this new arrangement suited him before he gave too much information to the enemies of his native country.

Leznikov walked past the door that led to the apartment where the meeting was to take place. He didn't notice anyone following him, but he was too early for the meeting. Leznikov did not want to give the impression he was too eager to betray his country. He walked to a café table and sat down. He placed the attaché on his lap. He watched the cars speed by him, their occupants not interested in what was occurring on the sidewalks. People walked along the avenue not interested in him at all. It was late morning, and the sun warmed Leznikov's face. He took a quick look up and down the street before he decided it was time to meet with Sean.

Sean's contact, Pierre Beaumont, had arrived first. The apartment where they were all to meet was that of Pierre's mistress. Pierre knew in the future that Leznikov would also enjoy the woman, but that did not bother him. Pierre had no intention of leaving his wife and family. They provided the perfect cover for his work with the DST. His wife was dutifully raising their children, and as long as the money was available for the bills and their needs, she did not find it necessary to know what her husband did with his time. It was a perfect arrangement for both of them.

Sean and Nicole arrived fifteen minutes after Pierre. Sean greeted the tall, thin man with a hug. "Pierre, it is good to see you again."

Pierre's eyes focused on Nicole. She was still standing in the hallway waiting for the embrace to end. "This cannot be my contact from Russia?" Although there was a hint of hope in Pierre's voice, he knew his fortune was not that good.

"No," Sean confirmed.

"Then who is she and why is she here?" It was clear by the tone of his voice, Pierre was not happy that someone he didn't know would be joining them.

"This is Nicole. I told you about her the last time we met."

"It is a pleasure to finally meet the woman who stole MI6 of their best field agent," Pierre said, eyeing Nicole. "But I see no reason for her to be here."

"She won't be a problem," Sean countered. "She stays, or I'll find someone else."

Nicole didn't speak. Up to this point, Nicole thought the espionage world was free of the bogus ass kissing that filled the confines of Washington, DC. She wanted to roll her eyes at Pierre's comment that she somehow stole Sean from his work. It wasn't true. Pierre took an unoffered hand from Nicole's side and gave it a subtle kiss. The gesture was his attempt to cover over his faux pas. She removed her hand from Pierre's grip and cleared her throat. "Don't you two have some work to do?"

Pierre laughed. "You described her perfectly to me," Pierre directed to Sean. Nicole wasn't sure how Sean described her to Pierre, but she also knew that she didn't care. Pierre closed the door after Nicole had entered. "Come and sit here," he instructed. He motioned to a small table in the very compacted kitchen of the two-room apartment. The kitchen and sitting area melded into one room. The closed bedroom door prevented a look inside.

"While we are taking attendance," Sean began with an inquisitive tone in his voice, "where is your mistress?"

Shocked by Sean's accusation, Pierre began his denial. "I don't—"

"Stop," Sean interrupted. "Don't play me for a fool. Where is she?"

Pierre swallowed. "She is in the bedroom."

Sean shook his head. "I'm not sure I like that." He looked at his watch. There was very little time to wrestle her from the apartment. "Tell me, would you trust her with your life?"

"As much as you trust Nicole with yours," Pierre shot back, insulted by the question.

Nicole had to cross in front of Sean to move to a couch by the window. "Are you sure you want Slick here to be the contact?" she whispered as she passed him. Sean bit his lip to contain his amusement at Nicole's given nickname for Pierre. Nicole continued to the couch, looking out the window.

Pierre had heard Nicole's question but ignored it. "No, no," he said in reaction to her retreat to the window. "Come join us. I will get more chairs."

"Your mistress knows not to come out of the bedroom?" Sean asked. The question stopped Pierre from gathering more chairs.

"Of course," Pierre replied. "You know this. It is not the first time we have conducted business here. She is listening to music with headphones." Pierre changed the subject. He looked at Nicole. "Please come sit with us," he said to Nicole.

"I'm fine here," Nicole countered as she took a seat on the couch.

"Just the three of us at the table," Sean ordered. "As we discussed, we will not be joining you in the future for these meetings. It is too risky considering my position in Moscow. It is up to you to convince Leznikov to become a double agent." Sean looked at Nicole and then back at Pierre. "After we determine that the two of you can work together, Nicole and I will be leaving."

"My understanding was that you would be here for the full meeting the first time," Pierre said. His discomfort was evident. "How do I know he is not offering shit?"

"I don't know what exactly he is offering, and I want to keep it that way," Sean replied. "We've ruffled enough feathers between the Soviet government and our embassy." Sean shot a look at Nicole. Nicole rolled her eyes and looked away. She knew Sean was referring to the way she had handled the situation with Katrina. She shook her head as Sean started to speak. "It is best not to contact us with details or arrangements in the future. If Leznikov needs extracting or a special circumstance arises, then I suggest you call and invite me to Paris."

"I understand," Pierre replied. "I don't have to like it, but I understand."

"Good," Sean said as he sat down. "Leznikov retrieved the information for the meeting place this morning."

Pierre eyed Sean, not asking the question that was on his mind. He wanted Sean to continue, so he just raised his eyebrows.

"I saw him," Sean said with a smile.

Pierre, too, was at the station but did not see Sean. "I don't care how much you deny it. You miss the field, my friend. The smile on your face confirms this to me."

Nicole studied Sean while Pierre was stating his observation. Sean's smile increased in agreement. She turned her head as she realized Pierre was correct.

"I saw you as well," Sean confirmed.

"I could never find you," Pierre admitted. His frustration was apparent and referred not only to this morning but also their past.

There was a knock on the door. No one moved. A second knock occurred as per the written instructions. Sean stood up to answer the door. He peered through a small peephole before he opened it, standing behind it to shield himself should something go wrong. Leznikov did not speak as he walked through the door.

"Welcome," Sean said as he shut the door. He motioned to the table. Leznikov took a few steps and looked at Pierre, who was not standing. "Pierre Beaumont, this is Dmitry Leznikov."

Leznikov acknowledged Pierre with a quick nod of his head, not offering his hand. He turned his head and noticed Nicole. He smiled at her. "If you keep—how does one say it—popping up?" Nicole cocked her head confused at what Leznikov was trying to say. "I think, yes—if you keep popping up with this person," he pointed to Sean, "we will classify you as a spy as well."

Nicole smiled. "Popping up is the correct expression."

Leznikov smiled back at Nicole. "You didn't deny it."

"I don't think you'd believe me if I did," Nicole shot back. "I'm not British."

"CIA?" Leznikov questioned.

"They probably have a file on me, but it is not because I am employed there." Nicole's eyes shifted to Sean and then Pierre. "Please pay me no attention. Your meeting is with Sean and Pierre." Nicole turned her head to look out the window. It was the job Sean gave her. She was to make sure that no one suspicious was loitering downstairs on the street.

Sean motioned to the vacant chair for Leznikov to sit. He glanced over at Nicole, who gave one, quick shake of her head, indicating she did not identify anyone she considered suspicious on the street. Sean joined the other two.

Leznikov placed the attaché on the table and started to open it.

"One second," Sean interjected. "I want to discuss the arrangements before we begin. As I informed Pierre, he will be your contact. I will not be attending any future meetings."

"That is unacceptable," Leznikov responded. He retracted his arms from the case and folded them. "I do not know this man."

"And he does not know you," Sean reminded Leznikov.

"I assumed that you would be involved. I am more comfortable dealing with you," Leznikov asserted.

Sean shook his head. "I told you at the chess club I could not be involved. Only in a dire emergency are you to contact me. If you need extraction, I'll do my best to get you out."

Leznikov and Sean were locked in a stare down. After a few seconds, Leznikov nodded his head. "With your assurance to help in an emergency, we can move forward." He looked at Pierre. "I can only hope that you are as trustworthy as Sean."

Pierre eyed Leznikov. "I believe our connection to Sean speaks to our integrity. I am as much at risk as you."

Sean wanted to cringe. Before Leznikov could speak, Sean said, "No, Pierre, you are not. Let me explain. Our friend here is sitting within the Kremlin and diverting documentation to you. He is the most at risk." Both men stared at Pierre. "If you can't understand that, I'm afraid I will have to find a different contact. I thought I explained this the last time we met."

"You did," Pierre confirmed. "But how do we know these documents will be what he says they are. Are you translating these documents into French?"

"No," Leznikov said. "They are in Russian. I can go over them with you."

Sean shook his head at the direction the conversation was going. "Gentlemen, we knew the documents were not going to be translated. Dmitry, there will be no need for you to go over the documents with Pierre. That only heightens the risk you are taking. The less time the two of you spend together, the better. Don't give me the impression that I have two fools running this operation. Stop this farce immediately."

Both men looked silently at Sean. Pierre was the first to speak. "How do I know these documents are not something frivolous?"

Sean turned his head, taking in a deep breath. He had forgotten how difficult Pierre could be. Just as Sean was about to answer, Leznikov snatched the attaché off the table. "This man is impossible," he complained.

Nicole, still looking out the window, gave a quick chuckle. The three men looked at her. "Imbeciles," she muttered under her breath. She felt their eyes on her. She turned her head to look at them. Without saying a word, she turned to look out the window again.

Sean stood up. "We're done here." The two men looked at Sean. Nicole stood up to join him.

"Wait," Leznikov urged Sean, grabbing his sleeve.

"You can't leave," Pierre asserted.

Sean shook his head. “I delivered my end of the bargain. Pierre, I brought you a man who is willing to risk his life to provide the French with information on Line X’s operations. Dmitry, I provided you with a contact as you requested. What happens after this,” Sean motioned for Nicole to join him. “I don’t care. Work together. Don’t work together. It is up to you.” With Nicole by his side, Sean reached for the door and opened it. Without saying a word, they left.

When Nicole and Sean were back downstairs on the street, Nicole said, “What do you think will happen?”

“Leznikov will share the information.”

“What makes you so sure?”

“Because each has risked enough to get to the place they are in,” Sean replied. “They were only interested in keeping me in the loop so that they felt more secure. I don’t care to know what they set up or what information passes between them.”

“Liar,” Nicole said. “You’re dying to know.”

Sean didn’t say anything. They took a few more steps when Sean added, “I said I don’t care what information passes between them. I didn’t say that I’m not interested in what information Bobby receives.”

Montebello, Quebec, Canada—Château Montebello

Pierre Thibeau, prime minister of Canada, patiently stood by a grassy field next to one of the seventy lakes on the approximately sixty-five thousand acres of Château Montebello. He was waiting for the first of six helicopters to arrive for the G7 summit, each carrying a leader of the six other major industrialized nations of the world. Canada was the seventh nation to take part in the summit.

Following the 1973 oil crisis and the world recession, French President Romain Eschete invited six leaders to meet informally to discuss the economic situation. That summit, held at Château de Rambouillet in France, was so successful, a variation of the six nations met regularly under rotating leadership. This group was referred to as the Group of Six throughout the seventies.

The leaders of France, West Germany, Italy, Japan, the United States, and the United Kingdom met to resolve differences and provide encouragement amid difficult times. In 1976, Canada was asked to join, and the Group of Six became known as the G7. Thibeau offered to host the summit in July of 1981 and set the agenda in coordination with Gaston Gaudet, the European Commission president. Thibeau thought that although the G7 was to be an informal gathering, layers of complexity existed. He was hopeful the beautiful setting of the château would soften the complexity and provide ample opportunity for the world leaders to hold bilateral meetings, which would keep the formal meetings on topic. The group's focus during this summit was on unemployment, interest rates, and aid for less developed countries—a criticism the G7 had been facing in the past.

The first to arrive was Chancellor Helmut Scheidt of West Germany. Scheidt was considered a true statesman, always poised and ready to serve his country. He had been part of the Hitler Youth Movement but was sent on leave because of his anti-Nazi views. From his experience during World War II, Scheidt's straight talk and moralistic views were grounded in his belief that West Germany needed to draw the most stringent lessons from the catastrophe of the war. Promoting European integrity and international stability was at the forefront of his agenda since he felt his country lived in the shadow of Hitler and Auschwitz. The European Monetary System, a means of uniting Europe under one economic system to control the fluctuations, was established with

Scheidt as the main political architect. He felt that the creation of the monetary system tied his country to the West. The dashing, firm-jawed, gray-eyed Scheidt was a Social Democrat and made no apologies for his proudly held convictions.

British Prime Minister Geoffrey Adkins arrived after Scheidt. Geoffrey had received a letter from Sean a few days before he left on the trip. Sean asked his brother if he would act as an intermediary should François Millet, who didn't particularly care for Jenkins, not be amenable to meet with the president of the United States. Geoffrey's helicopter arrived, landed, and Geoffrey greeted Thibeau whom he had met on several occasions before this.

Jenkins was the third guest to arrive and sprightly hopped out of the chopper, followed by Chris. Their prior war experience exiting helicopters was evident. Whittaker, older and not as confident, carefully vacated the craft, turning back around to grab his briefcase. After having a brief chat with Thibeau, Jenkins and his staff were off to their rooms.

Thibeau greeted the remaining guests as he did the previous three. Next to arrive was the French president, François Millet. He had an additional aide, who was carrying a rather large briefcase. When Thibeau greeted him in French, Millet gazed at him. Thibeau had heard that the socialist was a bit cranky and set in his ways. Millet let Thibeau know that he did not appreciate arriving in a military helicopter, finding the ride too turbulent. Thibeau apologized, but it was clear that Millet's mood was not going to improve. Thibeau whispered to one of his aides to take a cart and pull a nice bottle of red wine—Château Pétrus or Château Haut-Brion, whichever Millet preferred—and have the sommelier serve it to the guests. The aide acknowledged the command and sped off to the lodge to find the sommelier.

After Millet, Giovanni Spaziani, the prime minister of Italy, Suzuki Tokuda, the prime minister of Japan, and Gaston Gaudet, president of the European Commission, arrived in that order. The only person whose attitude matched that of Millet's was Gaudet. He had faced many reporters who were all asking about the scandal—the wife of his chief aide killed her husband and then electrocuted herself. Gaudet, from Luxembourg where he had served as prime minister, was still gathering the details of the murder-suicide. There was an air of confusion and frustration around Gaudet. Thibeau would not be surprised if the council president, Prime Minister Adkins, would become the default leader of the formal gatherings.

With all the members of the G7 present, Thibeau climbed into the last of the golf carts and headed to the conference room. The first bilateral meetings would begin within the hour. Thibeau moved to a podium in front of the white-clothed tables. There was a table for each country and enough chairs for the heads of state and their aides. When Thibeau reached the podium, all eyes focused on him. The press took a few photographs and settled down when Thibeau began to speak. He formally welcomed everyone to the summit and quickly went through the binder of information placed on each table. It contained a schedule and key information on each topic to be discussed. He then noted that it was time to break into the scheduled bilateral meetings.

Jenkins looked at the schedule quickly. As he started to close the binder, Chancellor Scheidt approached him. Jenkins stood and greeted the leader of West Germany. "Helmut, it is good to see you."

"I think we are to meet first," Scheidt said, straight to business.

"Yes," Jenkins agreed. "Perhaps we could take a walk by the lake?" Jenkins pointed to the door to the right of them.

"That would be acceptable," Scheidt said as he turned and began to walk toward the doors.

Jenkins leaned over to Chris. "Secure my binder," he said, pointing at it. "And rescue me in forty-five minutes for my next meeting." Chris acknowledged his statement with a grin as Jenkins walked away from him. "Chancellor, how was your flight from West Germany?" Jenkins called to Scheidt as he walked briskly to catch up to him.

Scheidt turned and looked at Jenkins as he said, "It was uneventful but a little long."

The two men walked out of the conference room and began their stroll by the lake. Scheidt was unsure of the young and, in his opinion, untested Jenkins. Scheidt also believed in being direct and cuttingly honest. West Germany had lived through unstable times, seeing their growth drop and inflation skyrocket. Scheidt's re-election occurred during an upswing in job growth. However, 1981 was not a good year for West Germany or Scheidt. Growth was falling, and inflation was unabated. His people were questioning whether Scheidt could be trusted and if 1980 was a manufactured upswing to keep Scheidt in power.

"Times are rough in my country," Scheidt began, his hands clasped behind his back as he walked. "And you are inexperienced in your job. West Germany has always worked closely with the United States and has always welcomed its advice in the past. But now, I wonder if the US is in a position to help its allies. I worry that it has become weak."

"Weak? Why would you think that?" Jenkins asked, surprised by Scheidt's statements.

"You have many of the same problems we have," Scheidt said.

"I think you will find that these problems exist in all our countries. There is a world recession, and I believe we are here to discuss options available to us globally," Jenkins countered. "Unemployment is too high for us all, and we need to find a way to get people back to work." He stopped walking and eyed Scheidt. "Dismissing any suggestions brought to the table by me would be foolish. If you see me as weak on the economy, that is because you and your staff have not done their homework reviewing my experience. Let's not get off on the wrong foot, Chancellor. America has always been proud to help West Germany and call her our friend and ally. If you feel you have been slighted in some way by the previous administration, tell me now, but don't insult my intelligence."

Scheidt studied the feisty, young man standing before him. "I meant no disrespect to you personally, Mr. President. The conspiracy and its aftermath seemed to have engulfed your country and perhaps divided it more deeply than first imagined. I was merely questioning if your country is still strong enough to lead."

"Our domestic agenda is well defined, and we are beginning to deploy initiatives," Jenkins assured Scheidt. "We allow freedom of expression, so while others see that as a division or weakness, we see it as a strength—an opportunity to communicate." Jenkins smiled. "I'm sure to outsiders America seems like a dysfunctional family, but I assure you, we unite when needed." While Jenkins knew his country was fractured, he was painting a much brighter picture than was truly accurate. The two political parties were finding more reasons not to work together. There was a new movement in the House of Representatives that didn't sit well with Jenkins personally and was far too self-centered for his liking. He made a mental note about creating a strategy to address that new caucus. "As you know, Chancellor, democracy isn't a speedboat. It's more like a cruise liner. It takes a while to turn the ship."

"I hope we are not on the Titanic," Scheidt growled.

"Only if another country decides to be an iceberg," Jenkins shot back. The two began walking again. Jenkins knew his comments were biting. He tried to smooth it over. "We're here to find answers that will help us."

"Too many times have I sat in these summits. My country was promised aid and certain assurances, only to have your country back out of them. Your predecessors were unable to get your Congress to pass the necessary measures," Scheidt lamented. "What makes you think your presidency will be any different?"

Jenkins thought for a moment. "Chancellor, it is true that in the past, the US had a divided Congress. I was a senator during that time, and I was able to reach across the aisle to draft legislation that ultimately passed because of its bipartisan support. I don't believe my ability to do that has suddenly left me because I became the president. It is through negotiation and compromise that we achieve success."

Scheidt nodded his head in agreement. "Communication is key."

Jenkins gave a little chuckle. "One can talk all he or she wants, Chancellor, but if no one is listening, it doesn't matter, does it?"

Scheidt laughed. "That is true! Perhaps I judged you too harshly. But rest assured Mr. President, I will be watching," Scheidt said. Then he added, "and listening."

"And participating in the process, I hope," Jenkins replied. He continued to walk along the lake with Scheidt. To Jenkins's dismay, too much of the conversation focused on his youth and what Scheidt called inexperience. As they were returning from their walk, Jenkins was relieved to see Chris walking toward him, right on time as instructed.

After excusing himself from Scheidt, Jenkins started walking with Chris; his body language was different than the message Chris brought him. Jenkins was intentionally sending a message to Scheidt that Chris's message was important. "Who's next and how long do I have?" Jenkins asked Chris.

"You have about ten minutes before you meet with President Millet," Chris replied.

When Jenkins heard the French president's name, he stopped walking. "So soon?" Jenkins remarked trying to cover his abrupt reaction.

"Is everything all right, sir?"

"Yes," Jenkins responded. "Where am I meeting him?"

"He asked that you join him in his room. He wanted to make sure it was a private meeting," Chris told him. He handed Jenkins a note with Millet's room number.

"Thank you," Jenkins said. Before he left for his room, Jenkins informed Scheidt that he had an urgent matter to attend to before the next bilateral meeting. They shook hands, and each returned to their rooms where they freshened up before their next meetings.

Jenkins knocked on Millet's door and entered when instructed. Jenkins gave Millet his best campaign smile; a smile he had forced on his lips too many times to count. While he knew Scheidt would ultimately work with his administration, he wasn't at all sure what Millet would do. The Socialist had won his election with the promise of lower unemployment and rapid growth just a few months before the summit. It was clear to Jenkins what the theme of the summit was quickly becoming. Each country was grasping for solutions and looking toward the United States for ideas and leadership.

Jenkins shook Millet's hand and took the seat across the table from the French leader. Millet pointed to an open bottle of wine. Jenkins declined the unasked question. It was a little early in the day for Jenkins to have a drink. An aide walked into the room carrying a large briefcase. Millet pointed to the table, where the aide positioned the large briefcase between the two presidents.

"I believe you will be interested in this," Millet said. "My intelligence director says that you are waiting to receive this information."

Jenkins was a bit surprised that Millet knew he would be expecting the intelligence. Jenkins decided to play dumb for the sake of appearances only. "I'm sorry, I don't think I understand."

"These papers are from a contact, a spy, in the Soviet Union. It is my understanding that you knew I would pass this on to you. A test by you, no doubt, to see if you can trust me," Millet spat out. He had no problem showing Jenkins his anger.

"You've studied the information?" Jenkins asked, uncomfortable with Millet's ire.

Millet rolled his eyes. "Yes, we are studying it. We have a copy. Don't act like you do not know what it is."

Jenkins shifted in his seat and dispelled a slight breath. "I don't know what it is and I don't believe like what you're insinuating."

"I don't care if you like it or not," Millet announced. "I find the level of your trust in me and my country insulting. This little ruse that you and your MI6 friend concocted to see if I would share intelligence with you—it is preposterous. Why should I trust you?"

"Mr. President, I don't know what to say," Jenkins paused for a moment. "Can you tell me what the documents are?"

"The Soviet mission objective of their Directorate T, specifically their Line X project. They are using the West to build their technology and computer systems. There are also documents that identify Soviet spies in Western facilities all over the world."

Jenkins's mouth dropped open. "What?" Millet looked at Jenkins and realized his surprise was honest. "What did you say?"

"You heard me," Millet replied, his anger starting to soften. "You didn't know?"

"I was only told that I should make sure I meet with you. I had no idea you had this kind of information," Jenkins countered, knowing that what he said was only half true.

"We have set up a system of exchange," Millet continued.

"You mean there is more coming?" Jenkins asked, astonished.

"Yes," Millet confirmed. "The Soviet spy has a connection to one of my agents in the DST. They have a schedule of meetings where this Soviet, who we call Eagle, will provide us with more intelligence."

Jenkins wanted to jump for joy. "This is marvelous! These documents should allow us to disrupt their program."

"France cannot be involved in that," Millet declared.

"No, of course not," Jenkins agreed. "You should focus on the exchange of documents. We'll focus on disrupting the program."

"Need I remind you that you don't have a CIA director in place?"

Jenkins looked at Millet. "No reminder is necessary. I'm addressing that issue." Indeed, Jenkins's mind was churning with the possibilities. "If you'll excuse me, I'd like to get this information secured."

Millet stood up. "I hope you will share your counterintelligence measures with us."

"Most definitely," Jenkins said, hoping that Millet didn't pick up on the mental finger crossing he was conducting in his head. Jenkins had no intention of discussing their covert operations in detail. "Thank you, Mr. President, for bringing me this information and for continuing this operation. All of our allies will benefit from this."

"I hope so, Mr. President."

Jenkins shook Millet's hand, snatched the briefcase off the table, and left the room. He breezed through the door of his room, much to the surprise of Chris, who immediately stood up. Before Chris could say a word, Jenkins started barking orders. "I need Kevin Thompson up here immediately." Jenkins set the large briefcase on the table in the sitting room of his suite. "Get Whittaker back here."

Chris was dialing Thompson and making a mental note of the rest of the demands. "The president for the director," Chris said when Thompson's secretary answered the phone. "Hello, Director Thomp—"

Jenkins's adrenaline was still surging. He motioned to Chris that he'd take the phone. Chris handed it to him. "Go get Whittaker," he told Chris. "Kevin, I need you up here. I don't care how you get here, but I want you here before nightfall."

Thompson looked at his watch. "That doesn't give me much time, sir. What's wrong?"

Thompson's question made Jenkins stop to think. There wasn't anything wrong. Everything was fine. Millet fulfilled his part of the bargain. He contacted Jenkins with the intelligence Sean said would be coming his way. Why was he acting as if the whole world had collapsed? Jenkins exhaled a breath and tried to slow down his thinking. He had waited so long for this day to arrive. He realized he was finally in a position to do something instead of waiting. Jenkins's decisions required impeccable execution. Lives depended on that. "Nothing is wrong," Jenkins replied. "We have been handed a great opportunity. I need people I can trust to help me. I'll explain more when you arrive."

"Yes, sir," Thompson responded. "I'm on my way."

Jenkins hung up the phone. He walked over to the briefcase and opened it. He sat down as he picked up the first set of documents. Chris and Whittaker enter the room to see Jenkins's face contort into a scowl. He tossed the set of papers back into the briefcase. He turned and looked at the two men. "Do either of you speak Russian?"

Chris shook his head as Whittaker said, "No."

"Great," Jenkins quipped.

"Should I call the director back and instruct him to bring along a translator?" Chris asked.

"No," Jenkins replied. He started to rummage around the briefcase as Whittaker walked over to the table. "I don't want them translating these documents here. Thompson can take this back with him. I'll explain more when Thompson gets here."

Jenkins had to rush off to his next bilateral meeting according to Chris. Whittaker returned to his meeting with the other chiefs of staff from the other countries. Thirty minutes after the sun had set, Thompson arrived at Montebello. An hour later, Jenkins and Whittaker entered Jenkins's suite.

"I'm not ready to concede to that trade deal," Jenkins said as the door opened. "Not when I think there is a better deal to be made with Canada. I'm meeting with Thibeau in the morning. Geoff said what Thibeau is offering makes a lot of sense, and I want to hear him out." Jenkins saw Thompson, who, like Chris, was now standing. Jenkins offered his hand to Thompson. "Thanks for coming up here, Director."

"My pleasure, Mr. President," Thompson responded.

"Have a seat," Jenkins instructed. He began to loosen his tie as he sat down in a chair. He showed Thompson the large briefcase and brought him up to speed on its contents. "We have a unique opportunity to set up a counterintelligence operation that, if done properly, could end the Cold War," he said. Surprise took Whittaker and Chris. Whittaker's head whipped around to look at Jenkins—an action not lost on either Thompson or Jenkins. "He doesn't believe me," Jenkins said, jerking his head in Whittaker's direction. "Am I wrong?"

Thompson thought for a moment. "A lot depends on what is in the briefcase and what comes our way in the future. If what you say is true, then yes, a thoughtfully planned out counterintelligence operation could do just that. It would be a huge undertaking and involve both the CIA and the FBI."

"See," Jenkins said to Whittaker, "I wasn't bluffing." Thompson and Whittaker both smiled. Jenkins cleared his throat. "I don't want to waste a lot of time. Which part of this operation is more crucial—the CIA or FBI?"

"It depends on the operation, but I would think the international aspect would be critical. You wouldn't want Russia to find out they have a mole too quickly. I also think at some point that mole will want to defect. That would be the most delicate part."

"I thought so too," Jenkins nodded. "That's why I want you to be my CIA director."

"What?" Thompson asked, his voice rising with surprise. He cleared his throat. "Excuse me, sir. Did you just say you wanted me to be the CIA director?"

"Yes," Jenkins confirmed. "And I want you to tell me who I should appoint as your replacement. It needs to be someone you trust and have worked with before."

"But, sir—" Thompson began before Whittaker interrupted.

"Mr. President, Congress won't go for this."

"This was what I was referring to earlier, Fred," Jenkins stated. "This is the big ask. Thompson moves to CIA director, and the approval gets through Congress quickly no questions asked, no push-back. At the same time, we appoint a new FBI director, whose confirmation is quickly confirmed by Congress." Jenkins noticed a reluctant scowl on Whittaker's face. "Fred, we have an opportunity to end the Cold War with America coming out on top. We have to make this work, and I only want people I can trust in these positions."

"Mr. President," Thompson began, clearly uneasy with what he was about to say. "It is true, sir, that I work at the pleasure of the president, but, as you know, the FBI director reports up through the Justice Department. The CIA director reports to you through the Cabinet. Our reporting relationships are the way they are to prevent what you are suggesting."

"To prevent espionage?" Jenkins asked.

"No, sir," Thompson started. "To prevent a situation where the leader of the free world could directly influence two intelligence directors' actions."

Jenkins shook his head. "No, that's not what I'm asking. I'm not going to change any of the reporting relationships. The attorney general and the Director of National Intelligence cabinet member will be a part of this. I want to make sure that the CIA and the FBI work together. Kevin, we both know that Jefferies left a mess behind. Stanton told me he resigned because Barker had something on him. I can't have Barker's moles involved in this. I'm not asking for you to do anything other than giving me recommendations for your replacement at the FBI. As for you becoming the CIA director, you know and have worked with someone involved." Jenkins waited for Thompson to realize Jenkins was talking about Sean. "I need the best."

"But you want Congress to lie down and accept this," Whittaker said.

"And you said we can always strike a deal. How do I make that happen?"

"Meet with the Gang of Eight," Thompson stated flatly. "You'll have to tell them why this is so important."

"I can't bring too many people in on this," Jenkins countered. "Someone always has a big mouth. Someone always wants to prove how important they are and will end up talking about it at some stupid cocktail party."

"I don't think that is a fair assessment," Whittaker said. "You were on the Intelligence Committee. How many people knew about the Sipes tape?"

Jenkins wanted to laugh. "Yeah, well, case in point. I was the only one who knew about that tape and look at what happened there." Jenkins was referring to Nicole publicly exposing the confession tape in the United Kingdom followed by Nicole being shot and almost killed. Jenkins then formed a committee to investigate President Andrews's assassination which lead to President Stevens removal and several convictions of co-conspirators.

"OK, so that wasn't a good example," Whittaker deadpanned.

"No, it wasn't," Jenkins concurred.

"My point is, you and that committee knew a lot of things no one else knew," Whittaker said. "How much of that information leaked out?"

"I understand what you are saying," Jenkins confirmed. "If it is a matter of national security, we can trust our members of Congress."

"I think we can," Whittaker agreed. "I'm more concerned with the information in that case being a Russian cookbook. Until we have translated documents confirming what we think is in there, I don't think we do a thing. The Gang of Eight would be the first group we talk to." Whittaker studied Jenkins. He could tell that he hadn't convinced him. "No one wants to beat the Soviets more than the leaders of Congress. You should know that. You were once one of them."

"Beating the Soviets isn't what I'm worried about," Jenkins responded. "Taking credit for beating the Soviets is what concerns me. No one loves bragging and accepting credit for success quicker than Congress. But just one little mess up—just one little mistake—and they are even quicker to lay the blame elsewhere." Jenkins paused. "I need Congress to confirm my nominees, and then I need Congress to fund the operation—"

"That's the Intelligence Committee's responsibility. You have friends there," Whittaker said.

"—And then I need them to keep quiet about it for a few years," Jenkins finished his comment. "Do you think they can do that?"

"What have you heard about our operations in Afghanistan and Iran?" Thompson asked.

Jenkins looked at Thompson. "I'm briefed on them. Why?" A sinister smile crept across Thompson's lips. "Are you saying things are going on there I don't know about?" Thompson continued to smile. Jenkins shot Thompson a stern look. "I don't know if I should be upset that you know something I don't or if I should be more upset that I don't know."

"I'm just saying, sir, there is a reason our intelligence operations are covert. What is briefed to certain individuals depends on their clearance and the objective of the operation. In one form or another, you receive information, and you or your predecessor have approved operations, but you don't know every minor detail of certain operations."

"Thompson," Whittaker interjected. "That's enough."

Jenkins sat staring at Thompson. He was angry at Thompson's accusation that he didn't know everything that was happening in the covert world, especially if it involved his agencies. His mind was working through what Thompson had said. "Why wouldn't I know?"

"Two words," Thompson said. "Plausible deniability." Jenkins nodded his understanding. "We can't put someone at your level on trial in front of the whole world. Someone at my level…" Thompson's inflection implied a question. "We're here to take a bullet for you, sir."

Jenkins looked down. "So, are you saying that I wouldn't be briefed on this operation after we get it in place?"

"No," Thompson said. "I'm saying don't ask about Afghanistan and Iran. This one, you'll be briefed on any time you want. You are in this one too deep already." Thompson stood up. "I think Fred is correct. The first step is to make sure we don't have a recipe for the many different ways you can cook stroganoff. Let me get started on translating the docu—"

"You speak Russian?" Jenkins interrupted, surprised.

"No sir," Thompson replied. "But I know someone at the CIA who does. I'd want him on this operation. He'll do this quietly on the side as a favor for me. I'll take a few of the documents to him and sit on the rest." Thompson stood up. "Just for the record, I will work closely with whomever you appoint. Unlike you, I don't see the need to move me to the CIA. I do have some names; if you'd like me to forward those to Mr. Whittaker, I can do that."

"That sounds good," Jenkins said. Jenkins pointed to the suitcase. "When you have some of these translated, let me know what they say."

"Of course, sir," Thompson said, taking the case off the table. "I'll lock this up in my safe back at the FBI."

Jenkins walked to the door of his suite with Thompson. "We've got a lot of work to do."

"Yes, sir," Thompson said as he left the room. He hurried back to Washington, calling his friend from a pay phone at the airport. He asked him to meet him for breakfast the next morning.

London, England—Buckingham Palace

"It's only the private secretary to the sovereign, Nicole. You can shake his hand if he offers it." Sean wanted to laugh, but the look on Nicole's face indicated the panic of doing something wrong. Sean exited the limo, turned, and offered his hand to Nicole. She exited the car, grasping Sean's hand. Sean moved to the private secretary.

"Philip," Sean said, taking the hand of the private secretary. "So good to see you again." Sir Philip Morris smiled as he shook Sean's hand. "May I present, Nicole Charbonneau."

Philip, who would have been slighted by anyone else calling him by his first name, greeted them with grace. "Ms. Charbonneau, it is a pleasure," he said offering his hand to her. Nicole greeted Philip with a smile as she shook his hand. "It is good to see you again, Sean. How's the Soviet Union treating you?"

"Surprisingly well," Sean replied.

"That is good to hear," Philip said as he turned and led them inside the palace. "I have you across the hall from President Jenkins and his aides as you requested. The queen has requested your presence at the rehearsal dinner. I assume you have no objections."

Sean wanted to laugh. He was a guest in her residence, a servant of her government, and she was requesting his presence, how could he possibly say no? "It would be an honor to join the royal family," he replied. Nicole, who had taken Sean's offered arm when they began walking, dug her fingernails into the sleeve of his suit coat. Sean placed his hand over hers and gently pried her fingers from the grasp on his arm. Without taking his eyes off of Philip, he patted Nicole's still-tense hand twice. "As in the past, the queen's support of our family is graciously accepted."

They arrived at the room, and Philip opened the door. Before they entered, Philip turned and faced the rooms on the other side of the hallway. “President Jenkins is in that room. His aides are in the three rooms down the hallway there.” Philip pointed to the rooms. He entered the suite. He pointed as he spoke, “Your suite and the bedrooms, bath—and should you need anything else, just ring us up and someone will take care of it.”

“Thank you, Philip,” Sean said. “I’m sure we’ll be fine.”

“Your bags should arrive shortly,” Philip said as he turned and walked to the door. “The cocktail party will start promptly at six. The wedding party should arrive by 6:30. Dinner will follow shortly after that. Goodbye for now.”

“Goodbye and thank you,” Nicole called as the door to the suite was closing. “I don’t think I know how to curtsy,” Nicole remarked, referring to the inevitable, upcoming meeting with the queen.

“Don’t look at me. I’ve never curtsied in my life,” Sean quipped.

“Great, I’m doomed! The queen will always remember me as that stupid American girl who didn’t know how to curtsy properly,” Nicole lamented as she walked to the bathroom.

“I think Dad and Geoff will be by before the party. If anyone can talk you through it, it will be Dad,” Sean replied, kissing her cheek as she passed him. He started for the bedroom when there was a knock on the door. He opened it to find Jenkins standing in the hallway. “Hello, Mr. President,” Sean said.

“Hello, Sean,” Jenkins greeted him. He knew Mr. Ambassador was a more fitting response, but Jenkins wanted their friendship to be intimate and free of formalities. “If you have some time, I’d like to talk about the information passed to me at the G7 summit a few days ago," Jenkins said as he stood aside, indicating he wanted the conversation to take place in his suite.

"Of course," Sean responded. He waited at the door for Nicole to join him.

The two men and Nicole walked into Jenkins's suite. Jenkins walked to a door that was open. He instructed Thompson in the other room to join them. Jenkins walked to formally greet Nicole, who had just finished giving Chris a quick hug.

"Hello, sweetheart," Jenkins said as he embraced her. He kissed her cheek. "It is good to see you," he whispered in her ear. He gave her one last squeeze before he released her. "I've asked Kevin Thompson to join us." Jenkins watched the expressions change on his friends' faces.

Thompson walked out of the other room with a rather large briefcase. He smiled as he extended his hand to Sean, who accepted it and pulled him closer to give a quick chest pump. "It's good to see you again."

"I quite agree," Sean responded, stepping aside so that Thompson could hug Nicole.

"Nikki, how are you?"

"I'm fine, Kevin. Are you enjoying your new job?" Nicole asked. Thompson's had been in the role of FBI director for approximately six months. Nicole finished her hug and stepped back. She smiled as she waited for Thompson's response.

"There is never a dull day," Thompson finally replied.

Jenkins invited everyone to sit as he sat down in the chair closest to him. "Sean, as you know, Millet approached me at the G7 and gave me a briefcase full of documents. They were in Russian, and Kevin believes they are the originals."

"I would hope so," Sean said.

"We are in the process of translating the first batch, and it steadily continues to arrive. What Kevin brought in that briefcase is what we have so far. If the rest of the documents are so…" Jenkins's voice trailed off as he searched for the accurate word. "Revealing, and if they are true, we have an opportunity before us to defeat communism without firing one shot."

Nicole looked at Sean. Sean turned his gaze to Thompson, then to Jenkins and said, "I knew this was a game changer."

"Whoever this person is, their placement within the KGB is a very trusted position, and that is very opportunistic for us. The documents we've translated—they've provided us with the very objective of Line X," Jenkins declared.

"The intelligence community was beginning to think it was a decoy because we couldn't find anything concrete about it. We couldn't confirm its existence," Thompson added. "What we've found out is how the Soviets orchestrated the leaps and bounds they have made in technology. We suspected what they were doing, and we knew that one of the cosmonauts for the Soyuz mission was a KGB agent," Thompson bobbed his head from side to side, adding, "Well, we found out when it was too late. Through that one agent, the Soviets extracted a large amount of technological information."

"Kevin is formulating an interesting plan. It's a counterintelligence plan, and it is going to take a partnership between the FBI, CIA and the companies at the forefront of the technical revolution," Jenkins said.

"For it to work, we'll need to keep it very quiet," Thompson said. "If word gets out, well, it could quickly start us down the path to war."

"What do you need from us?" Sean asked.

"Nothing right now, except—" Thompson began as he shifted in his chair. "Keep this asset safe. If there is any chance that he becomes compromised, we should extract him. We can't afford to lose him."

"Understood," Sean said. "I can't promise anything, but I am sure he will be in attendance at various affairs."

"Good," Thompson said. "Make sure he knows he has a way out if he should ever need it."

Jenkins looked at Nicole, whose face betrayed her concern. He looked at Sean. "You don't see all of this as too dangerous?" Jenkins asked.

"Not any more dangerous than it already is," Sean replied when he saw Jenkins exchange a concerned look with Nicole.

Jenkins looked at Sean and could see Sean was annoyed by his concern of Nicole. Jenkins decided to clarify his position. "You've had training, and I wouldn't put it past the Soviets to apply pressure on you by going after Nikki in some way."

Sean smiled. "Nicole is quite capable of taking care of herself." He thought back to Nicole's handling of the spy placed by the Soviets who resembled his late wife. "To answer your question, I don't believe this compromises either of us. I have told you in the past, our security forces are first class, and the foreign office upgraded our munitions. The meetings take place in Paris. I don't know when they meet. We shouldn't be in any more danger unless this asset decides to turn us in and that would not benefit him at all."

"The punishment for spying is harsh, Sean," Jenkins said. "I mean, they wouldn't just expel you, and since Nikki is by your side, it puts her at a greater risk of being accused of spying as well."

"Yes, well, I know I'd be tried in their court and probably convicted as a spy if they wanted to go that route," Sean retorted. "And I understand the risk Nicole is taking. From rescuing your pilots to setting up this pipeline of information, there's no turning back now."

"Maybe it would be better for you to ask for a transfer," Jenkins encouraged. His concern for his friends was evident in his voice.

Sean gave a shake of his head. "I've worked too hard to run away now. We'll be fine."

"Are you sure about that?" Nicole asked.

Sean touched her cheek and smiled. "We'll take it day by day." He looked at Jenkins, then at Thompson. "As you know, our alliance has always been about trying to make a difference in this world. I need the assistance of MI6 to accomplish what we want. If this KGB agent turned US asset needs extracting, I would need full MI6 support. I'm meeting with Kensington while I'm here to bring him up to speed personally."

"Just MI6? More like Her Majesty's army," Jenkins said, flippantly.

"That's not funny," Nicole chided him. "You are very close to the truth. This isn't a game."

"We're well aware of that, Nikki," Jenkins said, the tone of his voice sounded more like a reprimand than agreement.

Nicole looked at Jenkins. "Don't get that way with me, Bobby. You're safe in the White House surrounded by Secret Service who would willingly take a bullet for you. We are on the front lines," she scolded him. Sean took Nicole's hand in his, but Nicole pulled it away as she continued. "We have a lot more on the line then you do. Our plausible deniability doesn't exist. Your protection is degrees higher than ours."

Jenkins, as president, wouldn't have allowed anyone to talk to him the way Nicole just did. Thompson knew that and was waiting for the dressing down to begin. Instead, Jenkins gave Nicole one of his infamous stern looks. Nicole didn't back down. She knew him too well, and she had received the anger behind those looks many times. After a few seconds, Jenkins broke off his gaze as he suppressed the corners of his mouth from curling into a smile. "I'm well aware of the position you and Sean are in. You have to understand, Nikki, I can't send in American troops to rescue you if something happens. Your queen can, Sean."

"She won't," Sean said flatly. Sean looked at Nicole. "You don't send in the military to rescue one spy."

"But—" Nicole started and was interrupted by Sean.

"There are other ways," Sean said giving Nicole a wink. "I'm not even sure how we got onto this topic. It seems a bit senseless to talk about this type of scenario. Bobby, do what you want to do. We'll be fine."

"We're still in the planning stages," Thompson said. "We'll only get one chance to set up this counterintelligence operation. We don't have the luxury of making mistakes. Because of our compromised embassy, would it be possible to put a few agents in your embassy?"

"That's a bit risky. Valesky was having a fit over the two pilots he knew were there but couldn't find. It limits our options if something does happen. Is it necessary?"

"I'm not sure yet. I will be meeting with the new CIA director next week. I know he'll ask," Thompson responded. He looked at Jenkins, proud of the fact that Jenkins didn't go outside what Thompson felt were the boundaries established by the Constitution.

"Get the plan worked out," Sean instructed. "The United Kingdom will always support her ally. If you have to plant some agents, at this point, I can only promise to extract them in a dire situation. We'll revisit what is needed." Sean paused and then with slight hesitation added, "You know you'll always have my eyes on the ground there."

Thompson nodded his head in acknowledgment. He looked at the briefcase on the table in front of him. "Do you want to see any of this, or did I carry it here for nothing?"

Sean gave a quick laugh, sat forward and waited for Thompson to open the briefcase. "I thought you'd never ask."

Thompson opened the briefcase and grabbed the first packet of information. "This talks about Line X's operations. How they used the détente that the Andrews administration championed to gain information from companies in the United States. There are times when I think they know our regulations better than we do." Thompson handed the folder to Sean, who started to page through them. "One of my favorite tricks was the double-sided sticky tape on the soles of their shoes when they visited Boeing and Lockheed." Sean and Nicole looked at Thompson, then back at the documents.

At one point, Nicole looked at Jenkins. Her comment was unspoken, but Jenkins knew what she was thinking. Nicole knew if Congress saw all this information, their consternation would be unbearable. After forty-five minutes, Thompson had walked them through the majority of the papers. Leznikov had provided a treasure trove of information including gathering techniques used against the United States as well as an incomplete list of agents working not only in the United States but within her ally countries as well. Sean asked for a copy of the list. Thompson balked at first, but after some convincing arguments, Thompson's only recourse was to agree that it would be sent to the intelligence agencies to use.

"There's one final document that was handed to me by our analyst right before I left for London," Thompson said. "You haven't even seen this one, Mr. President." Thompson reached for a manila folder he had set aside when they started the meeting. "If you think the list of spies was extraordinary, well, hold onto yourselves because this will truly blow you away." Thompson handed the document to Jenkins first.

The information contained in the one-page document wasn't very long. Jenkins read it, continued to look at the paper, and then read it a second time. Nicole, Sean, and Thompson watched the blood drain from his face at first, and then quickly return, turning his skin color red with anger. He handed the paper to Sean. Nicole peered over Sean's shoulder.

"My God," Nicole uttered. "Can they be that…" her voice trailed off as she searched for the words. "They can't possibly want to…"

Jenkins watched Nicole struggle to communicate what her mind couldn't seem to grasp. "Are you asking if the objective of Line X is to gather technical information and use that information to annihilate us in a nuclear war? Do they honestly believe if they achieve their objectives that they can survive a nuclear war with us? Yes—to both questions."

Sean cleared his throat. "I think the objective is rather clear. They aren't interested in keeping the military might on par with their enemies in the West. They want to obliterate their enemies. I agree with Bobby."

Jenkins looked at Thompson. "We have to stop these bastards at all cost. The end of the free world will not happen on my watch."

Sean handed the paper back to Thompson. "Whatever report you give to FVEY, make sure this document is among them. That objective needs to drive our efforts to thwart Line X."

"FVEY?" Nicole questioned.

"The Five Eyes," Jenkins replied. "It's the term used for the five nations who work together; sharing intelligence and operations." Nicole was still confused, so Jenkins continued. "Australia, Canada, New Zealand, the United Kingdom and the United States comprise the Five Eyes intelligence community."

"Not the Mossad?" Nicole asked.

"We share intelligence with Israel, but it is directed more toward the situations in the Middle East at this point," Jenkins replied. Jenkins looked at his watch. "It's almost time for the cocktail party and rehearsal dinner. I have a few things to do before then. Will you excuse me?"

Sean stood up first. "Of course."

Jenkins turned to walk to his bedroom but hesitated. "Sean, I know this probably doesn't need to be said, but let the United States lead with this information. I don't know what you are going to discuss with Kensington, but we need to prepare a comprehensive report to the intelligence community. We can't have information of this nature trickling out without the support of this evidence." Jenkins pointed to the briefcase. "Can I trust you to allow us to disseminate this information before you share it in detail?"

Sean looked at Jenkins. He knew he would have to tell Kensington some of the information to get the support he needed in case of an emergency extraction. "You can trust me, Bobby. You know that."

"I do," Jenkins said. He looked at Nicole. "That goes for you, too. We don't have a good history in regard to keeping secrets and trusting each other to do what is necessary before informing the rest of the world." Nicole knew Jenkins was referring to the Sipes tape.

Nicole rubbed her throat, the scar of the attempted assassination Barker ordered still visible to those who knew where to look. "I think I learned my lesson. You can trust me on this one, Bobby."

Jenkins nodded his appreciation. "I'll see you shortly." He walked to his bedroom and closed the door.

Nicole and Sean bade farewell to Thompson and Chris before they returned to their suite. They walked to their bedroom where their luggage was waiting for them.

"Sean," Nicole said as she sat down on the bed. "Bobby looked like he had the whole weight of the world on his shoulders after he read that last document."

"Yes," Sean agreed.

"Is it truly that bad?"

Sean walked over and sat next to her on the bed. He took her hand in his and looked into her eyes. "Yes."

"But the Cold War and détente—it's about keeping these two superpowers at parity. How do we know Baranov is changing that?"

Sean swallowed. "Because that last paragraph of the paper we read says so. Those comments were made to a closed-door session of the Politburo and then they became the objective of Line X. They don't want parity; they want to be superior and secure in the knowledge that they will win a nuclear war." Sean looked down and then back at Nicole. "I do not doubt that Leznikov will supply some documentation that discusses ways to cripple the power grids of their enemies which would prevent retaliation. To say this is a big deal is an understatement." Sean could see the worry on Nicole's face. He put his arm around her and pulled her to him, kissing her forehead. "And the rest of the world will be looking to Bobby to make sure they don't succeed."

London, England—Peter Adkins' House

The day after the royal wedding, Sean and Nicole met with director of MI6, Jack Kensington. After bidding farewell to his son and Nicole, Peter left for his office before Jack arrived at the house. After exchanging pleasantries, they moved to the dining room and got down to business. Sean informed Jack about Operation Eagle, Leznikov, and how the Americans were setting up a counterintelligence operation.

"This is all very interesting, Sean," Jack began. "However, I have to say, for someone who sought out a quiet embassy in which to work, your embassy seems to have been anything but that." Sean didn't respond. "Look at what has occurred in only seven months. You rescued American pilots and housed them at the embassy. You've turned an agent—"

"I haven't turned him," Sean interrupted. "He sought my help."

"And you gave it to him. I'm not even mentioning the unfortunate incident with—what was her name?—oh, yes, Katrina something or other." Sean didn't bother to look at Nicole, who folded her arms in an attempt to show the anger she knew she couldn't voice. "Through all of these incidents, you have acted on your own. You've sought no instruction from us, let alone the foreign office."

Through clenched teeth, Nicole said, "The Katrina incident, as you called it, I executed without Sean's knowledge."

Jack turned his head and ire at Nicole. "I don't give a fuck! Tell me, is it supposed to make me feel better that an American in a United Kingdom embassy had a Soviet spy killed?"

Nicole sat forward. "Is it—"

Jack ignored Nicole, shouting over her voice at Sean. "AND NOT A WORD OF YOUR ACTIONS WERE REPORTED BACK TO THE HOME OFFICE," Jack paused when he realized Nicole had stopped talking. "Or MI6."

"And yet," Sean calmly began, "you seem to know about each one of them."

"From the news, Sean, we heard about them on newscasts," Jack replied. He understood what Sean was implying. He also knew his response was weak.

Nicole eyed Jack suspiciously. "Katrina's death was not on the news. The location of the pilots while in the USSR was not public knowledge either." They continued their stare down. Jack's jaw moved as he gritted his teeth.

When it became apparent that Jack was not going to speak, Sean added, "She has a point, Jack. We know I didn't report what happened. Are you watching me?"

Jack looked at Sean. “You know Elliot is required to update his database and also send reports.”

Sean became livid. “YOU HAVE ELLIOT SPYING ON ME?”

Jack slammed his hand on the table. “HE IS NOT SPYING!” he screamed back at Sean. Jack took a few breaths to calm him. “He is required to file reports on all activity he witnesses. You know that is standard procedure. Don’t make Elliot out to be a bad guy for doing his job.”

“Did he report that there is a mole in MI6?” Sean asked. Jack cocked his head. “Did he?”

“No,” Jack replied.

“Now it’s your turn not to make Elliot out to be a bad guy,” Sean repeated. This also told Sean that while Elliot was fulfilling his job requirements, he was still loyal to him. “The question now is whether I can continue to trust you.”

“Of course you can trust me. Any other agent and I would have recalled them by now,” Jack insisted.

“Yes, well, you seem to forget that I have always operated the way I am now,” Sean said.

“My question is this: Are you more loyal to Jenkins than to your own country?” Jack asked. “Jenkins has an embassy in Moscow as well as other cities in Russia. There was no reason to do what you did.”

“An ally asked for assistance. He has a compromised embassy.”

“That’s his problem, not ours,” Jack spat back at Sean. “Where do your loyalties to the crown fall? Is it before your loyalty to Jenkins or after? The United States and the Soviet Union were teetering on the brink of war—"

"Oh, for God's sake," Nicole interrupted. "While the situation with the pilots was tense, neither country was going to go to war. It wasn't the first time an operation like this occurred. In fact, I'm sure you, your country, benefited from the gathered intelligence of that failed mission. An ally needed our help. If the Soviets captured those pilots, the incident would have stewed for months. What irritates you the most Jack—that Sean doesn't report every step he takes or that he doesn't ask for permission to do something?"

"Right now what is irritating me the most is you," Jack retorted.

"You poor baby," Nicole slowly replied, not taking her eyes from him. Sean closed his eyes waiting for Jack's inevitable response.

"Don't push it, Nicole," Jack warned her. "You are a guest of this country, and you are at the embassy as a courtesy. You have already caused enough trouble. I have vouched for you with Parliament on numerous occasions. It is a damn good thing Peter likes you. Your ability to stay in Moscow with Sean is hanging on one very short thread."

While the notion that the United Kingdom could make her leave their embassy had never crossed her mind, it had crossed Sean's. Nicole sat back from the table without saying a word.

Sean ignored the threat that Jack issued. "You asked where my loyalties fall, Jack. You, of all people, should know that I serve this country first."

"Do you?" Jack questioned. "Then why did you go to the DST with the Soviet asset and not us? Why is France cultivating intelligence that we should be the purveyors of? Your instructions weren't for this DST agent to turn the information over to us. It was to give it to the Americans! How is that serving your country first?"

"Do you want my honest answer?"

"No, Sean, I want you to be dishonest with me." Jack's sarcastic response revealed the depth of his anger and perhaps his distrust.

"Because you have a mole in your agency," Sean replied, not blinking or looking away. "Your agency is compromised. Eagle's information will be shared with FVEY when the United States feels it is appropriate. Not to mention that if I had brought the asset to MI6, I would have put myself and, in the worst possible scenario, our embassy in a position to be searched, at the very least, or relinquished without time to destroy our classified information. I would have put myself and my staff in a position to be arrested and tried as spies." Sean paused. "If you can't see that, then shame on you." There was a moment of silence before Sean spoke again. "I have mentioned twice that you have a mole inside MI6, and yet you have failed to ask me how I know this or if I know who it might be. I can only deduce that you don't believe you have a mole. What's going on, Jack?"

"That's right, I don't believe I do," Jack replied. "I think it is an accusation you are using to justify Nicole's actions."

Sean huffed at the suggestion while he suppressed a laugh. "It's not an accusation, I assure you. Someone knew six weeks before we did—" Sean pointed to Nicole and then himself, "—that we were going to Moscow. In that six-week time period, someone decided to alter Katrina's looks and have her placed at the embassy. That someone has ties to Kent, who in turn coached Katrina to become Sarah. You have a mole, Jack. Your resistance to believing this information will influence my decisions in the future. I hesitate even to discuss the reason I asked that we meet today." Sean eyed Jack while he waited for Jack's response.

"I have no evidence supporting what you are saying," Jack stated.

"Did you not see the report that Elliot requested on Katrina?" Sean asked.

"I was not privy to the detailed report," Jack said. "Only that he requested information on a Stacy Cambridge, who turned out to be Katrina Natalinsky."

"When did you know we were going to Moscow?" Sean asked.

"I will not justify that with an answer," Jack shot back. "How dare you make that accusation!"

"Look at the report again, Jack," Sean said, ignoring Jack's indignation. "And when it dawns on you that you have a mole, then we can talk. Until that time, I will do what I think needs to be done without clearing it with anyone at the home office. Right now, in my mind, MI6 is as compromised as the United States embassy in Moscow." Sean stood up, took Nicole's hand prompting her to stand up, and said, "Good day, Jack."

CHAPTER TEN
OCTOBER 1981

Cairo, Egypt—Outside Seddik's Palace

It was five o'clock in the morning on the day of Egypt's celebration of the crossing of the Suez Canal. Kent and Maggie arrived early to prepare for the assassination that Kent was paid to perform. Kent had received the permits to enter the six-story apartment building across from the Seddik's reviewing stand a few days earlier. President Hayyan al-Ashear made sure the required papers would allow them unimpeded access to the building.

They entered the building encountering one security guard, who disregarded Maggie completely as he looked over the papers that Kent presented him. The guard noted Seddik's signature on the papers and waved them into the building. Kent breathed a sigh of relief when the forged signature passed the guard's inspection. Kent walked to the elevator with Maggie following behind; who was seething at the role Kent had placed her in—that of a domestic servant. They entered the elevator and proceeded to their room. Inside, Kent began to set up for his task. The room had a bathroom off the main sleeping area. It looked more like a hotel room than an apartment. A small refrigerator was snuggly placed in a corner with a small microwave oven sitting on top of it. Blackout curtains covered the one window in the room.

Kent reached through the curtains. He opened the window and cursed. He had done the same thing a few days earlier when he first inspected the room and hid the case that contained his sniper rifle. There were no good alternatives for him. If he sat among the crowd in the reviewing stand, it would surely result in his capture and death. The organizers of the parade had selected a wide boulevard with few buildings across from the stands. Kent called the street a runway because of the distance, at least a football field, between where Seddik would sit and any structure that would provide adequate shelter for Kent to perform his task. Maggie assembled the gun while Kent looked through the scope at the chair in which Seddik would later sit. Kent, now in the full mindset of the Serpent, reviewed his execution plan.

Down the road, the military leaders in charge of the parade began to stage the personnel, equipment, and armaments. It was hectic and loud, with orders being shouted and countered. As the time for Seddik to arrive approached, the staging was coming to an end. One general was in charge of placing the arriving troops onto troop trucks. His assistant was checking the names of the troops off a list.

"Who are you?" The assistant asked the man who had two other men flanking him.

"I am Lieutenant Khalid Elrashidy. These two men have replaced—" Elrashidy looked at the assistant's clipboard and pointed, "—these two men, who are violently ill. The last thing we want is weak soldiers vomiting from the truck."

The assistant agreed and told Elrashidy and his men which vehicle to board. The three men walked to the truck, climbed into it, and sat on the bench. They watched the others perform the same actions.

Kent finished positioning his sniper rifle and mounted the scope on it. Maggie had discarded her Egyptian clothing, now dressed in jeans and a blouse. Kent had changed to an all-black outfit just a few minutes after he had drawn the heavy drapes. He turned to Maggie and said, "He should be arriving in a few minutes. Is there anything to drink in here?"

Maggie moved to the refrigerator and opened it. "No," she shot back, still upset about the role Kent forced her into playing.

"Run down to the street and buy something," Kent demanded. Maggie huffed out a disparaging sigh as she grabbed her purse. She opened it, secured some money from her wallet and shoved it in her pocket. She shot Kent a dirty look, which Kent did not see as his back was to her, and grabbed her papers. She quickly grabbed the Egyptian clothes she discarded and threw them over her jeans and blouse as Kent said, "Be quick about it too." Maggie left the apartment, slamming the door behind her.

Maggie showed her papers to the guard, who paid them little attention as she walked past him. Unbeknownst to Maggie or Kent, an impromptu festival had sprung to life on the street outside the building. Proud Egyptians were singing and dancing to lively, celebratory music. The festive music made Maggie smile for a second before she turned to weave her way through the dance party. She would walk and then peer above the crowd as best she could trying to locate a store or vendor. She continued her search, moving farther away from the building. The distance back to the building unsettled her. Her MI6 training had her instincts on high alert.

Seddik arrived on time and exited his car, walking with his guests and bodyguards to the first row of the reviewing stand. Those who had already gathered sprang to their feet and applauded Seddik's arrival. Seddik acknowledged their applause first with a salute and then with a wave or two of his hand. He turned and sat down. It was time for the military parade to begin.

Finally securing a soda from a vendor, Maggie began her return trip to the building. She dodged and weaved in between people, ducking below the raised arms of men and women. After ten minutes, she arrived back at the building. She looked up when the deafening roar of Mirage fighter jets and the stiff gust of wind from their afterburners surrounded her. The parade had started. Seddik was in his place. She needed to get up to the room. She had no idea when Kent would pull the trigger, but it wouldn't be long. As quickly as she could, she moved to the front doors when all hell broke loose.

Kent was looking through his scope and thought that his luck had changed. A troop truck had stopped. Kent prepared to take his shot, his finger beginning to tighten on the trigger. It was perfect. Seddik stood up to salute the one soldier who had jumped from the truck and moved toward him. There was Seddik, standing, caught in the perfect stillness of his salute. Kent started to pull the trigger when an explosion occurred. Kent looked up to see that a second soldier from the troop truck had thrown a grenade that exploded just in front of Seddik. Chaos ensued.

Lieutenant Elrashidy shouted at his comrades. The group of assassins jumped from the troop truck and ran the thirty yards that separated them from Seddik with AK47 assault rifles in their arms. Elrashidy grabbed the rifle being carried for him by one of the other soldiers and started shooting. The three men riddled the reviewing stand with a barrage of bullets.

Seddik fell to the floor, hit by bullets and shrapnel from the grenade. His bodyguards and those around him began to place chairs over and around his body in an attempt to shield him from more bullets. Seddik's security forces were petrified. They couldn't believe their eyes.

"Move!" came the command from their leader. "Stop these assassins! Get them! MOOOOOVE!"

Seddik's security forces sprang into action forty-five seconds after the shooting started. The reviewing stand emptied, as the scared, panicked people ran. The attack lasted for two minutes.

Kent watched the assassination through the scope of his rifle. He didn't fire one shot. His brow wrinkled with confusion. Why would Ashear pay him to kill Seddik only to have Seddik's army kill him?

Maggie was trying to get past the guard who had moved to a position in front of the door to the building when the grenade went off. "I have papers—look!" Maggie yelled, showing the papers to the guard. "Let me inside!" The guard picked her up and tossed her aside. She stood up to try again. Suddenly, Kent ran out of the building, hitting the guard's shoulder as he passed. "Kent!" she yelled. Then the oddest thing happened. Kent looked right at Maggie barely stopping, turned, and ran down the street away from her. One of the other guards, who was clearing the street of the festival goers, looked in the direction that Kent was running. Maggie started to run after him. "Kent, wait!" Maggie shouted after him. "Kent!" As she started to run to him, the guard, who had thrown her to the ground, grabbed her arm. "Let go of me!" she yelled. The guard waved to two other guards to come and take Maggie. Kicking and screaming, Maggie kept yelling for Kent as she was pulled away from the door. But Kent just kept running away from her, away from the commotion. He knew that he had been set up. He didn't know why or by whom. He needed to get out of Egypt as quickly as possible. Maggie watched Kent dart and dash his way through the crowd when suddenly she felt a horrible pain on the side of her head. Everything went dark. One of the guards had hit her on the head with the butt of his pistol. The second guard covered her head with a black cloth bag. They dragged a semi-conscious, groggy Maggie to a cargo van where two other men opened the back doors, and one of the guards held her up. They tied Maggie's hands behind her back and tossed her into the back of the van. As the two guards began to close the doors of the van, one of the kidnappers began to bark out an order. The second man from the van jumped in the back just before the doors closed. The man who was shouting orders pointed down the street in Kent's direction, instructing the two guards who had delivered Maggie to the van to follow and apprehend Kent. Content that he had deployed the two guards, the apparent boss moved to the driver's side door. He got in and sped off.

The two guards left behind looked at each other and quickly started off in pursuit of Kent, but they did not run. They moved through the crowd with no sense of urgency. It wasn't indifference to the command that kept them from executing it. Theirs was a bigger role to play—a longer range mission. They didn't see the value of capturing the woman or the Serpent. They knew that they needed to give the appearance of following the order to keep their cover stories intact. These two men were undercover agents for Mossad. As they reached the edge of the chaotic, panic-driven crowd, they picked up the pace to keep their eyes on Kent.

Kent was to meet Amsu to pay him for all the information he had supplied. Kent knew that meeting would never take place. Just like Saverio, Kent would have killed Amsu. Kent turned down an alleyway, stopping to see if anyone was following him. He didn't think of Maggie or what her fate was. Like the coward that Sean always thought Kent was, he was more afraid of losing his own life. He caught his breath, knowing he had to get out of Egypt and back to France. He started to jog down the alley, rounded a corner, and found a young man getting out of a car. It wasn't much, but it was faster than running. He needed to get to a seaport and stow away on a cargo ship. That was now his mission.

He walked up to the young man, tapped him on the shoulder, and sucker punched him as he turned around. The man fell to the ground, blood pouring from his nose and mouth. Kent grabbed the keys out of the man's hand, got in the car, and off he went. Six hours later he boarded an oil freighter in the port of Benghazi. Kent didn't care where it was going. He had money to hop a jet at the first port of call. Only when he thought he was safe and the adrenaline was calming down, did his thoughts turn to Maggie. He wondered if he would ever see her again. Then he told himself she would have slowed him down. It was better this way.

Washington, DC—White House Residence

Jenkins was finally sound asleep after a few hours of tossing and turning. As the decoding of the documents continued, the counterintelligence plan's scope increased. He was confident in both Thompson and the new CIA director Hugh McGuffey. McGuffey had served in Vietnam, working in the Military Intelligence Division. After the war, he returned to college to finish his political science degree after which he decided to run for his hometown's council. McGuffey ran for governor of Minnesota the year Jenkins was elected president. Jenkins had met McGuffey on the campaign trail and was impressed with his credentials. McGuffey's political affiliation prevented Jenkins from campaigning for him, and McGuffey lost. Jenkins had been under a lot of pressure to nominate a Republican to head the CIA. His prior nominees for various appointments consisted mostly of Democrats.

What Jenkins liked about McGuffey though, was that he put country before party.

Sleep was never elusive to Jenkins before becoming president. Now he considered four hours of uninterrupted sleep a blessing. It was 4:15 in the morning when the phone next to his bed rang. He opened his eyes on the first ring, sighed, and rolled over. He looked at his alarm clock and cursed at the hour. On the fourth ring, he had gathered enough patience to answer the phone. "This had better be good," he said into the receiver.

"Sorry to wake you, Mr. President," McGuffey started. "I'm afraid I have some terrible news. There has been an attack on Amon Seddik during the military parade. They are transporting him to the hospital."

Jenkins sat up in bed at the news. "What happened? How did it happen?" He was in shock. He had just talked to Seddik two days ago regarding the use of military advisors in Egypt. "At the parade? Were others shot?" Jenkins tried to clear his head.

"Yes, sir," McGuffey replied. "The situation is still in disarray. We are still gathering intelligence. I can brief you at the White House in a half hour if you would like."

"Yes," Jenkins said as he reached for his prosthetic leg. "I'll meet you in the Oval Office." Jenkins hung up the phone, slipped on his fake lower leg, and then grabbed the phone again. He waited for the White House operator to respond. "Wake everybody up," he told the operator. "They need to be in the Oval Office as soon as possible. Wake Whittaker first and tell him he has fifteen minutes." Jenkins hung up the phone and walked to his closet to dress. Fifteen minutes later, he was walking into the Oval.

Whittaker joined him via the door that led from his office to the president's office. Jenkins was sitting at his desk, the television in the corner tuned to WNN. Steven Harrigan was providing news coverage of the assassination attempt on Seddik.

Jenkins looked at Whittaker as he entered and bemused, "This is becoming an interesting world. I don't know if it is a good thing or a bad thing that the press knows more about what happened to Seddik than I do."

Whittaker looked at the television and then at Jenkins. "I'm going to venture out on a limb here and say that within the next twenty minutes you'll know more about what happened than the press does."

Jenkins frowned. "That doesn't make me feel better." Jenkins released a deep sigh. Chris knocked on the door and entered the room with a tray. On the tray were coffee cups, a pot of coffee, sugar, and cream. "Thank you, Chris. You read my mind."

"You're welcome, sir," Chris said, setting the tray on the bar located among the built-in bookcases. "Can I get you both something to eat?"

"I need some sugar—get the doughnuts and pastries," Jenkins said. "Throw some bagels and cream cheese on there for when my conscience kicks in and tells me I shouldn't eat another doughnut."

Chris smiled. "Yes, sir." He looked at Whittaker.

"That will be fine. Thanks, Chris," Whittaker replied.

As Chris opened the door to leave, he noticed the CIA director waiting in the outer office. "Sir, Director McGuffey is here."

"Send him in," Jenkins said as he poured himself a cup of coffee. "Would you like a cup, Hugh?" Jenkins asked as McGuffey walked into the office.

"No thank you, Mr. President," McGuffey replied. "I've had three cups already."

Jenkins acknowledged his comment with a nod of his head. "Any more information?"

"Yes, sir," McGuffey began. "Eleven doctors are working on President Seddik, but our intelligence indicates he was DOA." Jenkins sat down and took a drink of his coffee waiting for more information. "Seddik's security forces abducted three men; a fourth killed at the scene." McGuffey pulled a photo out of the folder he had carried with him into the room. "This man, Lieutenant Khalid Elrashidy, was the leader of this attack and is in custody. We have information on him that ties him to the Egyptian Islamic Jihad terrorist organization." McGuffey went into the details of the attack that Jenkins and Whittaker had witnessed on WNN a few minutes prior.

Jenkins wiped his face with his right hand. He didn't want to imagine what the people in the reviewing stand went through. "Are there other casualties?"

"The information we have right now states the Cuban ambassador, an Omani general, a Coptic Orthodox bishop, and the Egyptian Central Auditing Agency head official are dead. There are twenty-eight wounded including Egypt's vice president Hazem Mustafa."

Jenkins closed his eyes. "Dear God," was all he could muster. "Is Egypt in turmoil? Who's leading the country?"

McGuffey swallowed. "That isn't very clear right now. Sir, four of our military liaison officers were also wounded."

Jenkins slowly released a long breath. "OK, Hugh, get back to CIA headquarters and keep me informed. Do you have the names and conditions of the four officers?"

"Yes, sir," McGuffey handed Jenkins a slip of paper. "Emergency contact information is listed for each as well."

"I want their conditions confirmed before I make any calls," Jenkins demanded. "I'm not going to call and tell someone their loved one is alive only to find out they are not. I won't put a family through that."

"Of course," McGuffey said. "The Joint Chiefs have better information. I'll have a man coordinate with them and provide Chris with updates."

"Thank you," Jenkins responded as he took another sip of coffee. "I assume we'll be talking to each other a lot in the next few hours."

"We will," McGuffey confirmed. "If you'll excuse me—"

"Thank you for the update," Jenkins said. McGuffey turned and started for the door. "Hugh," Jenkins called. "I'd appreciate it if the CIA could keep me a few steps ahead of the press on this issue."

"We'll do our best," McGuffey returned. He walked out the door and closed it behind him.

"I want to talk to our Egyptian embassy. We may need to fly in a few more troops. I'm assuming our ambassador was at the parade. Let's see what they know about the situation," Jenkins told Whittaker. "I'm sure I will be hearing from Isreali Prime Minister Baruch before long."

"I think you can count on that," Whittaker said as he started for his office. "I'll get our embassy on the line."

"Send in my press secretary and the communications director," Jenkins called out. "We need to issue a statement."

Atlanta, Georgia—WNN Studio Headquarters

Two hours had passed since the attack on President Amon Seddik. Steven Harrigan, who had only slept a couple of hours before being called back into the studio, was low on energy. Perhaps his tiredness was appropriate given the gravity of the situation. At one point, he grew frustrated at the lack of confirmation on some facts supplied to him, and he lashed out at his staff. "We are responsible for broadcasting truth, not fiction," he yelled. "And, certainly, we are not responsible for sensationalizing an already dire situation. Two independent sources confirm it, or we don't broadcast it. Understood?" The staff nodded and returned to their work. The stage manager counted down, pointing at Harrigan when the broadcast was back on the air live from a taped segment on Seddik.

Harrigan finished up the hastily pulled together segment regarding Seddik's rise to power. His staff was researching the Egyptian Islamic Jihad terrorist organization for a piece that would air in the next hour. Harrigan announced there would be more news to come after a short break. When the stage manager cleared the studio by stating they were in commercial, Harrigan reached for his coffee cup sitting to his right out of view of the camera. His assistant walked up to him with a paper in his hand. He gave it to Harrigan and said, "We just received word from two different sources, one of which is Seddik's press secretary, that Seddik is dead. There's a statement regarding the cause of death from his doctors. Also, Jenkins will be addressing the nation in thirty minutes."

Harrigan read over the information. "That's President Jenkins," Harrigan corrected his assistant. "Are we ready to lead with this when we come back from the break?"

"Yes," the assistant confirmed. He walked away from Harrigan as the stage manager began the countdown back to the live broadcast.

Harrigan paused for a few seconds as he looked at the monitor. Displayed on his right was a photograph of Seddik with his birth year and death year. He cleared his throat and began, "We have just received word that President Amon Seddik died after eleven doctors operated on him for two hours. According to his doctors, he died of—and I am quoting here— 'violent nervous shock, a collapsed lung, and internal bleeding in the chest cavity, where the left lung and major blood vessels below it were torn.' As we have witnessed over the last two hours, this man who sought peace died most violently." Harrigan paused. "We'll have more on President Seddik's legacy and reports from our correspondents in the Middle East. We have also received notice that President Jenkins will address the nation in approximately thirty minutes. We will carry his speech live." Harrigan moved the paper aside as his producer informed him of the next story. "We go now to our correspondent in Israel for an update."

When the report ended, Harrigan introduced their White House correspondent who then filled the airtime until President Jenkins walked down the hallway to the podium centered in the East Room. Everyone stood as Jenkins entered the room. As he reached the podium, the solemn Jenkins removed a tri-folded paper from the inside pocket of his black suit jacket. He unfolded the paper as he looked out at the reporters. "Please be seated," he said. "I stand before you now to remember a man that I will admit I did not know very well. While I have worked with President Seddik closely in the last few months, our time together was brief." Jenkins paused. "President Seddik was dedicated to Egypt, his family, and to peace. He courageously ventured into the peace accord, an agreement that brought scrutiny from his allies and enemies alike. In the end, a terrorist group opposed to the president's work ended his life, but not his vision of peace. In this time of mourning, we have expressed our nation's condolences to the nation of Egypt and President Seddik's family and friends. I have spoken to now President Hazem Mustafa. He has assured me that Egypt remains committed to the peace accord. As vice president, Mustafa worked alongside Seddik brokering agreements and had visited Israel many times. Prime Minister Baruch looks forward to working with President Mustafa and acknowledged the loss of a man who had become a good friend. Differences of opinion were always present as these two countries walked toward peaceful resolutions. Respect for the love of their countries and the hope of peace for generations to come kept President Seddik, Prime Minister Baruch, and now President Mustafa committed to a bright future. The future will not be extinguished or diminished by the cowardice acts of men whose only voice is the rattling of machine guns, grenades, and violence. The United States stands ready to assist Egypt, Israel, and all of our allies in that region. We are fully committed to peace in the Middle East." Jenkins paused and shifted his weight to his other leg. "In remembrance of President Seddik and sympathy with the Egyptian people, I order all American flags to be flown at half-mast for the next seven days. We thank President Seddik for his courage and vision of a peaceful, strong, and gallant Egypt."

Jenkins picked up the paper he had placed on the podium. He had not looked at it once during his speech, having memorized it beforehand. Jenkins walked back to the Oval Office in silence. He walked to his desk and looked out the window. He watched a Marine in dress uniform lower the American flag to half-mast. With no one around to see him, Jenkins stood at attention and raised his hand to his forehead as the flag traveled down the mast to its new resting place. He finished his salute and wondered if a new manner of war was commencing. He sat down in his chair resting his jaw in one hand as he thought about how he could alter the path the world seemed destined to travel down.

London, England—MI6 Headquarters

Jack was sitting at his desk, reading the latest intelligence report. It matched the information that had been reported on the news. He set the report aside and glanced over at the television set that was always on with the volume muted in his office. Just as he sat back in his chair, there was a knock at the door. Jack had sent his secretary home hours ago. “Yes, who is it?”

Charlie Dawson, Sean’s contact at MI6 while he was in the field tracking the Serpent, opened the door. “It’s me, sir. I received some information of which I think you need to be made aware.”

“Come in, then,” Jack said. Charlie entered and walked over to the chairs opposite Jack’s desk. “Sit down.” It was then that Jack noticed the single piece of paper in Charlie’s hand.

As Charlie sat, he said, “I’m afraid I have some bad news. It appears that Kent was in Cairo with one of our agents, Maggie—”

“Yes, I’m aware of her mission,” Jack interrupted. He rarely had the patience for Charlie’s flare of dramatics. “You aren’t going to tell me Kent did this,” he said pointing to the news on the television screen.

“No, sir,” Charlie began again. “It was the Egyptian Islamic Jihad. However, Kent was hired to assassinate Seddik according to Maggie’s last report. We had taken the appropriate steps to ensure his chances of fulfilling that contract were mitigated.”

“Then what’s the problem?”

“Our agent, Maggie, well sir, she’s been captured,” Charlie finally managed to say. “The Mossad forwarded this report to the Americans, who sent it to us.”

Jack snatched the paper from Charlie and began reading. Except for Sean and Nicole, no one knew that Maggie was his daughter. Jack read the report and then placed it down on his desk. He tried to control the emotions that were surging through him. He wanted to order a raid to extract her. He wanted to fly to Cairo to locate her. He wanted to do so many things but knew he couldn't. "This is very sketchy. Does anyone know where she is or who has her?" he asked as calmly as he could.

"Not yet, sir," Charlie replied.

"Why were the Americans given this information? Why didn't the Mossad notify us directly?" Jack demanded.

"It appears that the United States is working closely with the Mossad to place more agents and military advisors in Egypt in response to the peace accord." Charlie looked at Jack.

"Yes, well, I suppose that makes sense," Jack responded. "Any idea who has her?" Jack asked again. His mind was still reeling from the news.

"That is a bit unclear," Charlie said. "We aren't sure if she was taken to the EIJ's base camp or if the General Intelligence Directorate has her. The Mossad agent that sent the report also indicated that there is a possibility that the Syrians took her."

"So, let me get this straight," Jack began, his temper starting to show. "She is either a captive of a terrorist organization who just killed Seddik, or she is a captive of the Egyptian intelligence directorate. Those two possibilities I can understand. How the fuck does Syria enter into all of this?"

"It was Ashear who hired Kent. We also believe that the Soviets were backing both Ashear's attempt and the EIJ," Charlie informed Jack.

"But we thought that connection was a ruse," Jack responded.

"It still could be, but we can't rule out involvement in some way given Maggie's last report." Charlie stood up. "I will naturally keep you informed. I've sent word to the Americans to tell the Mossad we need to know her location and circumstance as quickly as possible."

"Did they respond?"

"Yes, sir," Charlie replied. "They understood our concern but doubted that the Mossad would risk their agents' cover to get us that information quickly." Charlie looked down. He balked to add the rest, given all the emotions that Charlie witnessed on Jack's face during their conversation. "I hesitate to add…" His voice trailed off.

"What?" Jack exclaimed loudly, irritated both by Charlie and the situation in which he found himself and his daughter.

"She may already be dead, sir. I'm sorry." Charlie bowed his head. "I need to get back to my desk." Charlie didn't wait for his dismissal. He peered out from his bowed head to see Jack lower his head, not at all sure if there were tears in his director's eyes. Charlie told himself that he imagined those watery eyes as he turned and left the director's office.

As the door closed, Jack looked up. He sat back in his chair. There was only one thing on his mind. He needed to get out of there. He folded up the piece of paper that Charlie brought him and stashed it in his trouser pocket. He grabbed his hat and coat and then walked in a daze to the train station, where he mindlessly boarded a train heading north.

He didn't know what time it was when he reached his destination. He didn't care. He had called earlier in the day and reported that he would be late. He knocked weakly on the door of the little cottage in Inverness.

The door opened. “Hello, my love.” Gillian threw her arms around the man she had loved all these years. At first, she was furious with Sean for telling Jack he had found her. But Jack was persistent. He had won her back, traveling to see her as often as he could. It was only this past June that Gillian confessed to Jack that Maggie was indeed his daughter. Jack, however, had not confided to Gillian that Maggie was an MI6 agent. He let Gillian continue to believe Maggie was working for the advertising agency—the cover story that Maggie had told Gillian. “What’s wrong, love? It looks like you’ve lost your best friend,” Gillian remarked.

Jack pushed through the door, taking his coat off and throwing it on the closest chair. He removed his hat and tossed it aside. “Gillian, you need to sit down. I have something dreadful to tell you…” His voice trailed off. “It concerns Maggie.”

A Note from the Author

It has been so much fun writing this first book of this next trilogy! I envision the Blind Series as trilogies. I am researching and creating the next trilogies as this book launches.

When I began writing this series, I expressed to friends that I felt the 1980s were a turning point for our government. Throughout the eighties, on through the nineties, and up to today, the split in the United States has grown exponentially. The underlying question that started me on this journey was: "What if one drastic thing had occurred back in the 1980s, that put us at an obvious crossroads, and one politician had the courage and finesse to lead, where would we be today?"

The books are inspired by historical event and secret operations. At each turn I ask *"What if this happened instead?"* It's a fun question to ask and answer—that is where the fictional characters come into play. They are free to make their own choices.

Thank you for your continued support. You can find me on social media (Facebook and Twitter) and my website, www.LindaFisler.com where I share many things—including recipes! Want more behind the scenes Blind Series? Become one of my patrons (aka super fan!) over on Patreon: https://www.patreon.com/LindaRiesenbergFisler I'd be eternally grateful!

I wish you all the best.

Thank you with all my heart for reading *Cloaked*!

Respectfully yours,

—*Linda Riesenberg Fisler*

Made in the USA
Lexington, KY
24 September 2018